I mus
at the
but un
the ev ...... my head like an
action replay. Then I realised what had happened.
The rest of my party thought that I was taking
Claudine home. Jonathan must have leapt up on
impulse and rushed after us without explanation. I
hadn't gone back into the dining-room after that.
Any witness outside the restaurant would have
seen a couple coming out, behaving with the easy
manner of close familiarity. She stays by the restaurant door while he goes to flag down a taxi.
Bang! And then bang again, leaving no face to
recognise, even for those with the stomach to look
closely. So it had been assumed that it was
Jonathan who had burst from the restaurant to find
that appalling scene, and who had scooped up
Claudine to protect her from the sight of her husband – me! – lying, a bloody bundle, in the gutter.
'*Take care of the lady*!'

'Something wrong is there?' The two policemen
came back into focus.

'You could say that.' Normally, I enjoy a dramatic opportunity, but this one was as enjoyable as
the sight of an open grave – dug for me. 'I think
you must be under the impression that I am
Jonathan Cassell.'

It was their turn to gawp. 'Well I'm buggered,'
the older one got out. 'You're not? Then you must
be—'

'William Warner. And glad to be alive.'

Also by Martin Sylvester in Sphere Books

A DANGEROUS AGE

A LETHAL VINTAGE

Martin Sylvester

SPHERE BOOKS LIMITED

AUTHOR'S NOTE

Chapter headings are from *New Introductory Lecture on Psychoanalysis*, first published in 1933 by the Hogarth Press, translated and edited by James Strachey and re-issued in the Pelican Freud Library in 1973. Freud himself complained (Lecture 34) about being quoted in novels. But here, in the master's own words, is what he actually said about the famous Freudian slip etc. Readers who think that Freud was doing all right without my help can skip – they have his blessing!

Reproduced by permission of Sigmund Freud Copyrights Ltd, The Institute of Psycho-analysis and the Hogarth Press.

SPHERE BOOKS LTD

Published by the Penguin Group
27 Wrights Lane, London W8 5TZ, England
Viking Penguin Inc., 40 West 23rd Street, New York, New York 10010, USA
Penguin Books Australia Ltd, Ringwood, Victoria, Australia
Penguin Books Canada Ltd, 2801 John Street, Markham, Ontario, Canada L3R 1B4
Penguin Books (NZ) Ltd, 182–190 Wairau Road, Auckland 10, New Zealand

Penguin Books Ltd, Registered Offices: Harmondsworth, Middlesex, England

First published in Great Britain by Michael Joseph Ltd 1988
Published by Sphere Books Limited 1989
1 3 5 7 9 10 8 6 4 2

Copyright © Martin Sylvester 1988

Printed and bound in Great Britain by
Richard Clay Ltd, Bungay, Suffolk

To Jane

CHAPTER 1

A Shot in the Dark

Here are happenings rich in unsolved riddles!
SIGMUND FREUD

'Are you sure you don't mind?'

'My pleasure, and my privilege,' Jonathan said with grave courtesy, taking a firm hold of my wife's fur-clad arm.

'Oh, I'm so sorry,' Claudine murmured.

Jonathan and I bowed to each other with exaggerated solemnity, mirror images in our dinner jackets. His bow tie was sagging, and I straightened it for him. 'Take care,' I advised. 'Shall I get you a taxi?'

'You go back in,' Jonathan said. 'Go on – I'll look after her.' I watched, irresolute, as he manoeuvred her gently towards the door which a waiter was holding open. *'Bonne nuit, m'sieu, madame. Bonne nuit.'*

'Tell everyone goodnight from me,' Jonathan called as the door closed him out into the night.

A final closure. And eternal night.

That evening, Les Trois Pigeons had been pushing the boat out for us, and we'd been most of the way through a five-course dinner, a different wine with each course, when Claudine's migraine got the better of her. I hadn't noticed her struggling with it, but the French tend to be like that – all go or all stop, and nothing in between – so I wasn't surprised, and wasted no time in arranging to take her home. We left to a chorus of sympathy, just as a ripe Brie and a bottle of Pomerol were being delivered to the table. Ah well.

Then Jonathan Cassell caught us up in the passage – it's one of those restaurants converted from a terrace house, and we

7

were dining in the room at the back – and offered to go in my place. Perhaps I shouldn't have agreed – I didn't at first – but he was very insistent, and it was my party, so when Claudine herself said I should stay and look after our guests, I weakened and then accepted. But I felt uneasy. One of the signs of approaching middle age is that you can remember moments, unrecognised as such at the time, when some small decision changed your life, and you start to look out for them. Perhaps this was one such moment . . . I wasn't sure. Neither was I sure of Jonathan. But the decision was made, and Claudine had to be got home.

I can still clearly recall that image, of the glass door closing behind them: through it, blurred by reflections, I can see Jonathan's arm moving to encircle Claudine's shoulders. Claudine – my beautiful, dutiful wife. I turned away. She wasn't feeling well, after all. She needed comfort – and he always affected that courtly manner. No, this isn't one of those turning points, I decided firmly. I began to climb the stairs to the cloakroom. Pomerol, Sauterne and maybe brandy still to come, and I needed to make room.

I was halfway up when I heard a loud bang from the street outside. A car's backfire – but then something about it made me hesitate in mid-climb. Then I heard it again, followed immediately by a woman's scream.

Claudine!

And in an instant retrospect I recognised the double blast of a shotgun, spaced as it might be by a deliberate left–right at a high-flying bird. A familiar sound in the country – but not in a London street. And the only game here was of my species.

I practically fell down the stairs, colliding at the bottom with a waiter coming down the passage with a tray of coffee cups, which was sent flying: he stood, empty-handed, gaping after me as I charged through the hallway, burst open the glass door, and found myself on the pavement, gasping with terror at what I might find. I could spare no time for precautions: to get out there, find Claudine, was my only thought.

She was standing just outside. *Standing, yes!* She had the lapels of her fur coat held to her face with both hands. I reached her in three steps and took her hands in mine, trying to ease them gently away, to see her face. *Oh no, not her face . . .*

'Let me see, darling. Please let me see. Are you hurt?'

She shook her head, still holding the coat over her face. Not hurt! But then, why the coat?

'*Pas moi,*' she said, '*pas moi.* Johnny!' Her shoulders began to shake, slowly at first, then more and more violently.

I looked away from her, across the pavement. All my attention had been on Claudine, but now my eyes focussed on the wider scene. Curious faces were collecting round us, pale blobs in the lamplight, but they left an open pathway to the kerb. At the far end, half on the pavement, half in the gutter, lay a bundle of black and white evening clothes. Black and white and red. The shotgun had made Jonathan into this. Jonathan! – who only minutes before had been alive and laughing . . .

Somebody, a man's voice, was saying they'd get the restaurant to telephone for an ambulance. 'Thanks,' I heard myself say. He was going, then. His voice called back: 'Look after the lady.' A woman's voice, hushed but still penetrating, was saying 'Is he dead . . .?'

I didn't need to go closer to see that. And Claudine had already seen too much. I put my arm round her, and began to lead her along the pavement, away from the thickening crowd and the faces hungry for drama. Soon, the police would arrive and she'd have to answer questions – that would be soon enough to go back to the restaurant. Meanwhile, the faces were turning away from us, back to the bundle in the gutter. A few more steps, and we were clear of them; it was like breaking through waves into clear water. We came to a corner; I steered us round it into a side street, where it was quiet, and where Claudine might tell me what had happened.

We stopped outside a tourist agency's shop window, in which a spotlit silver airliner was jetting to freedom against a background of cardboard palm trees. Claudine was sobbing audibly, and I could feel her weight increasing against my supporting arm. No, she wasn't nearly ready to talk, not yet. Perhaps if I could find somewhere for her to sit down – but it wasn't the sort of street to be equipped with benches. Nothing for it, then,

9

but to run the gauntlet of the crowd again, and make our way back to the restaurant.

'Darling – we'll have to go back. There'll be somewhere you can lie down. Don't look – it'll be all right. Hold on to my arm. Ready?'

She gave a small mewing sound, and shook her head. '*Non, non, je ne peux pas, non . . .*' She shuddered violently. Normally so controlled, she was now close to hysterics – there's no middle way with her.

But there was nothing else we could do – we had to go back. I began to ease her along the pavement, back towards the street corner. We reached it. I glanced towards Les Trois Pigeons – there was now a large crowd outside. We started towards it. I could feel Claudine's resistance, though she said nothing between her sobs.

Sixty yards to go, then fifty.

A taxi drew up just ahead of us, and a young couple got out. If only – but of course we couldn't, the police . . .

'*Claudine!*'

She had twisted away from my arm, was heading for the taxi . . .

'Wait! – you *can't* . . .'

Oh yes she could. She *had*.

Well, what should I do? Remonstrate – or show solidarity at a time of stress? But she was already signing to the cabby to move off. I had to climb in after her, or be left behind.

'Church Street, Kensington.'

There must have been other witnesses. And our friends at the restaurant would give the police our address. I could ring them when we got home, and explain. Wife hysterical – French, you see, no tradition of sang-froid . . . though why, then, is that *their* phrase?

The taxi hadn't moved.

'Well, let's go then,' I said angrily. It would be worse to be caught in the act.

'What's going on there? You see anything?' The cabby was staring through his windscreen, still immobile.

'Accident. Look, my wife's ill. Got to get home. *If* you don't mind.'

'What happened, then?'

'No idea. Look, I just told you . . .'

'I heard you,' he said. 'Never fear. Have you home in a jiffy.'

And so we left the scene. I was afraid there'd be trouble about it – and there was. But you'd have needed a Roman sense of civic duty to march Claudine back in there, that night. Lacking which, I had no choice; not really.

Inside the taxi, Claudine huddled against me, shivering and silent. I held her close, and waited for her to recover enough to tell me what had happened. Outside, London nightlife reeled past our windows, the glaring neon of theatres and cinemas filling the cab with successive waves of multicoloured light which grew, revolved, and receded. We turned north off the King's Road, away from the bright lights, and rattled along Chelsea's narrow residential streets between painted and por-ticoed terraces, cavernous and quiet. Then back into the bustle again, turning west along Hyde Park, joining a shoal of taxis in a torrent of traffic as Saturday night began the long decline into Sunday morning.

Ahead of us, the final right turn at the bottom of Church Street, and the lights were red.

'Almost home, darling.'

Claudine stirred, looked up. She watched, still silent, as we passed up Church Street with all its familiar sights and sounds. The shop came into view. I leant forward, and spoke through the partition.

'On the corner there – William Warner Wines. Go a little way up the side road, will you please? There's another entrance there.'

The driver nodded. He turned into the side road, and pulled up. I had the fare ready, got out, and paid him. Then I helped Claudine out. The driver watched her with an air of concern, but he didn't move. Of course. Nothing shifts a London taxi driver off his seat, short of damage to his paintwork. But he was moved to remark: 'Hope you'll be better in the morning, luv.'

'Yes,' Claudine said, attempting a smile. 'Yes. Thank you.'

We left him lighting a cigarette, and I unlocked the gate in the garden wall. It was dark in the garden, but there was enough light from distant street lamps for us to see our way. Julian, my architectural student son, was at home in his room over the garage, I noted: the roof lights were ablaze, throwing the big plane tree outside in the street into theatrical relief against the night sky. Looking towards the house, I could see no light in the girls' bedrooms. But, as neither Nichole nor Sylvie ever go to bed until forced, they were probably watching the Saturday night horror film on television. Somebody, probably Julian, had thought to leave the hall light on. I ushered Claudine up the flagged path towards it.

Once in the hall, with the door shut behind us, our arms went round each other and we stood, swaying in mutual sympathy. Crisis pulls us together, and this wasn't the first we'd shared. 'Oh William!' she said in a tremulous voice: her shoulders began to shake again. 'Don't think about it,' I said. 'Just hold everything until we've got you into bed.' I helped her off with her fur coat, dropped it on a chair, and urged her upstairs.

Our bedroom is on the top floor, converted from the original attic; it's got beams and sloping ceilings, and it's a haven of peace and quiet where the din of teenage female adolescence hardly penetrates. On the way up, we passed a partly open door from which issued screams of terror, and I put my head in. 'We're back,' I said, 'and Maman's got a headache. Turn it down, will you, and let's keep this door shut. Goodnight both.' 'Goodnight, Papa,' they replied in unison, their little angel faces lit by whatever flickering horrors were taking place on the TV screen. Better than rape, or documentary-style violent death, I supposed.

Violent death. I went up the stairs to the top floor, and straight to our bathroom. Yes, I thought so – there were some powerful painkillers, supplied on prescription, for Claudine's occasional but ferocious migraines. I took them into the bedroom with a glass of water. Claudine was sitting on the edge of the bed, pulling her shoes off.

'I'll switch the blanket on,' I said, 'and here are some of those knockout pills – the strong ones. What else can I get you?'

'Nothing, *chéri*. I think perhaps I will get into bed now.'

'Of course.'

She stood up, undressed, and slipped into the bed. It's a big pine four-poster, and she looked somehow smaller in it tonight, like a child. Diminished. I've noticed before what a little space we occupy when we're not on our feet, strutting and fretting.

'William?' she murmured. She lay on her side: only her head showed above the bedclothes.

'Yes?'

'I must tell you now. The police . . .'

'I'll deal with them. Talk when you're ready. Not before.'

'But I must tell you. Johnny and I –'

'Tell me what happened, then,' I said quickly.

'But –'

'Just what happened. He left you by the door . . .'

'And went to call a taxi. He saw a free one coming. There is a motorcycle parked a little way down the road. Before the taxi can pull in, this motorcycle starts, and it drives up to Johnny. A man jumps off – not the driver, there are two of them – and points a big gun at Johnny. He shoots, and Johnny falls. Then . . . then he leans over Johnny and . . .'

'Shoots again.' I knew what he'd done – I'd seen the result. The killer had made sure, with a second shot into the face at close range.

I asked, partly to distract her: 'What did the men look like?'

'Both of them wear helmets – you cannot see their faces. The one with the gun wears a dark *pull*, and blue jeans. He is not so tall as you, but bigger.'

'Anything else you can remember?'

'Then you came out.'

That would do for the police tonight. I expected them to telephone at any minute. They'd have to wait for the rest until the morning.

'Take these pills, darling, You can have three, it says. I'll switch off the bedside phone, and when you're safely asleep I'll wait downstairs in the office for the police to ring. They'll want to talk to you in the morning, but nobody's going to disturb you tonight.'

I put out a hand, smoothed her hair on the pillow. Then I bent to kiss her cheek.

13

'William –'

'Go to sleep now, darling. Try, anyway.'

'It wasn't, you know, *really* anything . . .'

'Don't know what you're talking about. Sleep!'

'But they might say –'

'Let them. I'll leave the bathroom light on.'

I waited, sitting in a corner of the room, until I was sure she was asleep. Then, down in my office, I poured myself a large brandy, the missed conclusion of my dinner. I could, some might say should, have gone without, in respectful remembrance of Jonathan Cassell, fellow diner, who had been similarly deprived. But, either he was where the best brandy was part of the service, or he was now non-existent. So it would have been a meaningless gesture. I drank to his memory instead.

Jonathan was an architect, and his firm, Cassell and Charrington, had taken on the refurbishment of these premises which, until recently, had stayed as they had been when I took them over following my father's death a few years ago. The business had been in my family for three generations, and needed a facelift. As well as wine-importing, I wanted to improve the retail side, to take advantage of the boom in wine consumption that was already well under way and which, I'm glad to say, has grown as the British take to wine with exponential enthusiasm.

Cassell and Charrington had a reputation for shopfitting work, an in-house graphic designer, and could provide us with the complete new corporate identity – which we needed. So I rang them and, at the appointed time, Jonathan – whom I had not met before – turned up with his sketch pad, his tape measure, and his courtly manner. The shop was to have white walls, black shelves, and a stripped-pine floor, he informed us. Modern, but simple; let the bottles speak for themselves. Yes, we liked it, Claudine and I. Let it be done, I commanded. And so it was.

We were delighted with the results. Well, until the bill came in; but in time we managed to forget that. And Claudine, whose nesting instincts had now been thoroughly stirred up, persuaded me to let Jonathan loose on the rest of the building, which had always been cramped and uncomfortable. It was Jonathan's idea that we should convert the attic into a private suite of bedroom and bathroom, where marital bliss could be practised undisturbed by racketing kids. We rose above all that, up the neat little spiral stair that Jonathan provided for us. And into a world of colour-coordinated tiles and towels, duvets and draperies, flowers and fripperies, which Claudine chose and changed and agonised over until it was all to her exacting satisfaction. Jonathan helped, I think. No, I'm sure. It was after that orgy of creativity that he became Johnny. Vital decisions had to be made in Berners Street and Knightsbridge, time-consuming and exhausting, and Claudine would return flushed and with garlic on her breath. Never mind. Came the night, and I would swing into the nest to find her waiting. Wow! And afterwards she would say dreamily, I think, *chéri*, the blue is a leetle bit too pale. And I would agree, even though I knew it meant back to Berners Street.

Yes, nesting turned her on, all right. But as long as I was Mr Blackbird, I was able to stay mellow. After all, I've had outside interests of my own and there would have been garlic on *my* breath, too, from time to time, if I had not been influenced by a more dissembling nature to avoid the treacherous delights of escargots or coquilles St Jacques and chose, instead, some potted shrimps and a *bon bouteille*, in bed. That, in any case, is better fuel for a man of action. A restaurant, as its name implies, is for afterwards – a *restoring*.

So maybe Claudine's garlic was the scent of innocence, a mere meal. Maybe it was a warning shot across my bows. If so, it was not followed up by any change in her behaviour, in bed or out of it. That proves nothing: Claudine is French, indelibly so, and the French know how to be discreet when it suits them. There may, or may not, have been anything to be discreet about on her side, I never knew. Like battles, a discretion only takes place by mutual consent, and I didn't *want* to know.

Then, some months ago, Jonathan's wife Barbara threw him out, having, I suppose, weighed garlic against courtly manner, since when he'd lived in a studio apartment on Notting Hill with Italian furniture and quadrophonic sound, not ten minutes' stroll from us. So I wondered, and sometimes I found myself watching, though I tried not to. But now I need wonder and watch no longer.

Here's to you, Jonathan! Wherever you are.

The police didn't telephone, as it turned out. The front door bell rang and, as I went through the shop to answer it, I saw a panda car parked on the double-yellow lines just outside, under the yellow glare of a street light. There were two of them in uniform, and I unlocked the door prepared for trouble but quite sure, now I'd seen Claudine into bed, that I'd done the right, the husbandly thing. Take it calmly, I was telling myself – don't be too apologetic . . . Ridiculous how self-conscious the sight of an approaching policeman can make you.

Their car radio was going oy-oy-oy and ah-rah-rah, as they do. 'Good evening,' I said. 'Come on in. I was expecting you, of course.'

They stepped past me as I stood by the door, each in turn giving a slight nod, a minimal greeting, their faces impassive. They looked young, and appeared to my inexpert eye to be no more than constables – not what I'd expected to see on an enquiry like this. I led the way through the shop to my office. 'I've been waiting here for you to ring,' I said. 'Please sit down. What a terrible business this is.' I moved the brandy bottle and my glass to the top of a filing cabinet. They weren't, it seemed, going to sit down. They kept their caps on. The effect, in my small office, was alarmingly formal. What did it mean? Did they keep caps on for murder, take them off for housebreaking? Was it a criminal offence to leave the scene of a serious crime? What should I . . .?

'Now, sir, I'll put you in the picture,' the older of the two said. 'We're from Chelsea District. Our CID officers are still at the restaurant, taking names and addresses of witnesses, and preliminary statements. You should still be there, sir – yourself, and Mrs Warner.'

'Well, I'm sorry, but you see . . . I thought that in the circumstances . . .'

'I take it that Mrs Warner is here now, sir?'

'Yes. She's upstairs, in bed.'

'Not injured, is she?'

16

'No. But badly shaken up, though. She's taken some sedative pills and I'm afraid that's it for tonight. She really wasn't up to questions. I'm sorry if you were hoping to get a statement from her, but I'll have to ask you to accept that it just wasn't on.'

'I see.' Both policemen looked glum. 'I'll report that back, sir. They're not going to like it, you know. Has she been seen by a doctor?'

'No. She had the pills already – they're for the migraines she sometimes suffers from.'

'She told you that, sir?'

'Told me? Well, I knew that, yes, of course.' Odd question!

'All right, sir. Well, we'll report all that. They may want to send a policewoman round to see Mrs Warner, or they may not.'

'You don't want a statement from me?'

'That's not up to us, sir. That's for CID. You can expect a visit from them as soon as they've finished at the restaurant, or in the morning if they decide to see Mrs Warner at the same time. Now, sir, will you be staying here, or getting off home?'

'Home?'

'Yes, sir. Let's make sure we've got it right.' He consulted a notebook. '5 Scarsdale Studios, Notting Hill.'

I must have stood there for several seconds, staring at the young policeman's face, hearing his words but unable to make sense of them. The events of the evening went reeling through my head like an action replay. Then I realised what had happened. The rest of my party thought that I was taking Claudine home. Jonathan must have leapt up on impulse and rushed after us without explanation. I hadn't gone back into the dining-room after that. Any witness outside the restaurant would have seen a couple coming out, behaving with the easy manner of close familiarity. She stays by the restaurant door while he goes to flag down a taxi. Bang! And then bang again, leaving no face to recognise, even for those with the stomach to look closely. So it had been assumed that it was Jonathan who had burst from the restaurant to find that appalling scene, and who had scooped up Claudine to protect her from the sight of her husband – me! – lying, a bloody bundle, in the gutter. *'Take care of the lady!'*

'Something wrong, is there?' The two policemen came back into focus.

'You could say that.' Normally, I enjoy a dramatic opportunity, but this one was about as enjoyable as the sight of an open grave – dug for me. 'I think you must be under the impression that I am Jonathan Cassell.'

It was their turn to gawp. 'Well I'm buggered,' the older one got out. 'You're not? Then you must be –'

'William Warner. And glad to be alive.'

Back in my office, I poured another brandy, and took it to the desk. I dropped heavily into my chair, and began to think through the implications of all this. After a few hurried words, the police had left, and I saw one of them busy with the car radio as they drove away. I looked at my office clock. Just after midnight – about an hour and a half since it happened.

A mixture of guilt and relief – that's what I felt. Normal, no doubt, in this situation – as when somebody takes your place on the plane that crashes. It should have been me that walked out of Les Trois Pigeons with Claudine on my arm.

But no – it's not the same situation, of course it's not. This wasn't a natural disaster, but man-made, deliberate. They were after Jonathan, not me. If he hadn't come out then, they would have waited and got him later, when the party was over.

Clear enough. Not surprising that I feel shaken up – who wouldn't after what I'd seen? – but there's nothing I can do now except tell the police all I know and hope they can find who did it. How many murders go unsolved? What on earth can Jonathan have got mixed up in? Questions for the police, not for me. I haven't a lot of faith in authority, it's against my instincts to expect much from any large organisation – they're all too busy sealing themselves off in worlds of their own to have any time for the rest of us, except when they need our money. But this is one time when authority can take over, and welcome. Jonathan was my friend, but his death is not my problem.

And yet, and yet . . .

18

I've a feeling there's something I ought to do, an opportunity I ought to take . . .

No point, though, in sitting here getting more cold and tired by the minute – that isn't going to help me work it out. Better to continue this in comfort, in bed.

I swallowed the final drop of brandy in my glass, switched off the office light, and made my way upstairs. Claudine was sleeping soundly, her breathing light but regular. Pills must be working, then. I undressed and slipped in beside her.

Now, this thing at the back of my mind . . .

CHAPTER 2

Freudian Slip

In order to explain a slip of the tongue (for instance)
we find ourselves obliged to assume that the
intention to make a particular remark was present
in the subject.

SIGMUND FREUD

Rain woke me, great gobbets of it, splashing and sliding down
the sloping rooflights of our attic bedroom. Through the
streaming glass, a dark grey sky was just becoming visible, still
stained with the yellow glare of street lights, heavy and oppressive. The same colours seemed to prevail inside my head,
an underworld of foggy shapes lit by an occasional shooting
star as a thought flared and failed. One, more insistent than the
rest, burnt a hole in the sleepy murk – *something had happened.*
Drink, yes – but something more. The hole widened.

Jonathan.

Some decision had to be taken. What time was it? I levered
myself upwards, propped my weight on my left elbow. Across
the softly rolling landscape of duvet that covered Claudine, the
green eyes of the bedside clock blinked back at me. Twenty past
seven. I stared at it in dislike. As I did so, it blinked again –
another minute gone. Emperors hang the bearers of bad news.
One of these days I'll confiscate its battery. I slumped back into
the pillows.

What did I have to do?

A night's sleep should have given my subconscious time to
come up with the answer. Sleep on it, people say, when they're
stuck for a solution. It's good advice – we're full of bits and
pieces of information, random facts and impressions, all held
down in some lower part of the brain by the upper, conscious
part because, if all that information were all available all the
time, we wouldn't be able to handle it, there'd be an information
overload, we'd be in a permanent state of dithering indecision. I

20

read somewhere that operations of thought are like cavalry charges in a battle, only to be used sparingly at decisive moments. Most of what we do is automatic, predigested, buried in the subconscious. The brain is built that way – right hemisphere for instinct, left hemisphere for verbal and logical skills. So they say – and after forty-odd years of observing the erratic behaviour of myself and fellow humans I can believe it.

So – what messages are there for me this morning?

Left Brain, which should have worked out a status report overnight, was silent. Right Brain was being as inscrutable as ever.

I yawned. More time was needed, perhaps. The night was hardly over. I should sleep some more, let the night shift take over again, and hope they'd have everything sorted out before I woke up again. It was too early for questions and answers.

At my side, Claudine was still fast asleep. I listened to the soft hiss of her breath, noted the slight stirring of the duvet over her ribs in the hollow above the swell of her hips. A warm wave of affection flowed through me: for all our difference of temperament and nationality, in spite of extra-marital adventures carefully papered over (or *because* of them?) we had built up a good life together, and I couldn't imagine it without her as queen bee. I slipped my arm round her familiar form, and let my eyes close.

Sleep didn't come, though. The exhaustion – and over-indulgence – of the night before was wearing off, now, and my mind refused to be shut down again. Thoughts and images nagged at me, demanding attention, action maybe. What should I be doing? The police might arrive at any minute, and I ought to get myself sorted out before that. There would be a sharpish interview, of course, but I would say that ... well, what would I say? Perhaps I ought to agree it with Claudine.

'Are you awake, darling?'

No reply. Strong pills, those. Should have worn off by now, though. Still suffering from shock, probably. Bad idea to remind her of what happened last night, anyway, before it was unavoidable. The police would do that, must be used to dealing with shocked witnesses. They never sent a policewoman to check that Claudine really was here and in a drugged state, must have decided it wasn't necessary. Or didn't have one available. Or forgot. Just like the rest of us, when it comes down to it – muddling through with limited resources and less than perfect efficiency. Only the neat uniforms make you expect otherwise. But, take those two last night, for instance: the eyes under the official cap brims were far from penetrating: they were watchful but not perceptive: I had a collie with eyes like that and that's what most policemen are: straightforward, muscular, woof-woof, move along there. I was fond of my collie. And I shan't get those two into trouble if I can help it – no need to point out that they didn't check my identity at the outset as no doubt the rule book says they should. It was an easy mistake to make, and caused an extra ten minutes delay at most.

Wasn't that the doorbell?

I listened. It was.

A relief, really. My thoughts weren't getting anywhere useful. I slid hastily out of bed, and wrapped my dressing gown around me. My slippers had gone missing. They have a life of their own and I suspect them of trying to escape from my service. All right, then – have to go down barefoot. I swung down the spiral stair, across the landing past the girls' rooms, and down the main stairs. The bell sounded again as I reached the bottom; it was the shop door at the front. I pounded through the shop, the polished pine boards cold under my feet. Halfway there, I saw an unmarked grey Rover outside – must be someone senior. I unlocked the door.

Two plain clothes policemen this time – no need of uniforms to tell me who they were. One stood on the step, close to the door, to escape the worst of the rain which fell in curtains of icy water from overflowing gutters high above our heads. The second still sat in the passenger seat of the car, his face turned towards us, waiting. For me to be identified, I assumed.

I stepped back to allow the man on the step to come inside, into the dry. He moved just through the door, running a hand round his collar to catch raindrops making their way down his neck. His face was official, unsmiling. He said: 'Your name please, sir.'

'William Warner.'

His eyes swept over me once, taking in my dressing gown,

22

bare feet, and no doubt dishevelled hair and bleary eyes. Then he stepped back to the doorway and nodded towards the second figure in the car. The car door opened, and then slammed, and this person crossed the pavement to join us, plunging through the rain with the dignified haste of senior rank caught in an uncomfortable situation, like a general under fire. Behind him, the street lights still shone yellow, reflected in the shimmering black of the street surface, where raindrops swirled and pattered in the grip of the wind. Overhead, the sky was scarcely lighter, or less oppressive, than at daybreak. I shut the door.

'Filthy day.'

The newcomer gave me the same sweeping glance as his companion: it was as if all my vital statistics were being recorded. I was reminded of a supermarket checkout, where the bar code is swept over the laser. Did he now know my stock number, product category and price? What date would I be best before?

'Filthy day, sir, yes.'

My turn to record details. A tall, lean man, forty-five-ish, clean-shaven, greying hair. What use is it to know things like that? Not much. It's the dynamics that matter, the things that make him tick. He *thinks* – I can tell that from the way he looks at things, including me. There's an air of *bitterness*, suffering almost – I can tell that from his mouth, which is too tight, too closed. Not the sort of policeman I'm used to – but of course I haven't come across senior detectives before. Why should I care? Because I have a feeling that this one is going to affect my life. That this is the start of an invasion.

'Is this going to take long?' I asked. 'Because, if so, I'd better put some clothes on.'

'Do that, sir. And I'll need to see Mrs Warner as soon as I've had a talk with you. I hope she's sufficiently recovered.'

'She was still asleep when I came down, but I'll try to wake her.'

He nodded. 'It is important.'

'Of course,' I said, and showed them into my office.

I climbed back up the stairs. I didn't have to wake Claudine: she was lying there with her eyes open. She watched me as I approached the bed, but said nothing. Well, it couldn't be

23

avoided, not any longer. She was going to have to go through this. I said, gently: 'It's the police. I'll have to get dressed – they want to talk. And then they'd like to see you. I'm afraid it can't be avoided, darling.'

I stood by the bed, looking down at her. 'Of course it can't,' she said. 'And *I* want to talk to *them*, to tell them everything so they can catch these people who did this.'

I sometimes forget that Claudine has a core of steel. Of course she would want to do that. Last night's breakdown was over. Today she would do what was necessary. Sometimes it strikes almost chilly, this ability of hers to sweep aside the past, so much water under the bridge, and get on with what's next. It's her Bordeaux background, perhaps, the ability of the bourgeois French to pick themselves up and try, try again. They're survivors. No time for sentimental moppings and mowings. Useful, of course, when they're on your side.

'I'll come up and tell you when they're ready,' I said.

'*Entendu, chéri.*'

Down in my office it was time, it seemed, for formal introductions. 'I am Detective Superintendent Priestly. This is Detective Sergeant Cooper.'

I nodded. 'Please sit down. My wife is awake, and getting dressed.'

There was a short pause, during which Priestly's eyes stayed on me. If it was one of his little ways, an interview trick to see what was on his interviewee's mind by letting him speak first, I found it more irritating than alarming. But perhaps it was just to let some tension build up.

Finally he said: 'As you'll be aware, Mr Warner, it is your duty to assist me in this enquiry. But you need not answer any questions if you do not wish to do so. Is that clear?'

'Perfectly,' I said. 'I'm only too anxious to help in any way I can. Jonathan was a friend of mine.'

'We'll come to that,' Priestly said. Nothing, his tone seemed to say, would be taken for granted. What could be more obvious than to claim friendship with your victim? Was that what he was thinking? Oh come *on*, now – that's pure imagination, he's just taking things in order, that's all. And why should I be nervous, for God's sake – I've done nothing criminal . . .

'... must surely have been aware that you should not have left the scene, nor your wife, before police had taken charge.'

The scene of the crime. They *did* use these phrases. But I shall deal with this in my terms, not his ... 'As I explained to your officers last night, my wife was badly shocked, almost hysterical. There was nothing I could do for Jonathan – an ambulance was being called for. So I brought her away. If that's some kind of offence, I'm sorry, but I still think it was right in the circumstances.'

'You are aware of the confusion that was caused?'

'Yes. But I don't understand why it lasted so long – Jonathan must have had some means of identity on him – wallet, cheque book, credit cards ...'

'It's not so simple, Mr Warner. Uniformed officers were first on the scene. They are trained, in a case of suspected criminal homicide, not to move the body or interfere with the scene. The body had to be screened while everything was recorded – this took some time. Identity is a secondary consideration, and took place after the body had been removed to the mortuary for detailed examination, accompanied by an officer.' Priestly's look was severe.

'Well,' I said, 'of course, I didn't know all that. But even if I had, I don't think I would have wanted to make my wife go back. A crowd was gathering. She was badly shocked – well, I've told you the state she was in.' I didn't know what else I could say, but surely that was enough? And so far, Priestly had shown no sign of sympathy, formal or otherwise. I glanced up to find his eyes still on me, and still severe. He's overdoing it, I thought suddenly – he's using this situation to put me on edge. Interview technique again. Bloody hell! – I may have made a mistake, but it wasn't deliberate, my wife *was* ill. And anyway ... 'It can't have made much difference, or you'd have been here before now,' I told him sharply.

'That's for me to decide.' He spoke just as sharply as I had, but it was a standard defensive remark which he didn't attempt to justify. And he took his stare off my face.

We moved on to the central event of the shooting. Sergeant Cooper's ballpoint skated rapidly over the pages of his notebook. I couldn't think there was much of importance in what I could tell them – I'd been offstage, as it were, when the important things were happening.

'We'll have that read back, Mr Warner. Tell me if there's anything incorrect, or that you think has been left out,' Priestley said.

Cooper read it back in a flat voice, frowning over his writing.

'Well?' Priestly asked.

'It's correct,' I said, getting to my feet. 'Do I sign it now, or do you have it typed out first?'

'I was just checking our interview notes,' Priestly said, 'not taking a formal statement. Thank you.'

I sat down again. Had he finished with me? Apparently not.

'You say that Mr Cassell offered to take your wife home?'

'Yes. It was my party – I was the host. Kind of him to offer, so that I could stay on.'

'This was because she was ill?'

'I told you. A migraine.'

'Does she often get migraines?'

'Sometimes. Not often.'

'Once a year? Twice?'

'Not more than once.'

'How many in the last, say, five years?'

'I don't know,' I said, irritated. 'Two or three, perhaps.'

'She gets them quite rarely, then?'

'If you like.'

'I don't *like*, Mr Warner. I simply want to *know*. Rarely?'

'Yes.'

Another sharp exchange. True, my answer had been woolly. But so had his question. I felt I was being treated like a hostile witness although, in my statement, I had tried to be helpful, to give more than was being asked. But Priestly was not in forgiving mood, it seemed. I watched him as he studied his own notebook, saw him blink, and then stretch his eyes wide as he read. Must have been up all night, I realised, organising his men at the restaurant, taking statements, making sure he'd got all he could before evidence disappeared. Perhaps he already knew what had happened, or thought he did.

'What else can I tell you?' I asked. It sounded impatient, not what I'd intended. 'Jonathan was a friend of mine,' I added, to correct any wrong impression. Then I remembered I'd already said it.

Priestly nodded. 'I understand that, sir.' He pursed his lips, seemed to be considering alternatives. 'It would be useful,' he said at last, 'if you would describe your relationship with Mr Cassell. From when you first met him. If you please.'

'Of course,' I said, and told the story of our house alterations, Jonathan's idea of the attic bedrooms and spiral staircase, Jonathan's help in dealing with the builders and so on, during which he became a personal friend. 'Always prepared to spend time to get things just right,' I said. 'We appreciated that. Especially when it came to the decorations.' These trivialities could have nothing to do with Jonathan's death, of course. But by listing them I hoped to straighten the account with Priestly.

He listened in silence. Then, when I'd finished, he asked: 'Did you choose the decorations yourself, sir?'

'No, not really. I left that to my wife. She's got strong ideas about wallpaper, colours and so on. Good ideas, too. I left her to it.'

'So she told Mr Cassell what she wanted?'

'They sorted it out between them.'

'And you stayed out of it?'

'More or less. Except for the money side. It cost more than expected. Building always does.'

'Your wife found Mr Cassell quite easy to deal with?'

'Oh yes. They got on very well.' I smiled, remembering the evidence of garlic lunches, Claudine flushed and happy with creativity.

'Yes. Well, thank you, Mr Warner. I'd like to see Mrs Warner now, if I may.'

'I'll tell her. Would you both like some coffee?'

'Very kind. If it's not too much trouble.'

'No trouble at all.' I left the room, feeling that I had regained some ground with him.

Claudine was in the bathroom, where she keeps her potions, applying the finishing touches in front of the mirror, her dark hair already sleek with brushing. She's meticulous with make-up: always has been, always will be, regardless of the current trend towards looking well-scrubbed and sporty. I confess I like it – I want a woman in my life, not a hockey player.

'They're ready for you, darling.'

'*J'arrive.*'

'And they'd like some coffee. I'll go down and make it while you're finishing off. Sure you feel all right?'

'Of course. You go down.'

I went, pausing to glance at the bedside clock. Ten past nine. On the landing I paused again. No sound from the girls' rooms. And down in the kitchen no sign of Julian, who slopes into the house from his room over the garage for breakfast, but doesn't appear until after ten on Sundays.

I put the kettle on, ground some beans, got the coffee pot out, laid a tray with milk and sugar. The kettle was just coming to the boil when Claudine arrived, dressed in a black wool dress with a deep red scarf at the neck and matching nail varnish. Her decision to wear black was understandable, if a little overzealous, but, wool being what it is, the sobriety of the colour was more than offset by the contours beneath. Claudine's contours – well, there's a German novel that begins: 'She had buttocks like a horse – a thoroughbred mare, *natürlich*.' That puts it in a nutshell. But Claudine doesn't see herself like this, or chooses to ignore this aspect of her otherwise slim and distinctly elegant figure.

'Darling . . .' I began.

She saw the direction of my gaze. Her face clouded. 'Oh,' she said. 'Oh. You think this is not suitable. I think perhaps you are right. I couldn't make up my mind. I will go and change.'

'No, don't,' I said quickly. Priestly had already been kept waiting ten minutes. 'No, I was just going to say how right you looked. You'll brighten their morning, no doubt about that. They've been up all night, I think.'

She regarded me doubtfully. I gave her a confident smile. Well, she'd be sitting down, after all. That would help a lot.

I led the way into the office, carrying the coffee tray, Claudine following behind. The two policemen rose to their feet, Priestly first, Sergeant Cooper taking his cue some seconds later. 'Coffee,' I said brightly. 'Do you take milk and sugar, Inspector?'

There was no reply, and I looked up. Superintendent Priestly's eyes were taking in Claudine, from head to foot and back again. A policeman is entitled to look at people more directly than the rest of us – required to, of course. He'd done it to me. But not quite like this. He seemed, suddenly, to be aware of the silence that had followed my question, and his eyes switched abruptly to me. 'Both,' he said. 'Thank you.' Too late, though. For a second, Superintendent Priestly's mind had been an open book. For adults only.

I introduced them to Claudine, got her safely seated, dispensed coffee, and turned to go. Nobody was looking at me. Claudine was looking down, her hands in her lap. Sergeant Cooper was turning to a new page of his notebook. And Superintendent Priestly's gaze was turned to the window, with its view down the garden, where the rain still fell from a sodden sky and lay in pools on the muddy grass. He wasn't seeing it, I felt sure. His thin, thinker's profile was turned away from all of us, concealing whatever expression it might have carried. We might all, for the moment, have ceased to exist.

'I'll leave you to it, then,' I said.

Sergeant Cooper looked up and nodded. No one else moved or said anything.

The Sunday papers had been delivered, thrust hurriedly into the letterbox of the side door, half in, half out. The outer half was soaked, and tore as I pulled it through, decapitating a prominent Northern Irish clergyman and Member of Parliament, and damaging a Savile Row suit worn by Prince Charles. I was sad about the suit. I took the paper to the kitchen, and spread the wet pages out to dry, scanning them quickly as I did so. Yes! – there it was, inside page, squeezed in at the bottom of the News In Brief column: CHELSEA SHOOTING – *man understood to be wine merchant shot dead outside luxury restaurant late last night ... Police are interviewing witnesses ... statement expected tomorrow.*

It was odd, reading that. Sent a shiver up my spine. But I'd wanted it to be there ...

Abstractedly, I wandered round the kitchen, looking for the coffee pot. Then I remembered it was still in the office with

Claudine and the police. I've never mastered the art of making coffee in a saucepan, so coffee would have to come later. Meanwhile, some toast perhaps.

Wanted to be reported dead . . .

Julian appeared at the garden door, under an umbrella. I went to let him in.

'Hi, Dad. The studio rooflight's leaking.'

'Badly?'

'I've put a bucket under it.'

'Has your course got on to leaking rooflights yet?' Julian is a fourth-year student at the Architectural Association.

'Don't worry, I'll fix it when it's dried out a bit. Just needs some mastic down the sides. Where's the coffee pot?'

'The police have got it.'

'The *police* . . .?'

He's fairly laid-back, Julian, so his uncharacteristic squawk of surprise brought me out of my speculations. I told him what had happened the night before. He found it hard to take in.

'Claudine saw this?' She's his stepmother, so he calls her by her name. His own mother, my first wife, died in a road accident when he was ten.

'Yes. I brought her back home straight afterwards – she wasn't in any state to answer questions – and the police are here now, taking her statement.'

He whistled – a long descending note. Then, putting two pieces of bread in the pop-up toaster, he leant against the dresser, watching me. 'Is that something about it in the paper?'

'Yes. But they've got it wrong – here.'

I handed him the paper. My mind was elsewhere. *Understood to be a wine merchant* . . . after trading for a hundred and twenty years on this site that's all the impact we've made . . . bypassed by Tesco's . . .

'Wow!' Julian said. 'They thought it was *you*!'

'Yes,' I said absently. 'Good, isn't it.'

'*Good?*'

'Well . . .' *Did I mean that? I must have done, according to Freud.*

A sudden metallic crash made me look up. Electronic wizardry everywhere, but nobody can produce a silent, civilised toaster.

Julian came to sit at the table. He had his thoughtful look on.

Reaching for the butter, he said carefully: 'Makes you wonder who else could have got you and Jonathan mixed up.'

'What do you mean?' I was fairly sure I knew, but I wanted to hear him say it.

He seemed to be struggling with himself.

'Say it,' I urged.

'All right. Look, Dad – you're in quite a state, I can see that. So it's probably occurred to you as well. I mean, that it might not have been Jonathan they were after.'

So I'm not alone. But . . . 'Nonsense,' I said firmly. 'I've had a rough night, that's all. I don't have enemies like that.'

'Did Jonathan?' Julian asked quietly. 'You wouldn't have thought that, either.'

He was right, he was right . . . 'The difference is,' I said, 'I *know* I don't have enemies like that. None of us knows – knew – that much about Jonathan.'

'The thing is,' Julian said, 'it's such a weird situation, you can't help working out the combinations. It must really have been Jonathan they were after – it's unlikely anyone would make such a colossal mistake, is it? You're quite sure you can't think of anything . . .?'

'I can't,' I said firmly, 'think of any reason for anyone to want to knock me off. No.' *Well, there wasn't, was there? . . . not that I'd been able to think of . . .*

'Anyway,' Julian said, 'you've got today to think about it in perfect safety. Because, officially, you're dead. How does it feel?' He smiled his dry little smile.

Yes! That's it exactly! Safety, and time to think. Provided gunmen read newspapers . . .

'I don't suppose you'd feel like going up to the newsagents to get some of the other papers?' I asked him. 'I don't think I ought to go out while the police are still here.'

'Of course. I'll go now, before they're sold out.' He got up to go.

'Thanks. You're being more help than you know. If only you could make coffee in a saucepan you'd be perfect.'

'No problem. When I get back, OK?'

'Fabulous boy,' I said warmly.

He left. I stayed at the table, riffling through the news section of the paper looking for any other reference to the shooting, but found nothing. Found nothing much else either. I don't know why I keep on with Sunday papers: the fatter they get, the less there is in them. You sit there munching words as a cow munches grass, consuming acres of newsprint for a minimum of nourishment. But at least it ensures a restful Sunday morning silence. The girls didn't appear. Normally Claudine would have chased them downstairs by ten, but this morning it was better to have them out of the way until the police had left. If they ever did leave. Claudine had been in there an hour, now.

After ten minutes, Julian reappeared with an armful of newspapers. The promised coffee was made, and then we both got to work. We found virtually the same short news item in most of the papers. None mentioned my name, but all described the victim as a wine merchant.

'Must be an agency item,' Julian said.

'Because they're so similar? Yes, that would explain it. It's good they didn't get hold of my name, or decided not to publish it. I'd have had to have been on the telephone all day, reassuring relatives.' And how long would everybody have taken to get used to the idea of a world without me? I wondered. Not long, I fear. A day or two of 'Alas, poor William, I knew him well' and the waters would have closed over my head. Except for family, you sink with scarce a ripple, I have observed.

So let's make good use of the here and now, starting with this famous Freudian slip. 'Good' to be reported dead, is it? Yes, I'm beginning to see the advantages. But there's some planning to be done. 'I think, while the police are finishing with Claudine, I'll go upstairs and be horizontal for a while,' I said. 'Last night is catching up with me.' I got up, stretched, and made for the door.

'I'll tell her when she comes out.'

'Thanks.'

'Meanwhile, er . . .'

'Yes?'

'Rest in peace,' Julian said.

CHAPTER 3

Evil Illusion

> . . . belief in the 'goodness' of human nature is one
> of those evil illusions by which mankind expect its
> life to be beautified and made easier while in reality
> they only cause damage.
>
> SIGMUND FREUD

'Hello?' said the telephone. It wasn't Pete, as I'd expected, but a
girl's voice, breathless and suspicious.

'Give it 'ere, yer silly bint.' That was Pete in the background.
There were sounds of struggle, some giggling, and then Pete
came on, louder. ''Ullo?'

'You're still in bed,' I said, 'I'm sorry.'

'Oh, it's you. Well, Sunday morning, innit? Time for all good
men to make up for Saturday night disappointments, on account of 'aving 'ad a jar too many. I mean, I got company.'

'Understood. I'll be brief. You haven't seen a paper, I suppose?'

'Not likely.'

'Well, there's been a bit of bother up here, and I badly need
to talk to you. I wouldn't ring at this time, otherwise. Could I
meet you at the warehouse at twelve? That'd give you an hour
and a half.'

''Ang on a mo'.' He turned away from the telephone, and I
could hear him explaining. 'It's my guv, 'e's got trouble.' There
was a muttered consultation, and then he came on the line
again. 'You're on. Twelve, you said?'

'That's it. Thanks, Pete. Sorry about it.'

'Pleased to oblige. See you.'

I used the bedside telephone to make this arrangement. Afterwards, I lay back and thought for a few minutes, planning what
I would ask Pete to do for me. It wasn't by chance that I had
an employee with underworld connections: if you've got a

33

warehouse in Wapping stuffed with hoistable booze, it's only sensible to choose a van driver from the area who knows who's who and what's what. The fact that Pete had brushed with the law in his youth was to me a recommendation – he knew that I knew, and we soon came to a tacit understanding on the number of bottles that might go missing by way of overtime. No one else from his manor was likely to poach from us while he was in charge, and any strangers would be instantly spotted. In fact, while wine does get stolen, it's spirits that attract most attention, and everyone knew we had none of that. So far so good.

I heard voices downstairs. It sounded as though the interview was breaking up. I got off the bed, put my shoes on, brushed myself down with both hands to chase some of the creases from my clothes, and descended. Claudine and the police were in the hall bidding each other a subdued farewell. I hoped they had finished and wouldn't hang about – I longed to hear from her what had been said, and why it had taken so long. Priestly turned to me as I reached the bottom of the stairs.

'That'll be all for now, Mr Warner. But, unless I'm very much mistaken, there will be further questions. Have you any plans to leave London at all? We may need to see you again at short notice.'

'No,' I said, 'none.'

He nodded. Cooper was stowing away his notebook.

'Any help I can give . . .' I began.

Priestly gave a small, wry smile. The black mark was still against me, it seemed.

Pointless to say any more. Only deeds, not words, would count with him now. I led the way through the shop to the front door where the car was waiting. Priestly paused by the claret shelves. Was he a fancier? I would have guessed that, if he liked wine, claret would be his tipple – dry, tannic, austere. He was peering at labels in the gloom.

'I'll put the lights on for you,' I offered.

'Château Pichon-Longueville, Comtesse de Lalande,' he read slowly. 'A wine-making lady.'

'In fact, yes,' I said, 'but not the old countess; it's now run by a mere madame. The estate changed hands in the twenties.'

34

'Twenty-one pounds a bottle,' he read.

'Good year, '76. Would improve with another year or two's keeping, probably.'

'Would it, now?' he said quietly, almost to himself. I recognised the drift: every wine merchant gets to see himself as others see him, especially others who reckon the wine trade a means of conning large sums from snobbish suckers. Countesses, vintages, fancy French names. At twenty-one pounds a bottle. Don't know why you bother, sir, a customs officer said, totting up the little collection I was bringing back by car, I-don't-know-why-you-bother. All this duty to pay, which you needn't if you make your own, like me, from a Boots Wine Kit . . .

'It's a lot of money,' I said. 'Not often I get to drinking one of those. But anyone who likes wine should have a really good bottle once in a while. It puts the whole thing into perspective.'

'Does it, sir, yes?' Priestly murmured. He straightened up, walked slowly to the door, glancing from side to side, looking as if he were shaking his head in despair. Sergeant Cooper held the door open for him. Outside, the rain was still sheeting down, and the gutter by the nearside wheels of the Rover was inches deep in yellow water. Priestly turned to me, inclined his head in farewell. 'We'll expect to contact you here, then, Mr Warner.'

'Yes. Can I lend you an umbrella, Superintendent?'

But he'd gone, stalking through the rain to the car, where a rear door opened to take him in. I saw his thin profile, obscured by the streaming glass of the car window, motionless as a waxwork. Then the car bore him away.

I watched them out of sight. Then I went to find Claudine, to ask about the interview. She was in the kitchen.

'What did he say?'

'I am making some fresh coffee, you would like some?'

'Thanks. What did he say? What did he ask about?'

Claudine's shoulders lifted, and dropped again. The genuine Gallic shrug. Expressive even when seen from behind, as now. Her face was away from me, towards the sink, where coffee grains made a dark brown whirlpool around the waste. 'What you would expect, *chéri*. About what happened at the restaurant, in such detail I could scream. And so slowly, *mon dieu*.

About why you brought me home, about the migraine I had. Surely you told him all that before? About Jonathan, and you, and me. On and on. He is a strange man, I think. All that silence, while he looks out of the window. You think perhaps he has gone to sleep but then, no, another question.'

'I couldn't decide if I thought him very clever or very stupid.'

'I don't know, *chéri*. Very, very *slow* – that is certain.'

She handed me a breakfast cup of milky coffee. I took a swig. Always tastes better when she makes it, but I can't see why. I asked: 'Have you seen the bit in the papers?'

'I showed her,' Julian said, handing his cup over for a refill. 'And I said you were glad they hadn't got hold of your name. There's no real harm done, is there?' He caught my eye while Claudine was pouring coffee into his cup. It was a look of male complicity – *Let's keep the little woman out of this*. I was amused but touched – he's fond of Claudine, whom he treats more like a sister than a stepmother. And, of course, I did want to keep her 'out of it' – at least until last night's experiences had receded to a safe distance.

'It passes the imagination,' Claudine was saying.

'What does?'

'That the newspapers can make such a mistake. How can it happen, a thing like that?'

'Oh well,' I said, 'it's always happening. Notoriously inaccurate, newspapers.'

'But, William, why did not the police . . .?'

'Well, it was late-night news, wasn't it? Only just in time to catch the morning papers, and too late for corrections. Anyway, as Jules says, no real harm done.'

'But some of our friends knew we were having that party! If they see this in the papers, they will think . . .'

'I know, darling, I know. 'Tricia did, for one – she rang up while you were still in with Priestly, and after that I put a message on the answerphone. She sent you her love, by the way.'

'Oh – I must ring her!'

'Well, if you're feeling up to it, darling, I suggest you ring anyone you're worried about and explain. Or I'll do it for you when I get back from the warehouse this afternoon.'

'You are going to the warehouse?'

'Didn't I tell you?' I said smoothly, having prepared for this. 'There's been an almighty cock-up, and I've arranged to meet Pete there to sort it out. Got to be done before he can make tomorrow's deliveries. We may have to send out some substitutes.' I avoided Julian's eye. He might guess I was up to something.

'I roast a piece of beef for lunch,' Claudine said, 'and you can have it cold for supper. With first, perhaps, a little *Gratin dauphinois* to warm you up. It will be cold at the warehouse.'

Some people would rearrange deckchairs, but Claudine would carry on cooking as the *Titanic* went down. A double tragedy if there wasn't time to eat it before the waters closed in.

'I love you, my darling!' You, and your *batterie de cuisine*.

I eased the Citroën out of the garage, and set off along drenched, deserted streets to the docklands of the East End. It's through the City, a mere fifteen minutes drive in light traffic from the Champagne-Charlie-land of Park Lane and Piccadilly to the Dickensian grime of Whitechapel and Wapping, from the haves to the have-nots. The East End is changing, with redevelopment gradually eating away the ancient warehouses and cobbled streets, but in the meantime life goes on as it has for centuries, a battle of wits against poverty and the police: it's an upside-down world, where families with histories much longer than that of the police take a pride in passing on the traditional skills of pickpockets and housebreaking, and where 'well-respected' does not mean respectable. East End crime has traditionally been small-scale, and murder frowned on as bringing too much close attention from the Law, but violence is on the increase, influenced by the lurid brutalities of the Richardson and Kray gangs in the fifties and sixties: taboos once breached tend to stay broken, and the younger generation of villains take violence as a matter of course.

So why do I have a warehouse in this alligator swamp? Well, the docks are there, which is convenient if not essential – I could pay more for road transport and operate from outside London. But most of my customers are in London – big-spending hotels and restaurants, some with accounts going back to my father's time and beyond. I have a strong list of private buyers in London, who appreciate the rapid delivery I can arrange. The premises are cheap, being on an ancient lease at bargain terms by the standards of today. And it's surprising how little you actually *see* to cause alarm, even though you know what's going on from the media. Somehow, so far, the crime statistics don't seem to have applied to me. Until yesterday.

I could see the firm's taxi sitting outside the warehouse as I turned into the long, cobbled chasm of Brewery Lane, lined on both sides with dark crumbling Victorian red-brick sheds and offices. Today the normal atmosphere of gloomy decrepitude was increased to the point of terminal depression: shut in by the solid grey sky, its sides spewing rain from broken gutters, its floor veined with rivulets of oily water sliding over cobblestones between blocked drains, Brewery Lane had a doomed, defeated air. The effect was increased by the lights which glowed every hundred yards or so in security offices, oases of light and warmth in this man-made desert: as I passed one I could see, through greasy steamed-up window panes, the blue-uniformed inhabitant slumped over a tabloid newspaper, mug of tea to hand. Not much chance of an alarm in this weather – the likely lads would be in the pubs, keeping dry.

I pulled up outside our warehouse, behind the taxi: it's driven by Pete and, looking like a regular taxi, saves time and much hassle with traffic wardens on London calls and there's room for a dozen sample cases of wine at my feet.

The little pass door in the warehouse frontage was open; I saw Pete's face there. I got out, slammed the car door, scrambled to twist the key in the lock, and made a dash for it.

'We'll be fishin' in the street if this goes on,' Pete greeted me. 'Can't hardly tell the river from the road, can you? There's a leak over the Coat de Rone. I've been shiftin' the crates before the labels come unstuck.'

People don't like buying wine with damaged labels: Pete knows his job. I thanked him, took a look at what he'd done. 'Must be a blocked gutter. Better get Ron to clear them all when the rain stops.'

Pete looked doubtful. 'You won't get Ron,' he said. 'Not wiv your lawyer wavin' writs in 'is face.'

Ron Green was a local builder whose reconstruction two years ago at the back of our premises had come unstuck: a gable end was already cracking and looked likely to get worse. Rebuilding seemed the only way out, but Ron said London clay was the culprit, not him.

'He ought to be covered by insurance, the lawyers say. It shouldn't hit him personally.' I hoped not – I liked him, and he'd done a lot of maintenance work for us over the years, with hardly any problems before this.

''E doesn't see it like that.'

'No, I suppose he doesn't. Well, who else is there?'

Pete said he had a mate. You can't be too careful with employing unknown builders about the place: too often they're the ones who tip off the lads looking for a hoist, having identified the best place to break in. But Pete's recommendation was as good as I was going to get.

That settled, I led the way to the office at the back of the warehouse, and motioned Pete to a chair. I gave him the Sunday paper, folded at the News in Brief, and pointed out the relevant item. He read it carefully. 'Bloody 'ell!'

'We were making an occasion of it, you see. Dressed up in dinner jackets, both of us. Same height, same shape, much the same haircut. The rest of the party saw me going out with Claudine, to take her home because she wasn't feeling well. Had a headache. But Jonathan met us in the hallway, and offered to take her in my place.'

I described the shooting, as Claudine had told me. 'I took her straight home – she was badly shaken, of course. You're supposed to wait for the police, but in a case like that ... anyway, I didn't. The rest of the party knew where we'd gone, and the police came round later. But they thought, everyone thought, that I was the one who went outside with Claudine, that it was me left lying in the gutter. That's how this story got about.'

'Proper turn-up, innit?'

'Sure is.'

'Must 'ave felt queer, readin' this 'ere.'

'Sure did.' I watched while he read it again, absorbing every detail. Then he shook his head slowly, and sucked in his breath. 'So it could've been you they was after. 'Course, you've thought of that.'

His immediate jump to this conclusion, reinforcing what Julian had said at breakfast, made me feel a lot better, much less out on a limb. It *was* a wicked world. It *was* sensible to take precautions, to look out for oneself. But, apart from the lack of any motive against me, I'd had time, while coming here in the car, to think of an obvious argument in favour of Jonathan being the intended victim – so obvious, I didn't know why it hadn't occurred to me before. 'I hope this isn't just wishful thinking,' I said, 'but the bloke wielding the shotgun fired the second barrel right into Jonathan's face – he must have seen him close up. Not much chance of a mistake there.'

'Glad to hear it, guv'nor,' Pete said. 'Makes sense, that does. Anyway, who'd want to settle with you? Don't owe anybody you shouldn't, do you? Or anythink like that?'

'Owe anybody?'

'There's people round 'ere gets a bit upset at being owed, know what I mean? Clubs, gees, grey 'uns. No, not your scene, is it. What about hanky-panky with somebody's missus? That Ginny you was seein' a lot of, for instance. Still goin' strong, is it?'

'Ginny Duff-Jones gave up the independent life and went back to her double-barrelled well-heeled called-to-the-Bar husband,' I said reproachfully, 'and is walking labradors in Wiltshire. It's a sore point with me. How did you hear about her?'

'Well,' Pete said, 'a word here, a word there. You put two an' two together, and there you are. You know how it is.'

'It left a hole in my life,' I said, after a pause.

'Oh dear. Sorry to 'ear that.'

'Thanks.'

'Didn't mean to upset you.'

'No, no. Of course you didn't.'

'Anyway . . .'

'It's all right. Go on.'

'That rules him out, then. This brief she's married to.'

'Oh, yes. A pompous prick and pillar of the Establishment. He wouldn't shoot, he'd sue. Anyway, it's all over now. Look, I

40

thought we just agreed that Jonathan was the likely victim – not me.'

'So we did. Well, know anybody that'd want to do 'im? What sort of a geezer was 'e?'

'A smoothie,' I said, and gave an outline, which included the courtly manner.

'Ah. Ladies' man. Didn't like 'im, did you?'

'I suppose not, if it comes right down to it.'

Pete was looking at me speculatively as I said this, but made no comment. I thought the time had come to explain my idea, something Pete could do without risk, by following his normal pattern of life, but a bit more so. Pub crawl. And listen to the grapevine. He'd just given me an example of how effective that was. In the East End, there's an information network that works faster than anything the CIA could set up: it covers employment prospects, manpower availability, official intentions – you could put it like that. Plus any other business. 'Things should be humming today, especially if it's thought the wrong man got shot – that's news, isn't it? What are the chances of picking up something useful?'

To my surprise, Pete looked a lot less than overjoyed.

'What's the matter?' I asked.

'Oh,' he said, 'well. Yeah, no harm in keepin' my ears open, I don't mind doin' that for you. I'll take my new girl round, show 'er the sights. But . . .'

'What's the problem? I don't want you to do anything at all risky.'

Pete leant towards me, his face as solemn as a priest's. 'It's not a question of bottle,' he enunciated. 'I'll do it, no bother. But makin' enquiries, naming names – now that's different. That's *'ighly personal*. Someone might not like it. Someone might think I was a mutt. Things can 'appen to geezers what ask too many questions round 'ere, with the river so 'andy an' all. Besides, I got me reputation to think of.'

I was appalled. 'Forget it,' I said – Pete *scared* was something I never expected to see. 'It's a long shot, anyway. It isn't worth it. And the police will have had the same idea, bound to. We'll leave it to them.' I made to get up, but Pete put his hand up to stop me.

'Like I told you,' he said, 'I'll do it, but there's a limit, an' I'll 'ave to watch it. 'Course, the lads what did it may not be from round 'ere at all, but I may pick up a whisper. If I do, I'll tip you off, but not on the blower, mind. You never know who's listenin'.'

This sounded like pure fantasy, but the East Ender is obsessively secretive, even when there's no need: at a time like this, caution would go into overdrive. 'Think I'll start up the Tickle,' Pete was muttering to himself, 'then maybe the Scrubber.'

'Tickle?'

'The Prince Albert,' Pete explained. To his own satisfaction – I didn't get it. But then, that's the idea, outsiders aren't supposed to. We both got up.

'Sorry again about this morning,' I offered.

'No matter,' he said, smiling reminiscently. 'There was time enough after.'

'A new girl?'

'Yeah. Social worker. Small, with specs, but a right little goer. She's reformin' me, see. Nothing pulls a bird faster than the chance of doin' good to you.'

'But you haven't been in trouble for years!'

'Ah. I was meanin' to bring that up. Due a bit of overtime, aren't I? Well, if I was to, like, nick a case of that Coat de Rone with dodgy labels, an' get caught sneakin' it into the flat under'and, she'd 'ave sumfink to get 'er teeth into, know what I mean?'

Driving back to the rich and righteous West, I thought some more about what I'd asked Pete to do, and why. He knew how to keep out of trouble, I was sure of that. Even if he slightly overstepped the safe limit, and someone noticed his ears were flapping more than usual, his reputation as a straight 'un would keep him safe. Regular informers – mutts, snouts, narks, grasses or whatever – are mostly known to be so, and so avoided: useful tip-offs normally come from a disaffected member of a group formed to do a particular job. Pete, I believed, was clear of all that, and unlikely to have any reason or need to curry favour with the police. On this occasion, it would be natural to take an interest in a dramatic killing, just as any member of the public might. Besides, at this stage I didn't want any names, it wasn't the identity of the gunmen I was interested in, *yet*, but the name

42

of the intended victim – Jonathan, or me. Yes, I was interested in that, all right. Although I was sure it was Jonathan. Certain. Almost.

That rings a bell, people say, when something half-understood niggles for your attention. A bell was ringing now, like a telephone call from the subconscious. Something important . . .

'Yes?'

'Left Brain here. The answer to your query – it's *wince*.'

'What?'

'Tickle and wince. You didn't get it.'

The Prince Albert. The Prince. Wince. Tickle and wince. *The Tickle*.

'Oh, yes. Thanks.'

Must have something better to do, surely?

CHAPTER 4

Abundance and Complexity

The deeper we penetrate into the study of mental
processes, the more we recognise their abundance
and complexity.

SIGMUND FREUD

Possible that, if I'd driven straight back to Church Street, I'd
have arrived in time for the tail end of lunch with roast beef.
The talk with Pete had taken less time than anticipated, and
the streets were emptier than ever, what with the rain still
pounding down and the good citizens all tucking into their meat
and two veg this Sunday lunchtime. But there were other ways
of spending my spare hour or two, useful ways, pleasurable
ways – or maybe both. Also, it is my firm opinion, tried and
tested, that cold roast beef (pink in the middle) is one of the
world's great dishes: to lessen the impact by eating hot beef for
lunch would be a shame. The situation called for restraint,
perhaps in the form of something light and fishy. How fortunate,
then, that I was within striking distance of Leicester Square,
where the brass-and-mahogany emporium known as Jackson's
exists to supply just such lunches, on Sunday as on every other
day. I turned north off the Embankment, negotiated Nelson and
his pride of Landseer lions, where the pigeons, grounded,
huddled and shivered against the granite. And found a choice
of parking places.

A wave of warmth greeted me as I pushed through the
heavy doors. Jackson's provides that red-plush solid comfort at
which the age of Edward was supreme. Muscular, masculine
comfort, built for men who ruled the world, and their wives
as well. In the private rooms upstairs, with their gilt mirrors
and gaslight, the geishas of the stage – all piled hair, huge
hats, swan necks, and wasp waists improbably corseted – were
wined and dined with intervals for the 'hurly-burly of the chaise

44

longue' as one lady unforgettably described it. Sad to think that the place is now owned by a vast catering group, beloved of the City. But at least they've had the sense to let it alone, so far.

'Half-a-dozen, Tony. And a glass of, let's see, this one.'

'Right, sir.'

Montmains, it was, a *premier cru* from Louis Michel. I'm not well stocked with Chablis, so you could call this research. Well, *I'm* going to. Anyway, I don't think it's fair to oysters to send them down with boring old Muscadet.

The best way to spend the afternoon, I decided, would be to call on Barbara, Jonathan's wife, or now, I supposed, widow. They had been unofficially separated for several months, otherwise the day after his death would, of course, have been too soon to call. It might still be too soon – you can be wildly wrong about how a separated couple feel towards each other: sometimes a separation improves a relationship by removing day-to-day hassle – a tendency of one partner to overbear, perhaps, or practical irritations like snoring or hairs in the washbasin. I know several couples who, although fond and far from wanting a permanent split, needed more space in their lives and made it by living apart some of the time, often for reasons connected with their work. Maybe this is to do with more people working at home, without the outside interest an office provides. When I first read in Alvin Toffler about the 'electronic cottage' that technology can now provide us with, where work is piped in to VDU consoles, and there's no need to commute to work, it all sounded very cosy and delightful. He sits at one work station juggling commodity prices, while she sits at another selling airline tickets. The trouble is, with house prices rocketing as they are, we're all having to make do with smaller and smaller houses, and we don't want to spend all day every day at home. If we, as couples, except for the exceptionally well-integrated few, ever did.

Barbara and Jonathan, I suspected, had come to some such impasse. It was second-time-round for both of them, which must have increased the strain of living and working together since tolerance of one's marital partner, alas, varies inversely to age. Youthful illusions butter over a lot of dry bread. Reality, by definition, is not what you want but what you have to put up with. Most people, not being very good at putting up with things, bend reality a bit to suit themselves. Successful couples bend in unison, or one bends and the other complies, or a bit of both. I didn't know either Barbara or Jonathan well enough to see how they stood according to this theory, but a few seconds on Barbara's doorstep would provide some clue.

The doorstep in question was situated in Edwardes Square, off the south side of Kensington High Street, less than a mile from my house. Neat, terraced houses with small gardens fronted by iron railings; built, I think, for officers returning from thwarting Napoleonic ambition in Europe, which would make them about 1815 or so; they have that sash-windowed propriety which contrasts so well with trees and grass, and makes a London square the archetype of gracious town living. Not much of a porch to shelter under, but I had my umbrella. Would it ever stop raining?

I didn't hear the bell ring when I pressed the bell push, and after a half-minute decided to try the brass knocker. I was just reaching for it when the door was opened. Barbara stood there, looking at me with a mainly blank, slightly worried expression. It's disappointing not to be remembered, especially by someone as pretty as Barbara. I'd forgotten how pretty – a slight, youthful figure, and long pale hair of an indeterminate colour with lighter streaks in it, expertly cut. Her face was smooth and unlined except for a faint effect of time, difficult to say exactly what, about her green, thoughtful eyes. Which continued to search me for my name. I opened my mouth to tell her.

'No!' she said quickly, 'no. Don't. I'll get it in a moment.'

'Let me give you a clue,' I offered, smiling. Already I could see the answer to my own question: this was not a woman in mourning, and Jonathan, by the time of his departure, could not have been very dear.

'It was at a party, here, about a year ago, just before Jonathan and I separated,' she said. 'Yes! – of course. You're William – William Warner. How could I be so stupid – I was talking to the police about you this morning. You were at the restaurant last night – that must be what you've come about. Please don't

46

stand there in the rain – come in. You can put your umbrella there.'

'Barbara, only if you're sure. This dreadful thing . . .'

'It's all right,' she said. 'Really it is. I'm glad to see you. Let's go in here.'

I parked my dripping umbrella, closed the front door behind me, and followed. She led the way into a small sitting-room overlooking the square. It was tricked out in fabrics and wallpaper that were a bit much for my taste. Tables were swathed, curtains were thickly gathered, pelmets swooped. Little lamps and objects stood all about, vulnerable to the careless elbow. White carpet flowed wall to wall. There was a large mirror over the pine-framed fireplace, and groups of little pictures. Definitely boudoir-ish, I thought – made me feel a clumsy male with big feet. Facing the fireplace was a deep sofa loaded with cushions. It looked tremendously suitable for hurly-burly.

'What a pretty room! Not Jonathan, I guess.'

'Thank you,' Barbara said lightly. 'No – not his style, is it? I had the whole house redecorated after he left. I don't think – do you? – that men are very good at interiors.'

I had a sudden picture of her standing in this room, planning that revenge, exorcism, annihilation which a thorough re-decoration provides.

She indicated the big sofa, and installed herself at one end of it, curling her legs up beside her as comfortably as a cat. I took the opposite end. We smiled at each other. She shook her hair back, and her green eyes glowed.

'I'm so sorry about Jonathan,' I said. 'I'm not sure why I've come, really, but I was out and about and I thought I should – we live so close, after all. And I thought you might like to talk to someone who was there, when it happened.'

She looked down, the hair falling forward again, her hand stroking a cushion, and said in a matter-of-fact voice: 'As you see, I'm able to be quite detached about it. Jonathan and I had been living apart for a year – but you know that, of course. We hardly ever saw each other. It didn't work out, you know, except at first. Oh, we seemed to hit it off so well at first. We had so many shared interests – design of course, and travel, and building things up. He had his architectural practice with

47

Bill Charrington, and then I started Nature Store – you know about the shops?'

I did, of course. Barbara had started a chain of small shops selling a combination of health foods and natural cosmetics, brown rice and coconut oil lotions. She had told me I should eat more fibre, and had given Claudine a selection of small pearly globules to dissolve in the bath and soften the skin. I tried them once and came out of the bath stickier than when I got in. Not my sort of thing. But I'd recently seen a piece in the financial section of the paper about Barbara, describing her as the 'Darling of the Unlisted Securities Market', so her shops must be popular.

'Know about them? Who doesn't! How is it going?'

'Quite well. No, to be honest, it's going *very* well. I can't really believe it. The shops are spreading like weeds.'

'Like wild flowers.'

'Oh, William, do you think so? I wish you really meant it. I can't help identifying with them, with how they look and so on, and I so much want people to like them. My accountants think it's wrong to get personally involved – they think you should stand back, keep detached, treat it as a marketing operation, nothing more.'

'That's why they're accountants. Trained to keep their feet on the ground, and their eyes on the figures. But no amount of juggling with figures is going to do any good if a business hasn't got a clear idea behind it. You had a vision, Barbara. That's what makes the thing go.'

'You understand it *perfectly*! Oh, but of *course* you do – it must be the same for you. And your business has been going a long time, hasn't it?'

'Family firm. I didn't really feel it was mine until the shop was revamped and brought up to date – by Jonathan, of course. It was like slamming a door on the past, on my father in effect. But it had to be done – we were beginning to slide. I don't think he'd have minded, really.'

'I'm sure he wouldn't,' Barbara said warmly.

'Well, you didn't know my father. Nothing short of imminent bankruptcy would have persuaded him to change the old shop. But Jonathan's scheme kept the best of the old – the Victorian shopfront, some of the fittings – but removed the gloom and the air of decline and fall. It's all stripped pine now, white walls, black lettering. Quite sharp. Haven't you seen it?'

'Isn't it ridiculous, no, I haven't. Except from the outside, driving past.' Barbara looked a touch uncomfortable.

'Perhaps you're not into wine?'

'Well, I don't know much about it. I think I'd feel lost in a shop like yours. I'm afraid I get mine at the supermarket round the corner.'

'Barbara!' I launched a few well-used comments on the better value offered by real quality.

Barbara smiled and nodded, but I saw her mind was elsewhere, so I cut it short. 'Sorry. Can't help it – we're under pressure, and it's a problem to know how to handle that kind of competition.'

'I was thinking,' Barbara said, 'that we had Jonathan in common. He set up the Nature Store house style, of course. The whole image, from shopfittings to letterheads. And it really worked for us.'

'Green and off-white. Like lettuce and fresh cream.'

'With little strips of mirror, and brass light fittings and door handles to give an upmarket feel. Yes, he was good at that, wasn't he?'

We sat in silence for a moment. That had been the best side of Jonathan – dashing about the shop, head down, like a hound on a trail, seizing on this feature and that, knowing what to suppress and what to emphasise, ruthless in pursuit of an image which exactly fitted the business, the public face of your trade. Before Jonathan, I'd thought designers were fairly useless people who fussed endlessly over superficialities, the precise shade of a coat of paint or pattern of carpet. I hadn't expected his depth of analysis. 'What *is* your business, then?' he'd asked. 'What is it you're trying to do? Once I know that, I can help you put it across. That's what shopfitting is all about.' And he was right, of course.

'Yes,' I said, 'he was good at that.'

The talk so far had skated round the main purpose of my visit. It could be avoided no longer.

'Shall I tell you what happened, as far as I can? Or have you heard enough from the police? I didn't actually see it – I was inside when I heard the shots. It was Claudine –'

'Oh yes, I *know*! Poor, poor Claudine! How is she?'

'Claudine,' I said, 'is a lot tougher than she looks. She had over an hour's grilling from the law this morning, and emerged tail up and talking of potato gratin for supper. I think she took a dislike to Inspector Priestly – did you have him?'

'No, a detective sergeant. Bruce, I think he said his name was, and another man. Very non-committal. They worked through a list of questions, got me to confirm that my answers had been taken down correctly, and then left.'

'But he told you what happened?'

'Oh yes, thank you, William. Yes, I really don't want, I don't *need* to hear any more. I can picture it – that's enough. It must have been quick, mustn't it?'

'No doubt of it. Instantaneous.' No need to dwell on that space between the two shots, or how it must have expanded for Jonathan, as the barrels swung and re-aligned. Had his life passed in review, as it's supposed to, in those two concluding seconds?

Time for the big question. 'Have you any idea *why*?' I asked.

Barbara shook her head, brushing the pale hair back with one hand. 'It's the sort of thing that happens to other people. My mind just goes blank when I think about it. It's impossible to imagine anyone doing that. Or what Jonathan could have done to deserve it.'

'Retribution of some sort, you think?'

'Oh, I don't know. What *do* people get killed for?'

Six reasons, I'd read somewhere. Retribution was one. Money, jealousy, lust, for a principle, for the pleasure of killing. All too simple, too pat. Human motives, surely, were always mixed and more complicated than that.

'Did you know,' I said, 'that last night everybody thought I was the one who'd been shot?'

'I saw it in the papers,' Barbara said, 'and the police gave me an outline. But they weren't saying much about anything, mainly asking. That was extraordinary, William.' She gazed at me, frowning.

'Interesting, too. Who will send flowers? How big will the

bunches be? What was my true worth in the eyes of the world? – all that.'

'I see.'

'Unfortunately we decided not to let it go to the test. When I left this morning Claudine was about to pass the word that I'm still extant.'

Should I tell her about Pete and his mission? I think not. Although they were separated, she's still Jonathan's widow. Best to leave it at that for the present.

Barbara was shifting her position on the sofa. Resettled, she gave me a quick, estimating kind of glance, and then switched her green eyes to the fireplace. It was equipped with one of those very realistic everlasting coal fires which are really fired by gas. But the room also had radiators and was quite warm.

'Are you cold? Shall I put that thing on for you?' I offered.

'Cold? Yes, I think I am, just a bit. Would you?'

I turned the gas on, and lit it. Soon the bogus coals would begin to glow, a practical illusion even though the idea is absurd. I turned from the fireplace, and stood looking down at Barbara. She had been watching me, it seemed, as she quickly slid her gaze away, murmuring, 'Thank you, that's better.'

'Still raining?'

'Yes.'

I felt there was something she wanted to say, and stood there for a few moments, waiting. But perhaps Jonathan's death was only just sinking in; perhaps she felt it more deeply than she cared to admit, either to me or to herself.

'Barbara, I think I'd better be off.'

She looked up. I held out my hand to say goodbye. Slowly, she took it, but, instead of a brief pressure, she held on to it, and drew me down to sit on the sofa again, only releasing it when I was installed. The green eyes looked into my face, closer now. 'I'm going to tell you,' she said. 'I think I ought to.'

That always sends a shiver up your spine. Mostly because, put like that, it can only be bad news. 'Out with it, then,' I said.

'It's about Claudine,' Barbara said.

No no no no! I don't wish to know that! I especially don't wish to be told that! This could upset the whole carefully loaded applecart. How can I stop her?

51

'Don't say anything,' I said quickly. 'There's nothing I need to hear about Claudine. It's not necessary. Thank you for the thought, but no.'

'I mean, about Claudine and Jonathan –'

'I know, but there's nothing I want to hear about that.'

'I see.'

'The police were asking, I suppose?'

'Yes.'

'In detail?'

'I don't know any detail, William.'

'But they asked? They want to dig up every scrap?'

She didn't answer, but it was written on her face. The spades were out. And the earth, crudely excavated, would turn into mud.

'How,' I said, mostly to myself, 'does one translate the subtleties and complexities of a relationship, built up over years, into terms that the police understand and can accept? Jonathan, I'm sure, would have moved on by his own choice, maybe already had. He didn't need to be pushed.'

Barbara put her hand on mine. 'I know,' she said quietly, 'what it's like. We really did have Jonathan in common, didn't we?'

'He gave you a hard time?'

'He believed, he said, in being "honest".'

'But it was "honesty" with a certain glint in the telling?'

Was that plausible claim ever more than a cover for guerrilla warfare in the battle of the sexes? A camouflage for the working-off of resentment? Or, in Jonathan's case, no more perhaps than simple egotism, as a man might arrive home bursting to tell his best-beloved about A Good Day at the Office? No, of course not. There had to have been spite in it.

'A glint,' Barbara said, 'yes. That was there. You're so right, William.'

I glowed a bit, under her green gaze. Well, nothing in it really – anyone could work that out. Still satisfying, though, to hit the nail on the head.

'You realised that, of course?' I said.

'That "honesty" was just an excuse? Well, I suppose I did. I didn't really think about it like that.'

'But he must have had some reason, something he held

52

against you? Oh, I'm sorry, Barbara – you won't want to go all through this now – it's all water under the bridge. I'm just naturally nosy – always have been. Sorry. Forget it.'

'It's very nice of you to be interested – don't be sorry. And I don't think you're nosy, not at all. I think you're very sympathetic, and I like talking to you. Kind, too, coming to see me on a filthy day like this.'

I glowed a bit more. But forebore to explain that my motives had not been entirely altruistic. Sympathy is a plant which thrives best on selective truth, especially at the early stages. Who knows where this could lead?

Barbara still held my hand in a light, forgotten kind of way. It was quiet in the room: the effect, it might be, of the swagged, ruched, pleated and draped materials that surrounded us, tucked us in, two birds in a nest. Outside, the rain drummed on the window sill; an occasional car splashed round the square with its dripping trees waving green arms in response to the wind. In front of us, the phony fire hissed and glowed red, sending a flickering and soporific warmth into the depths of the big sofa. How does it go, now? – 'Isn't it a lovely day, now we're caught in the rain/You were going on your way, now you'll have to remain.' Did she feel that, this little Barbara? An electricity, the stirrings of a delicious tension, were, I sensed, beginning to build up. Our silence had that quality of awareness which makes thoughts almost audible, or visible. It couldn't go on. Something had to happen.

It did.

The door opened.

Barbara slipped her hand away, and turned her head. The door itself prevented me from seeing who was there. But anyone, at this moment, was one too many.

'Hugo darling!' Barbara said, 'come in, do.' It was a warm enough welcome – too warm, to my way of thinking, my line of thought. Warm enough to succeed, that is.

It did. Hugo darling moved round the end of the sofa into my area of vision. I heaved myself vertical, being, even at moments of opposite intention, helplessly polite. But I was on autopilot.

'Hello.'

'Hello.'

Hugo darling, I remembered even as Barbara was announcing our identities, was her son by her first husband, who had been, probably still was, a German sculptor – quite famous, or notorious, for works of heavy symbolic intensity and minimum visual appeal, usually in iron with tattered scraps of canvas attached, preferably charred. Somebody had described his Tate exhibition as '*objets brulés*', which was near enough. His son Hugo, now standing before me with his back to the fire, was a slight, pale youth of about eighteen, wearing jeans and a red check shirt buttoned to the neck. He was tall and stooped slightly, which gave his beaky, earnest face an uncomfortably questing air. A chip off the old block, I guessed.

'You should put a sweater on, darling,' Barbara scolded him.

Hugo nodded. His eyes, after a brief glance at me, were fixed on the floor. Barbara continued to inspect him anxiously. I thought I might as well take my leave. You can't compete for the attention of a mother hen.

'Thought it might be time for tea,' Hugo said to the carpet.

'Yes, darling,' Barbara cried, leaping up. 'Good idea. You'll stay and have some with us, William, won't you?'

I played the got-to-go tape – much as like to, things needing attention, Claudine expected, better not, good lord is that the time. Etc.

Barbara saw me to the door, while Hugo darling sloped kitchenwards. At the door, she offered her cheek for a farewell peck, and gave my arm a little squeeze. 'Thank you so much for coming.' It sounded as if she meant it, and I felt a little rush of returning warmth. Perhaps I should invite myself again, in a day or two. There was still plenty to discuss – further thoughts on why Jonathan had got shot, more about what the police had said. After which, it seemed possible, we might move on to Any Other Business. Yes, we should meet again, soon. I opened my mouth to suggest it –

'Can't find the sugar,' Hugo's voice, tinged with complaint, echoed along the hallway.

'I must go,' Barbara said. 'Hopeless boy.' She smiled complacently. I began to open the door. Jesus! I was going to get wet.

'Wait,' Barbara said urgently. I shut the door quickly, and spun round to face her. 'Your umbrella!' She thrust it into my hand. Oh. That.

I watched Barbara's slight figure recede down the hall as she hastened away to the kitchen, leaving me to let myself out. Slight, but not skinny. A woman retreating at speed, glutaeus maximus at full quiver, is a sight that draws a programmed response, disapprove it as they may while hopelessly hauling down the back of the cardigan. We can't help it: we may dissemble, switch the glance, assume an air of clerical innocence and detachment from the ruder things of this world, but it's there all right, even in those of us too genteel to shout, "Ullo darlin'! Wot's the 'urry?' Equality begins –

The door bell rang. Barbara had disappeared, so I answered it.

In the background the rain was an almost solid wall of water. In the foreground stood a tall figure dressed in a very dark blue or black suit, with a white shirt open at the neck, and the business end of a toothbrush showing above his breast pocket. He was about my age. His hair was long, dark, and lank. His face was gaunt and unshaven. Brilliant pale blue eyes stared at me from either side of a strong, hawklike nose. He held an umbrella in his left hand, and in his right, as though it were a weapon, he gripped a single red rose, its stem wrapped in silver foil. His stare seemed to have in it something of enmity, as though I was the intruder, instead of vice versa. The rose, probably, was the key. He had expected the door to be opened by Barbara. An annoying thought – pretty widows not being all that plentiful.

'Yes?' I said shortly.

'Krantz.'

'You are Krantz?'

'Of course.'

I made way for him. All was explained. This was Hugo's father, Barbara's first husband. I didn't know they were still in touch.

Barbara arrived, having heard the bell. 'Ludwig!'

Ludicrous name.

'I have come again,' Ludwig said. His accent was slight, but his careful articulation made this sound like a public

55

announcement. The Second Coming of Ludwig. I decided I should go before our instinctive dislike was cemented by a snigger. This would be inescapable the moment he began on the presentation of the rose. The comparison with *Rosenkavalier* – a favourite opera – would certainly be too much for me.

'I must be off,' I said, and slid out of the door. Neither of them seemed to notice. I closed it behind me.

Back in Church Street, tea was also in progress. The girls were there, the first time I'd seen them since the previous night. They're just coming up to teenage, and I get a sinking feeling whenever I think of it, like the captain of the *Bounty* on hearing that the men have got at the rum. All it will need is a spark to fire their barely bottled-up insubordination – most likely in the form of some contemptuous youth with dyed hair and monosyllabic conversation – and mutiny will explode, our whole ship will go up. This, in spite of my fine, my formidable First Mate.

'Nichole! Make room for Papa.' Claudine acknowledged my return with a rather distant smile. She was looking tired, I thought, but no wonder. Nichole, who had spread herself across one end of the table, edged her chair across to make room for another. I sat down beside her, and gave her a little squeeze by way of greeting, which she accepted impassively, her mouth full of bread and jam. Sylvie, on the far side of the table and out of reach, gave me a smile of unnerving brilliance, and batted her eyelashes vampishly. Just practice, I realised – yesterday the mirror, today dear old Dad, tomorrow the world, God help it.

'Some tea, *chéri?*' Claudine passed me a cup. 'It is all arranged, at the warehouse?'

'All sorted out – I left Pete to finish off. On the way home, I called to see how Barbara Cassell was. She's all right, taken it very calmly, in fact. They weren't close, were they?'

'Not, I suppose, since Jonathan left,' Claudine said, dabbing her lips with her napkin.

'Sylvie and I are glad it wasn't you that got bumped off,' Nichole said suddenly through her bread and jam. 'Aren't we, Sylvie?'

I was touched at this rare display of sentiment, freely offered. Maybe, somewhere deep inside, beneath those exteriors of seamless tungsten, little hearts had paused in their pit-a-pat for a millisecond at the thought of losing me.

'Thank you, my treasures. I am glad to be still with you,' I replied. The future seemed a little lighter, somehow.

CHAPTER 5

Findings and Difficulties

But I can set myself no other aim than to give you
an impression of the nature of our findings and of
the difficulties involved in working them out.
SIGMUND FREUD

Monday morning in the office. According to the daily paper I
was alive again. On a day like this, it was a doubtful privilege.

I shut the door, crossed to the desk, switched on the brass
desk lamp with its green shade, and stood for a moment beside
the dark brown leather executive chair, staring out through the
window down the length of the garden. I wasn't ready to be an
executive, not yet, not this morning. The rain had slackened a
little, but the sky had taken on an angry tinge of purple, and
there had been thunder in the night; an occasional rumble still
erupted like celestial indigestion. In the garden, weighed down
with water, japonica sagged away from the high brick wall
along the side street. Dead leaves, driven into corners, had been
pounded to a mush. I switched my stare indoors. On the desk, a
tray of letters, invoices, problems lay waiting. It would be an
hour and a half before the next cup of coffee. Why was I here,
struggling for existence in this inhospitable island, next door
but one to the arctic circle, when I could be reclining under
tropical palms accepting free-growing abundance from the soft
hands of dusky beauties? A historical accident, is all. Time I left
the scene of it.

Meanwhile – all of life seems to be meanwhile – I'd better get
on. I sat down, wincing at the clammy grip of executive leather,
and pulled the tray towards me.

Some time later, there was a tap at the door, and Maggie,
our mainspring rather than just our manageress, entered
briskly. Her hands were empty. I stared – had we run out of
coffee? Had the grinder broken down?

'Peter is here,' she said. 'He'd like a word.'

'Fine, ask him to come in. Er, Maggie, what about coffee?'

Maggie looked down at her watch, and then at me. Her glasses flashed disapproval. 'Mr William,' she said in her severe ward sister manner, 'there's half an hour to go yet.'

I looked at the clock. She was right, as usual.

'Oh come on, Maggie,' I wheedled. 'We ought to see Pete refuelled before we send him out in this weather again. Oughtn't we?'

Maggie considered this. An appeal to her motherly instincts usually wins the day. It did. She left, promising coffee and shaking her grey curls at my unfair tactics. I sometimes wonder whose firm this is: mine by title, certainly, but she's been here since I was a schoolboy, and is still the backbone of the place. Control of the coffee is her way of ensuring set times for consultation, I'm sure.

Pete appeared in the doorway, his black bomber jacket speckled with rain. ''Ere I am,' he said. 'Bright an' early.'

'Hello, Pete, come in.' I studied his face. Was he charged with news? Was it good or bad? He wore his usual cheerful, wily, city-dweller's mask – a friendly fox. Impossible to tell anything from it. 'Shut the door, and sit yourself down. You can hang your coat up there.'

He hung his jacket behind the door, where it dripped gently on to the carpet, but I was too impatient to care. 'Any luck?'

Pete sat in the visitor's chair, and looked across the desk at me. Then he smiled slightly, enjoying the moment.

'Come on then!'

'Nuffink much,' he cautioned me. 'No names, nuffink like that.'

'Never mind. You've heard something?'

'Yeah. I'll give you the whole story, right?'

'Right.'

After he'd left the warehouse, he said, there'd been time to call in at a couple of pubs on his way home, starting with the Prince Albert. And there, almost before he'd collected his Guinness from the bar, he'd struck lucky. Sitting in a corner, with a little group of cronies, was his Uncle George.

'Who's Uncle George?'

'"Aven't I never told you? Ah, well, 'e's a character, old George. Retired now, got a bit tucked away, got 'is old age pension, 'e's quite comfortable. Still does a little job now and again for fag money, but 'e's lost 'is 'ead for 'ights, see. Won't go up ladders no more.'

'What did he do?'

'Old George? Well, you know, the usual. Bit o' this and that. Only ever got put away twice – 'e was a dab 'and, 'e was. Well respected. 'Course, 'e's not really me uncle, but 'e was a good mate to my dad, close as that they were.'

'Say no more,' I said, joining in with the spirit of the thing. 'I've got the picture.'

'Right. Well, Uncle George, 'e's old-fashioned, see. 'E don't 'old with young tearaways what carry shooters on the job, beat up old ladies, and that. Unprofessional, 'e says. 'Course, 'e says, they don't know no better – come from nuffink, most of 'em. They're rubbish.'

'Right.'

'Well, old George seems quite chuffed to see me, an' so I joins 'is little group of old codgers. And we're in luck, 'cause they're all rabbitin' on about your shooting, see. There you are, says old George, jus' what I'm always tellin' you. Scumbags, the lot of 'em. So thick, they can't even shoot the right feller.'

Pete paused, watching me. 'Wait,' I said, 'wait. Got to work this out. Had Uncle George seen the Sunday paper?'

'"E 'ad one there. That's what started 'im off, see.'

'And it said that I'd been shot? Gave my name as the victim?'

'Yeah. Saw it meself.'

'Then,' I said, 'what made Uncle George think the wrong man had been shot? Didn't say that in the paper, did it?'

'No, that's the point, see.'

I didn't see, not at all. Monday morning fog still embalmed my brain. Coffee, a sometime luxury, was at this moment a vital necessity. Where are you, Maggie?

Heaven heard me. A rattle at the door, and Maggie came in with a tray, dead on cue. 'Bless you, Maggie!'

She parked the tray on the desk, and tapped the small pile of papers beside the filing tray with her forefinger. 'Shall I take these? Cathie needs something to get on with.'

'Yes, do. And there's that indexing, as well.'

She nodded, and left. I pushed a cup towards Pete, and took a healing sip from mine – it was good and strong. Then, with the door firmly shut again, I leant forward and said: 'Please explain. If it wasn't in the paper, how did Uncle George get the idea that a mistake had been made?'

'Oh well,' Pete said. ''Eard it on the grapevine, didn't 'e?'

'I've got to get this right. The paper said *I'd* been shot.'

'Yeah.'

'And the grapevine was saying the *wrong man* had been shot?'

'Yeah. Like I said.'

'So I'm the wrong man. And it *was* Jonathan they were after.'

'That's right.'

Surely that was clear enough. Well, I hadn't ever seriously thought they were after me. But there had been that nagging possibility, and as a matter of fact, someone did once take a potshot at me, which led to all sorts of amazing events, and a lot more shots. So, and who wouldn't, I felt relief mixed with a slight sense of anti-climax. It wasn't my problem any more, never had been mine, but Jonathan's. Which now, poor sod, meant no problem at all.

''Eard it again in the evenin',' Pete said. 'Just a mutter. In the Blind Beggar, it was, up the Whitechapel Road. Geezer saw me listenin', so I took my girl away. That's the place where Ronnie Kray did a feller called Cornell, at the bar, in front of all the customers. Still remembered, that is. I was only a nipper at the time. Real nutter, 'e was.'

'They caught him, though.'

'Oh yeah. Put 'im inside. 'E's still there. Nuffink to do with 'im, not this caper. Makes you think, though, dunnit? There's things you're better off not knowing about, that's for sure.'

Pete left, and I had to get down to work then. It's a real chore, my office work. People usually show a more than polite interest when they hear you're a wine merchant – it's one of those occupations, like psychiatry, maybe, or working for the Foreign Office, that evokes in most people's minds a picture of a world one stage removed from ordinary life, furnished with its own set of attitudes and experiences, demanding from its practitioners a range of special skills, its mysteries preserved with all the care taken by medieval monks over a fragment of undoubtable True Shroud from the tomb of Our Lord.

We have our sceptics, too. I've learnt to recognise the evil glint in the eye of a host when handing me a glass of 'claret' for my opinion, hoping that I will fall for this and suggest some *château*, so that he can gleefully announce the stuff is cabernet sauvignon from Bulgaria, or California, or Australia, or whatever. Some wines are usually unmistakable – the top white burgundies, for example – but, with growers all over the world trying their hardest to emulate the best, it's wise to be cautious and avoid these party games except with your friends who understand the problems and are not out to score a point at your expense. One of the best 'clarets' I ever tasted was, in fact, a little-known Tuscan wine called Sassicaia. You couldn't blame anybody for not knowing it was Italian and not French. Doesn't prove anything, either, except maybe that wine is infinitely complex and variable, which is just the point your evil-eyed sceptic is trying to *disprove*.

Well, all that is the interesting side of being in the wine trade: I don't think I shall ever tire of it. But not a lot of my time is taken up with tasting, unfortunately; most of my work has of course to do with stock lists, haggles with transport contractors, invoicing, sales ledgers and unarmed combat with VAT inspectors, not to mention endless moans about rising overheads and increasing competition from supermarkets. And it's boring, boring, boring.

That's why, probably, while I wrote lists, checked prices and signed cheques, my thoughts drifted back to Jonathan, although it was now clear from what Pete had told me that I wasn't involved, that it was nothing to do with me. Nothing at all.

How did the Safetyfast Shippers van driver manage to take *two weeks* to get from Bordeaux to London? Even a girlfriend in Boulogne couldn't be that demanding, surely. They've got to be charging me for a lot of other deliveries slipped into the same trip.

*

Claudine had made a thick onion soup for lunch, with croûtons as it was such a cold and clammy day. We ate it, just us two, at the kitchen table. She wore a cardigan draped round her shoulders, and looked as pinched and miserable as any French housewife when the sun fails to shine. Crumpled, almost. Not her style at all – she's usually one for the straight back and the bright smile even in adversity.

Why did I say, or think *adversity*? Hardly the world to describe weather, unless you're halfway up the Himalayas.

'Are you all right, darling?'

She smiled slightly, looking up from her soup which she had hardly touched.

'I think perhaps I have the migraine again.'

'Shall I call the doctor? Saturday night, and now again today . . . I think you should see the doctor. Shall I?'

'Oh no, *chéri*, it is nothing much, I expect it will go soon. After lunch I will lie down for a while.'

'Good idea.'

Wine at lunch is apt to make the afternoon return to work more of an effort, but today it seemed a medicinal necessity. Just a glass of ten-degree plonk. Claudine shook her head as I reached over with the bottle towards her glass.

'Thank you, *chéri*, but no.'

'Do you good?'

'No.'

Perhaps she was right. Well, I didn't have a migraine. I took a swig and felt a warming glow begin to circulate. A litre a day kept Roman soldiers on the march, fighting fit. Though they didn't have to do office work on it. I looked across at Claudine, saw her replace the soup spoon at the side of her bowl. Why didn't she simply go and lie down? She seemed to be struggling against it. No need, surely.

Perhaps it was something more than a headache. Some kind of delayed shock. Or . . .

'Did the police upset you, darling?'

'The police? Oh no, no. Why should they?'

'I thought perhaps, well, something they said . . .'

'No.'

'You were in there a long time.'

63

Claudine pushed her chair back and stood up. She frowned, passed her hand over her eyes, and shook her head two or three times, as if dazed. Then she pushed her chair into the table, and picked up her soup bowl and spoon to take to the sink.

'I'll do that,' I said. 'You go on upstairs. Would you like a hot-water bottle? Comforting, you know, when you're feeling fragile.'

She nodded, and made the semblance of a smile, but her eyes, I noticed, were not included in it. She did not look at me, but made for the door as if it were a refuge.

I boiled a kettle and filled the old hot-water bottle which we keep for such emergencies, settling the woolly jacket round it. This old thing seems to console the sick better than an electric blanket, due to the localised warmth perhaps, or the woolly jacket that makes its plump shape feel like a friendly animal lying beside you. I went upstairs with it.

'Here you are, darling.'

No reply. She seemed to be asleep. I slid the bottle gently into the bed, and settled it against the small of her back, where it would do most good.

Back to the paperwork, then, until about four, when the phone rang.

'Mr Warner?'

'Speaking.'

'Inspector Priestly, sir. Will it be convenient if I call later today, say, at half-past five?'

The form of words was polite, but the tone gave little support to the idea that my convenience was uppermost in his mind. But then, why should it?

'I don't know what I can add to what I've already told you, but yes, that time would be as good as any.'

'Thank you, sir. I'll be there.'

Maggie appeared moments later, bearing more piles of paper.

'What's all that? Will today never end?' I complained.

'It's only four o'clock,' she pointed out.

'Time for the chairman to summon his Rolls and go home.'

'Delusions of grandeur,' Maggie remarked.

'And persecution.'

'If I didn't . . .'

'I know, I know. Just a routine grumble. You know how I hate this stuff. Couldn't we put it on computer?'

'Still got to be fed in.'

'Yes, but . . .'

'Someone else would have to do it?'

She had me there. More staff, more overheads. Impossible.

'Grrrr,' I said.

The police arrived on the dot of half-five. There was a lingering customer in the shop, and so they tactfully came to the side door. I opened it, and let them in, Priestly in the lead with Cooper close behind. Coming in from the dark, against the glare of street lights, they looked bulkier, more ominous than yesterday morning. Priestly sounded it too. Cooper avoided my eye after an initial glance. Well, all right, if that's how they feel . . . don't expect me to battle with the bonhomie all on my own. I led the way to my office in silence, indicated chairs. We all sat. I waited. Not for long.

'I understand,' Priestly said, 'that Mrs Warner had quite a — shall we say — close relationship with Mr Cassell.' He watched my face as he said this. So did Cooper.

In spite of myself, my stomach gave a lurch: suddenly, there was an acid taste at the back of my throat. I had to swallow. All of which must have shown on my face, however slightly.

'Are you asking me, or telling me?' I said sharply.

'Perhaps,' Priestly said, 'you'd like to tell us what you know about this relationship.'

'No,' I said, 'I wouldn't like to. Not at all. I will tell you, though, that it's got nothing to do with your investigation into Mr Cassell's death. Nothing at all.'

'You're not prepared to discuss it? You don't have to, if you prefer not to, or think that it would not be in your own interest to do so. But frankness is usually the best policy, I need hardly point out, especially in an enquiry into a serious crime such as this.'

'I can only repeat,' I said, 'that the friendship between my wife and Mr Cassell, however you may choose to describe it, is entirely irrelevant to your enquiry. Any time you spend on it will be wasted. That's all I've got to say on the subject.'

'I see, sir,' Priestly said. He looked round at Cooper, and nodded. Cooper snapped his notebook shut. They both stood up.

I showed them to the door. Nobody said a word until I had the door open; then Priestly paused, looking out into the street where the car sat waiting for him, rain making jewelled patterns on the roof where the street lights caught it. Then he said, without looking round: 'Let me know, Mr Warner, if you change your mind.'

He didn't push it, or threaten – I don't think they're allowed to do that – but the meaning was clear enough. Talk – or be under suspicion as a man with something to hide. Reasonable, too – from his point of view.

'Not a chance,' I said firmly. I could be frank in my refusal, at least – surely he could see from my manner, from the lack of any attempt at evasion or half-truth, from the straightforward refusal to discuss the subject – that I was simply not prepared to have my marital affairs dissected – unnecessarily – by the Metropolitan Police. To have my life, mine and Claudine's, transcribed by Sergeant Cooper into official language, crude and inaccurate – open heart surgery with a blunt axe. Surely Priestly could understand that. And if not, too bad. If he thought that was suspicious behaviour, let him suspect – I had nothing to hide. The worst he could do was to be a bloody nuisance. And I would put up with that, if I had to. So –

'Good night,' I said, and shut the door.

Brave words. But it gives you an uncomfortable feeling to get across the police. Well, it does me. And this was the second time I'd done it within two days. Perhaps I was making a mistake. Perhaps Inspector Priestly would prove to be more sensitive than I supposed. Perhaps we could have a little chat, explain everything, off the record, without Cooper and his moving finger eternally writing.

A tap at the door, and Maggie came in.

'All locked up,' she said, 'and there's the till slip.'

I looked at it, and winced. But then, Monday is never good, and it had been raining all day.

I gave the slip back to her and, on impulse, said: 'Sit down, Maggie, if you've got a moment.'

She had, it seemed.

I outlined my dilemma, in general terms. 'They seem to think that Claudine and Jonathan might have been a bit more than just good friends. Asked me what I knew about it. I told them it was nothing to do with their enquiry, and therefore I refused to discuss it. Would you think that made me a suspicious character, if you read a report of it in the paper?'

'Not in the least,' Maggie said indignantly. 'They've got no business poking their noses into your home life. What can it possibly have to do with poor Mr Cassell getting shot by hooligans?'

'Well, they weren't exactly hooligans. It's likely somebody hired them.'

'Even so ... well ... that couldn't be anything to do with you, could it?'

'Why not? I mean, I agree with you, but what's your reasoning?' I smiled at her – dear old Maggie, known me almost all my life, that's why I can talk to her like this. She probably knows me better than anyone else on earth, with the sharp and surprising realism of many aging spinsters. Does she detect the man of peace beneath my façade of male chauvinism? 'Why couldn't it have been me, Maggie?'

'Because,' she said briskly, 'if you'd wanted Mr Cassell shot, you wouldn't have hired hooligans – you'd have done it yourself. I'll see you in the morning.'

Thank you, Maggie!

But how can I tell that to the police?

CHAPTER 6

Unconscious Need

It seems that this factor, an unconscious need for
punishment, has a share in every neurotic illness.
SIGMUND FREUD

The bedroom was in darkness. Claudine, I supposed, was still
asleep. She must have felt worse than she had let on, or had
realised, when she said she would lie down for an hour. Six
o'clock, now. Well, I'll come back at seven and see how she is –
better not to disturb her yet.

I moved quietly to the door and was just closing it carefully
when there was a sound from the bed and the bedside light came
on.

'William?'

I braked, stepped back into the bedroom, closed the door
behind me. Claudine was lying against the pillows, her head
turned towards me. She drew her left arm back from the light
switch, and slid it under the pink-patterned duvet, back into
the warmth, a gesture of fragility. I crossed the room and stood
beside the bed. 'How are you feeling, darling?'

'Oh, not too bad. Thank you.'

There was an odd note of formality in her voice. Being ill
does that sometimes: makes a feeling of division between the
sick and the healthy, each concerned with their separate worlds,
interests, timescales. Poor thing!

'William –'

'Yes?'

'The curtains . . .'

'Of course – I'm sorry.' Should have thought of that. The
skylight was a black hole, sucking light and warmth from the
room. I pulled the curtains across, behind the brass rail that
held them to the slope of the ceiling, and the room took on its

68

customary night-time cosiness, enclosed and comforting. 'There.'

'Thank you.'

I sat on the bed, leant over to put my hand on her forehead. She shut her eyes as I touched her. Quite cool. No fever, or anything like that. I took my hand away. Her eyes stayed shut.

Yes. Well, it takes the possibility of loss to make you feel your dependence. And I've never felt it quite like this before. I was always the king pin, the one in charge. In marrying me, she did the correct, the traditional thing. The houses of William Warner and Dubuisson Frères were joined in permanent alliance, to the greater glory and profit of both. Or, to be realistic, their house and my cottage. I wasn't that much of a catch, but an old-established English merchant, though small, is the sort of son-in-law they like to collect, down there on the Quai des Chartrons. No doubt about that.

It wasn't a one-way bargain, of course. I got what I wanted, a beautiful dutiful wife, and a certain amount of licence – the French understand that. It wasn't chilly, either – Claudine has an earthy side, otherwise we'd never have got off the ground. Once I found that out, and with all the practicalities pressing in our favour, the thing was a foregone conclusion. We virtually had the Bordeaux bourgeousie at our bedside, waving crossed flags and urging us on, so *cordiale* was the *entente*. Henry Plantagenet and Eleanor of Aquitaine couldn't have been better encouraged.

So, how are we now?

I would have said we were fine, in the context of our particular relationship. That the stresses and strains of living together, always so unpredictable until you actually do it, had been weathered and adjusted probably better than most, in spite of – or maybe because of – the existence of a few no-go areas of imperfect understanding, inevitable in a marriage of mixed nationalities. A little mystery does no harm, can even be exotic.

No, I would have said that, as long as the chemistry is still there, as it is for me, there's no cause for alarm. I wouldn't have worried about a thing; I didn't worry, not even when Jonathan came on the scene. What was there in his attentions, however courtly and entertaining and smoothly conducted, however luxuriously staged amid soft music and flaming dishes and even, let's admit it – I've seen the ludicrous thing – on his burping, wobbling professional seducer's water bed – what was there in all that that she didn't get from me, or better? A meeting of minds? Ballocks! Jonathan's interest in women was never intellectual, never. He told me that himself.

What, then?

Because there's *something* wrong: the machinery is not humming as it should; there's an undercurrent of distress, of imminent breakdown. I think, I *think* it's just the effect of the police enquiry, throwing us off balance.

But there are other possibilities. Perhaps she has been feeling neglected, God knows why, and I was meant to make a big fuss and objection, a reassuring demonstration. Banish Jonathan from the house, I demand, strong and decisive – darling, you are so right, it was getting dangerous, she murmurs. Let bygones be bygones, I reply, squaring my shoulders; let us live happily ever after. End of story. And only a story – I must have read it in a magazine at the dentist's. Real women are not so coldly calculating, not once they're past the age of eight.

Perhaps, again, she was driven by something I will never know and could never understand, some entirely female compulsion or caprice. Who knows what women really want, or whether they'll be happy once they've got it? Can you believe a word they say, or must you always look for the hidden objective? What part do the tides and concatenations of the planets play in all this? Oh yes, truly, Suff'ring is the Lover's part.

And I *am* suffering, I find to my surprise and considerable annoyance. The balance of power has shifted. Whether she intended it or not, she's got me hovering round her, anxiously in attendance. I'm not worried about her being ill – that doesn't seem anything much. No. What I'm worried about is *what she's going to do next*.

In other words, I no longer feel king pin. I've been made to realise my dependence, to question my identity even. It's usually worse for men when families split up and wives go off, taking half the money and all the children. Good riddance, says the poor sod, as he starts to ring up old girlfriends; I can do without them. But he can't do without his identity, and she's gone off with that, too.

'Claudine!'

She opened her eyes, startled. It had come out louder than I intended.

'Are you feeling better?'

'Yes, I think so, *chéri*.'

Already I was ashamed of myself. Negative thinking. No good at all. Of course it was just a momentary feeling, that sense of limbo. At the end of a hard day's work.

'Would you like something to eat? Or drink?'

'No thank you, *chéri*.'

'Pills?'

'No. But –'

'Yes?'

'*Embrasse-moi.*'

Just a momentary feeling. She needs me, really. We haven't become strangers, and things are just as they were.

'Mmmmm.'

I looked down at her when she'd released me. Dark hair, and dark eyes – which seem either dark brown or dark green depending, maybe, on mood or weather. Tonight they seemed dark brown, intelligent, dependable.

'The police came. They wanted to see me again,' I said.

Claudine sat up, pushing pillows into place behind her. She pulled the duvet up, and huddled it round her breasts. She said: 'Why?'

'They wanted me to talk about what they called your relationship with Jonathan.'

She was studying the pattern on the duvet. Swirling pinks, in fine lines, like a child's scribbles. She didn't comment.

'I refused.'

She nodded.

'I told them it wasn't anything to do with Jonathan getting shot, in any case. I shouldn't put it like this, but what a bloody nuisance it all is. I'm afraid they won't leave it at that.'

She nodded again.

'Maggie said,' I added, 'that if I'd wanted Jonathan shot I'd have done it myself. I think she meant it as a kind of compliment. But I haven't yet worked out how a preference for *crime passionnel* can be presented to the police as proof of innocence. They'd more likely think it suggested a wild and unstable temperament which would be better behind bars.'

'*Merde*,' Claudine whispered to herself: her voice was low, but I caught the intensity in it.

'Don't worry, darling,' I said, 'they'll catch the thugs who did it, and then they'll be all smiles and apologies.' Well, not smiles maybe, not Priestly . . .

'I suppose so.'

'You go back to sleep. I'll bring you up something in about an hour. Scrambled eggs be all right?'

'Yes. Thank you.'

She wriggled down into the bed and I settled the duvet round her familiar form. Her eyes looked up at me as I gave her a parting kiss: they looked intelligent as always, but troubled, frightened almost. What had I said?

'Cheer up. Maggie's right, you know. It wasn't me. And Jonathan wasn't really that much of a threat, was he?'

Damn! Shouldn't have said that. What would I do if she suddenly burst into floods and cried Yes, he was, he was . . .?

'No,' she said, closing her eyes again.

So must bomb disposal experts feel when the fuse comes out intact.

But then, I thought, watching the girls plunder the kitchen for their supper, what else *could* she have said? What would have been the point, with Jonathan no longer among the available? Claudine isn't one to be racked by useless emotion, or to indulge in an orgy of guilt and self-recrimination. Pale and interesting is definitely not her style. Under the gloss, there's a practical bourgeoise, her tiny trotters firmly on the tarmac. She won't be weeping by the casement or crying into the wind – it wouldn't be profitable, it wouldn't be *French*. They're not really romantic or poetic: they like to think they are, and they go on about it the whole time, but it all has a feeling of detachment, of academic remove, they aren't really feeling it, no matter how flowery or elaborate the sentiment. Brilliance, humour, intelligence – yes. But real feeling, which only comes from a muddy wrestle with reality – no. They, rather than us, are the nation of shopkeepers. But then Napoleon, who so rudely insulted us from the depths of his Corsican ignorance, hadn't heard of *qui accuse, s'accuse*. Claudine, true to form, will be over this and back behind the till in no time. All we need is a period of calm, tact, and mutual grooming. And the absence of Inspector Priestly and his inquisition.

Not bananas with *marmalade*, surely?

'I'm going to do some scrambled eggs. Wouldn't you like some?' I affect an almost total incompetence in the kitchen as a matter of policy, but my fatherly conscience was pricked by the sight of the tray the girls were about to stagger off with, loaded down by a sickening assortment of their favourite items, up to the telly.

'*Ça va, Papa, merci,*' Nichole replied. They go to a French school, and sometimes forget it's not the official language of the household. Why do I surround myself with Frogs? Because, of course, though their poetry is insubstantial, their skill at domesticity is sublime. Known for it.

'See you later.' They left, twittering between themselves like birds. Hard to believe, but they must soon start to emerge from this era of gastronomic anarchy and become Claudine replicas, fastidious and demanding. Though it might take a Frenchman to inspire it.

I may eventually be forced to agree with those who think that eggs and wine make an unhappy marriage. But I like to drink something with my eggs, so I keep on trying. Last time it was a Portuguese Dão, a roughish red, which held up well enough though the eggs made it taste somewhat metallic. Tonight, I was going on the opposite tack with a smooth white, a Bulgarian Chardonnay, the poor man's white burgundy. At the worst, it was an affordable mistake. Competitors grumble that the price reflects Eastern Bloc desperation for Western currency. Maybe the KGB are behind it. Let's leave that to politicians. I'm for drinking, not thinking. I took the tray up to Claudine. She looked as though she'd been asleep. Struggled upright, managed a smile of sorts. I plumped the pillows, settled the tray on her lap, hovered indecisively.

'Oh, thank you, *chéri*. Wine too!'

I explained the experiment. She tasted critically, frowning. Then she nodded.

'Ça passe.'

Better, I decided, to leave her to it. There's been quite enough discussion for the time being. Better to have an end of words, and let the life of the house just carry us along, dissolving the tension.

'Anything else? Tea? Coffee?' There was already fruit on her tray: an apple, and some grapes, contributed by Maggie.

'Nothing.' She was smiling again, more convincingly this time.

'What is it?'

'Oh. Well, you know, men look funny, nursing. So . . . *big.*'

That's more like it. Normality is on the way back.

'Eat up your egg,' I growled as I went.

Later that evening, while I was (secretly and unobserved) washing up, I heard the telephone ringing in my office. It's on a separate line from the house, and therefore meant business. Sometimes I put it on the answering machine, but tonight I hadn't, in case Pete had some news for my ears only. I reached the office, pushing the door to behind me, and picked up the phone.

There were noises at the other end, not background but some kind of argument in which the telephone was for the moment being ignored. Dialled the number, and then forgotten the call, I supposed.

'Don't you tell me what I can and can't do!' the telephone quacked. 'If I want to ring him, I'll ring him. Couldn't care less, couldn't care less if he don't like it. Couldn't care less. I tell you I couldn't –'

'Who's that?' I asked, bored with this. The voice at the other end sounded familiar, but I couldn't place it. Highly charged with emotion it was, certainly; drunk, probably. A man with something on his mind. Was mine the number he had meant to dial?

'Hello!' I shouted.

There was a sudden silence. Then there was a woman's voice in the background, warning of catastrophe.

'Shut up!' the man's voice blared. Then, for the first time, words were addressed to the instrument, at a slightly lower volume. 'Is that you, Mr Warner?'

'Maybe,' I said cautiously. 'Who wants to know?'

'Ah. You may well ask. Yes, you may well –'

'Look. Tell me who you are, and what you want, or I'll put the phone down. I've got better things to do –'

'Mr Green here,' he said.

Ron Green, our builder. Of course! With a skinful, and something on his mind.

'Oh, Ron!' I said. 'Hello. What can I do for you?'

There was a pause, with heavy breathing. Then: 'Sarcastic bastard,' he said, with as much feeling as Laurence Olivier could put into it.

I remembered then. The cracked gable end, due to be rebuilt once Ron's insurers had bitten the bullet and paid up.

In the background the woman was letting him have it. I could hear her quite clearly: 'Talking to him like that won't get you nowhere, you listen to me for once, you'll make it worse, you will. Talk civil, why can't you? It'll end up in the courts else, you mark my –'

'Ah, *shut up!*'

Another pause, more heavy breathing. My turn to try pouring oil on the waters.

'Listen, Ron. If you've got something to say, I'm ready to listen. No need to shout. What is it?'

'Call your dogs off. Just call them off. That's all.'

'What do you mean – my dogs?'

'You know well enough what I mean.'

'Do you mean the lawyers? Are they giving you a hard time?'

'Listen to him! Did you hear that Kath? He says, are the lawyers giving us a hard time! – as if he didn't set them on. As if it was nothing to do with him! This is what you get, after years of cut-price jobs and not charging for all those little extras he kept adding in – "while you're at it, just run me up a little this or a little that". This is what you get. A bunch of bleedin' lawyers forcing you to sell your house. A lot of thanks that is. You –'

'*What?* Listen, Ron –'

'*Mr Green* to you. You don't fool nobody.'

'I'm not trying to. Just explain what you just said, about selling your house.'

'Got no choice, have I? Don't have a stack of readies at the bank, like some people.'

'But *why?*'

He gave a snort of disbelief.

'Look,' I said, 'do us both a favour. Just give it to me straight. Why are the lawyers trying to make you sell your house?'

'Well. Damages, isn't it?'

'For rebuilding the gable end?'

'And a lot of other stuff they've added in. I'm not doing it myself, don't think I am. I wouldn't come near it, not after this. You can get some other poor sod to do it.'

'But your insurance company will pay. I understand there was no doubt about that.'

'You understood wrong.'

'It's not likely.' It wasn't either. Simpson, my lawyer, was an expert on claims. 'I think you'll find your insurers will pay up. That's what I was told.'

There was silence.

'What reason,' I asked, 'are they giving for refusing to pay?'

'Who?'

'Your insurance company.'

'Not bloody well insured, am I?' he said.

'Not at *all?*'

'No. Not since four years back. Never been any need, see.'

'Oh.'

Now I understood. I didn't ask why he dropped his insurance. Ron Green wasn't the gambling type, just a small-scale, odd-jobbing builder, honest but not very bright. Probably, like us, he'd been squeezed by mounting overheads. And so made this dangerous economy.

'Ron – er – Mr Green?'

'What?'

'We'll have to get together on this and sort something out. I've been leaving it to the lawyers, but I'll go and see them and find out what's been going on. It wasn't my idea that they should be heavy-handed with you.'

76

'They want me to sell my house.'

'So you said, I've got that. It was the insurance money we were after.'

'I'm not insured, I told you . . .'

'Yes, yes. I understand.'

It sounded as though the aggression was wearing off, and he was getting to the maudlin, repetitive stage. I told him to leave it with me, not to worry, and that I'd be in touch later in the week. Then I rang off.

He'd been a fool, of course, and it was going to cost me, I could see it coming. But it was also true that he'd saved me a lot over the years. Maybe if he did the repair work, and I paid for the materials, something like that . . .

A few minutes of thinking about Ron Green and his problems left me feeling quite calm, soothed almost. It was such a simple problem, comfortably remote from the emotion-stirring dramas of the last few days. Not that it would feel like that to Ron, of course: he had sounded emotional, all right – desperate wouldn't be too strong a word. Poor old Ron.

CHAPTER 7

Character Studies

You yourselves have no doubt assumed that what is
known as 'character' – a thing so hard to define –
is to be ascribed entirely to the ego.

SIGMUND FREUD

I like the sound of Tuesday. It's light, happy-sounding, floral
almost. There are girls called Tuesday. And it means that
Monday is over and done with. To the world's workers, among
which Maggie is determined that I should be numbered,
Tuesday brings a glimmer of hope, a feeling that the cavalry
are just over the horizon with a waggonload of weekend.
Goodnewsday.

The bedroom skylight was brighter, too. Not much: the sky
was still a uniform blanket of grey, but paler, a shade less
sombre and depressing. I rubbed my eyes and racked them fully
open. Yes, it was true. No raindrops on the glass. After the last
few days, it seemed a kind of miracle.

I turned towards Claudine, sliding out an arm. Nothing
lustful, not after yesterday's frailty, just a snuggle to start the
day right. Though you never know what may –

She wasn't there.

I sat up with a bound. Her behaviour yesterday, that odd
formality, the eyes closing when I leant over her, those signs of
separation – I'd thought I'd made too much of it, read too much
into what could have just been the effects of her malaise. But
maybe I hadn't, maybe those signs were just the tip of the
iceberg, maybe there was more, much more underneath, suc-
cessfully hidden to give her time to *plan* . . .

Oh.

The bathroom light is on. There is a sound of running water.
Yes, of course, after much of yesterday as an invalid she would
want a longer than usual session in there, on the work of

restoration. So that she can assume, once again, the role of beautiful dutiful wife. According to our understanding.

She appears in the bathroom doorway.

'Bonjour, *chéri!*' she smiles. Her tone is cheerful, her hair brushed and gleaming, her face impeccable.

I am an idiot. Worse, I have the green poison in my veins, sapping my balance, my bounce, my libido. I need a displacement activity. I shall go to see Charrington, and talk about bricks.

Come at once, I was told when I telephoned. Admin is best cleared away in the mornings, to leave the afternoons free for real work. Not the most complimentary of terms in which to couch an invitation to (I trust) a valued client, but then bluntness is Bill Charrington's style, take it or leave it. He's from Yorkshire, and they believe in plain speaking. It must be a hereditary privilege, as you can't reply in the same manner without causing serious offence.

So that was why he teamed up with Jonathan Cassell, who was quite prepared to bewitch men as well as women with his smooth line of chat, as long as there was the prospect of a job in it. Even if you knew his type, you couldn't help being swept along: he used a light, humorous touch, always careful in discussion to avoid giving the impression that he had any interest in the outcome other than your own. That's too hard on him because, as I've said, he had a genuine feeling for design which also came across, and without which his soft sell would have had no hope of success. A big talent in public relations, Jonathan had. How Bill Charrington would get along now, without it, was a question that might well be keeping him awake nights.

The office was a small terrace house in Treadgold Street, up in the Notting Hill area. I could have walked it, but that would have certainly tempted the Gods to turn on the rain again, so I got out the Citroën and was there in ten minutes. Nice houses up there in W11: a mixture of late Regency, Victorian and Edwardian, brick or rendered, mostly with white sash windows and period porches. Prices are much lower once you get north of Holland Park Avenue, but with Latimer Road tube a stone's throw away, and access to the Westway trunk road not much farther off, it's highly convenient, if a little downmarket. But that will pass. Bill Charrington had made a good investment when he bought it, something like ten years ago.

I trotted up a short flight of stone steps to the porch, and pushed open the new plate-glass door which had CASSELL & CHARRINGTON – ARCHITECTS stencilled on it, in small plain white letters. Bill's wife Shirley looked up from behind the reception desk, a Tipp-Ex brush in her hand. She showed no sign of recognition though I had met her several times when going back to the office with Jonathan. She was a rather sad creature, I always thought: thin, with straggling, mousy hair and a withdrawn expression.

'Tell him to get you a new one, with automatic erase,' I said.

'Pardon?'

'The typewriter. Messy fingers are a thing of the past, tell him. You don't remember me, do you? William Warner. I've got an appointment with Bill.'

'Oh, yes,' she said, her face clearing. 'I remember. You've got an off-licence by Notting Hill Gate. If you'll take a seat, I'll tell him you're here.'

All right. Let's admit it – that's not quite the description I'd choose for myself. But if that's the way she sees it, that's the way it has to be. An off-licence. Uh-huh. By Notting Hill Gate. Well, I suppose it *is* . . .

Behind the desk, a cork pinboard was cluttered with postcards, photographs of buildings, posters of classical concerts. The walls elsewhere were lined with dark brown hessian, beginning to peel at the edges. The inevitable rubber plant, its broad green leaves cloudy with dust, stood in a corner next to a small dark brown corduroy sofa. I began to wander towards the sofa, over the dark brown ribbed haircord carpet. That, too, had seen better days. Though a forceful hoovering would have helped. Was that up to Shirley, I wondered?

'Morning, William.'

I looked up. He stood by the door to his office, a big man, not quite my height, but heavier. He had a seadog's beard, full and bristling, with more ginger in it than his hair, which was short

80

at the sides and as thick as a brush on top, with a centre parting. Not much could be seen of his face except his eyes, which were deepset under a strong brow. He wore, as on all the other occasions I'd seen him, a red rollneck pullover and blue jeans, with blue trainers to match. He radiated energy.

'Hullo, Bill. Good to see you again.'

'Come on in.'

He went back into his office, and Shirley slipped back behind her desk, giving me a shy smile. I followed him in. We sat in a pair of chrome and canvas chairs on either side of a low table.

'Coffee?'

'Never known to refuse,' I said.

'Do us some coffee, Shirl, there's a love,' he called. His voice went with the beard – it would have carried in a storm. I find them reassuring, voices like that. There's more credibility in a rumble than a squeak.

'Terrible thing, that, about Jonathan,' I said.

'Shocking,' Charrington said. I remembered that his style of speech bordered on the Trappist – talking to him, I was always made to feel garrulous.

'Have the police been to see you yet?' I said.

'Oh yes. We've had a chat – yesterday morning, it was. To fill in the details. It was all a bit rushed, Saturday night.'

'*Saturday night?* The night he was killed?'

'I was called in to identify him. At the mortuary.'

'Were you? I didn't know that – it can't have been very pleasant.'

'Someone had to do it. Better me than Barbara. They asked her, as next of kin, but said I'd do.'

'Her suggestion, then?'

'I suppose. Not that I wasn't glad to do it for her. He was a mess.'

'Good of you.'

'Oh no. I've seen more of him than she has, this last year since they separated. Much more.'

Of course that must be so, I realised.

'So,' Charrington said, 'got a problem, have you?'

Straight down to it. Well, why not? I outlined yesterday's telephone conversation with Ron Green. 'It seems to me the only way out is to get expert advice on exactly what needs to be done, and then split the liability. If he'll agree to do the work, I'll pay for the materials. The only alternative is an expensive legal battle, since he's got no insurance.'

'Bloody fool.'

'Yes. But he's done all right by us in the past. I wouldn't like to see the lawyers tear him in shreds, even if he's technically in the wrong this time.'

'Hope he appreciates it.'

'I don't think he understands much of what's going on. He's a jobbing builder, fiftyish, with ladders and pigeons in the back yard, employs casual labour. Letters from lawyers send him straight to the pub, where he waves them about as evidence of my ingratitude. I don't want that: it's like a family down there, and one of these nights some of the lads may decide to work off their beer and even the score by setting my warehouse on fire. Or worse.'

Or worse? What did I mean? Would they have –

'This work he did. Who instructed him?'

No, of course not. Though, if they were really pissed – 'What?'

'Who told Green what to do?'

But no, I forgot, it was Jonathan they were after –

'Oh yes, sorry. Nobody did. It was just a bit of rebuilding, a gable wall, and some other work. I thought it would be simple enough, he'd done a lot of other work for us over the years, and he didn't ask for help, just gave us a price and got on with it.'

'District Surveyor consulted?'

'I left that to Ron. I know nothing about it, assumed he did.'

'And now the wall's cracked. Could be clay. It can be a right bugger, building on that.'

'Could be. Will you take it on?'

'I think I can fit it in. I've got other work down that way: that'll save my time in travelling. I must warn you, it'll not be cheap.'

'Oh?'

'No, it won't. It's the liability, you see. I'll be taking that on once I touch it. Some people don't realise that. Do someone a favour, a bit of a sketch on the back of an envelope, and the next thing you know you're in court, on the sharp end of a claim for negligence, with some smart-arse in a wig holding up your bit of sketch and asking if all your working drawings are, heh heh, to the same level of competence. A thing to avoid, is that.'

'Yes, I see. Well, so be it. Can you give me an idea of cost?'

'Oh yes. Tell you what I'll do. Next time I'm that way, which should be later this week or early next, I'll take a look and see what's what. I'll need the address. How about getting in?'

I gave him all the details he needed. It was a relief to have him involved. I'd relied more heavily on Ron than I should have done, by the sound of it, but things would get straightened out now. It had to end without hard feelings, if at all possible. Perhaps, in a while, I should go over and talk to Ron's wife, as she had sounded more level-headed than he. Yes, I hadn't fully realised all the implications before. With a warehouse full of booze, you've got enough risk from regular thieves without having the natives against you as well. Bill would handle it well, I felt sure of that: it would be difficult for Ron to find cause for more resentment in that matter-of-fact manner of his.

'Well, that's it, then,' I said. 'Thanks, Bill, very much. How's everything going, otherwise? What's this job you're doing down our way?'

'Dockland redevelopment,' Bill said. 'Big stuff. Housing, shops, leisure centre. Just the job.'

'Sounds like the big time. Congratulations!'

'Oh,' he said, 'haven't got it yet. But we're – I'm in there with a good chance. It'll mean expanding the office.'

'Well, best of luck. Of course, you're a one-man-band now. You must be missing Jonathan, I suppose.'

'I suppose,' he said, with a wry smile.

'I thought you needed each other? He was good at getting the work in, wasn't he?'

'He *was*, right enough. But not lately.'

'Oh? I'm surprised to hear that. I thought he could hardly help picking up work, that it was a sort of game, a way of life to him. Why did he go off it?'

Charrington shot me a curious glance. 'Other fish to fry,' he said shortly.

83

'What do you mean?'

He shrugged, but made no reply. His large hands were occupied putting the top on and off his felt tip pen.

'I'd like to know,' I persisted. 'Jonathan got shot for a reason. Something was going on in Jonathan's life which caused this. So far, nobody seems to have any idea, especially the police.'

'What makes you say that?' he asked.

'Because they don't seem to have anything better to do than crawl round my house. The idea seems to be, though they haven't yet come straight out with it, that the one who-done-it is me. Maddened by jealousy, because Jonathan took Claudine out to lunch a few times, and maybe a bit more. I'm not asking.'

Charrington looked up from his pen. 'So you know that,' he said.

'Well, of course I do. Claudine and I are, let's say, established fellow travellers down life's highways and byways. We give and take a little space when we need it. I'm not saying it's always easy, but neither of us gets homicidal. Anyway, I *know* it wasn't me. So it was someone else. I would be interested to know who, mainly because it might get the police off my back.'

'I've already told them all I know, which isn't much,' he said.

'Was it a Superintendent Priestly?'

'That's the name.'

'Did he have a go at you?'

Charrington shrugged again: it was characteristic of him, I realised, a big man asserting his bulk, rising above irritation like a whale from water. 'You could call it that,' he said. 'Asked about the partnership. Who did what. Whether Jonathan earned his keep. I told him straight what I've just told you.'

'That he didn't, not lately?'

'They haven't been back to arrest me,' Charrington said with a flicker of a smile. 'Not yet they haven't.'

The door opened, and Shirley backed into the room, carrying a tray with two mugs of coffee on it, the line of her thin back twisting as she strove to avoid bumping the door frame with the tray.

'Shirl,' Charrington said with resignation in his voice, 'we've almost done.'

She turned round with the tray and stood there, looking from one of us to the other. 'I know,' she said breathlessly. 'The milk was off, you see. I had to go to the corner shop.'

'Well, never mind,' he said. She seemed stuck to the floor. He got to his feet and took the tray from her. 'Might as well have it, now it's here.'

'Thank you, Shirley,' I said. She gave me her weak smile and went out. We sipped the coffee. It was instant. Oh well. What were we talking about? The police . . . 'What else did the police ask about?'

'Nothing much. Said they might want to see the partnership accounts. Good luck to them.'

I would have liked to put a few questions myself. If Jonathan's interest in this office was slackening, what had been taking its place? What had Jonathan been living on, with his Italian furniture and playboy water bed? Charrington might know, even though theirs was essentially a working partnership, a combination of talents and very different personalities, unlikely, for that reason, to spill over into their social life outside office hours. I stared into the tasteless coffee. I should risk being rebuffed, I decided, and ask. How else was I going to find out?

'They'll find there's just enough work for one,' Charrington said.

I looked up, and realised he'd been watching me – I'd never make a poker player.

'So what did he use for ready?' I asked, the way now seeming clear.

'He was a director of Nature Store,' Charrington said, sounding surprised at the question. Oh yes, of *course*! He was fixed in my mind as a designer, a fee-paid man, but I think I had heard that Barbara had secured him a place in the firm, long before it really took off. As a tax dodge, probably – I couldn't imagine Jonathan doing more than token time behind a desk.

'And she kept him on, even after they separated?'

'Always good to him, Barbara was.' Too good, his tone implied.

'Until he pushed her too far.'

'Too far?'

'The girlfriends. He didn't even try to be tactful, she said. He was one of those people who get as much kick from telling as from doing. Maybe more.'

Charrington said nothing, but began to fiddle with his pen again. I watched him take the top off, put it back on. Off and on, off and on. Time I was going.

'What do you think of her?' I said, on impulse.

'Barbara?'

'Yes.'

He thought for a moment. Then he said slowly, without looking up: 'I wouldn't have treated her like that.'

'No. Nor would I.'

We both looked up then, and our eyes met. It was a moment of recognition: Charrington was better concealed behind the furry façade of his beard, but his eyes gave him away; I knew he thought what I thought, and that we had indulged the same daydream, cherished the same image. A small image, slight but not skinny.

I smiled, and, after a moment's hesitation, so did he. Nothing more was said. I just had time to reflect that he wasn't likely to be serious competition: not with that red sweater, that beard, and with Shirl weeping floods in the background – enough, I felt certain from what I'd seen of her, to extinguish all passionate tendencies in the whole area north of Notting Hill. Then I got up to go.

Shortly after I got back to my office, the telephone rang. It was Ted Soper, our young, earnest bank manager at Child & Co. on the corner of Church Street and Kensington High Street. He sounded reserved – I soon discovered why.

'Ah, er, William,' he said. I always think it must be bank policy to get on to Christian names with clients; it doesn't come naturally to him.

'Hullo, Ted. What's up – have we been paying our bills too soon?'

'Oh,' he said, 'no. No, nothing like that – your account is well within bounds, I believe. No, it's just that ... well, er,

William, we have the police here. Making enquiries. They have an authority to inspect your statements of account. I'm bound to comply, of course, but I thought that you should be informed.'

I felt a surge of alarm, followed by an unreasonable rage. 'Sneaky buggers!'

'Well er . . .'

'They might have *asked*! I could hardly have refused.'

'Quite.'

'Is it an Inspector Priestly?'

'That is the name, yes.'

I contemplated having a few words with Priestly, but decided against it. He would only play me some scratchy old number about the necessity of routine procedures to save time, that this was an enquiry into a serious crime, that he had to do his job as he thought best . . . I could hear it all. And it would be true. My feelings were not his primary concern. Especially if he thought that I . . . 'Would you tell him –'

'Yes?'

'Oh, nothing. Just say I'm happy for him to look at anything he wants. And give him my best wishes. The sooner he gets to the man he's after, the sooner we can all go back to normal life.'

'Yes, indeed,' Ted said. 'I'll certainly pass that on. Goodbye now.'

Of course, I thought, sitting back and gazing through the window at the muddy garden – even my best wishes might carry the wrong message to Priestly. He might take it, in these circumstances, as a *sneer* – as though I really meant to imply 'and the best of luck!' In other words: 'my tracks are covered, I saw this coming, and you won't get anything on me!'

Then I realised it didn't matter what he thought. Because, of course, there wasn't anything to find.

I must stop being wrong-footed by Priestly. There's no need, no need at all.

CHAPTER 8

Noticeable Plasticity

The sexual instincts are noticeable to us for their
plasticity, their capacity for altering their aims, their
replaceability ...

SIGMUND FREUD

I had lunch in the kitchen with Claudine, who had been
shopping with one of the multitude of cronies she retains just
for this purpose. Or so it seems: I seldom get to meet any of
them except briefly when they're setting out armed to the teeth
with cheque books and credit cards, or on their return, flushed,
laughing and opinionated, on a high of consumption. Claudine
works, of course, and a sharp sense of the value of money runs
in her Gallic blood, but some of her little chums have no such
inhibition; they must each have an Arab princeling in tow, or a
spare key to the Bank of England.

'Ah, it was *une merveille*, and the stitching, oh! – *im-pec-cable*!'
Claudine sighs.

'And the price?'

She looks at me, and smiles. Then she recites the exact sum.
My soup spoon rattles against the side of the plate. Astronauts
have been to the moon for less, surely. If these expeditions ever
tempted her beyond a merely vicarious satisfaction ...

'I have seen a pattern not so different,' Claudine says, 'and I
think, with some little changes, you know, and a good
material ...'

'Good idea, darling.'

Never was any risk, of course, not really. Not from my beautiful dutiful wife.

Simpson, my solicitor, could spare me a few minutes later that
afternoon. I hadn't seen him, face to face, for a year or more,
and a meeting, however brief, would, I felt, be better than trying

to sort things out on the telephone. It would be against all his bulldog instincts to let poor Ron Green off the hook, and I was going to have to make a forceful representation in person to make sure my feelings got across, and to get Simpson back on his lead and under control.

Maggie was letting me off lightly today, and the small pile of paperwork was soon dealt with and removed. Time on my hands, to think – about new sources of supply, about finding new customers, about coping with competition. Circular thinking, mostly. Ours is not the sort of enterprise where you can break out in dramatic new directions, plot crafty takeovers, and lateral expansion. I'd already considered the question of owning our own transport but had come to the conclusion that, apart from local deliveries here in London, it wouldn't pay – we're too small, and we buy from too many widely separated sources. No, if we survive – and I worry about it as competition is increasing – it will be through quality and not price-cutting. I'm sure of that. There is more money about – among our customers at least – and upmarket is the way to go. And that's a thought: upmarket not only means better wine, it also means better service. Quicker, more reliable. Perhaps it would pay us to have another van, and some extra help for Pete.

I decided to talk to him about it. Inspect the warehouse, and see how we could improve it. I rang, and left a message on the answerphone for a meeting tomorrow morning, then sat back with a feeling of achievement. If only that was all there was to it . . .

What next?

Suppliers, customers, new ideas. New directions, opportunities.

Opportunities. *Slight, but not skinny. With long, pale hair . . .*

No, no.

Well, perhaps just a quick call, to keep in touch.

Hard work, telephoning high-powered people. I'd never visited Barbara's office, but I could picture it now – her position at the hub of Nature Store was well defended. I worked my way past Switchboard, was waylaid by Sales and then, after re-direction through Switchboard, was brought to a halt by an assistant whose instructions were clearly to guard the inner temple with her life if need be.

'If you would care to tell me the purpose of your call . . .?' enquired this soft-voiced but determined guardian.

My purpose, well. Tentative, as yet, but employing Meursault and potted shrimps possibly, candlelit conversation probably, to ease our egos into a comfortable proximity from which, with the smooth inexorable swoosh of a ship being launched, your mistress and I may progress to the merging of Yin and Yang according to nature and ritual. In other words. I want to –

'It's a personal matter,' I replied, equally firmly.

'I'm afraid –'

'And important. Just give her my name.' In a confident tone, which may or may not find justification.

'Very well. Hold, on, please, Mr Warner.'

I waited. Then Barbara came on the line. 'William?'

'Look, Barbara, I'm sorry to ring you at your office. If you're really busy I'll ring off.'

'No, that's all right, William. What is it?'

'I could give you some cooked-up excuse. But the truth is I've been wanting to ring you, and the opportunity came up, so I did. I felt there was more to be said than we had time for on Sunday.'

Oh, yes. That's how it goes, this game. I pat the ball into her court. She considers, pats it back – or lets it go by. How often have I done this? How often has she?

'How very odd.'

Odd? Dear Barbara – you can refuse to play, but it isn't *odd* of me to ask! 'Well, never mind. Just an idea, that's all. I'd better let you get back to work.'

'No, I mean it really *is* odd. I nearly rang you this morning, but decided not to. Telepathy, it must be.'

'Minds in tune across the teeming city, Barbara.' And a fine, strong return of service! Aha! Play on! 'What did you decide not to ring me about?'

'Well, it's Ludwig – my ex.'

'I met him on your doorstep. The *Rosenkavalier*.'

'Yes. The idiot.' Barbara didn't sound entirely displeased. 'He wants us to get together again.'

'Barbara, he looks a complete nutter! And didn't he beat you up?'

'It was all right in the early years,' Barbara said, 'when his work was going well.'

'When you were doing his PR. It was probably due to that. You were always good at PR.'

'Well, to be frank, my promotion probably did help his early success, yes. And, of course, his type of work was in vogue then. A lot of artists rose with the sixties, and then died with them.'

'Barbara, watch out!'

'Yes,' she said, 'I know. It isn't me he wants, it's my promotion. But even if I wanted to do that for him again, I wouldn't have time now – I've got my hands full with Nature Store.'

'Of course you have.'

'I managed to get him out of the house, but he said he wasn't going back to Germany, not yet. He's trying to make a comeback and he had some galleries to talk to. The best thing would be if he could persuade one of them to take him on. That would take the pressure off me.'

'He's quite determined, then?'

'Ludwig,' Barbara said, 'believes in the power of the will. *His* will. He never gives up.'

'Oh, Jesus! One of those. A real nutter.'

'I'm afraid so. And William – that's what I was going to ring you about.'

'I'll be glad to give you any help I can, Barbara – you know that.'

'Oh, that's sweet of you, William, it really is. But it wasn't quite that, though I do appreciate it. No, it was to warn you.'

'Warn me? Against Ludwig?'

'Yes. You see, I'm afraid he's got the impression that you're the reason why I won't see him.'

I was amazed at this. Then a little gleeful spark began to glow: if Ludwig felt this, it couldn't, surely, be as a result of that brief encounter on Barbara's doorstep, no, she must have said something to reinforce the idea. Something I would have liked to hear. Sweet William.

But then, this wasn't all good news.

'Why do you say "warn me"?' I asked. 'What can – or could – he do about it?'

Barbara hesitated. Then she said: 'People don't change as they get older, do they – whatever they are to start with, they just get more so. Ludwig was always violent and irrational – proud of it. He used to say that an artist, more than other men, must obey his impulses, be uninhibited, must live dangerously.'

'Couldn't he train tigers? Join the Foreign Legion?'

'No, I'm serious, William. I think Ludwig isn't able to bear having become a nonentity. I think it's made him desperate.'

She sounded as if she meant it.

'Tell the police, Barbara,' I suggested. 'Perhaps they'd put Inspector Priestly on it; I'd like to see him gainfully employed. At present he's wasting his time investigating me.' I told her about Priestly's visit to my bank.

'Oh,' she said, 'what's he looking for?'

'No idea. Whatever it is, I'll probably hear in due course, whether he finds it or not.'

'How horrid.'

'Yes, it is rather.'

There was a pause. Then Barbara said: 'I think I'd better go, William. I'm so glad you rang. It's so good to have you to talk to. Listen, I'm not going to tell the police about Ludwig, and I'd rather you kept all this to yourself: now that I'm, well –'

'Famous, Barbara. The "Darling of the Unlisted Securities Market", the papers call you.'

'Well, hardly. But I don't want the papers to get hold of it. It doesn't take much to make the shareholders nervous, and this on top of the Jonathan affair could be a disaster.'

'Of course. I won't say a word to anyone, not even Claudine, just in case.'

'Oh, thank you. And William, remember what I said about Ludwig.'

'I will,' I promised. 'But let's keep in touch. Call me at once if there's any trouble, or if you need anything.'

'You're very sweet,' Barbara said warmly.

'I mean it.'

'I know,' she said.

We exchanged goodbyes and rang off. Altogether a successful

call, I felt: definite signs of growing sympathy, and Ludwig providing a touch of useful menace in the background, practically throwing us together. Knocking women about was the kind of violence he was into: men who indulge in that aren't usually the sort other men are scared of, and I thought I could handle it. In any case, he'd have to go back to Germany sooner or later, as he clearly wasn't going to get anywhere with Barbara. Yes, things were going well. I'd better make sure I had a good Meursault in stock – it's the buttery flavour that goes with potted shrimps, and you need an old one for that.

Simpson looked up from his desk as I was shown in. Although we'd had occasional telephone conversations, I hadn't seen him face to face for about a year, and my immediate impression was that he had changed. In his early forties, with fewer dark strands now left to decorate his dome, he nevertheless looked younger, sharper, more energetic. He propelled his swivel chair back from his desk, braked it, stood up, and shot out his hand. He was a head shorter than me.

'William. Good to see you. How's the world of wine?'

'Hello, Paul. People are still drinking it.'

The old Simpson had been firmly from the traditional mould of English solicitors: bony-faced, soberly suited, slightly dusty. All that had gone. As I looked at him more closely, I realised that the differences were not much in themselves – it was the total effect which told. He was wearing a white shirt and dark blue tie – nothing remarkable to that except for the gleaming crispness of the shirt and the glitter of gold from cufflinks which I felt sure he never used to wear. He was still soberly suited, but the trousers – or what I could see of them above the desk – were of expensive but un-English cut, Italian probably. The jacket was displayed on a hanger against the far wall as though too good for ordinary occasions such as this: like knightly armour, it waited to be worn in Simpson's trials of strength, his courtroom jousts and boardroom skirmishes.

We sat down, and Simpson shuffled papers on his desk with a nervous intensity.

'It looks,' I said, 'as though things are going well for you.'

Simpson glanced up from his papers. His eyes met mine

93

briefly, and then darted back to his desk. 'It's all work,' he said. 'Excuse me one moment.' He picked up his telephone, and waited, drumming his fingers impatiently. 'Come on, come on! ... Rachel? How are you getting on with ... yes, that's the one. It must go today, first-class post. No, better – send it by hand. Call City Express. Make sure of that, won't you? All right. Thanks.' He put the telephone down, and sat for a moment without speaking, frowning. I waited. Then he nodded to himself, scooped up some papers immediately in front of him, tapped them on edge to square them off, and pushed them into a folder which he slapped to one side. 'Sorry. You were saying?'

'Nothing much. You looked different, I thought. Younger, fitter, richer ... if you don't mind my saying so.'

'Squash twice a week. Tennis at weekends. I don't know about richer ...'

'You look well on it.' Not quite true – there were signs of strain around his eyes, which were never still but moved constantly from me to desk to window and back again, as if on sentry duty against imminent attack.

'Of course,' Simpson said, 'you know I married again.'

'No! Congratulations.' Now he said it, I remembered I had heard: she was an American girl, quite a lot younger than him ... aha, that explained a lot ...

On Simpson's desk was a large framed photograph of himself posed with his arm round a blonde girl as tall as he was, the two of them in ski gear against a background of snowy chalet. In my mind, Simpson existed only in the context of his office: I had to make a rapid readjustment. Trendy clothes! blondes! – or one at least ... In the picture, he was wearing jumbo-sized aviator shades pushed up on to his forehead, where they hung, huge and black, like a vampire bat.

'So this is the second Mrs Simpson,' I said, gesturing at the photograph, to gain time to take it all in.

'What? Oh yes, that's Maryanne,' Simpson said. He spun the picture round, took a quick inventory of its contents, and turned it back again.

'American, isn't she? – it's coming back to me now.'

'Californian. I met her while I was over there, at a conference.'

94

'Lucky chap,' I said. Hidden depths – he must have hidden depths. It was unsettling – solicitors ought to be reliable and dull, as Simpson was before recycling. 'Was it a useful conference – in other ways as well?'

'The world's a small place, now,' Simpson said. 'This country is now on the sidelines, an outpost of Europe which itself is still living in the past. The United States is where changes come from – we can't afford to ignore that. I went to see for myself. Yes, it certainly was useful.'

'The French have always been over-impressed by things American,' I murmured, 'and look what's happening to them now – they're about to be turned into a giant holiday camp, a theme park. Disneylands are coming, did you know that? All over the place, acres of them. In the country of Molière and Debussy, they're building plastic replicas of Mickey Mouse and Donald Duck, forty feet high. There should be rioting in the streets, not welcome banners. Then there's the hideous spread of fast food . . .'

'Oh, that,' Simpson said, 'yes, well, I don't know. It was the legal system I was talking about. Ours has got to be brought up to date – attitudes, manners, *methods*.'

'I suspect it all hangs together,' I said, 'and if you start importing chunks of another culture rather than developing your own you may find yourself with an identity problem.' I hadn't at all meant this to apply to Simpson individually, but even as I said it I realised that it well might. 'Nationally speaking,' I added.

'With respect,' Simpson said, his eyes checking the contents of the room more nervously than ever, 'I think that's a somewhat eccentric view. Changes have to be made: no way can we avoid it.'

'Oh yes, I can't argue with that,' I said. 'It's not change I'm against, but the wholesale importing of it. National differences can be like those wines that taste terrific in the taverna, but horrible when you get them home. But I know I'm over-cautious – I'm getting to the age when I want everything to stay just the same for ever.'

'Can't agree with you there,' Simpson said, shaking his head emphatically. 'No way! I'm for moving on.'

And up. I didn't doubt. Must be a thruster, this Maryanne, to have wrought such a change in him. I hoped he could stand the strain.

'Well, anyway,' I said, 'you're busy, and I'd better tell you why I'm here. It's about Ron Green. I'm afraid your new methods are causing drunkenness and marital strife down Wapping way, and I'm going to ask you to tone it down a bit.' And I told him about Ron's anguished telephone call.

Simpson listened, frowning, as he jotted down the points I made. 'You've called an architect in, then?'

'Yes, to tell us what needs to be done to restore the gable end to stability. Look, Paul – I appreciate what you've been trying to do on my behalf, putting pressure on to get the best deal for me. But I don't want to drive Ron to drink or bankruptcy: I want to settle on a compromise which will leave him in business and me not too badly out of pocket.'

'I could do much better for you than that,' Simpson said. He didn't seem to be getting my message. I was going to have to put it more strongly.

'I don't *want* to do better than that. Also, you've got to understand that it's a jungle down there – it doesn't do to fall out with the natives, not if you've got a warehouse full of drink.'

'Ah, right. But the man's liable, you know – you can take his insurance company to the cleaners, no problem. Papers are already with Counsel for him to draw up the Statement of Claim.'

'I don't want you to go for him, Paul. I want a compromise. And he hasn't *got* an insurance company – I told you.'

'You don't want to believe that, William. Every builder has insurance – it's basic. Never came across one that didn't.'

'You have now. I believe him – he's just a small-time jobbing builder, a fair workman, but hopeless with admin.'

I looked across the desk at Simpson, who had a stubborn look on his face like Napoleon called away in mid-battle. As I watched, it faded. 'Well,' he said, 'if you're sure.'

'I'm sure.'

'Is your architect going to be able to handle it? Will you leave it to him now?'

'Yes, I think he can. He's big and bluff, just what's needed. It's Bill Charrington – do you know him?'

Simpson suddenly became very still. It was only for a second or two, but it was noticeable. Then he seemed to come alive again. 'Sorry,' he said, 'I was thinking of something else. Who did you say?'

'Bill Charrington – Cassell and Charrington.'

'Oh yes. Heard of them.'

'Perhaps you saw about Jonathan Cassell's death in the papers? He was –'

'I believe I did. Shocking affair. Well now, William – if that's all . . .'

'Thanks, Paul, it is. I'm sorry if I've disappointed you.'

'No problem,' Simpson said automatically. He came round the corner of the desk to show me to the door. Something shiny caught my eye and I looked down. He was wearing Gucci shoes with gold buckles. It's the sort of thing women do, to write a man off because of a loud tie or crooked haircut, but I think it was at that moment I knew I'd have to get a new solicitor, one that stayed more or less the same from day to day, year to year, the sort that Simpson used to be – earnest, sober, and unrepentantly English.

'Have a nice evening,' he called after me.

Swinging Simpson.

I had taken a taxi to Simpson's office off Tottenham Court Road and, as my return taxi came up Church Street, I saw the now familiar grey Rover parked outside the shop. Half-past five, I noted, and beginning to rain again: departing commuters hurried by under umbrellas; neighbouring antique shops were rattling down their window grilles and switching off all but their night lights; somewhere in the distance an alarm bell was triggered briefly as a front door was locked. The feeling I'd had several times since Jonathan was killed, of things closing in, returned to me. Quite irrational, of course. Left Brain pointed out: a drop in barometric pressure can do that. Right Brain was silent. I paid off the taxi and went in by the side door.

Priestly and Cooper were waiting in my office, Maggie told me. 'I thought it best, with customers still in the shop . . .'

'Right, Maggie, fine. And I'll see if they can be persuaded to park the car in the side street, if these visits are going to become a habit.'

I went into the office. They were standing by the window, looking out at the rectangle of garden lit by yellow street lights, and turned as I came in.

'Good evening,' I said briskly, 'please sit down.' I drew the curtains, and sat behind my desk. It was the scene as before.

'Mr Warner,' Priestly said in a flat voice emptied of all expression, 'I have here copies of bank statements for your personal and business accounts covering the year up to the end of last week.'

'Ted Soper told me you wanted to see these, as you know. You could have asked me; I would have had no objection. So?'

He got up, and placed a statement on the desk in front of me, my way up, then returned to his chair. 'In that statement, from your business account, there is a debit of four thousand five hundred pounds, representing a cash withdrawal.'

I looked down the list of items. Yes, there it was.

'That's correct,' I said.

'Would you,' Priestly said in the same flat voice, 'please explain the purpose of that withdrawal?'

I thought for a moment. The item was dated April last. Surely that was – I looked at it more closely, read across the line.

'Yes,' I said. 'We have a house in France. That money was used to pay for some building work we had done. That is why the withdrawal was made in French francs.' I sat back with relief. Surely he could have worked that out for himself.

'I am aware of that possibility,' Priestly said, 'of course. There are two previous withdrawals during the year in French francs. Both of these were made by direct transfer to a branch of Crédit Lyonnais, in Périgueux. Will you explain why a cash withdrawal was made on this occasion, instead of a direct transfer? Four thousand five hundred pounds' worth of francs is a large sum to carry about in banknotes, is that not so?'

I hesitated, and Priestly, who was watching closely, must have seen the expression on my face as I realised what was coming. Well, there was nothing I could do but plough on.

'Some French builders insist on being paid in cash,' I said,

98

'and as builders are in short supply, you have to comply if you want to get the job done.'

'I see,' Priestly said. He looked down, into his lap. In the silence that followed I could hear the little brass carriage clock on the mantelpiece ticking busily, a tinny sound that was so much a part of this room that I only normally became aware of it when it stopped. What next? I didn't have long to wait.

'In that case,' Priestly said, 'you would be able to produce invoices or receipts accounting for the money?'

Shit! This was the question I didn't want. Because, of course, that money had gone on under-the-counter payments, nudge-nudge, wink-wink, good for you and good for me, moonlighting, *le travail noir*. Untraceable cash, ex-tax, ex-VAT, the existence of which would be denied with shrugs and blank faces by René, Georges and Bernard.

'Maybe,' I said. 'It's all very rural and informal out there, you know. Many of the builders are farmers as well – they don't go much for paperwork. Some can barely sign their names.'

'I must ask you to produce what evidence you can,' Priestly said. He looked up to reinforce his words with a stern look. This is serious, it said. I knew it was. Dead serious. *The price of a murder . . .*

'I'll do what I can,' I promised. I was buying time, that was all. There wasn't really anything I could do. Or, if there was, I had yet to think of it.

Priestly rose. Cooper followed suit. I showed them out.

'Don't delay, Mr Warner,' Priestly said from the doorstep.

'I won't. Superintendent –'

He turned, his face expectant. Of what? *Superintendent – I can't stand this any longer, you're right, I did it, I hired them, the swine was after my wife, my life, my all, my universe was about to be destroyed . . .*

'I wonder if you would mind parking your car in the side road, if these visits are to continue? Our customers . . .'

O, splendid stroke! Well played, Warner!

I closed the door and bowed to pavilions ringing with applause.

CHAPTER 9

In Phase Again

Thirdly comes the *phallic* phase in which in both
sexes the male organ (and what corresponds to it in
girls) attains an importance which can no longer be
overlooked.

SIGMUND FREUD

Genuine guru, or cunning charlatan? Gurdjieff could have been
either, or both, it seems to me, not knowing much about it.
Julian, however, is convinced that, in spite of his passion for old
Calvados and fast cars badly driven, the man held at least some
of the secrets of the universe, embedded in a smokescreen of
jokes and confidence tricks. I met Julian in the hall, on his way
to a session at the nearby Gurdjieff Institute to find out more.

'Hi, Jules.'

'Hi, Dad.'

'What's on tonight?'

'A talk on overcoming Indifference and Hostility.'

'That,' I said with some enthusiasm, 'is knowledge I could do
with right now. Take notes, my boy. Fill me in on it when you
get back.'

'It doesn't work quite like that,' Julian said. 'It's only one
aspect of Whole Being. You have to work through all of
Harmonious Development before you even begin to see what
he's getting at.'

I let him go. With the barbarians already at the gates, it was
too late to sign on as a sorcerer's apprentice. The spells might
be dud, anyway.

But the Calvados I could copy; there could be mysteries ready
to be revealed by that. I went down to the cellar, and brought
up a murky bottle bearing a stained handwritten label which
we'd acquired from a farm Somewhere in Normandy on last
year's journey back from the French house. Fifteen years old,
they'd assured us, with a price to match, and we'd taken it on

trust, though, by the look of it, this bottle might as easily contain sump oil as smooth old apple brandy. I marched it to the kitchen and stood it on the table. The moment of truth had come.

'Ah, *voilà!*' Claudine cried, recognising it.

'I thought, with the pork chops, to make a change . . .'

'*Pourquoi pas! Mais doucement, hein!*'

'Oh yes, just a drop or two. Leave room for the new red Listel with cheese.' Powerful stuff from the Camargue, that – organically grown, natural-tasting, stands up to cheese. Good whites, and an excellent Listel blanc de blanc sparkler are also finding favour with us at present.

I scraped the wax off the top of the Calvados bottle, and eased out the small stained cork, which looked second-hand. A moment of suspicion there – why economise on corks when you're charging a hundred and twenty francs for the contents? Peasant mentality would see nothing odd in that, of course, and – yes! – the aroma's coming out now after the cork, and it's smelling good. Old apple lofts, plenty of pong and nothing dry or chemical about it. Let's taste!

'*C'est bon?*' Claudine asked, smiling at my gestures of ecstasy.

'*Vachement bon!*' I held the glass out to her.

She tasted, nodded, and handed it back. 'I think the chops are almost ready,' she said. 'We eat in the kitchen? Or –'

'Let's be proper tonight,' I said, and went to prepare the dining-room.

The girls didn't want any cheese, and left us to linger over it alone. I topped our glasses up with the Listel, and dealt us each a slim wedge of Brie. In the dining-room we always eat by candle-light: the soft flames reflected on the polished mahogany table, the pink plates, the twin hemispheres of ruby wine in the large glasses. Should it be boring to sit thus, tête-à-tête with a wife of many years? – I don't find it so. Two or three times a week we do this, enjoy a feeling of communion in this room dedicated to the worship of food and wine, our rituals conducted in an atmosphere of calm, order, and companionship. It's a fragile ceremony, easily disrupted by the presence of a single unbeliever or discordant spirit. By Indifference and Hostility, in fact – but at this moment, Priestly seemed far away, belonging to another world. I decided not to tell Claudine about the real purpose of his visit. It would only revive the ghost of Jonathan, and today it had seemed that Claudine was succeeding in shutting him into the past, in closing the book on him. Or in convincing me that she was doing so. By which, in time, she would convince herself. Yes, the ghost was fading. If Priestly would only leave us alone now . . .

I looked across the table at Claudine. She sat in her usual upright posture, elegantly straight-backed, her right arm lying on the table with the fingers just touching the stem of her glass: her fingernails matched the wine. As I watched, she took a firmer hold of the stem and turned it this way and that, the base of the glass remaining on the table, and the wine swirling gently against the side of the glass like a woman's skirt at a twist of the hips. Her dark eyes were fixed on the moving liquid. It was a thoughtful gaze.

'What are you thinking?' I asked.

She looked up, startled. Perhaps my face looked anxious, because she released the glass, smiled, and slid her hand across the table to cover mine with it.

'About you, my William,' she said.

'What about me?'

She made no immediate reply. Then she said reflectively: 'How long is it we are married? Thirteen years?'

'Um, yes,' I said, settling for that. I'm not good at dates.

'No, it is fourteen,' she said.

'So it is.'

She took her hand away, but kept her eyes on me.

'*Je ne regrette rien*,' I intoned. Edith Piaf did it better – much.

Claudine made a wry face. 'That song,' she said, 'I think perhaps you forget. It was the end of an *affaire* – she sings that the past is gone, she doesn't need the memories. She is going to start again, with someone new.'

'Not what I mean,' I said, appalled. 'Not at all.' I hate these games that women sometimes feel like playing – sport, perhaps, is a better description. Emotional kung-fu. 'As you very well know,' I added.

'Do I?'

I stared at her. 'Of course!' Her fingers were twirling the wine glass again. 'Surely you know that?'

'I know that – I think I know that. But what I *see* is not quite the same thing. You are quite *distrait* these days, William. It is not usual, that.'

Oh my God. She's got it all wrong. If I seem distracted, it's because I'm worried about *us*, about the stability of our castle with the rat Priestly gnawing at the foundations, hoping to find dry rot where there's been no more than a touch of damp, soon cured and floorboards nailed back in place. She knows that, I'm sure she does. Then why does she –?

Ah.

Well, I'm slow, but I get there in the end. This isn't a complaint, except on the surface. She doesn't want to fight. No, it's the opposite – an invitation, in fact. A proposal. Let's put all that behind us, she's saying, let's get together again. She's feeling insecure – as I am too. All very discreet, as she prefers emotional matters to be. Leaving room for manoeuvre, personal space, excursions and adventures. Which Barbara ... but time to think of that tomorrow, or next week. Tonight, there should be a re-building of battlements, a demonstration of solidarity, England and France uniting in pageantry on the Field of the Cloth of Gold, up the spiral stairs and make sure the door is firmly shut. A tournament, yes! – flags up and knickers down.

'My darling,' I said, putting out my hand to capture hers, 'you've got it all wrong. It's because you're a foreigner, you see –'

'Oooh!' she exclaimed. '*Ça alors!* You! – *you* are the foreigner. I can tell you, to marry with an Englishman, that is to –'

Her eyes flash, her cheeks are taking on colour, her hand quivers in mine. Oh yes! To make sure of a long flight, you must first climb to a high place ...

'We are foreigners to each other, at present,' I suggested, 'and that is why we should abandon words and make haste to the land of that other language, unvisited for too long, where our differences are of nature not nurture. "*Vive la différence!*" And screw the washing-up.'

A pause while she disentangled this. Then she got it. She

smiled. She nodded – emphatically. We rose as one and, also as one, blew out the candles.

Then the telephone rang.

Claudine and I looked at each other. 'I'd better answer it, I suppose,' I said. 'You go on up, darling. I'll be with you *tout' suite.*' My eyes followed her departing form. Ah yes! – this was how things should be. I went into the kitchen, and scooped up the telephone. 'Hello?' I said in a brisk and breezy tone, 'Who calls?'

'Mr Warner?' enquired a well-known, a *too* well-known voice. The sap stopped rising in my veins, began to sink down again.

'Mr Priestly. Whatever this is, could it not wait until morning? I . . . we're having a little party here, a reunion. It *is* quite late.'

Useless, of course. Priestly didn't even deign to reply, but allowed a heavy silence to impress on me the frivolity of such a protest in such circumstances. 'Well, what is it then?' I asked, 'if it won't wait.'

'I expected to hear from you in the course of the day, Mr Warner,' Priestly said. 'You were going to look out some accounts to show expenditure on building works in France. What progress has been made?'

'Did I promise that for today? I certainly don't remember that I did.'

'I made it clear to you that this information is required without delay,' Priestly said.

'And I think I made it clear to you that it isn't a simple matter. Most if not all of the invoices are in France, and copies of some of them may have to be got from the builders – if they've kept them, which isn't certain. It was all on a very informal basis. I thought I'd explained that.'

'Yes, you did,' Priestly said. 'If you are unable to provide complete documentation, however, you should still let me have whatever is available. As a matter of urgency, please.'

'All right,' I said. 'But it's certainly going to take more than a day or two.' Perhaps Maggie would be able to dig up something to keep Priestly happy. 'Is that all?'

'Yes, Mr Warner – that's all. Good night.'

'Good night, Mr Priestly.'

Well, it could have been worse. I put the telephone down,

and went upstairs. I met Claudine coming out of the spare bedroom where we keep the television, having just said good night to the girls. I thought I'd give it a miss – the sight of Claudine and myself trooping off early to bed is sometimes taken as an excuse for knowing giggles.

'It was Priestly,' I said. 'Nothing that wouldn't have kept until morning. At least that should be the end of him for tonight.'

'*J'espère bien!*' Claudine said with a smile.

'Let's go!' I whispered in her ear, ushering her to the foot of our spiral stair. She started up it. Then –

'I don't believe it!'

The door bell had rung.

We could have ignored it. But I didn't guess what was in store, and chose – once again – to get rid of the caller while Claudine went upstairs and prepared for bed. In the event, it wasn't that simple.

I trudged downstairs again, hearing the bell ring a second time. It was our private entrance – the side door. I opened it.

A sharp shock of *déjà vu* went through me. Solid rain in the background: in the foreground, under an umbrella, a tall figure in a dark suit, long of hair, gaunt of face. No toothbrush in his breast pocket this time, though. And no rose in his right hand.

'Krantz,' he said, or barked, as before.

'I remember,' I said.

'That,' he said, 'does not surprise me.'

Well I thought, *be* like that! And stay on the doorstep. In the rain.

'I wish to speak with you,' he said.

'Sorry,' I said, 'but this is a most inconvenient time. Tomorrow would be better. If you don't mind.'

'Now is better.'

'I've just told you –'

'*Now* is better. This will not wait.'

Oh, shit. Well, just for a moment, then. I stood out of the way.

'This must be quick,' I said firmly. 'My wife is ill. We are expecting the doctor.' I showed him into my office. 'It may be infectious,' I added. Like all Continentals, Germans are terrified of germs. I shut the door, and gestured at the chair Priestly usually sat in. I sat behind the desk to assume, I hope, the air of master of the situation. This plan was wrecked by Krantz, who ignored the chair on offer, and stood in front of the desk looking down at me. He inclined his tall frame, and leant on it, all knuckles and thumbs.

He said: 'I am here to tell you this. You will not see Barbara again.'

'Really?' I said, blinking deliberately. 'This is very sudden. Going abroad, is she? Or has there been an accident?'

'No accident. You will not see her. It is my wish.'

'Rather up to her, isn't it?' I said, or rather drawled. Other nations shout their insults. Crude, and far less annoying. 'I mean, you're not married to her, or even anything to do with her any longer. Are you?'

'We are to be married again,' Krantz said. His eyes were remarkable, really. Strange how such a pale blue could support that powerful stare. The eyes of an eagle, fierce, hypnotic. But no indication so far of anything more than a bird-brain behind them.

'Married?' I said. 'Really! When did she agree to this?'

'She will.'

'But not yet?'

'She will. And that is why you must not see her.'

Perhaps because threats are infrequent utterances in the relatively polite, repressed corner of society which I inhabit, my stock of conversational gambits of an aggressive sort is practically limited to those overheard in pubs. 'Are you asking me or telling me?'

'I am telling you,' Krantz explained simply.

What comes next? I tried to remember, but failed. At some stage, the exchange should crystallise and consist entirely of repetition – you did, I didn't, you are, I'm not, you will, I won't. After that, warfare – actual or symbolic. Did I want to go to war with Krantz? Probably not. Definitely not, I remembered, with Claudine ready, willing, and waiting. A bloody nose was not what I needed just at this moment. An opportunity to retire with honour must be taken.

'What else have you got to say that might convince me?' I asked. 'So far, I can't say you've inspired me with sympathy for your cause.'

'You do not agree? You mean to meet with my wife again?'

'She isn't your wife,' I pointed out, 'and no, I'm not convinced. Now, if I thought that Barbara herself wanted this ...'

Krantz had straightened up, lifting his hands from my desk. His stare seemed to have intensified. His right hand was moving towards his jacket pocket, unhurriedly, but in a gesture familiar from innumerable films starring Humphrey Bogart, George Raft, Edward G. Robinson. I looked at the pocket. There was something in it, all right – the cloth was dragged downwards by a squarish object of considerable weight. Why hadn't I noticed that before? Probably, I thought, because the eyes had it – my attention, I mean. Must be useful, having eyes like that. Also because I had figured Krantz to be a joke – Ludicrous Ludwig. He still might be. But, now I'd seen more of him, I wasn't so sure. Barbara had sounded quite serious when she warned me that he was desperate – and the joke might be on me.

'All right,' I said, 'I'm convinced. Mind you, I think you might have said "please".'

The hand halted, inches away from the weighted pocket. Perhaps he would laugh, now, and produce a tobacco pouch, a pocket edition of Goethe. *So! I haf a fool of you made, dumkopf Englander!* No, I thought not. He had a gun in there and, whether he would have used it or not was a question I wasn't prepared to press, not at the moment.

'You are wise.'

'Known for it,' I said.

'So you will not change your mind,' he said softly, giving me the blue glare at full voltage, 'I say to you: *Remember Cassell!*'

I gave him a stare now – a poor thing but mine own. I couldn't compete with his, I wasn't trying to, mine was involuntary – shock and amazement must have been clearly visible in it. Playing games with guns to frighten people is one thing, but this was in a different class altogether. Laying claims to murder ... I hadn't expected that. I didn't know what to think, what to say, or do. His eyes held me, and I sat for several seconds, frozen to my chair. Then he switched his eyes away, and moved to the door, where he paused and turned his face again to where I still sat behind my desk.

'*Remember!*'

Then he was gone. I heard the side door open and click shut. There was a damp patch on the carpet by the fireplace where he had stood his umbrella. And a taste of acid at the back of my mouth.

I stood up and shook myself. Gradually, my sense of normality returned. Of course, I realised, he'd have to say that, to reinforce his threat. Possession of a gun means little – you must show yourself prepared to use it. And he'd given a brilliant performance of that. A failed artist, maybe, but Krantz had shown me an alternative talent that could solve all his problems. Artist to actor – what was he waiting for?

I spent a few more moments pulling myself together. Then I ran upstairs, turning keys and switching out lights as I went. In the bedroom, only the bedside lights were on, and Claudine was inspecting her naked self in the long mirror. I threw off my jacket and came up behind her, capturing her breasts and giving them my patent firming massage and manual uplift.

'*Ma biche*,' she murmured, watching the mirror.

'This will make them better than ever,' I whispered in her ear.

'Ah. Oh yes – that's nice.' A pause. 'They are not bad, for thirty-seven?'

'As good as when I first made their acquaintance.'

She smiled at me in the mirror. I nuzzled her ear and smiled back.

'Who was it at the door?' she asked.

'A man about a dog,' I said.

'A dog? You want to have a dog? In London that is not –'

'I'll tell you about it tomorrow.'

'But, my William –'

'Tomorrow. I have other plans for tonight.'

'Ooh-hoo! Tell me!'

'You'll never believe this.'

'Tell me!'

'Well, first you . . . and then . . . and next it's my turn to . . . and then we . . .'

'*Impossible!*'

'And to finish up with, we both . . .'

'*Ah non!*'

'Shall we begin?'

'You are still dressed.'

'Let's have a countdown. Ten, nine, eight, seven, six –'

'Wait!'

'What for? *Cinq, quatre, trois, deux –*'

'My watch will not come off!'

'Who cares, it's shockproof isn't it? Right then – ONE!'

'Oooh!'

'Aha!'

Oh yes. This was the language I meant. It seemed to me we still spoke it pretty well together. All I needed was for someone to rid me of this pestilent Priestly.

'Wow!'

'Ah, me too, *chéri!*'

'Good. I mean, yes, wonderful!'

Wonderful it was, but not the cause of my sudden bliss, not this time. No – it was the thought I'd just had. How to get rid of Priestly and Ludwig at the same time. Blindingly obvious, if I hadn't had these distractions. It's nothing new, of course; empires have been lost by an ill-timed legover. And now that's sorted out, I shall concentrate on the job in hand.

'How about this?'

'Oh yes, *chéri*, oh yes!'

Things always seem to work out best when you least expect it.

CHAPTER 10

Passing Judgement

After a short time the conversation turns upon
psychoanalysis and you will find the greatest variety
of people passing their judgement upon it, mostly in
voices of unwavering certainty.

SIGMUND FREUD

And in the morning, as I got the Citroën out of the garage and
set off for the meeting with Pete at the warehouse, the feeling
was still with me. I was getting back on top of things. The
waves caused by Jonathan were receding, and my household
was being restored to an even keel. Claudine seemed to have
come out of her depression, state of shock, whatever it was,
and resumed her normal role as queen bee, the calm centre
around which the rest of us revolved. And I now had a delightful prospect ahead, that of setting Priestly on to Ludwig,
thus ridding myself of both of them at a stroke. Temporarily,
perhaps – but at least it meant I would be setting the pace for a
while, to *do* instead of being done to. Passive endurance isn't
my style. And, in that while, Jonathan's waves would have a
chance to melt away to a flat calm. The boat could stop
rocking.

But first, the meeting with Pete. I had telephoned the police
first thing, and left a message for Priestly to ring me in the
morning, but there had been no call by nine, so I left for the
warehouse, glad, in fact, to have some extra time to think
about the best method and style of presentation – important if I
was to put the boot into Ludwig with maximum effect.

Best to play it fairly cool, I decided. To give the facts and let
Priestly decide whether to take the episode seriously or not. If I
gave it too much build-up, or told the tale with too much
obvious pleasure, the effect would be correspondingly less;
whatever I said, and however I put it, Priestly was likely to
hear me with scepticism. He was well aware that I resented his

prowling about the place, and I'd got off on the wrong foot with him right from the start. He probably wouldn't think I'd go so far as to invent a diversion, but he would certainly think me capable of exaggeration to that end.

Trouble was, Ludwig's visit, viewed in the cold light of day, had taken on a much less menacing aspect than it had last night, in the glare of those pale blue eyes. To be honest, I believed it less and less myself. Almost certainly, he was just a sad, disappointed man, clutching at straws, trying to recapture his golden age by empty threats.

Oh well. Even if there was nothing in it, Priestly would be distracted for a while. And Ludwig might be scared off, back to Germany. That was the other thing. I wouldn't be able to see anything of Barbara while Ludwig was still around, if she thought he ought to be taken seriously.

These thoughts, and variations on the same theme, had kept me from noticing much of the familiar route to the warehouse: I got there on autopilot, hardly aware that I was driving until the bumping of the car on the Brewery Lane cobbles shook me out of my reverie. Ahead, I saw the firm's taxi sitting unoccupied at the side of the road – Pete must have already arrived. I pulled up behind it, got out, locked up, and stepped through the pass door in the warehouse front.

Voices could be heard coming from the back of the building, behind the pallets stacked with wine. Pete's, certainly, but there was another I didn't recognise, higher pitched, and sounding like that of a boy or a young woman. I started to walk down the aisle between the rows of bottles. My footsteps echoed as I went: ker-lap, ker-lap. It's that half-second delay from footfall to echo that gives the creepy effect, the sensation that someone is following you. And when you stop to catch them out, you always succeed – they're half a second too late to avoid detection. Ker-lap.

A figure moved into view at the end of the aisle. Heard me coming, no doubt. Not Pete. Not Ludwig, either. No, it was a girl. She stood, looking in my direction. Then Pete appeared beside her.

'Hullo!' I called.

'Morning!' they both called back.

I ker-lapped the remaining few yards, and came face to face with them. The girl was, I guessed, in her late twenties; slim, and with a confident, upright carriage. She wore a plain black pullover and jeans. Shoulder-length, rather mousy hair framed a round pink face, shining bright and free of make-up. Small shrewd eyes inspected me through round, wire-framed specs. I guessed who it was even before Pete said: 'This 'ere's Miss Mullarkey.'

'Good morning,' Miss Mullarkey said, holding out her hand with a smile which showed small, very white teeth.

'Hello,' I said, shaking her hand. She had a firm grip for a woman – so many seem to aim at the wet dishcloth effect.

'Got a week's leave, see, so she's givin' me a bit of an 'and,' Pete said. 'Told 'er the guv'nor wouldn't mind. 'Ope I was right?'

'From what I hear, you'll be an asset, not to mention a good influence,' I told her. 'This is a lonely job at times, and it'll be nice for Pete to have some company for a change. As long as the deliveries go out on time, I've got no objections, quite the reverse. What are you on leave from?'

'I'm a social worker,' Miss Mullarkey said. I remembered that Pete had told me that.

'Oh yes,' I said. 'Visiting broken homes, and trying to keep lads like this one on the straight and narrow. If you look after this area, you must certainly earn your leave. But I'm afraid you'll be bored.'

'Oh no,' she said. 'I like to see behind the scenes. Many of the problems I have to deal with have their origins in the work situation. This is a good chance for me to get a new perspective.'

'That's all I am, see – a suitable case for study,' Pete said in a mournful voice.

'Yes,' Miss Mullarkey said briskly, 'but give me a few days, and I'll have you straightened out.' She smiled, showing the little white teeth again.

I remembered something else Pete had said, that she was a right little goer. What with those teeth, the shrewd eyes and the confident air, I could believe it. Once these intelligent girls get switched on, there's no holding them. I hoped Pete realised what he was letting himself in for.

I suggested we got down to business, and led the way into the office at the back of the warehouse. This used to be a spirit store, and is built like a fortress – reinforced concrete walls and ceiling. Going in there is like entering the Führer-Bunker at Berchtesgaden except for the lack of machine-gun embrasures. It's a tomb. Miss Mullarkey evidently felt this too; I saw her shiver as we went in.

'One ought to feel safe in here, not nervous,' I said to her as we sat down round the trestle table that serves as a desk.

She considered this for a moment, then said:

'I think that's because you feel cut off from the outside world, from reality. Withdrawal from reality is, of course, a sign of mental ill-health. Many people, if shut into a room like this, would in fact go mad in quite a short time. That's why I think that prisons – oh, I'm sorry.' She put her hand over her mouth.

Pete was looking at her proprietorially, and now gave a proud smile. 'Eats dictionaries for breakfast,' he said. 'She can't 'elp it.'

'Don't be sorry,' I said to her, 'I'm sure you're right. I hadn't ever got around to trying to work it out, the feeling of unease you get in places like this. But you're right – there've been experiments, haven't there?'

'Sensory deprivation,' she said, 'yes. Deprived of all sensation in a specially built chamber, people can't stand more than a very few hours.'

'Yeah,' Pete said, 'that's true.'

We looked at him.

'I go mad meself,' he explained, 'if I don't get me share of stimulation.' He returned Miss Mullarkey's gaze with one of perfect innocence.

The balance of power was fairly even, I reckoned. Intellect needs a nudge in the ribs now and again.

'Now, about our delivery schedule,' I began.

No need to go into the details, but half an hour later it seemed that, with some additional part-time help with the actual driving, leaving Pete in full command of the warehouse and our vulnerable stocks, we could make some worthwhile improvements in average delivery time. It was left that Pete would look for a reliable and trustworthy part-timer, if such a paragon were to be found. If not, we'd have to think again.

While this discussion was going on, an idea had occurred to me. No harm, it's said, in asking. And Miss Mullarkey already knew the background of what the newspapers were calling the 'Cassell killing', since she'd been with Pete on his pub crawl into the underworld, when Uncle George had confirmed that the wrong man had been shot.

'You get some psychological training in your job, I suppose?' I asked her.

'It's quite basic,' she said, 'but yes. Though most of what I do doesn't need much more than a little common sense and a lot of experience. No, it's more of a hobby with me, psychology, and I study a lot in my own time. Trying to understand what makes people tick. The problem is that everyone is different, and it's very hard to fit theory to practice. Exceptions are the rule, you could say.'

'If I tell you about someone I know,' I said, 'would you like to give me your opinion on their character? It could be very useful. For instance, I'd like to know whether you think they're sane and calculating, or halfway round the bend. I know that –'

'If you're goin' to talk about me,' Pete said, 'I'm off to shift some crates.' And he left, giving Miss Mullarkey a wink as he passed her chair.

'Well,' she said doubtfully, 'as I told you, Mr Warner, I'm not properly trained for this.'

'Have a go?' I pressed her.

'Well . . .'

'Just between ourselves, and I won't quote you or get you into any trouble – I promise that. I think you'll find it interesting.'

That got her, as I knew it would.

'All right, then,' she said.

So I told her all about Ludwig.

The twin discs of Miss Mullarkey's spectacles seemed to take on a deeper, a more searching brilliance as I talked; and Pete's noises off – a crashing of (I hoped) empty pallets being stacked, the arthritic groaning of our ancient fork-lift truck – faded from our consciousness. Even before I'd finished, I was aware of a bond between us: we both liked to "see behind the scenes"; we both had a kind of lust to know what made things tick. I described every detail of my two encounters with Ludwig, not forgetting the toothbrush, the rose held like a weapon, and the unnerving effect of the pale blue eyes. When I got to the hand moving towards the coat pocket, Miss Mullarkey gave an excited 'Ooh!' and hitched her chair closer. At the close of my account we both had our elbows on the table, and our faces inches apart.

'Well,' she said, 'that *was* interesting, as you said.'

'I'm afraid it isn't much to go on.'

'Oh, but what there is, is so clear. Absolutely textbook. Fascinating!'

'The important thing is,' I said, 'to know whether he's just acting a part, or really dangerous.'

Miss Mullarkey was silent for some moments. Then she said: 'Well. I see it like this. Adler says that to be a human being means the possession of a feeling of inferiority that is constantly pressing on towards its own conquest. Unlike animals, human beings are self-aware – of being ignorant, powerless, and condemned to die. They try to overcome this feeling by various means – accumulating money, power over others, being sexually attractive, and so on. By being *effective*. This is why unemployment is so hard to bear, and has such a destructive effect on the psyche.'

I gulped. Well – I'd asked for her opinion ... I said: 'And Ludwig is an unemployed artist, once famous, now not. Yes, I'd got that far. He thinks Barbara can make him famous again.'

'Which she won't.'

'I don't think she could, even if she was prepared to try. His sort of work was a sixties phenomenon, now disregarded.'

'What was it like?'

'His art? Well, bits of rusted iron and charred canvas, sometimes sprayed with black paint.'

'Titled?'

'Accident One, Accident Two, things like that.'

'Oh *splendid*,' Miss Mullarkey said with enthusiasm. 'This is really most interesting. I haven't had the opportunity to study the creative personality before. According to Freud, the artist is expressing the primitive impulses of the id – which, of course, is that submerged part of the psyche which contains our unconscious instinctual drives. In the artist, these primitive impulses are channelled through the ego into socially acceptable forms – he produces works which society will buy, a mark of social approval. But artists are always uncomfortable about this – they want the money, but they don't like the implied restriction on their freedom of expression. If the id is put under too tight a control, the quality of work will suffer – chocolate box painting.'

'Quite,' I said, 'I think I've always . . .'

'Now,' said Miss Mullarkey, 'there is a school of thought that believes artistic effort to be a compensation for a pathological condition. Beethoven, Goethe, Swift are quoted as examples of near-schizophrenic personalities. Whether this is correct or not, there is reason to believe that artists have a tendency to be neurotic, and in some cases will progress from this to being psychotic – the ego overwhelmed by the id. And here is the interesting point following what I've said – in such people *there is only a thin barrier between daydreams and action.* There!'

'Gosh.'

'Yes indeed,' Miss Mullarkey said with satisfaction. 'Yes indeed. Here we have a man used to indulging his primitive impulses for creative purposes, which have now been stopped up. His individuation is threatened. He seeks to re-open the creative outlet, but without success. He is possessed by a feeling of impotence. His art shows a morbid obsession with disaster – the death instinct. This is dangerous if inwardly directed, so (unconsciously of course) he turns it outwards, in the form of aggression against others. This is an automatic act of psychological self-preservation. Also, as Fromm points out, it is much easier to get excited by anger, rage, cruelty or the passion to destroy than by love and productive effort.'

'Yes,' I said, 'and that explains why . . .'

'Hate and aggression are derived from insecurity, from the struggle of the ego to maintain itself in striving for significance. To quote Fromm again, the sense of being condemned to ineffectiveness is one of the most painful and almost intolerable experiences, and man will do almost anything to overcome it, from drug and work addiction to cruelty *and murder*.'

We stared at each other across the intervening inches, Miss Mullarkey and I. Her spectacles shone with irrefutable perspicacity: I believed her, every word. We both gave sighs as the tension began to ebb away: it was post-coital, almost. Slowly, we drew apart and leant back in our chairs.

'Miss Mullarkey,' I said, 'you're really something. When you look at me now, I feel transparent through and through.'

She gave a little smile. 'It's only theory: I could be wrong.'

'But it makes such sense – everything fits.'

'Please treat it as a guide – no more. We don't know what stage Mr Krantz has reached, even if the process is as I've suggested.'

'No, we don't. But he must be taken seriously – that's quite clear.'

'Yes,' she said, 'I really think he must. It would be very dangerous not to.'

I stood up, and held out my hand. 'Miss Mullarkey – thank you very much. If there are developments –'

'Oh, please tell me,' she said. 'I'd like to know everything.'

'I certainly will,' I promised her.

'Oh good. I can hardly wait. Now, I'll go and help Pete. Could I drive the fork-lift truck, if he'll let me?'

'Miss Mullarkey,' I said, 'you can do anything and everything as far as I'm concerned.'

I drove back to Church Street on autopilot again, in the second daze of that day. Food for thought, it's called, and I had a lot of digesting to do. I stowed the car in the garage, and walked slowly up the path towards the house. It had rained again earlier that morning, and everything in the garden was still dripping. Will we ever see the sun again? I wondered. Or was London really about to succumb to a new Ice Age, ever-thickening grey skies, followed by endless rain turning to snow, followed by paralysing cold turning all this damp into a sheet of hideous crystal. Frozen stiff, if we haven't all rotted first. Time I went south to check if the sun still exists. Trouble is, I might not want to come back up.

Through my office window, I saw that I had visitors. Priestly and Cooper were in there – must have parked in a side street, as I'd asked. So, I was annoyed to see, was Claudine.

I quickened my pace, reached the door of the back lobby, and charged into the house, bursting straight into the office without warning. Claudine was behind the desk where I usually .sat: one look told me that she was close to tears.

'What's all this?' I said angrily. 'I'm the one that wanted to talk to you. My wife's had enough of all this: she's already told you all she knows.'

'That's all right, sir,' Priestly said impassively. 'I've no further questions for her at the moment. If you'd like to take her place . . .'

'You go, darling,' I told her. 'This won't take long. I'll see you in a minute or two.'

She glanced at me – that detached feeling was back again, I noticed. What had Priestly been stirring up? Then she nodded, rose, and went out without a word. The eyes of all of us followed her: I looked away and at Priestly just in time to catch him at it again. Oh yes. His expression said it all. Just our luck, to get a policeman who puts a high value on big bums.

'What would *you* do to keep her?' I burst out, as soon as the door was shut. 'Worth a murder, would you say? That's how it strikes you, isn't it?'

Priestly swivelled to face me. 'Now sir,' he said, 'since you bring it up, it can't be denied that Mrs Warner is a very attractive lady. There's no ignoring that fact: we must take it into account in our investigations. It's what we call one of the regular motives, that. But, of course, it's not often as simple as that. Usually, there's a financial factor involved, or a threat to family security. In this case, Mr Warner, there could be all three. I'm being frank with you, because I want you to understand that, in these circumstances, there are questions that must be asked – and answered. I hope I make myself clear.'

'Clear enough,' I said impatiently, 'but what you don't seem to understand is that all these questions put a considerable strain on us, on my relationship with my wife. I'll be frank with you, and admit that we don't run a strictly conventional household here; there's a certain amount of give and take, always has been. I'm afraid that what might seem a potential upset to you isn't so to us. We've learned to live like that, and we prefer it. But the whole thing's dependent on tact and leaving certain things unsaid. It's doing us no good at all to have you steaming in here and saying them. Is *that* clear?'

Priestly had continued to look at me while I said this. When I finished, he said nothing for a while. Then he looked away, and said in his flat voice: 'These ideas of yours, sir – is Mrs Warner in agreement with them?'

'We don't discuss it. I told you – some things are better left unsaid. They have to be. Discretion in marriage is a French tradition. You're forcing her to go against all her instincts with these questions. I must ask you to stop it.'

He frowned slightly. 'I can hardly do that, sir,' he said. 'Perhaps I should remind you there's been a murder done. And, whatever the French tradition may be, they have murders there too, sir.'

'Well, of course they do. When the system breaks down. *Crime passionnel –*'

'Doesn't apply to this case, Mr Warner. We believe that this murder was planned, cold-blooded, deliberate. A contract killing. It has all the signs of one.'

'Well, that lets me out then. If ever my wife and I set about killing each other, it'll be *crime passionnel*, I promise you.'

Priestly received this in silence, without even a flicker of a smile, though I saw Cooper give what appeared to be an appreciative nod over his notebook. He must get pretty pissed off, I guessed, having to trail round with dry-as-dust Priestly.

'Can we get on now, sir?' Priestly said.

'If we must.'

'It was you telephoned me. Early this morning. About the cash withdrawal, I assume?'

'No,' I said, 'not about that. I had just had a visit from a man called Krantz, Mrs Cassell's ex-husband. He threatened me with a gun.' I tried my best to keep the satisfaction from my voice.

Both Priestly and Cooper looked up at this. 'Threatened you?' Priestly repeated.

'That's what I said. With a gun. He seemed to think that I was after his ex-wife.'

'Why should he object to that, sir?'

'He wants to re-marry her.' I explained briefly about Ludwig's motive. 'I understand he feels his future depends on her. At present, he is suffering from acute insecurity, lack of identity, and so on.' How had Miss Mullarkey put it?

'How do you mean, "lack of identity"?' Priestly asked.

'His, er, individuation took a knock when his work stopped selling. He used to be famous. Work on show at the Tate and so on. Artists tend to be neurotic, and this seems to have pushed him over the edge.' I wasn't putting it very well.

'I'm not quite with you, sir.'

'It's quite simple,' I said sharply. 'Artistic effort is thought to be compensation for a pathological condition. Many artists have been schizophrenic. Beethoven, for instance.' *Oh shit.*

'Beethoven, sir?'

'Look,' I said. 'Think of it this way. This man, an unstable artist, accustomed to letting his id out for a walk, as it were, because creativity is based on primitive impulses, has crashed the barrier between daydreams and action, and become dangerous. He threatened me with a gun, for heaven's sake. What more do you want?'

Priestly went into one of his silences, digesting this. Cooper coughed, and said: 'What kind of gun was it, sir?'

'I don't know – I didn't see it.'

'Then how –?'

'He had it in his pocket. I could see the shape quite clearly. Flattish. An automatic, probably, rather than a revolver.'

'I see, sir,' Cooper said, subsiding.

It might be best to leave it at that, I thought. No good telling them about the amazing pale blue glare. Not after Beethoven. No, wait –

'And that wasn't all. As he left, he threatened me again – warned me to keep away from Barbara – Mrs Cassell. And said, "Remember Jonathan!" Just that – "Remember Jonathan!"'

'And what do you think he meant by that, sir?' Priestly asked.

'He wanted to frighten me. By implying that he was responsible for what had happened to Cassell.'

'And did he succeed in that, sir?'

'As a matter of fact, he was quite convincing, yes. Convincing enough for me to telephone the police about him.'

'Yes,' Priestly said, in a tone that might as easily have meant no. He thought briefly, and then asked: 'And have you been seeing Mrs Cassell?'

'I don't know her at all well. As you'll know, she had been living apart from Jonathan for some time. I called on her once since Jonathan's death, to see if she was all right, and I've also talked to her on the telephone once, when she warned me that Krantz was blaming me for her refusal to consider the idea of re-marriage, and was desperate enough to be dangerous. That's all.'

'She telephoned you to warn you of that?'

'Yes. No, she was going to ring me, but in fact I rang first.'

'For any particular reason?'

Time to see this coming, fortunately.

'I'd met Krantz as I left her house, and thought he looked like trouble. I rang to ask if, in fact, he had been.'

'After which he came here and threatened you?'

'That's right.'

'Anything to add, Mr Warner?'

'No, that's it.'

Priestly looked round at Cooper, who was scribbling to catch up. When he had, Priestly said: 'Have you turned up any documentation on the matter of the cash withdrawal?'

'Not yet, no. It's not going to be easy, I keep telling you that.'

'Nevertheless –'

'Do you really need this, when you can see from the statement that the withdrawal was made in French francs? That's clear enough evidence of what the money was intended for, isn't it?'

'No, sir. Currency can easily be exchanged.'

'But would anyone –?'

'Yes, sir. They would.'

He was right, I supposed. I might have chosen to take out

francs and change them, reasoning that some smokescreen was better than none.

'I'll go on looking. And you, I hope, will look for Krantz. Barbara says he could be dangerous, and she should know.'

'I'll look into it, sir,' Priestly said in his flat voice.

And I knew then that, on the Priestly list of priorities, Ludwig was last. I had failed to convince him, even with all the ammunition provided so efficiently by Miss Mullarkey. He would report it, of course, but there would be no intensive search, no knocking on boarding-house doors by discreetly armed officers, no arrest and interrogation. In short, I'd blown it.

When the two policemen had left, I went back into my office and sat down again. The sight of Claudine holding back tears, of her face frozen into a stranger's mask once again, was still with me. Priestly wasn't going to let up, that was clear. My attempt to explain how Claudine and I ran our lives had done more harm than good. He was right to think that I would react strongly to any attempt to invade my household and capture Claudine. Not violently, perhaps – but you never know yourself until the time of trial arrives.

Which – a sudden, earthquaking thought – *maybe it had*. The invader was Priestly; the result would not be capture, but it might be destruction, the end of all this, my kingdom come and gone. We might survive it – a short while ago I would have said we certainly would, this and much worse – but now I wasn't so sure. I didn't know, and couldn't ask, what Jonathan had meant to Claudine but, from her demeanour since he was killed, I'd say he'd been more than I'd reckoned.

Yes. The invader is Priestly. And it's time for me to react, before any more damage is done. Nothing will stop him, except the proof of who killed Jonathan. I'll have to see what I can do about that. At least it will be better than sitting here amid the crumbling walls. And I know where to start.

There was a tap at my door and Maggie came in.

'Ah, Maggie! Just the person I want.'

'I've brought these to sign,' she said.

'Right. And while I'm doing it, please see if you can book me on the Harwich–Hook of Holland ferry tomorrow. I'm going to Germany for a few days.'

'What on earth for?' she exclaimed.
'Sell wine, don't we?'
'Yes, but –'
'And they grow it. What more do you want?'
'But we don't stock German wine.'
'That's why I'm going. To see what they're up to.'
In the land of Ludwig.

CHAPTER 11

Unhesitating Certainty

When you first meet a human being, the first
distinction you make is 'male or female?' and you
are accustomed to make the distinction with
unhesitating certainty.

SIGMUND FREUD

There was no trouble with the booking. Although October can
be one of the best months for Continental sightseeing, with
bursts of surprisingly warm weather and autumnal colours in
the woods, most people go for summer holidays or winter sports,
and the car ferry to Hook of Holland was half empty. We landed
at seven-thirty in the morning: two hours later I was at the
German border.

This was Friday morning. I've skipped Thursday, a day of
scrambled preparation which took place in an atmosphere of
re-emerging gloom. It was probable that nobody believed this
sudden need to research German wine, although I make such
trips to Germany or elsewhere at least once a year. Normally,
before deciding to go, I hold consultations to agree on the most
likely new source of suppliers. This trip was too sudden to be
entirely credible. But it didn't matter. We were all aware that
there was a tension in the house, which might be eased by my
departure for a few days, and the excuse I gave was as good as
any; we were all oppressed by the same web of work and
domesticity which was normally our prop and our pleasure but
which just now, made visible by Priestly, seemed to draw tighter
day by day, a restriction instead of a support. There's a torture
in which lovers are bound face to face, and left until at last,
filthy and hateful to each other, each is ready to buy release
with betrayal. The evening after that last interview, Claudine
was again stricken by migraine, or said she was: all the warmth
of our night of rapprochement seemed to have leaked away,
and she was again silent and withdrawn. If I needed any more

encouragement to action, the sight of her face that Thursday evening was it. And if what I was doing turned out to be useless, as it probably would, at least it got me out of the house and away – away from the increasingly stifling atmosphere, from the questions, and from the endless grey London skies and the rain.

There'd been time to telephone Barbara and get Ludwig's address, which turned out to be near Munich, a place I'd been to several times on business and pleasure. I told her what had happened, and what I intended, which was to see where he lived and collect all the information I could on his character and background: I hoped to arrive there before he did. Barbara sounded non-committal about this, which I supposed was better than being downright discouraging, but nothing she said would have made any difference – I was determined to go. Keep this strictly to yourself, I warned her. I then wrote a note to Priestly, who was obviously going to think my sudden disappearance from London in the middle of his investigation a most irresponsible if not suspicious thing to do: as I didn't want him to prevent it, he would have to be notified by letter arriving after my departure rather than by telephone: a transparently wilful device but one which he'd just have to accept, or refer to Interpol. Of course, I said nothing about Ludwig, and everything about wine. Imperative that I get on with my work, the note explained. And so I scooped up some deutschmarks from the bank, did a little hasty shopping, and left.

No, not quite. There was one other item of preparation, which was to get out the old Webley revolver I keep locked away in the bottom drawer of my desk. My father brought this back from the First World War, and so I look on it as a souvenir more than as a weapon, although the police might not agree – it isn't licensed. I used to have two bullets for it, but one misfired at a critical moment in my life, so I mistrust the other. As you can't buy bullets without a licence, I keep it loaded with .410 shotgun cartridges which fit well enough, though the effect would be minimal except at very close range. I'm not sure why I do this: maybe it's a sign of paranoia. Or the chance of peppering a burglar's backside – we live in a high risk area. I lifted it out, and unwrapped the oily duster it lives in. Lying on the desk, gleaming black under the lamplight, it looked even more enormous than I remembered. Next time, I thought, next time Ludwig reaches for his pocket *I* shall come up with *this*. No pistol can be more impressive.

And so I was armed, the Webley safely tucked under my seat, as I arrived at the border of our erstwhile enemy, and was waved through with barely a glance. A middle-aged business-man in a big grey Citroën – what possible trouble could I represent?

Dark green and black, the brooding landscape of Germany: pine forest and shadow; camouflage and Iron Crosses; *Grünwald und Schwarzwald*. I don't go to Germany often, but whenever I do I get the same tingle in the spine, the same stirring of childish bogies: the smell of gas masks; the sound of air-raid sirens; the sight of grown-up faces frowning over the wireless set. Later, I was sent to join BAOR in the land of the bogeymen, and saw them for myself, looking down from the turret of my tank as my fifty tons of Centurion broke their bridges and churned up their crops. And, on the whole, they accepted our rule and the reverse in their fortune: *'Jawohl, Herr Leutnant!'* snapped my driver as I stepped into the dark green Volkswagen, just as though I had been an SS officer, or as if we were both taking part in *Escape from Colditz*. It was black comedy, like so much about Germany, that land of extremes. On the one hand, perfect order – *'alles in Ordnung'*; on the other, permanent incipient hysteria. Furious energy, and tortured introspection. So my English spine tingles; what could be more alien? Comfortable compromise left behind at the border, and I've got to stiffen the sinews, summon up the will.

I had all day to do it. It was another four hundred miles or so to Munich from the border. There's no speed limit on the autobahn, and at first the Mercs and BMWs were rocketing past me, but I soon got into the spirit of it, and belted the Citroën along with accelerator booted to the floor. You soon realise why German cars have such massive pedals – they'd get broken off otherwise. I stopped for an hour at midday to give myself and the Citroën time to get our breath back. *Kaffee und Käsebrot* was all I had – no alcohol for once – and then it was back to the racetrack.

Munich came up ahead just before six, and I plunged off the autobahn straight into the rush-hour traffic jam. In some ways it was a relief, and allowed the landscape to settle around me as I moved slowly towards the city centre. Half an hour later I had booked in at a hotel just off the Leopoldstrasse, in Schwabing, the equivalent of Chelsea. I parked the car in the basement car park, out of sight. Then I went up to my room with my own small case, locked the door, ran the bath, and got in feeling content. The troubles and traumas of Church Street already seemed far away. I must ring Claudine later; we needed distance, but not total separation. In the meantime, a good soak, and then perhaps a stroll to the Münchener Freiheit before dinner, to see some Bavarian café life.

I went back to the hotel for dinner, not being in adventurous mood. Their restaurant was small, and the menu limited; local trout, I supposed, was the thing to have, with *Bratkartoffeln* and a green salad.

'*Und was trinken Sie?*'

Well, I could get in some research here. I chose a bottle of '76 Iphofen, to remind me what a good Steinwein should taste like. It was pleasant enough, but pricey. Better check, like Pooh Bear's jar of honey, that it's the same all the way down to the bottom. It was. Surprise, surprise.

Afterwards I took another stroll before bed, in the nearby Englischer Garten, a meandering park criss-crossed by little paths. The evening was quite warm, and pairs of happy Müncheners were also strolling, lustfully involved with each other. I felt a twinge of loneliness.

Time I went to my solitary hotel bed. The call to Claudine would add a female touch to the end of my day.

There were several entries under Krantz in the hotel telephone directory, I found when checking the address Barbara had given me. The one I wanted was among them, so there seemed no problem there. Reassured, I went into the restaurant for breakfast. If you could call it that. Though it was offered with confidence, and everyone else was gnashing at it, I can hardly think of anything less appetising at nine o'clock in the morning than black pumpernickel bread with a slice of clammy yellow cheese on it. I settled for shelled boiled eggs which came in a glass, and strong black coffee. After that I felt prepared to take on the day, and went back upstairs to my room for a tactical conference with myself.

First, I guessed the approximate location of Krantz's house according to the address of the nearest village, which I found to the east of Munich. Less than an hour in the car, I reckoned, even allowing for getting out through the city traffic. I plotted a safe approach route, coming in from the south on minor roads, just in case Ludwig had arrived back before me. If I kept to that route, it was less likely that we would meet on the road, and I didn't want a confrontation until I'd done all possible background research. If I had bad luck and we did pass on the road, I'd taken some simple precautions to try to avoid recognition. These were: my wire-frame tinted glasses in place of my usual black-framed pair, and some clothes of a type I never normally wear – a black bomber jacket and blue jeans. The car was the problem: a right-hand-drive Citroën which, even with the GB sticker taken off, was going to stick out in German farming country like a hippo in the home pasture. I could hire a car, of course, but I hate doing that – they always stink of stale cigarettes. No, I'd take what precautions I could and let fickle fate decide the rest.

I descended to the basement car park some time before ten. It was deserted, and I slipped quickly into the bomber jacket and jeans. Then I drove up the ramp into the street, blinking at the sudden ascent into brilliant daylight. I had the route memorised, and took the Karl-Scharnagl-Ring to the south, turning off on to the Salzburg autobahn. Foreign cars would be commonplace on this road. Perhaps I was an opera fan heading for the Festspielhaus at Salzburg, or even for Vienna, to the State Opera. I like opera, especially if sung in German; it adds the final touch of lunacy to the language. Much of my limited German consists of one-liners from opera, especially *Rosenkavalier*, and especially Baron Ochs. '*Ohne mich, ohne mich, jeder Tag dir so bange!*' It loses everything if sung in English. 'Without me, without me, every day a misery.' No guts, no gutterals, just a flop. English is not a language to boast in. *Ohne mich, ohne mich . . .* here's the turning.

I turned off the autobahn and took a small road to the north, direction Grafing. That's the village the house was near. The landscape was more open here, with excessively neat green pastures like golf courses, and only small patches of pine forest. The villages were tiny; some boasted a gaunt *gasthof*; tall and forbidding, with rows of identical square windows. They all looked much more primitive than English villages must look to a foreigner.

I stopped at one of the larger places to buy something for lunch, and went into the only shop.

'*Grüss Gott!*' said the massive maiden behind the counter. I returned this greeting, and began to look along the shelves. She watched me, her head lowered like a cow at bay, curiosity mixed with caution. Not a local, so who could I be? – tourists don't come this way. I chose some pretzels and a bottle of Pils and put them on the counter.

'*Danke. Haben Sie sonst noch einen Wunsch?*'

I shook my head, handed over some money, and was given my purchases. I felt her gaze on my back as I went out.

Another ten minutes driving took me to a larger area of pine forest, with clearings in which small industrial buildings had been built: many of them were sawmills, but there were light engineering works and small warehouses as well. I passed a sign which said 'Grafing 2km'. Then I came to a T-junction with the main road from Munich coming in from the left and leading into Grafing on the right. What to do? I decided to follow it towards Grafing, and turned right. Although a main road, there was very little traffic; only a few small towns and villages between here and the Czechoslovakian border just the other side of the Danube. The beginning of Eastern Europe. And beyond, Russia.

I came on the place I was looking for almost immediately, though I'd been expecting a house and not the small warehouse-type building that now appeared. It was set back from the road, and flanked on either side by pine forests; that was why I hadn't seen it from the road junction. A long signboard, 'BILDHAUERKUNSTSCHULE KRANTZ', in stained white lettering on a black background, was fixed on low posts by the roadside: it looked clean by comparison with the building behind, which was built of dark green corrugated steel, smart enough in outline, but with the surface badly weathered and beginning to peel. A number of cars and motorcycles were parked in front; the cars were old models, Volkswagen Beetles, a couple of elderly BMWs, and German Fords.

This was all I had time to see, as I didn't want to attract attention by stopping. If it hadn't been for the sign with KRANTZ on it, I'd have missed it altogether. I drove on, and the next moment was entering the outskirts of Grafing.

Well, the easy part was over. The next approach had to be made on foot. I turned right in Grafing, drove out of the village, and stopped to consult the map. A short distance ahead, a minor road was marked that should bring me to a point half a kilometre from the back of the warehouse. Ideal! I drove on, found the track, and turned along it, stopping when a crossroads became visible a couple of hundred yards ahead: that would be the road from the south on which I had arrived, and meant that I must now be directly behind the warehouse. I backed the car up a forest track until it was hidden from passers-by, unless they were looking for it. Then I got out, stretched my legs, and found a comfortable tree to lean against while I ate pretzels and drank my Pils from the bottle.

It was one o'clock on the car clock when I got back in, and reclined my seat for a nap. I'd decided to wait until two-thirty before moving in: on a Saturday afternoon there might be a chance of falling in with someone going home early, perhaps after I'd managed to get a look inside the place. If not, I would drive away again and wait for dark, having noted a likely way to get in. One way or another, I should gain a good idea of the set-up. And that reminded me: I reached into the glove compartment for my pocket dictionary. What was the word? Ah yes – *Bildhauerkunst*. That's sculpture. Plus SCHULE, which is ... well, no need to look that up. Sculpture School Krantz. Those who can do, and those who can't teach – was that the case here?

The sun was playing on the windscreen as I put the dictionary away, and leant back in the leather seat. I fell asleep almost at once: the effect of the Pils, the warmth, and the scent of pine wafting in through the car windows sent me off, effortlessly drifting above the forests. Or so it seemed.

In the distance were the mountains, blue streaked with white, with the deeper blue of lakes between. I floated nearer, over the dark green undulating forest; no sound but the sighing of the wind. A white turreted building appeared, clinging to the mountainside – I knew what it was, Neuschwanstein, the fabulous castle built by mad King Ludwig of Bavaria. And there he was, standing in the courtyard, looking up and waving.

'I say!' he shouted, 'Come down and listen to Wagner!'

'Tausend Dank!' I shouted back.

But when I landed, he'd disappeared. I looked about the courtyard; it seemed deserted. Then there was a cry from above; I looked up. A blonde girl was leaning from a balcony at the top of a tall tower.

'Are you the one?' she called.

I knew what she meant: without me, every day a misery. 'Das stimmt!' I confirmed.

'Oh, super!' she cried. 'Hang on!' – and she started to let her hair down. It took a long time.

Someone came into the courtyard from the far end, and strode towards me, shouting; it was Hitler. 'Bloody well clear off!' he bawled.

'Was ist los?' I asked.

Hitler stopped bawling. He smiled. Then he reached for his upper lip and peeled his moustache off. It wasn't Hitler at all – it was Krantz, the other Ludwig. 'Ah-ah! Had you there, old chap,' he said. The glare from his pale blue eyes grew brighter and, as I stood there, transfixed, the wind became louder. And colder – I began to shiver.

And woke up.

Wind was making the trees sway and rustle. The sky was overcast. The dream was still with me: plenty of material there, I supposed, for a psycho-analyst to get his (or her) teeth into.

A glance at the car clock put an end to speculation. Nearly a quarter to three – I'm behind schedule. And only a couple of hours of daylight left.

I got going in a hurry, remembering to get the Webley from

under the seat and stow it inside my jacket before locking up the Citroën. Then I began to stumble through the forest in the general direction of the warehouse. After ten minutes of prickly orienteering, I saw light between the black tree trunks, and made in that direction. Another two hundred yards, and I could see the rear of the warehouse. I chose a good place to return to after dark, in case I needed to do that, and then went back to get the car. Time for the frontal approach. I started up, drove round the back of the wood up to the main road then, and a right turn brought me to the entrance.

Only one car was left, a red BMW 2002, but there were still six or seven motorcycles, with leather-clad figures clustered on and around them. From inside the building there was a sound of engines being revved. I walked up to the group, rehearsing my minimal German.

'*Grüss Gott.*'

One or two heads turned in my direction.

'*Wann kommt Herr Krantz, bitte?*'

Blank faces at this. I remembered that Germans are punctilious about titles.

'*Herr Professor Kra –*'

A shout of laughter from one of the group. Others joined in, followed by cheers.

'Listen!' I said, giving up. 'Does anyone here speak English?'

A tall figure in a crash helmet stepped forward: he turned to the joker who had started the laughing. '*Halt die Klappe, Heini!*' he called. Then he turned back to me. 'I speak English,' he said. 'I apologise for my friend. You wish to speak to the *Bildner* – he is not here, I think.'

'Well,' I said, 'I would like to leave a message, then. Where is his office?'

'Go in, please,' said the tall figure. 'His room is at the back.'

'Thank you.'

'*Bitte schön,*' he said politely. They all watched me push through the swing door into the building.

Inside was a small lobby, with lavatories on one side, and an empty reception office on the other. Ahead was another swing door; the sound of engines came from beyond. I opened it.

No sculpture school, this, but a motorbike repair shop. Several youths in overalls were working at their machines, and took no notice as I walked past, heading for the only door in the far end. The noise was deafening, and I was glad to go through and shut the door behind me.

Here it was, then, the Sculpture School Krantz. Now I understood the laughter. The place was a tip. The only sign of creative activity was a jagged assembly of twisted steel, roughly tackwelded, which leant against one wall: from the rust on it, it had been there years. Otherwise, there was nothing but piles of old timber beams with nails still in them, a collection of car fenders and wings, and a roll of rotting canvas.

Perhaps this was a storeroom, and there was a studio beyond? I threaded my way between the piles of junk, and found another door with strips of carpet nailed to the edges against draught, or noise. I knocked, as it had an air of privacy about it, There was no reply. I tried the handle. It wasn't locked, so I opened the door and peered in cautiously, ready to retreat with apologies if anyone was there. It was dark inside, and I groped for a light switch. A single bare bulb came on, and I saw a small room, furnished like a monastic cell, with a tall steel cupboard, a bookcase, an iron bedstead with folded bedclothes on it, and a metal table with two folding chairs. In one corner there was a sink and a small camping cooker. Everything that could be painted white, had been – walls, ceiling, furniture, and even the concrete floor. There were no rugs or cushions – the place was stripped to essentials, as if for a siege. There were no windows of any sort. I was reminded of the office in my own warehouse: there was the same sense of oppression, of being cut off from the outside world. But here, the feeling was stronger: someone chose to live like this, and the thought evoked a brooding presence that hovered in the corners of the room, watching and resenting my intrusion.

I switched the light off, and closed the door. It had to be Krantz's, of course, this white steel fortress. Miss Mullarkey would go into boggle overdrive when I described such a dramatic confirmation of her theories. Not that it would convince the police of anything: I needed conventional evidence, of motive and opportunity, to do that. But the sight of that room was an encouragement to press on with the hunt.

133

I retraced my steps between the junk to the door I'd come in by. The din of engine-tuning had stopped, but there were still sounds of occupation beyond. I'd omitted to close the door, I noticed, or else it had failed to catch – it stood open by a few inches. I grasped the handle and pulled it open.

Two figures stood just outside, facing me. Both were clad in jeans and biker jackets; both wore crash helmets with visors raised. I looked first at the tall one behind, whose face was on a level with mine. Was it the one I'd already spoken to, outside the entrance? If so, no explanation from me was needed – he'd invited me in. But I wasn't sure, and so began to put together some placatory phrase in German: Herr Krantz not at home, it seemed, if I could borrow a pencil to write a message . . . Then I looked down at the shorter, bulkier youth in front. And my words trailed off into silence.

I was looking into enormous blue eyes the colour of mountain lakes. Though extravagant description runs the risk of setting the cynical rocking on their backsides with derisory laughter, there are times when nothing else will do, so they'll just have to get on with it. Mountain lakes, I said. And worse is to come. She began to speak and, in spite of being a bit muffled by the helmet, her voice was like cowbells on mountain pasture. A subjective judgement, of course, but I'll stick by it, right up to and including pistols at dawn, if necessary.

It was English she was speaking. That blocked up the best line of retreat, for a start. She spoke it well, a strong accent, but with plenty of words. Conversation could be sustained indefinitely, it was inescapably clear. Communication offered no barrier, would be no problem, and no excuse. I knew, then, that I'd been handed a one-way ticket to trouble, and that the train was already on the move.

Jump for it, then! – there's still time. Still time – you assume too much from what you've seen and heard so far, lakes and cowbells for Crissake, but what of the rest? She can't be perfect, they never are. Hold to that, and jump! Go on man, do it! *Now!*

I'm on the brink, wanting to be wise, but held back by this feeling at the bottom of my stomach, this appalling certainty that, whatever experience, statistics, probabilities may be quoted in support of imperfection, in this case we have the exception that proves the rule.

I know this as a fact, with a certainty no less intolerable than that of ultimate doom. I know that, any moment now, I shall see the prison doors slam. I know, even before she completes the movement, that I shall see, as she removes her helmet . . .

Masses of golden hair. Being shaken about, of course, to free it. I expected that too, No use saying so, it's too late now. No use anyway – only failed expectations would have done any good, and there's no sign of those, no sign at all. It could, perhaps, be just another dream? No, it isn't. She has sneezed, and is blowing her nose on a blue handkerchief. Dreams don't do that.

We've talked for several minutes now, and the tall youth is getting restive – he hasn't understood much, if any. She's confirmed what I guessed, that the sculpture school failed, that the front part of the building has been let off for do-it-yourself car and motorcycle repairs, and that Krantz, when in Munich, lives in the white fortress. She helps with the running of the building, she says, as Krantz is often away. She looks at her watch: it's time to lock up and go home. A pause. Then she says that she hasn't quite understood what I wanted, but if I would like to give her a lift home I could explain it on the way, and she would be glad to give any further assistance she could. This agreed, the tall youth, who otherwise would have taken her, is dismissed with thanks. He clumps away in his leather boots, seeming to take this calmly. Me, I would have committed suicide on the spot. It's hard to understand the youth of today.

She will lock up then, and meet me at the car.

But first – she must have a name?

'My name is Eva,' she said.

Eva. Eva.

This is ridiculous.

CHAPTER 12

Objective Study

The first object of our study was only the sexual
instincts, whose energy we named 'libido'.
SIGMUND FREUD

'Good car!' Eva said, as she climbed in and threw her helmet on
to the back seat.

'You like it?'

'I like big cars.' She patted the seat. 'I like best big cars without a roof. So you can feel the wind.'

'You can open the roof of this one,' I said.

'*Ja*. That is good. But no roof is better.'

*O, I will be young, and go to Spain, and drive a sports car once
again.*

'Well, we'll get going then,' I said grumpily, feeling for the
ignition switch. 'Where to?'

'To my house, if you please. Towards München, about ten
kilometres. You are very kind.' She gave me a big smile, and I
sank a little deeper into the blue lakes. A drowning man. I never
would have believed it possible, not now.

I slid the roof back, and took off, working up through the
gears in a style long abandoned but not, I found, forgotten. Sober
outside, the Citroën CX Turbo will do 140 m.p.h. with a touch
of following wind; this wasn't the road for it, but you don't
need all that before the landscape begins to blur.

'Oh – *das ist prima!*' the girl exclaimed. She gave a merry
laugh. 'So! You like to drive fast, like us.'

'Like us?'

'My friends with big motorcycles. We like to go fast. It is
exciting!'

Bloody fools, the lot of us. I supposed their motives were the
same as mine. The slang word for a motorbike is *Feuerstuhl* –

firestool. And an exhaust pipe is an *Auspuffrohr*. There's a sort of mad simplicity about Germans that comes out in the language. A friend once persuaded me that the word for windscreen-wiper was *Flippenfloppenmuckenschpreader* – and I believed him, for a few seconds at least.

'Turn left here, please,' the girl said. '*So*. Good.' A minor road, and I could stop showing off. The girl gave a sigh, but of contentment.

'You liked that?'

'Oh yes! *Endlich habe ich wieder Glück!*' She gripped my arm and gave it a squeeze, laughing again.

Forget it, you fool. Drop the girl at her house, and call it a day. You've got all the information you're likely to get from her, anyway. And in the howl of engine, scream of wind – she forgot to ask why you wanted to know. Get out while the going's good. Nothing else is going to happen, anyway. What is she? – twenty or twenty-two? That merry laugh would soon get on your nerves. She might just be as much as twenty-five: that makes, let's see now, a difference of . . . Don't take it out on the gearbox. I wonder what they'll have for supper at the hotel. It'll be good to get into a hot bath, and I'll try some different Steinwein. Ah, wine is the thing. That's where experience counts.

'Slow down, please,' she said. 'We are almost at the house. Here, on the left. You can park there, in front. Good.'

It was an old building, part farmhouse, part barn, like the ones I'd seen earlier. All around were smooth pastures and blocks of pine forest like a giant golfcourse. In the distance, not very far to the south, were the blue and white of the mountains, reaching up to the evening sky already streaked with gold. When Eva opened her car door, I could feel the cool alpine air. A church bell was tolling. I could hear a tractor, but no cars. It was the sort of scene that jigsaws are made of.

'Come,' Eva said, pushing the car door shut, and starting towards the house.

'I must go,' I called after her. 'Got to get back to my hotel.'

She turned, and came back to the car. She opened the door, and leant in. 'But you must come in,' she said. The golden hair

137

fell forward about her face. 'I will make some coffee and we will talk some more. I will like that.'

'Well,' I said. Coffee, of course, coffee would be . . .

'Come!'

I sighed. I came.

I followed her into the house, through a heavy pine-boarded door, into a long, narrow hall with posters pinned on the white-washed walls. I could see through an open door into a large kitchen with a big wooden table and benches. There was an institutional smell – cabbage soup and floor polish.

'Who lives here?'

'We are a group of students and friends,' she said. 'Our students work in München, and we have bought it together. It is, as you see, an old farmhouse. It is very expensive to live in München, and so we are very lucky to find such a house – most are still lived in by the farmers. You think it is good?'

'Very good, yes.'

'We will go upstairs. There is the sitting-room.' She led the way along the hall to a steep flight of uncarpeted wooden stairs.

'Where are your friends now?' I asked, not sure what I wanted the answer to be.

'They have all gone to the mountains.'

Of course. It was the weekend, when everybody from the city suddenly stops working furiously, drives at full speed to the lakes and mountains, and starts playing furiously. It's what the English have to be persuaded to do at school – work hard and play hard. To the Germans, persuasion is unnecessary, they do it automatically. Bounding, boundless energy.

'This,' she said, 'is our sitting-room.'

It was a big square room which took up the whole of one end of the first floor of the house. I could see why they had chosen to put their sitting-room up here: at the far end was a huge picture window, with a spectacular view south towards the mountains. From up here, they looked larger, and nearer. An old telescope stood on a tripod near the window. The room itself looked well used, but was clean and well equipped: two sofas in crumpled art-nouveau covers, several assorted easy chairs, a television set, and a large bookcase taking up most of

138

one wall. Piles of books, papers and magazines lay about on the furniture and on the floor.

'*Ach*,' Eva said, 'so untidy we are.' She threw everything off one of the sofas. 'Sit here, please. Now I will go to make coffee. Then we will talk.' She nodded at me, smiled, and left the room. I heard her running down the stairs to the kitchen.

I strolled over to inspect the bookcase. It contained a mixed bag: novels, textbooks on politics and economics, collections of paintings and drawings, including exhibition catalogues, a translation of Agatha Christie, maps, handbooks on moun- taineering and motorcycle maintenance. A cover caught my eye, and I pulled out the catalogue of the 1968 Tate exhibition 'Contemporary Sculpture'. Was this the one? – I flipped the pages and found what I was looking for almost at once: '"Autobahn 11". Most recent of a series of works by the German sculptor Ludwig Krantz, invoking the powerful imagery of automobile wreckage to symbolise the inherent con- tradiction of man and machine. Steel and polyester sheet.' No price given. Who thought up that blurb? I wondered. Sympathy for victims was implied, but the sculpture might just as well be entitled 'Death Wish' – there was more destructiveness than pity in it.

I heard Eva climbing the stairs, and put the catalogue back in its place. She appeared in the doorway, and looked about the room for me. 'Here is the coffee,' she said brightly. She advanced to the sofa and, squatting, put the tray on the floor beside it. Then she straightened up and smiled at me. 'Here is the coffee,' she said again. As if I hadn't noticed. I knew it was there by the smell. But I hadn't looked at it. How could I?

She had taken off her heavy biker's jacket, and was now wearing a white cotton man's shirt, buttoned all the way up. It was too long for her in the sleeves, and she wore the cuffs turned up, and loose. It wasn't loose anywhere else. Oh no. It wasn't.

'Yes, with milk, please,' I said. She gave me the cup. At least, it appeared in my hand.

'I will shut the door,' she said, walking across the room. She shut it. Then she walked back. I tried to look away, but it was impossible. It wasn't just the size. It was the shape, and the way they shifted under the shirt as she moved. I'd thought, at first sight, in the helmet and heavy jacket, that she was a beefy youth. Ignorance, pure ignorance. Nor did she make any attempt to reduce the effect, as some girls try to do on finding themselves thus encumbered. Oh no she didn't. No rounded shoulders or huddling of the arms here. She wore them like flags, like a ship's figurehead, like . . . yes, that was it! – like the gilded fantasy on the front of mad King Ludwig's splendid sleigh that's on display in his palace in Munich, the *Nymphenschlitten*, breasting the snow on Alpine escapades, the king wrapped in wolfskins, the lanterns swinging, bells jingling . . .

'Now we will talk,' she suggested. Oh yes. Yes, what a good idea. We took our coffee cups across to the picture window. Oh Jesus. They waggle as she walks. She has burnt her *Büstenhalter*. Or never wore one. At her age, they stand up for themselves. Oh yes, we must talk. About something, anything.

'Which mountains are those?'

'Those?' She pointed.

I nodded.

'Those are the Bavarian Alps.'

'How . . . how high are they?'

'For high mountains, you must go on, into Austria. There we have the Glockner, two thousand five hundred metres. And the Gross Glockner, three thousand eight hundred metres.'

'Three thousand eight hundred metres,' I repeated, my voice unsteady. 'Three thousand eight hundred . . . what would that be in feet, I wonder?'

'In feet? Ah, yes, I understand. But I am sorry, I do not know.'

'It doesn't matter. Three thousand . . .'

She began to tell me about a week they had spent in the mountains, walking and climbing. I made, I hope, the right responses, but my mind was elsewhere, travelling back in time. What was I, thirteen, fourteen, fifteen perhaps, when I first got inside a girl's blouse? I can remember clearly that first voyage of discovery, though who the owner of those hidden treasures was is lost, probably for ever. The urgent fumbling with buttons. Don't! Oh come on! No, you mustn't! Why not? Well, all right. Oooh, your hands are cold.

'How cold is it, up there on the mountains?'

Shaming to still get like this about a girl's tits. What's so exciting about them anyway? Great wobbly lumps – it's absurd. Get a grip on yourself. Remember what you came for.

'Good coffee.'

'Would you like some more?'

'Thank you.'

She took the cup over to the tray, and began to refill it. I looked out of the window again, so as not to see her walk back. Three thousand . . .

'There's a motorbike stopping outside.' Or I thought I'd heard one.

'Perhaps it is one of my friends,' Eva said.

'I thought they'd all gone to the mountains.'

'Someone has forgotten something, perhaps.'

An overlooked alpenstock, a replacement rucksack. Rope, pitons, spare socks. Chocolate. You need a lot of equipment on the mountains.

Steps ran up the stairs. Then the door burst open. Eva gave a gasp, and backed against the bookcase. No friend of hers, apparently. Nor, I quickly realised, of mine.

The point of archetypes, as I understood them, was that they did not actually exist. An archetype was an idea, a generality – Mother/Father, God/Devil, Virgin/Witch, Hero/Villain. Symbolic significance was the phrase that had stuck in my mind. Useful, perhaps, in helping to understand real-life approximates, but you don't expect to meet them in the street. That's what I thought.

Not any more. The figure that now stood in the doorway, grinning with white teeth out of his bronzed face, shooting steely blue glances at me and Eva, but mostly at me, was, beyond any possibility of doubt, an archetype. I knew which one, too. Here was 'the splendorous blond beast avidly rampant for plunder and victory', all according to the specification laid down by Nietzsche, give or take a quarter-inch here or there. Over six foot; narrow waist, broad, powerful shoulders; arms like oak trees; a face deeply tanned by healthy exercise such as running up mountains; clean-shaven; square-jawed; short

141

yellow hair. His clothes were not quite up to standard: the Master might have felt that blue jeans were better suited to ordinary mortals, but the black leather jacket with wide lapels more than made up for them.

I snatched a quick look at Eva. She too had been taking all this in, and now switched her gaze to me; there was speculation in her eyes and also, I recognised with a chilly twinge in my spine, excitement. The bitch was looking forward to it. Whatever *it* was to be. I might have guessed this from what I already knew of her. In middle age she'll be one of those women who go to all-in wrestling matches, screaming for blood and hitting around them with their handbags. Living dangerously – at second hand. The Master had a word for her, too – 'Woman was God's second blunder'. They're never in the front line. *It's not fair!*

What does he want? What's he going to do?

He pointed at me – a dramatic gesture. Then he said: 'You! – come with me.'

'Not on your nelly,' I said. 'I'm staying right where I am. *Nichts zu machen.*'

He stared at me. Then he laughed, throwing his head back for it. '*So gut!*' he said contemptuously. '*So gut!* Then I must bring you!'

A terrible accent, but the meaning was clear enough – I was for it. Confirmation followed immediately, as he reached into his leather jacket and brought out nine inches or so of rubber hose with the ends taped to keep the lead shot in. It made my head ache just to look at it.

He paused for a quick brandish of it, and to give us a short aria about the deed he was about to perform. Then he came for me, leaping over the coffee tray, the cosh held high, his feet pounding on the bare-boarded floor.

There wasn't time to think about it. I acted instinctively, Right Brain in control. I saw my hands reach out and grasp him by those wide lapels, and then I was turning, waltzing almost, letting the weight of his charge carry him round and past me until his back was to the picture window. Then I pushed, as hard as I could.

He went backwards through the window with a bang and a

shower of glass. He began another aria on the way down, less confident than the last, but it was cut short. Eva and I ran to the shattered window. Oh my God, I was thinking, now I'm really for it. A broken neck; the police called; laboured explanations; a cell for tonight at least; a visit from the consul in the morning; all the complications of a foreign trial, endless and Kafka-esque. I looked down into the twilit garden.

Fallen on grass, thank God! As we watched, he struggled to a sitting position, shaking his head. Then he got to his feet like a hero, and stood for some moments, swaying, but apparently undamaged except for his left arm which he held awkwardly, and appeared to be broken or at least badly bruised. I expected him to look up and swear vengeance, but he staggered off round the side of the house without a backward glance, clutching his arm. We heard the motorbike start, and blat erratically away.

Eva and I turned to each other. What next? was written on both our faces. I still felt sore at her excited expression when battle was about to be joined. But not nearly so much, now that I had won. Hardly at all, in fact. Perhaps it was the outcome she had expected, from a man of my obvious experience, and had simply been interested to see me in action. Yes. Well, I certainly hadn't disappointed her, in that case. And it *had* been exciting, she had been right about that. The adrenalin was still buzzing in my veins. And probably in hers. There was only one thing I could think of that wouldn't be an anticlimax.

But would she, *did* she think the same?

I looked down into her deep blue eyes. Again, I had that sinking sensation. I had no choice, no choice at all. I would be welcome, I could see that.

But, if I had decided to be a fool about some things, I had been learning fast about others. And I knew there was something that had to be done.

'We'd better lock the front door, in case we have another visitor.'

'*Du hast recht,*' she said softly. She said, '*Du*'. I *was* welcome.

'I will lock it,' she said, and slipped away down the stairs. I drew the curtains over the broken window, and found a lightswitch.

'I have locked it,' she said, returning.

143

'Good. Now, I must telephone my hotel to see if there are any messages.'

'The telephone is in the kitchen,' she said.

'Be back in a moment.'

I went rapidly down the stairs and found the telephone. I took the receiver off and held it to my ear. There was no sound other than the dialling tone. I dialled a number – at random. Then I spoke. Were there any messages? Thank you – I'll wait while you look.

I put the phone down on the table, very quietly, and slipped my shoes off. I moved silently into the hall, to the door, and tried it.

It was not locked.

I moved back into the kitchen, pulled my shoes on while speaking. Thank you. No messages. I see. Well, thank you again. I shall be late back.

I climbed the stairs, feeling sad.

By the time I had reached the top of the stairs I was still undecided what to do next. I now knew what the risks were. There would be another visitor, of course. And she had to keep me here until he came. Well, I would play my part in that, although I no longer had any real inclination for it. And when he came, we would see. The advantage of surprise was now with me. I will make my plans while making a tour of the Alps. Great things are done when men and mountains meet.

She met me in the middle of the room. I looked again into the deep blue eyes. I thought I could now detect the treachery in their depths; an icy layer beneath the surface. She was too young for it to show on her face, but it was there in her eyes.

'You look sad,' she said in her new, soft voice.

'You are so beautiful,' I said. 'That always makes me sad.' It sounded a traditionally German sentiment; sentimental and tinged with *Weltschmerz*.

'Now *I* am sad, also,' she said.

Good! Soon we could start crying into our drinks if we had any, and work up a really enjoyable gloom.

I gave a heavy sigh, and started undoing her shirt buttons. She sighed too, and began to stroke my hair. We sank to the sofa, and she lay against the cushions, her face tilted back, eyes closed, her lips curved in the slightest of smiles. I worked my way down the buttons, parting the white shirt front as I went. The valley appeared, a chasm measureless to man. Then as the snowy fabric slid to each side in a gentle avalanche, the Alps themselves came into full view.

O, my Bavaria.

O'er the white Alps alone.

O, if thou care'st not whom I love, alas, thou lov'st not me.

As with a will of its own, my tongue alighted on the nearest peak, and circled in blind exploration. The mountains trembled at my touch. I skied slowly over the slopes; down, down in the valley far below, where the shadows deepened, down to the warmest depths where the scent of pine lay waiting. Then I was climbing, traversing the opposite slope in easy measures, up, up out of the valley and into the light again. I reached the tip at last, and slid to a halt, breathless. Again, the mountains shook beneath me. I planted my lips to secure the position. It had been a voyage to remember, an historic climb.

'Oh, oh, oh, *wie schön*!' Eva wailed.

I raised myself so that I could see her face. The blue lakes were brimming with moisture. As I looked, they overflowed. Large tears ran down her cheeks and splashed on to her breasts.

'What's the matter?' I said, startled.

'So sweet,' she sobbed, 'so gentle. I am so ashamed.'

'It's all right.'

'No, no. Not all right. You do not understand.' She sniffed loudly, and broke out into fresh wails of misery. More tears ran, and splashed. It must have been the best gloom she'd had for years. All it needed now, for a perfect conclusion, was *der Tod*. Death. Probably mine, though someone else's might do almost as well. German drama is notoriously indiscriminate about that sort of thing.

'Don't worry about it,' I said. 'I know what you've been up to. You telephoned from the kitchen when we got here, while you were making the coffee. And you haven't locked the door.'

She lifted her head to stare at me with the brimming blue lakes. 'You know?' she whispered. 'You know? But you were still so gentle?'

'So beautiful,' I said, 'so beautiful. I couldn't help it.'

'Oh, oh, oh . . .'

All right. I would have liked to continue with this scene, but I got too engrossed in the mountaineering to work out a plan, and I've got to beat *der Tod* to the door. 'Now I must go,' I said, and started to button her up.

She watched me without saying anything until I'd finished. Then she burst out: 'You must go quickly. They must be here very soon.'

'Thanks,' I said. 'That was the idea.'

We both stood up. She suddenly flung her arms round my neck and kissed me on the cheek. I took her golden head in my hands and kissed her on the forehead. That had to be it.

I started down the stairs, with images of her still revolving before my eyes. Otherwise I would have noticed the two figures flattened against the wall at the bottom before it was too late.

The images dissolved with a flash. I was spotlit on a stage, spinning in a waltz, singing. *Mit mir, mit mir, mit mir, mit mir, keine Nacht, Dir zu lang.* The end of the act. .

And suddenly, it was night.

CHAPTER 13

Men of Action

There are men of action, unshakeable in their
convictions, inaccessible to doubt, without feeling for
the suffering of others if they stand in the way of
their intentions.

SIGMUND FREUD

It was a church.

So this is what it's like. Consciousness does, after all, continue
in some form, even if only for a while. Fading slowly, perhaps,
as the brain cells decay and lose their charge; a battery running
down. It must be so; we must comply with the first law of
nature, the return to chaos. Do we all, then, by means of some
remnant of consciousness, attend our own funerals? Are we all
aware of the consuming fire, or the coffin's darkness? How can
they be told, the ignorant living, that they torture us in their
haste to put us out of sight?

Ouch!

O welcome pain!

Let me feel it once more! Oh yes! Oh ouch!

I ache, therefore I am. I am alive! If my nerves are working,
the blood must be flowing in my veins. My systems are go —
even if not at normal operating strength. Verification of post-
mortem properties will be resumed on a later occasion. Much
later, if You don't mind.

The size of the place, together with the dim light from a single
hanging bulb, had given me the impression that it was a
church. Now, as my senses gradually refocussed on my surroundings, I realised that I had been dumped in the barn which
was part of the same building as the farmhouse, sheltering
under one end of the same huge roof. Very little work had been
done on the place since it ceased being a barn and became a
garage, casual workshop and storage space: dust and cobwebs

were everywhere; wisps of hay hung from the old hay loft; the cow byre, with worn wooden stalls, was still in place and still smelt of cow. The floor was earth, stained with oil, the white powder of fertiliser, and crushed cattle feed. The beams were old, black and crumbling with woodworm. Far above my head, a chilly starlight was visible through every slip and crack of neglected slates.

I looked down. I was half sitting, half lying on the cold earth floor, propped against an inner wall which I supposed was the wall which divided the barn from the house. On the other side of it should be the kitchen; I could hear voices through it, but too faintly to make out the words. On my left was a rough workbench fitted with a large and rusty vice, but I could see no other tools. On my right was a plank door: it should lead into the hall at the opposite end to the staircase. At the far end of the barn, facing the huge and rickety old barn doors, sat its only other inhabitant besides myself – a member of the still ubiquitous horde of Volkswagens that remain Hitler's most lasting, and only cherished, memorial. Bright green, it was, and polished as though it had at least one careful owner. No flat tyres or visible incapacities, on my side at least. Given petrol, it might go.

Useless information: for the time being at least, I wasn't going anywhere. My feet and hands were tied behind my back; for extra security my hands were secured to my ankles, so that I had had to be propped sideways against the wall. My arms and legs were cramped and already ached painfully. I had been surveying the barn in the intervals between waves of pain which flooded my head and the back of my neck, causing my vision to blur, and bringing me to the point of vomiting before receding just enough to let me swallow and contain it. I had to struggle not to throw up.

What time was it? It was night out there, but it had already been dark when I left Eva and started down the stairs, so that told me nothing about the length of time that had passed. I could have been out for minutes, or hours – it felt like hours, but was more likely to be minutes, if what I could remember from reports of people being coshed was true. The depressing part was that, if I felt as cramped as this after being tied up for half an hour or so, I'd be crippled in an hour, and in agonies after two – I felt worse just at the thought of it. And this was the pain I'd first welcomed as a sign of life. But perhaps my legs and arms would go numb, and I wouldn't feel much after that. If so, how long would it take to get them working again if there was a chance of escape? National Service had given no guidance on this sort of thing – we were always assumed to be handing it out, not taking it.

What was it all about, anyway? Perhaps thinking about that would keep my mind off these discomforts. The Nietzschean Superman hadn't simply been a jealous boyfriend – there'd been no sign of that, no outrage or bluster or recriminations. Anyway, at that stage I hadn't laid a finger on the girl. No, he'd come in response to a call, either from the tall youth who'd been with Eva at the motorcycle workshop, or from Eva herself while she made the coffee. The object must have been to put me into storage until wanted. Some questions first, probably, and then a decision on what to do with me. Questions, because if they didn't want some answers, they could have put me safely underground by now, pushing up the *Gänseblumen*. Questions which I might as well try to answer as best I could without persuasion because, as all the world knows, these people are the experts in that dismal science.

And, just as I concluded this comforting train of thought, the door opened.

Probably I looked like next-in-line at the dentist, all thoughtful eyes and set expression, but I tried not to give away my inner alarm at their approach. There were two of them, both clad more or less identically in grey city suits, with clean black shoes, plain shirts, and dark ties. Stocky, middle-aged, and hard-faced: experts, I judged, in their profession. Watching their quiet but purposeful air as they checked my bonds, I had no doubt at all what that profession was, though I'm not sure what it's called. They were as far from the impressive but ultimately ineffectual Superman as a polar bear is from a teddy.

They stood back, having added a few extra knots to the cordage, and cast a cold eye on me and my prison. I thought I'd try a little conversation, see if I could learn anything useful.

'*Wieviel Uhr ist es?*'

No reply. Not the slightest change of expression, even.

'*Ich habe grossen Durst.*'

The one nearest to the door nodded to the other, who went out to the kitchen. I heard the tap running. He reappeared with a glass of water, and gave it to the first, who came up to me, squatted, took hold of my hair with one hand and pushed the glass against my lips, tilting it. I gulped at it, but much of the water ran down my chin. He pulled the glass away, and let my head go.

'*Danke.*' I thought I now knew which of the two was the leader, and christened him Sturm. His mate could be Drang. Storm and Stress. I couldn't remember who wrote it, but I understood it was a style-setting phrase in the old Germany. Which doesn't seem to be over, yet.

Sturm and Drang. They went on standing there, just looking. Perhaps they were making mental notes – my fingernail size, for instance. Or maybe they were just standing and staring, no more, no less. It's recommended, our side of the Channel; could be beginning to catch on here.

'Piss off, you ugly bastards.' I said it in the most polite tone I could manage, so as not to give the content away by the style of delivery. Sturm's face remained a mask, but Drang gave a slight shrug of incomprehension. It looks as though English is not spoken here, I thought, but I decided to try a guide book sample in case the first was too advanced for them.

'Is there a good restaurant round here?' Good British humour, you know, our support in adversity.

Not a flicker.

I tried a probe. '*Wann kommt Herr Krantz?*'

They kept staring, but didn't reply. Then Sturm gave Drang a nudge, and they moved to the door. Just before he went out, Sturm said: '*Morgen früh.*'

My probe successful, but it wasn't good news. By tomorrow morning I would be in a bad state to receive visitors. Even worse than now. Except that my headaches had started to ease off slightly. Brains, come in please. I need you.

Shortly afterwards, I heard one of them leave. I could hear them in the hall, talking, but I couldn't make out what was said. Then the front door slammed; moments later, a car drove off. Now there was only one to deal with. The thought encouraged me to struggle to my knees. I managed it, using the wall for leverage. But the knots were tight; the twine cut into my wrists and ankles; I didn't manage to loosen any part of the bloody stuff. The only useful thing I found was that, when kneeling, I could move my knees relative to each other by about an inch; this allowed a caterpillar progress across the floor of about a yard a minute – maybe even a little faster, with practice. It was about four yards to the door which, I'd noticed, Sturm had not locked when he went out. He – or Drang – would be on guard in the kitchen, with the kitchen door open, and could easily control the hall from there. No chance of getting past him while I was still tied up. Even if I got across the barn to the hall door, I wouldn't get any further. It seemed a pointless exercise.

I concentrated on keeping my legs and arms moving within their tightly restricted limits, and on working each set of muscles in turn. I've always found physical jerks intensely boring, useless, and narcissistic: who's got time for twenty minutes running on the spot just to work off half a slice of bread? Or cares that much about the body beautiful? But on this occasion I did it. Up an inch. Down an inch. And repeat it. Over and over.

Some time later, it could have been half an hour, I heard Eva's voice in the hall. She was laughing.

I stopped exercising, and leant against the wall.

Laughing. Her merry peals came clearly through the door. So much for her brief dalliance with remorse. I felt then, and now it was brutally confirmed, that she fed on emotion like cream cakes; bursting with merriment one moment, sobbing with despair the next; and none of it real. Pure unadulterated emotional indulgence – I hope she grows fat and sickens on it.

Footsteps outside the door. It opened, and there she was, backed up by Sturm, my keeper. Come to view the captive. I looked up at her. I couldn't keep my feelings off my face, but she seemed to find it amusing – she laughed again. Behind her, Sturm managed a crooked smirk, which was probably his Olympic best in that department. Obviously she'd been describing how the beast was captured; netted by her cunningly simulated interest; drowned in the big blue lakes. Yes, of course my pride was hurt. I've done some damage in my time, even if my time's running out now. But never like this. Never on purpose. And never with such consequences.

I turned my face away.

A final peal from her, and an amused grunt from him, and then I heard them go, her voice chattering excitedly to him in her own, her native tongue. They went into the kitchen. She would make him some coffee, she said. Oh yes, she could do that all right, the bitch. She made *me* coffee while she got the knife aimed at my back. He's going to have it black, he says, he's got to stay awake tonight, keep an eye on me. Though it won't be difficult, he says, with a girl like her to keep him company. Oh, thank you, sir, she laughs, a girl can't resist a compliment. Not difficult to think of them in your case, he says. And perhaps some apple cake, she asks. Well, perhaps just a slice; did you make it yourself? On and on they went. And on and on.

There was something about this conversation, this arch, banal, inane, maddening exchange of complimentary platitudes that struck me as excessive, even for a girl like her. I sat, propped against the cold wall, smarting at the sound of it as it went on and on. She could succeed, it was obvious, even with a squareheaded sod like Sturm who looked like nobody's fool. Perhaps he was a challenge, and she was practising. Well, he'd fallen for it all right. No doubt about that. For all his cool professionalism, just another score on her card. And yet, and yet ... there was something else that bugged me.

It was probably because of the headaches, still powerful enough to make me wince each time they came, that I was so slow. Otherwise I must surely have realised much, much sooner, what was the cause of my puzzlement. And, when I did realise it, I was seized by sudden hope mingled with a burst of furious speculation that set my brain buzzing.

I looked up. It was true.

The other thing that had been bugging me was, not *what* they had been saying in the kitchen, *but the fact that I could hear it!*

And the reason that I could hear it now, but not before, was that Eva had left the door very slightly open.

Of course, it might have been by accident. But I didn't think so: her chatty nonsense in the kitchen, since, had really been over the top for a girl like her who, I knew, was more than able to hold a conversation without sounding like a suburban strumpet of no brain and less sense.

I began to listen more carefully. I could hear almost all that she said, but not the whole sense of his deeper, more guttural tones. I rolled laboriously to my knees again, and struggled nearer to the door. Now the voices were clear enough. I concentrated, trying to understand the growling German. I'll never know for sure, but I think this was the gist of it.

Nothing more than an exchange of archery for some time. And then, the first signs of what I had been hoping. Oh, she was *brilliant*! How could I have doubted her? Clever, beautiful, treacherous Eva! I will love her for ever, or for as long as she's going to be treacherous to *them*.

So, she said, what is going to be done with the Englishman? In the morning, he said, there will be some questions, and then . . . we'll see. What has he done? she asked; nobody tells me anything. Perhaps I have made a mistake?

Sturm made reassuring noises: No, no, he said, there can be no mistake. We are fortunate that this man came here and fell into our hands: you have done better than you realised, my dear young lady. There can be no doubt that he came to collect information on the *fuhrwesen*, no doubt at all. Tomorrow morning, we will find out how much he knows, and who sent him.

But, she said, perhaps he is from the police?

I heard a chair scrape, and footsteps in the kitchen. Then there was the sound of something heavy thumped on to the wooden table. Then Sturm's voice again, with something like humour in it.

The English are obsessed by their old traditions, he said, and their policemen still do not carry firearms. But when firearms have to be issued, even the English give their police something more modern than this. Look at it! This is a revolver from 1914, a souvenir no doubt. It is loaded with only one good bullet – the rest are rubbish. So – this man is not from the police. He works for himself, looking for information to sell, perhaps. Or has been employed privately – we have competitors, as you know. This he will tell us, tomorrow.

There was a long silence. Then Eva said: If this is true, then what will happen – after he has told you what you want to know?

Ach, he said, a girl should not ask such questions! Oh, it doesn't bother me, she said brightly, what is necessary must be done. I did only what I was asked to do, and it was easy – it is for you men to take the decisions, and I know you will do what is best.

He grunted, and I imagined him sitting there at the kitchen table, gripping his coffee mug in one fist and his piece of *apfelkücher* in the other, basking in her clear blue gaze as she delicately inserted the needle and slid the honey into his veins. Would he fall for it? Yes, I thought he would. So had I; so would most men. We would all deceive ourselves willingly if we thought we were in with a chance. She was that sort of girl. She had the skill; she had the resources; and she used only the best butter.

I listened again, but the conversation seemed to have run its course except for an occasional increasingly drowsy comment. What did *fuhrwesen* mean? It seemed to be the key, and I had no idea. Something like an hour had passed; it was likely that Sturm would soon look in again to tuck me up for the night. A thought surfaced: he mustn't see that the door was ajar, or he would suspect Eva. I made a hasty plan: it was prompted by the realisation that I was bursting for a pee.

I struggled on my knees to the door, and butted it shut with my head. Then I went on thumping it six or seven times. Yes, it was nice when I stopped.

Footsteps in the hall, and then the door was pushed open; I fell over backwards. Sturm pushed his way in and, switching on the light, looked down at me, scowling.

'*Worum handelt es sich –*'

'*Toilette*,' I said.

'*Schade!*'

'*Ich muss . . .*'

He grunted with annoyance, and then nodded; perhaps he thought he should keep me in presentable condition, at least until the morning. He called for Eva, and she appeared in the doorway; he explained the situation to her, and then took an automatic pistol from his pocket and gave it to her, placing her several yards away where she could cover the door if I should try to make a break for it. The safety catch is off, he showed her; all you have to do is point it and pull the trigger. He took out a pocket knife and cut away all my lashings except those around my ankles. Then he hauled me to my feet; my cramped legs protested with a sharp attack of pins and needles.

'Ouch!' I complained.

He held me up until my legs could support me. I looked at Eva. She held the gun with both hands, pointing in my general direction. Now, I thought, now we can get out of this. His trust in her is about to suffer a painful disillusionment. As soon as I'm clear, she can shoot the bastard. And that's the end of this little drama; we'll be clear away with hours to go before anyone starts after us.

I could stand now, and began to hop towards the far wall for the much-needed relief. I was clear of him; he stood and watched me go.

Do it, Eva! Do it *now*! It's him or me. *Pull the trigger!*

I couldn't wait or look round. I got to the wall, and emptied my bladder, having to hop to avoid the little river which pushed across the dusty floor. When I heard the shot, I'd have to spring into action, finished or not. It was an undignified prospect, but I was prepared for it.

But no shot came.

Well, I thought, it's too much to expect of any girl. I shouldn't have pinned my hopes on it. Although there's still time, if she's going to do it. Perhaps it'll be when he's busy tying me up again, and distracted. I zipped myself up, and turned round. He gestured me towards one of the massive posts that held up the hayloft, above: tied to that, I would be completely immobilised. This man is no fool, he learns by experience; no more crawling about for this captive. I had no choice; I hopped towards the post and stood submissively against it. He had collected some more bits of twine from the hook where it was hanging, abandoned by the outgoing farmer, and began to lash my hands behind the post and my ankles to the base of it; I was going to spend the night standing up. At least that would torture a new set of muscles. I looked over his shoulder at Eva. Out of his line of vision, she had allowed herself to look miserable, and I realised what she was going through; she knew she should shoot, but she could not. She made a face, and gave a slight shrug of her shoulders; it was a silent, agonised apology. I risked a smile and a nòd; she couldn't help it. Perhaps she had some other plan of escape; I had some comfort in seeing her expression and knowing for certain that she was, she *had* to be, on my side.

Sturm finished lashing me to the post, inspected his work closely, and stood back with a look of satisfaction at a job well done. He'd used enough twine to make sure of King Kong; no medieval martyr met the flames in better bondage than this. Thank you, Herr Sturm. I hope I can do the same for you, some day.

They moved towards the door, Eva having handed back the automatic. He stood aside punctiliously to let her go out. She paused in the doorway, and turned to face me.

'*Mach's gut!*' she said sardonically, making me a little bow, and then in English, '*Wait for me!*' She went out.

Sturm was on to her immediately: what did you say? he called after her in an angry tone. Her voice came back from the hall; I wished him sweet dreams, of course, she replied, laughing. *Ach*, he said, you girls – you're worse than the men. We like to be on the winning side, she sang back, and it's obvious which *that* is.

Oh, Eva – you're too good at it.

Well, don't speak to him in English again, anyway, he told her. He turned to me, standing in the doorway with his back to the hall; he held the automatic in his left hand, and reached into his coat pocket with his right, which emerged with the magazine. I'd never noticed him take it out. He fitted it to the butt of the gun, and snapped it home with his palm. It made a precision click. All his movements were like that. He took a last look round the barn, and went out, shutting the door firmly. He could have been a factory foreman shutting up shop.

I took several deep breaths. *The automatic had never been loaded*, but he had implied to Eva that it was. He had been testing her, with the chilly efficiency he applied to everything. I could picture what would have happened if she had felt able to pull the trigger. The empty click when his back is turned. He hears it, turns, goes over to her, snatches the gun away, slaps her face for her futile deceit, then lashes her next to me. Two supermarket chickens trussed for the oven. Jesus! Thank God she didn't try it.

Wait for me, she'd said. She must have a plan. I'll wait for her.

Come to think of it, nothing else I *can* do. Wait, and wonder what that word means, the word Sturm used, the thing I'm supposed to be hunting after.

Fuhrwesen.

CHAPTER 14

Unloving Powers

Obscure, unfeeling and unloving powers determine
men's fate.

SIGMUND FREUD

It was a long, long night. Tied, as I was, in a standing position
against the post, I found I could keep my legs from going numb
by straining my toes against the floor, and then relaxing them.
My legs were better off than when I'd been tied into a bundle,
on the floor. But my arms were tightly lashed behind the post,
and the awkward angle at which they were held soon began to
cause cramp in my shoulders, which gradually spread to my
upper arms, and so on down, until after an hour or so I began
to wonder if I would be able to last the night without passing
out from the pain. I had no doubt that Sturm, who I was sure
never did anything without good reason and after careful
calculation, intended to put me through this. It was the sof-
tening-up which preceded question time.

The morning seemed impossibly far in the future; I would
never make it; when they came for me at six, seven, or perhaps
even as late as eight o'clock, they would find me hanging from
my post, unconscious, looking like one of those sagging wooden
figures that are nailed up behind every altar in Bavarian rustic
churches, the head lolling to one side, the torso tearing the arms
apart with its dead weight, the bony knees and stick legs
buckled and useless. They must have been mad, those country
carpenters, to make such sickening images; driving their chisels
along the lines of suffering and bodily indignity; chasing with
obvious relish every detail of masochistic delight; chopping out
these crude symbols of a misdirected religion with all the bru-
tality of a butcher's shop.

*

So, it was a long, long night. I wasn't aware that Sturm came to inspect my bonds again; of course, I may have slept, or passed out, from time to time. But, eventually, it came. *Morgen früh*. Morning – and question time. And there had been no sight or sound of Eva. The fickle bitch had changed sides again. Even if she hadn't, she'd left it too late. Daylight was brightening through the cracks in the slates and the boarded walls. I could hear sounds of breakfast-making in the kitchen, and voices. Sturm and Eva. Eva and Sturm. What had happened overnight? Why hadn't she come?

Then I heard a sound that made me give up all hope – the crunching of car tyres in the yard outside. The rest of the team had arrived. I heard footsteps in the hall, and the rattle of the front-door bolts. Here they come.

More footsteps in the hall, and the door flung open.

It was Eva. She was alone.

She shut the door quietly, but with maximum speed. Then she was behind my post, slashing at the twine bindings. She must have made sure she had a sharp knife – I was free in seconds.

'Quick!' she whispered urgently. 'The door. It must be made shut!' Her words were jumbled in her agitation, but the meaning was clear.

'Can't we lock it?'

'No lock!' she almost screamed. I realised she was terrified. So, to be honest, was I. It was like some nightmare; soon the door will open, and God-knows-what will come stalking, crawling, oozing in.

I looked frantically round the room. 'The workbench!'

I stumbled to it, and we started to slide it across the floor. My arms were useless; I butted it with my backside, while Eva pulled at the other end. We got it to the door and aligned it, end on, for maximum resistance. It wouldn't hold for long.

I risked wasting some seconds to look into the yard through a crack in the boarding. A big black BMW was out there, with Drang at the wheel, and yes! – Krantz was in the passenger seat. He was being given a progress report by Sturm, who was leaning on the side of the car. I looked back across the barn. Eva had disappeared. No, she was easing back the bolts on the inside of the big barn doors. Quietly, quietly. It was done. Then something caught her attention. I heard her give a stifled wail.

'*Es is nicht zu glauben . . .*' – her voice was trembling.

'What's the matter?'

'Locked! Locked outside!'

I looked. From what I could see there was a bar across outside, perhaps with a padlock.

'Were we going in the Volkswagen?'

'Yes,' she said, 'yes. I have the key here. It's mine.'

I looked at the barrier between us and freedom; the barn doors, huge but rickety, with gaps between the planks, some planks loose, all held together with rusty nails. Perhaps . . .

The inner barn door suddenly rattled. The enemy was at the gates. We would have to take our chances with the only escape route possible.

'Into the car,' I hissed. 'You must drive – my arms . . .'

The car doors were not locked, and we threw ourselves in. As we did so there were angry shouts from the hall. The hall door crashed violently against the end of the workbench. It began to slide across the floor.

Eva had started the motor, and now ran it up with a roar. It sounded healthy enough, although there were clouds of oily smoke jetting from the exhaust behind us.

'Let's go!' I shouted. It didn't matter how much noise we made, now. 'Back first, as far as you can. Then full speed at the doors. Bottom gear.'

She reversed with a wild, bucking motion until the rear of the car hit the rear wall of the garage with a thump. Then she slammed the old car into first gear, and took off like a drag racer, across the barn and into the big doors. As we roared forwards I saw the workbench slide further and the hall door battered half open. A face appeared round the edge of the door – Sturm. There wasn't time to note his expression.

We hit the barn doors with a rending crash. I remember thinking that a VW should be ideal for this: with the engine at the back, we were in no danger of smashing in the radiator. Planks flew everywhere as the door burst apart; the curved Beetle bonnet was suddenly dented as if hit by a giant fist. The windscreen stayed intact, but we might well have collected punctures from the rusty nails that pattered all around us and on the roof. Time to worry about that later. We were out – into the early morning light.

Across the yard we shot, past my Citroën and the black BMW, and then we were on the road. Eva wrenched the little car to the right, fought with the floppy gear lever until she found second, and we accelerated down the road towards freedom. I found myself laughing; Eva joined in, and we bowled along the narrow country road hooting like maniacs. I looked back: three figures were scrambling into the BMW, but we were already several hundred yards clear, and they had to turn their car before they could start after us. In any case, what could they do? The forest loomed ahead; another mile or two and we would emerge on to the main road to Munich. They couldn't shoot at us, or barge us off the road once we got there. We could drive on into Munich, and then come back later to collect my car. That would be the tricky bit; but I'd have time to plan it carefully; perhaps I could get a lift in a police car or breakdown truck, if I could think of a suitable story. Which, of course, I could. I could do *anything*! We were home and dry.

I looked across at Eva. She was wearing her biker jacket again; her hands gripped the wheel in a racing driver's three o'clock; her eyes searched the road ahead for potholes. She must have felt my gaze; she snatched a quick smile in my direction. She'd made a big mistake, but she'd taken bigger risks to put it right. I owed her, but I'd done something for her, as well. I had a sudden flush of fatherly feeling; perhaps the fool was becoming wise. It was a boring idea.

'How old are you?' I shouted over the clatter of the air-cooled engine.

'I am nineteen. Soon, I will be twenty,' she shouted back. 'What does it matter?'

Not at all, if you're nineteen.

We'll go into Munich, stick the car away in the garage. I must make a call to London, let someone know what's going on. But this evening . . .

'How about a celebration dinner,' I shouted. 'What's the best restaurant in Munich? We'll have champagne, lobster, Trocken-beerenauslese, everything. How about it?'

'I don't know, we do not go to such places, my friends and I. But I know other places, we will have a good time. Yes, please.'

Smoky cellars full of students. And the curious sideways glances of smooth, juvenile faces: Who's she with? What's he doing in here? Well, I could take it. If I had to.

'I know a good place,' she shouted, 'not too expensive. And not too many students.'

O my Bavaria – you read my thoughts.

'There, we can have good Hungarian goulash. And good beer.'

Ugh.

'That would be wonderful,' I shouted.

We bumped and rattled on down the road. The forest closed round us, and we were into the dark tunnel which led through it. Another mile; the main road couldn't be more than another mile. I looked behind. No sign of the BMW; but it would be there somewhere, behind the last rise, out of sight. Out of sight, and almost out of mind.

The engine stuttered, and the car jerked several times. It began to slow. 'It's all right,' Eva said. '*Benzin.* Petrol. But we have the reserve.'

She bent forward, groping for the tap under the dashboard, pushing in the clutch to let the car keep on rolling. She had a masculine competence with mechanics.

I suddenly knew there would be something wrong, even before she felt the tap and gave a wail of dismay. Bad news travels fast, all right; sometimes it travels so fast it precedes the event.

'It's already *on* reserve?'

'One of my friends has used the car; he has not told me. *Das ist doch eine Schweinerei!*' She began to beat the dashboard with her fist, throwing her head about, weeping with frustration.

'Out,' I shouted, 'out of the car and into the woods. It'll be all right yet. We must be near the main road.'

We jumped out, leaving the car where it had trickled to a halt at the side of the road, and I led the way into the pine forest, forcing a way through the clinging branches. Eva followed, holding the front of her jacket together with one hand and fending off the branches, which sprang back at her like whips, with the other. We made perhaps fifty yards before I paused to look back.

The BMW was just pulling up behind our abandoned Beetle, skidding to a stop in a spray of dusty earth, the big tyres howling.

'Get, down. *Get down!*'

I pressed Eva down with my hand, down into the forest floor thickly spread with pine needles and dotted with seedlings. She lay still, her face turned towards me, her eyes huge with fright. The nightmare had returned. The dark cathedral of black trunks and green vaults which surrounded us was oppressive: the man-made regularity of it gave a sense of impending drama, of readiness for an event already planned, the script written, the participants chosen, the action about to begin. Not make-believe, but a real-life drama, an affair of pounding blood and shrinking flesh, fought to a conclusion in this hostile place where creatures nightly scream and struggle in the jaws of their captors, and where the wind hisses through the trees like laughter.

I must get a grip on myself. Reaching out, I found Eva's hand and squeezed it. 'It'll be all right,' I whispered. It would be. It must be.

'But if they find us . . .'

'I'll think of something.'

'These men are . . . They will . . .'

'I know. We'll have to find a way out of here. Meanwhile, we must keep out of sight. They've got a gun, and we haven't.'

'Oh!' Eva said. She began to struggle with the zip of her jacket.

'Keep still, for God's sake!' I whispered urgently. But she had already unzipped, and now reached inside the jacket.

'Here!' And she handed me the Webley.

My hand grasped the chequered butt: I broke it open, checked the cylinder. Sturm hadn't bothered to unload it. 'Eva, you're brilliant!'

She managed a small smile. Of course, I remembered, Sturm had told her it was an antique, and practically useless. Except for the one bullet. But no one except me knew that a second, equally ancient bullet had failed to go off when the gun was last fired. That left me with a threat, at most. Still, that was much better than nothing. In a situation like this, a tiny advantage might tip the balance our way.

'Keep down now,' I warned her. 'I've got to take a look.'

I raised my head slowly above the tree root that was hiding us from the road. Sturm had the boot of the BMW open, and was lifting out a rifle. My heart sank. With that, they could pick us off at their leisure, once they'd located us. The threat posed by my pistol had now reduced almost to zero. Only fieldcraft could save us: keep in cover as far as possible; move fast when we had to break cover; avoid places where we might be expected and ambushed. If only the girl wasn't with me. But perhaps she needn't be.

'Listen, Eva. Why don't you give yourself up? They won't hurt you, will they? Just give me time to get clear, and then . . .'

She shook her head, violently. 'But surely they won't . . .'

'I will not,' she whispered. 'This is better. I know these men.'

'But . . .'

'No!'

I looked over the tree root again. Krantz had come into view from the far side of the car, and had taken hold of the rifle; Sturm was objecting to this, and they were both tugging at it; I could hear their voices as they argued. Then Sturm let go of it with an impatient gesture; taking his automatic from his jacket pocket, he waved his party on towards the forest. As usual, he'd kept to the essential point, which was to get after us without wasting time. Krantz, on the other hand, evidently had something more than that on his mind; I saw him work the bolt to load the rifle, and set off after Sturm with purpose in his every movement. I felt, more than ever, that there was something inevitable about this combination of forces against us: it was more than mere bad luck, this reversal of our fortunes – it was like a tide turning, unstoppable, irrevocable. How long would it be before I was looking into the muzzle of Krantz's rifle, watching his finger tighten on the trigger? How could I ever have doubted, failed to realise, the depth of destructiveness behind his threats? The evidence had all been there, but I had underestimated it, and him. Difficult, of course, to understand what goes on in the mind of a man like that, to recognise the smoke from invisible fires of obsession and resentment that makes one man a killer where others might simply shrug and pass on. But it happens – there *are* killers for no good reason except to themselves. And victims in no good cause.

Come on! There are born victims, as well as born killers – but I'm not one of them. The odds are daunting, but the first essential is not to give up. What's happening now?

They were splitting up, Krantz going off to the left, Sturm in command in the centre, and Drang taking the right. An error, certainly: I'd have had the rifle, with its much greater range, in the centre to cover both flanks: Sturm would too, but Krantz had sabotaged this. And given us our first slight advantage.

I gripped Eva's hand. 'Come on!' I leapt up, pulled her to her feet. Sturm was still a hundred yards away. We started to run. I led the way, trying to use the lines of trees for cover, dodging in and out at random, just as I'd had to do all those years ago on fieldcraft exercises. Sturm shouted, but didn't attempt a shot – we were still out of normal range, and he wasn't a man to waste time trying his luck. I didn't waste time looking round – I knew he'd be there pounding after us, kicking up the pine needles as he put maximum effort into the chase.

'Got to work over to the right,' I panted to Eva. She was keeping up well. We crossed one line of trees, then another, then a third. The ground began to fall away; a few yards further, and we could see light between the trees – that could be, must be, the main road to Munich. Not much traffic this early in the morning, but there would be a chance of stopping cars, a truck, anything to attract attention; would Sturm call off the chase if there were witnesses? If we could just keep running, keep far enough ahead of him until some sort of vehicle appeared, though the more people in it the better . . .

A shot popped from behind us: the harmless-seeming little sound that pistols make in the open air. But a splinter flew off a tree trunk before my eyes, leaving a yellow scar. Sturm's reasoning was the same as mine, and that shot was too close for comfort. He would make every effort, now, to stop us before we could get to the road. I had to take a quick look behind: yes, he had been gaining on us, and was already dangerously close. I glanced to my right. No sign of Drang, which didn't surprise me: he would always come second to Sturm in every way. Sturm was our nemesis: he'd lost perhaps five yards by stopping for an aimed shot, but he'd soon make that up, and next time he might score. Also, he evidently had no compunction about hitting the girl – a faint hope that had stayed with me until that near miss.

I ran on, aware that Eva was still close behind. Perhaps she could go faster without me? – perhaps we should split, and make a divided target?

'Eva' I panted, 'run ahead. Go as fast as you can. Go on! *Now!*'

'*Ich . . . kann . . . nicht . . .*' she panted back, '*unmöglich!*'

On the right, movement caught the corner of my eye: I turned my head for a second, and saw Drang, some distance away, but closing in. How far was the road now? The light between the trees was brighter, the spaces were getting larger. Another hundred yards, perhaps? And then, how far to the road? Would we emerge on the edge of it, or were there fields before the road? If there were fields . . .

There were fields. Or rather, I then saw, a single stretch of pasture, large enough to swallow up all hope of reaching the road before one of Sturm's seven (was that right?) remaining bullets reached one or both of us. No trees to disturb his aim, nothing but a smooth unbroken sward of green, green grass, faintly misted by the morning sun.

This was it, then. Once into this pasture, we had two choices: give up, or split and run – Sturm would surely aim at me first, and the girl might get away. Or we both might. She didn't want to give up – she'd said that. So, we must split, the moment we cross the . . .

A low bank appeared, formed of stones and earth dug from the ditch beyond. A ditch . . . could we . . .?

'Eva! Get down here!' I shouted, pointing. Almost simultaneously there was a second pop from behind – Sturm had seen what I intended – but I knew nothing of the bullet except that it missed. I arrived at the ditch, and flung myself into it, twisting round to face Sturm as I did so, and pulling the Webley from my pocket. The girl fell into the ditch beside me; by then I had the gun ready, and, spinning the cylinder to save the single bullet for later, fired off one of the five shotgun cartridges at Sturm's advancing figure. The gun leapt in my hand as the spray of tiny pellets left the barrel, but he kept coming: the spread of shot from the pistol's short-rifled barrel was too wide. I had to wait – seconds only, but seeming longer – until he was perhaps only twenty yards away, and raising his automatic: at that moment I fired again.

I didn't prevent his shot, which hummed past my head, exposed above the bank of earth. But this time some of my pellets found their target. He threw his left arm across his face with a grunt of pain, and swerved behind a tree, where he stayed. I slid as far down the bank as I could without losing sight of the tree: I'd stopped the attack temporarily, but an aimed shot from twenty yards could be expected to make a conclusive hole in my head if he got the chance to fire it.

I looked about me, hurriedly, without losing sight of Sturm's tree. Three feet to the left, a flat stone had been bulldozed out of the ground, and dumped on top of the bank. I moved towards it, motioning Eva to stay where she was on my right. Sturm's tree was a large pine, but too small for his bulk – I could see the point of one elbow, which would give me warning when he moved. Still watching the tree, I edged a second, smaller stone next to the flat one, leaving a firing embrasure. Sturm's elbow moved – I got ready to fire again, but the automatic didn't appear. Possibly he was mopping blood from his face. I patted the Webley – scorned, but still with a sting of sorts. Sturm must now be aware that, though unlikely to inflict a lethal wound at twenty yards, these pellets could injure and would certainly blind. And at close range the spread of shot would be an advantage – I could hardly miss with all of it.

A brief euphoria, no more. All we had was a respite, a chance to get our breath back. Where to go from here was the problem, so far insoluble. Sturm was held in stalemate, but somewhere out to his right was Drang, creeping no doubt into position after having come to a halt at the sound of firing. And, much worse, on the other side was Krantz, with the rifle. I looked past Eva, along the ditch we were in. Being German, it was cut in a dead straight line. Someone with a rifle could stand there, out of pistol range, and, sighting along the ditch, pick us both off at his leisure. Yes, we were sitting ducks. Even a pistol could do the job, given plenty of ammunition to allow for a few misses in between hits. And with my one proper bullet, I would have only one shot in return.

A muffled shouting started up. It was Sturm behind his tree. It wasn't the time to risk mistranslation.

'What's he saying?'

Eva listened. The shouting stopped. 'He says you must throw out the pistol. Then you must stand up with your hands high.'

Thoughts whirred in my head. Should I offer to do this if he agrees to let the girl go free, walk away across the green field to the road and safety? He might agree, he might understand that, as the situation was hopeless, I was choosing to go out on a high note, an act of chivalry for the sake of the girl, who's only a kid . . .

'Tell him,' I said, 'I'll do it when I see you step into a car on the road down there, and driven away.'

. . . but if so, he'd be wrong. I'm not stuck in medieval timewarp, and this isn't the age of selfless heroism but of shits and charlatans. When the time comes, I shall simply revoke the deal and decline to stand up. Then we'll be back where we are now, but without the girl . . .

'What?'

'I will not go,' Eva repeated.

I stared at her. The blue lakes were awash again; she gazed back at me with a misty expression on her face, her lips trembling but curved in a proud smile. Oh Jesus! – how can I explain . . .

No time, anyway. It's too late. Krantz has appeared at the edge of the forest a hundred yards to our right. He's seen us, and is stepping into the ditch. Now he's starting to walk along it, to reduce the range. With that rifle, he can't miss. We'd both better run – there's nothing else left to do.

Eva saw my horrified expression, and turned to look behind her. She seemed as shocked as I was – before I could stop her she gave a piercing shriek and half rose. I was looking in her direction, and failed to see Sturm's arm dart out from behind the tree with the automatic resting in it until too late.

The sound of his shot was simultaneous with a puff of dry earth from the top of the bank in front of Eva. With a second, despairing cry, she threw up her arms and fell back into the ditch.

I fired then, but too late – Sturm's arm was safely back behind the tree. My shot sounded louder than usual – had I fired the solid round by mistake? That was intended for Krantz. I glanced along the length of the ditch. Eva lay a yard away: I heard a moan – not dead then – at least not yet. Krantz was now much nearer, but standing, the rifle held ready, but not yet to his shoulder.

I switched my eyes back to Sturm's tree for a moment. Yes, his arm was coming back into view. Well – I'd have to deal with him first. I sighted the Webley on the arm, waiting for the automatic to appear. Curiously, his shoulder appeared instead – an unexpected carelessness for him. The shoulder began to move, not further out, but down the tree – was he going to try to crawl to a new position? Then, with a rush, all of the upper part of his body slid into view, seeming to collapse, and Sturm fell out from behind the tree, hitting the ground with an audible thud.

I watched for several seconds, unable to understand. Had my single bullet penetrated the side of the tree and found a vital spot? I made a hasty check of the Webley – the solid round was still intact, *had not been fired* . . .

No time to work it out. The important thing was that I still had one bullet to fire at Krantz, as I'd intended – it would have to be lucky, but it was our last hope. I swung the Webley in his direction, and gripped the butt with both hands, cocking the hammer for the most careful shot of my life . . .

His figure is a tall black shape beyond my sights, blacker than the shining barrel of the pistol. Good! – I'll have no trouble about the range, it is sideways alignment I must watch. There's no wind – that's good too. I steady my grip, begin a slow pressure on the trigger.

But wait! – he's still not taking aim but, gripping the rifle in both hands, he's advancing. I watch him take two, three, five paces towards me: the man must have nerves of steel – surely he can see the Webley aimed at him? Perhaps not – in any case, I'm not going to question this piece of luck. Every pace he takes increases my chance of a hit. Come on, Krantz – come closer! – I'm waiting. When he stops, as the rifle comes up, I'll fire.

Eva moans again. Nothing I can do now, poor kid. Have to finish this with Krantz, first.

She lifts her head, turns it towards me. That's a good sign – perhaps she's not badly hurt. Her eyes widen as she sees the Webley aimed, my face screwed tight with tension.

'*Nein!*'

'Keep down, Eva!'

'*Nein! Schiessen Sie nicht!* – Do not shoot!'

'But it's Krantz!'

She's on her knees now, blocking my aim. She puts out a hand, waves it frantically in front of the gun. I lower it at last, completely confused.

'But . . .?'

'He is my father,' she says.

CHAPTER 15

A Confession

There is a common saying that we should learn
from our enemies. I confess I have never succeeded
in doing so . . .

SIGMUND FREUD

The battle seemed to be over. I climbed out of the ditch and
approached Sturm. He was still breathing. Krantz's bullet
(which I now realised must have been fired at the same instant
as my last shot, just after Sturm had fired at Eva) had passed
through Sturm's chest from left to right: what the damage was
I couldn't say, except that it was bad. Drang appeared, hovering
in the distance between the trees; I suggested we should invite
him to throw his automatic down, and come to help carry
Sturm to the car.

Krantz was on a high of aggression, shaking all over, and
apparently ready to add Drang to his bag, but Eva persuaded
him to put his rifle up and do as I suggested: after some
understandable hesitation, Drang placed his gun at the foot of a
tree and came up to us. Eva, of course, wasn't hurt, merely
shaken and with a lot of dust in her eyes. She, too, was in a
highly charged state; after this, I supposed, ton-ups on motor-
bikes or in open cars were going to seem a trifle tame. But now
I knew where she got it from, on her father's side, that is. Who
her mother was I hadn't asked – not Barbara, was all I knew.
Probably one of Krantz's students in the sixties, the good old
days. Perhaps when the time came for talking I should ask him:
it might soften the hostility I could still feel coming from him,
even though he had kindly refrained from expressing it in
bullets.

But the time for talking was evidently not yet. Krantz had
slung his rifle and now stalked off ahead, leaving Drang and
me to carry Sturm. I took the feet, leaving the heavier end to

his partner, which seemed fair enough. Eva followed behind. We trudged back through the wood, stumbling on the soft carpet of pine needles. Nobody said anything, which made our procession feel even more like a funeral cortège. But there was going to be some conversation very soon, the moment we'd packed Sturm off on his journey back to the Underworld, alive or dead – I must admit I wasn't worrying too much about which it turned out to be.

We had to stop twice for a breather, but I didn't offer to change ends. Finally, we reached the other side of the wood, and laid our burden just inside the tree line, out of sight of the road, while Drang went to reverse the BMW as close to us as he could get. Krantz stood to one side, the rifle on his shoulder and in plain view of anyone that might pass on the road, but as it was an ordinary Heckler & Koch hunting rifle there would seem nothing remarkable in that.

Drang got the car to within ten yards, and came back to lift Sturm in. He was still alive, so we loaded him on to the back seat – if he'd stopped breathing it would have been the boot. Even Drang didn't take much care in the loading – I've seen potatoes handled with more finesse – but Sturm wasn't in any state to notice. Interesting, I thought, how everybody joins in to kick the bully when he's down, including his erstwhile mates.

Krantz did nothing but watch, and when it was done, he gestured Drang to drive away with a single flick of his hand, and without a word. It was a lordly dismissal. Drang didn't hesitate, but got back into the driving seat and gunned the car over the grass and away, direction God-knows-where. Krantz then set off along the road, past Eva's battered Beetle, towards her house: she and I followed, hand in hand like a couple of kids, a few yards behind. This was the moment I'd been waiting for. And I wanted some plain answers, this time.

My first question was, what did *Fuhrwesen* mean? 'Oh,' she said, sounding puzzled, 'that means "delivery service". Why do you ask?'

'Because, when you left the barn door open so that I could hear what was being said in the kitchen, that was the word Sturm (that's what I called him) used when he was telling you

172

what he thought I was here for – he said it was to collect information on the *Fuhrwesen*.'

'Oh,' she said, '*that* delivery service.'

'Yes,' I said, '*that* one – let's have it.'

She was reluctant, I could see that. So I stopped, swinging her round to face me, and taking her by both hands. The blue lakes looked up at me, and my pulse rate zoomed in spite of all I could do: it was unfair, unfair that I must soon drive away and never gaze into these depths again. Perhaps I would rather drown than reach the secrets hidden there. No! – godammit, she *must* tell me.

'At first,' she said slowly, 'it was a little thing. My father was asked to drive a car from here to Holland, that is all. He was to drive to an address and leave it outside a house overnight. Then he was to drive it back again. For this, he was paid some money. As he did not have much money, he agreed to do it.'

'I understand,' I said, releasing her. We walked on. 'And, as time went by, more trips – no questions asked.'

'Yes.'

'And Sturm –'

'This man you call Sturm came to see my father one day, on the part of clients – important people. I do not know their names. But my father was given much more money than before to make journeys to other places, sometimes to foreign countries, to London as well.'

'He liked to do this?'

'At first, yes. He liked the money. And he liked the excitement, because now he was told what was in each delivery, so that he could make his own arrangements for concealing it. He would do this at night in our workshop, welding a container to the underside of a car, or inside the petrol tank of a motorcycle. He is a good workman, my. father, although sometimes he seems strange.'

'Yes,' I said with feeling. 'And then?'

'And then there were more and more deliveries, so my father began to employ others. But then, last year, one of them was caught. And, although the one who was caught did not give my father's name to the police, my father decided he must stop deliveries until he felt safe again.'

'So now he's back to being short of money?'

'Yes. But he says he is going to live with his Barbara again, and make sculptures. He was famous, you know.'

'I know. I also know that she isn't *his* Barbara, not any more. She won't have him. She's too busy with her own firm, and anyway, she's just not interested.'

Eva sighed. 'You are sure?'

'I'm sure. He's hopelessly unrealistic, your father. Apart from being a disaster to himself and everyone else within range. Sorry, but it's true.'

'I know,' she said.

'And you were trying to protect him, of course?'

'Yes. But I did not expect . . .'

'Of course you didn't. Sturm – he's the organiser of all this, I suppose – was worried that his clients would be exposed, and that's why he wanted to eliminate me. It means little to a man like that. By the time he's recovered (*if* he does), he'll find that his clients haven't been exposed. So there'll be little point in his chasing after any of us and stirring the whole thing up again. I should think he'll keep away.'

'Oh,' said Eva, 'I hope so.'

We walked on in silence. Then I said: 'Why didn't you tell me that it was your father who had the rifle? I can understand why you didn't tell me earlier, but surely by the time we were being chased through the wood . . .?'

'I didn't know he was with them,' she said.

I thought back. In my mind's eye I saw Krantz wresting the rifle away from Sturm and setting off towards the forest. I saw Eva lying beside me, keeping her head down and *out of sight*, just as I told her. Yes. She couldn't have known he was with them.

Some explanations are so bloody obvious. Afterwards.

By the time we arrived back at the house, I was feeling that the day had already gone on long enough, although most of the world was not yet at breakfast. A whole range of aches and bruises, collected during the last twelve hours, were now clamouring for recognition, refusing to be ignored any longer. When Eva suggested coffee, I could hardly prevent myself from trailing after her into the kitchen and slumping into a chair while she made it.

But Krantz was already at work in the yard, knocking apart the remains of the barn doors Eva and I had crashed through a century or so ago: he worked with furious energy, bashing the heads off rusty bolts with a club hammer, and dragging splintered planks into the barn where he hurled them into a pile where they looked like nothing more than firewood. It might not be the right moment, but there might not be another for some time, if at all. In any case, I was too tired to bother with subtleties. I walked up to him.

'I must talk to you.'

'I do not think so.' He didn't even glance at me.

'It can't be avoided. Not after what has happened.'

'Nothing has happened.'

'Oh now, look here . . .'

'Nothing has happened.' He gave me the briefest of glances, before renewing his attack on a stubborn bolt head.

'The police –' I shouted above the din.

He paused in his work of destruction, turned to face me, the heavy hammer swinging loosely in his right hand. His pale blue eyes rested for a moment on my face. 'You have nothing to tell the police, because nothing has happened,' he said.

'That's where you're wrong. I've got plenty to tell, and they'll be very interested to hear it.'

He made no reply, but simply turned away and struck at the bolt head with a final well aimed blow: it broke off and flew away across the yard.

'Sooner or later,' I said wearily, 'you'll have to talk to me. Think about it. Meanwhile, I'm going in for some coffee.'

I went into the house, and leant against the kitchen door jamb. Eva was rinsing mugs at the sink. 'Your father,' I said, 'your father . . .' My voice was submerged by a huge yawn.

She turned, putting the mugs on the draining board, and came towards me, smiling: she took my arm. 'Come,' she said, 'come. You must lie down. You can be in my room.'

I allowed myself to be led along the corridor and upstairs. Yesterday, I thought drowsily, yesterday this would have seemed the final steps to the Promised Land – the girl's soft hand slipping into mine, tugging me gently after her, the faint scent of her hair, indefinable but recalling other tandem stumblings, whisperings, gigglings and clingings, along corridors lined with doors each concealing potential disaster – *Sshhh! they're asleep!*... But today, today is different, there's no anticipation, no tension, no rising sap or tingling urge. Here's the door. Here's the room – view of mountains, littered table, divan bed with tartan rug and large woolly lion in residence. His eyes are no more glassy than mine, his roar right now may well be louder.

'Thank you, Eva. Ah, that's bliss.'

Head on the pillow, eyes closing already. Poor old chap.

'I will bring you the coffee,' she says.

And she must have done, as I found it beside me when I woke up. A Mickey Mouse clock told me it was half-past ten. I drank some cold coffee, and considered. The short sleep had revived my brain, and I'd have to bear with the bruises for some time yet; no excuse not to get up.

I found a bathroom, washed and shaved with a borrowed disposable razor, and inspected the result. Face bleary, but undamaged: still, it was Sunday, the morning after the night before, and I wouldn't be the only one to show signs of wear. As I reached the top of the stairs, Eva appeared from the sitting-room.

'Do you feel better?' she said anxiously. And formally – while I slept, a gap had opened up, I could see.

'Much better, thanks.'

We stood, uncomfortably apart. What had happened?

'What will you do, now?' she asked carefully, her voice controlled but tense.

Ah! That's it, of course.

'I must talk to your father, Eva. Sorry, but I must.'

'He has gone,' she said, sounding nervous.

'Gone! Where?'

'He asked me not to tell you. He says he will not talk to you.'

'I know – he told me. And I told him that, after what's happened, he'll have to, like it or not. He told you what I want to talk about?'

'Yes,' she said. 'About a man who was killed in London. He told me. But –'

'It's important to me to find out what your father knows about this.'

'He knows nothing,' she said. 'Please believe me.'

'Your father came to my house, threatened me to keep away from "his Barbara", and said "Remember Cassell" – that's the man who was killed. Either he added that to make his threat seem more convincing, or he knows something about Cassell's death. I'm sorry, Eva, but I really have to know which it is. You said yourself that your father is a strange man: I think we both have to think of the possibility that he may, in fact, be ill – mentally ill. If so, it won't do any good to cover up for him – he needs help, he needs to go into hospital, for his own and everyone else's good, especially yours. Don't you see that?'

'My father is not ill,' she said. 'He is strange, yes, but ill – no.'

'How can you say that?'

'Because he is my father and I know him.'

'You want to protect him, even against his own illness?'

'He is *not* ill!'

'I've talked to someone with psychological training about your father. She told me that his behaviour is that of a man who may be mentally ill. He ought to see a doctor, a psychiatrist.'

'They will put him in prison,' Eva said in a low voice, almost to herself.

'If he's ill, he'll go to hospital, not prison.'

'Hospital, prison – either will kill him. He will die!' She was getting more and more agitated, pushing her hair back from her face with trembling hands.

'Eva,' I said as calmingly as I could, 'you must persuade him. You must! Try to understand. The police in London are already looking for the men who shot Cassell. They know about your father – it's only a question of time before they check up on him. If he was involved, the only thing that might then help him is a psychiatrist's report, confirming that he is ill. Surely you can see that?'

She stared at me, eyes brimming again. Her face now wore

an expression of mingled terror and determination, like a heroine about to make the supreme sacrifice. And that, I suddenly realised, was how she saw it, too – her emotional equipment was of the type that probes for the soft centre in each and every situation, and sucks it dry, regardless of consequences. Last night, this had worked to my advantage; but today, I was wasting my time.

I made one last effort to get through to her.

'Maybe the London police sound far away, not much of a risk to your father. But they'll get your police here to ask their questions for them, and they're going to insist on answers – your father will have to talk to them. So why not to me, first? I may be able to help . . .'

She shook her head, her hands pressing her temples. 'No! He will not . . .'

'Oh, for God's sake, be realistic, Eva! He can't refuse – especially after what's just happened here.'

She looked at me with a mulish expression which told me what she was going to say. What her father had told her to say.

'Nothing has happened. Nothing!'

I steered the Citroën past a line of lorries. It was a retreat, this dash back up the autobahn to catch the night ferry, I knew that – and felt it. Depression hung round my head, grey and prickly with irritation. Even the weather had caught the mood: the further north I got, the more cloudy and dull it became, until finally the last triangles of blue sky were covered up, I drove on, a grey man in a grey car, under a grey sky.

A retreat, yes. I couldn't cope with the land of Ludwig any longer. It was too much, it was over the top, it was relentless in emotional supply and demand. You had to be tuned up and super-energised to stand the pace. Yesterday – well, yesterday I'd gone in full of confidence, ready for anything, so I thought. Yesterday was golden and bright, a day of jumping nerves and pounding pulses, risky but intense. There was action, euphoria, gloom and ultimate survival. There was the girl – a figment, all right, but willing to lend herself to illusion, it seemed, for a day or two because here, brooding beneath their Alps, they understand the value of dreams ... But then I woke from this morning's short but fatal sleep to find the princess abdicated, the dream deserted. And in her place, Krantz's daughter, a fat and foolish *Fräulein*.

'Nothing has happened. Nothing!'

Would they get away with it, the pair of them, if I went back and gave Priestly the whole story? By the time I left the house, the garage doors were already cleared away – they were rotten and due for renewal, Krantz would say. The living-room window would, of course, have been broken by accident, since repaired. What else was there? – some shots heard in the forest, and some bullet and pellet marks on trees. Early morning hunters, that's all. My bruises? Inconclusive evidence, fast fading.

Yet I *could* bend Priestly's ear to it, and set the *polizei* sniffing after Krantz. I didn't owe him any favours. Eva had told me enough on the walk back from the forest (while the glow of our alliance was still with her) to make a case worth looking into. I needn't feel bad about doing that – I'd given her every chance to persuade him to talk to me first, and she'd refused. No, the question was: had he been involved in the shooting of Jonathan, or was that just his fantasy? Would it do me any good to find out? Would it remove the police presence from my house so that normality could be restored? Or would it result in more questions, more police, more upset instead of less?

I drove on northwards, undecided, under a darkening sky. When I'm tired, my mind makes a closed circuit, and the same thoughts go round and round. I was forced to relive yesterday, images and events, good and bad, over and over. Even the good bits added to my depression, by making me admit that I was lying when I said she was fat. Lying. Sadly.

CHAPTER 16

Life is Not Easy

Thus the ego, driven by the id, confined by the
super ego, repulsed by reality, struggles to master
its economic task of bringing about harmony
among the forces and influences working in and
upon it; and we can understand how it is that so
often we cannot suppress a cry: 'Life is not easy!'
                                    SIGMUND FREUD

It was business as usual in Church Street. Claudine went
through the motions of a dutiful welcome home, but her smile
had the precarious brightness of winter sunshine; there was little
warmth in it. Had there been another interview with Priestly,
or was this still the after-effect of last Thursday's interview,
which had had such a disastrous effect on Claudine?

'No,' Claudine said, 'he has telephoned, but not for me – it is
you he wants to see.'

'I suppose he would,' I said, taking the bowl of vegetable soup
she held out to me. 'Did he sound annoyed that I'd gone off
without consultation?'

'I think so. But with him it is difficult to tell – he has always
the air of disapproval when he speaks to me, although I try to
answer what he wants to know.'

'I'll ring him after lunch, to say I'm back. Though I'm sure
he's like that with everyone, it's his normal manner, the
lugubrious bloodhound on the trail. I shouldn't think he's very
popular with his mates in the police, either: it can't be much
fun having to work with him.'

'I do not understand it,' Claudine said. Meaning, I supposed,
Priestly's failure to show any of the normal male responses she
was used to. Having seen his eyes scan her when she wasn't
looking, I thought I knew the answer to her puzzlement – it
wasn't that he was indifferent, but the opposite. In his eyes, she
had to be the storm centre of this affair, the siren on the rock
luring all us hapless mariners to doom and destruction: a

180

genuine, original, made-in-France *femme fatale*. But lunchtime was no time to go into all that.

'Probably fancies you secretly,' I said lightly. 'Or has missed promotion to Chief Superintendent and is bitter about it – he must be forty-five, a dangerous age.' He'd got it wrong about Claudine – in spite of her glossy exterior, she's more housewife than houri. Or perhaps *I've* got it wrong – it may be just her particular combination of qualities that appeals to him, as it does to me. It wouldn't be the first time I've been outraged to find my choice confirmed by the most unlikely and unsuspected of competitors, my cherished individualism a delusion, lost in a shoal of similarity.

'Oh! – do you think so?' Claudine said thoughtfully.

'Certain of it,' I told her. She hadn't said which of my theories she was querying, but there was no need – she has the same order of interest as the rest of the world. The thought of which prompted me to add: 'If I get a chance, I'll ask Sergeant Cooper – he'll know.'

'Oh, but . . .' Claudine protested, reacting as I'd hoped.

'There must be a normal age for superintendents to get promoted,' I explained. 'Isn't that what you meant?' I grinned, knowing that it wasn't.

But Claudine wasn't playing. 'There is cheese,' she said with restraint. 'And while you eat it, you can tell me what you did with those two days in Germany. *Hein?*'

Well, it had to come. 'Dry whites are what we need, and it seems to me that the wines of Franconia . . .'

'William! *Ça ne va pas!*'

I looked across the table at her. Her eyes, dark and intense, stared back at me. Yes, it was time to talk: not because talking would necessarily solve our problems, but because it had become unavoidable.

Some seconds passed, each one a churchyard bell. Talking was unavoidable – Priestly had made it so – but the risks were grave. Things better left unsaid would be made explicit. Is there such a thing as a marriage, or relationship, of absolute honesty? Aren't we all, basically, strangers searching for another to share our ideals and illusions – up to a point? What happens when you're driven by circumstances beyond that point?

'All right,' I said. 'If you think it's time to talk, OK – I agree. But let's save it for this evening. Scenes like this are better played in bed, not across a table. We may need to grab each other if we're hearing things we don't like. *D'accord?*'

'*Entendu,*' she said, sounding stiff.

I reached my hand out and took hers. 'Come on! It'll be all right. I want it to be – don't you? We'll come through all this and out the other side, full of newfound wisdom and understanding, etcetera. That's what they say. It'll be like the psychiatrist's couch, but cosier. Then we'll forget it all and take up normal life again. It wasn't bad, was it? – if you can remember that far back.'

She looked down at our hands where they lay together on the table top. Then she managed a small smile.

'No. Not bad.'

'I'll go and do some work now. And ring the police to see what they want.'

'Yes.'

She didn't look up. I gave her hand a final squeeze and withdrew mine. It wasn't going to be easy, this evening.

Maggie hadn't expected me to be back so soon, and the tray on my desk was almost empty. By the telephone was a note in Maggie's handwriting – 'Inspector Priestly, please ring, urgent', with his number. The 'please', I assumed, was hers, not his. Better get it over with. I lifted the receiver and tapped the buttons. Sergeant Cooper came on the line first.

'Mr Warner?'

'That's what I said. I have a message here to ring Superintendent Priestly.'

'Ah yes. Just a moment, sir.'

Cooper had sounded surprised. Did they really think I'd done a bunk?

'Mr Warner?' It was Priestly himself, this time. The note of surprise was better concealed, but still there.

'You wanted me to ring.'

'I did, sir, yes indeed. Going abroad, Mr Warner, at a time like this – that was very ill-advised, if I may say so. Without notice, too – well sir, you can understand . . .'

'Mr Priestly, I'm a wine merchant. I go abroad frequently – it's a necessary part of my business. There's nothing unusual in it. I sent you a note to let you know where I'd be, and now I'm calling you to say I'm back. I don't see what more you can expect.'

'Your note, Mr Warner, reached us after you'd left.'

'I know that, but . . .'

'I have to ask you, sir, to contact me in advance if you should wish to leave the country again while the investigation into Mr Cassell's death is still in progress.'

'Well. If you insist.'

'I do, sir. That's to say, I am making a request for your co-operation, no more than that, at this stage.'

'All right.'

'Thank you, sir. Your visit to Germany – this was, I take it, purely on business?'

I had been expecting this. Besides myself, only Barbara yet knew what my real purpose had been, and I had asked her to keep it to herself. I'd decided to talk to her about Ludwig before telling the police anything. This meant that, for the time being, only a firm assertion would keep them at bay: if I had to retract later, so be it.

'On business, yes.'

Right or wrong, it was done. Priestly seemed to accept it, and asked no further questions. We rang off in an atmosphere of guarded civility. On the whole, my excursion had caused less fuss than I had expected.

I went to check in with Maggie, and got down to some work, then. For once, the routine was a relief, a pleasure almost. This panelled office, this passing of bits of paper from one pile to another, this sending of instructions to shop and warehouse, today seemed the centre of my life, the reason for my existence. Here, at the hub of my mini-empire, I felt real, I felt necessary. Work is the centre, I found myself thinking, and women should be peripheral. That's how things are when you're young: how it was for me until, or even for some time after, I met my first wife, and then Claudine, and, without even realising it was happening, lost my independence. Not lost, but *gave away* – for

183

which, in return, she appointed me head of her household, an honorary title in these emancipated times but bringing with it rights and privileges normally found irresistible by the homeless male: I mean good meals, clean socks, and a warm bed, all supplied with verve, energy and enthusiasm – my beautiful dutiful wife. Her *Moules à la Normande* – incomparable! Her style between the sheets – indefatigable! (No need to rhapsodise about the socks.) Oh yes, I know I'm being trivial, and cynical. There was also, maybe still is also, fundamental sympathy between us on the deeper marital essentials. But I don't intend to dwell on that, not now, with the whole show ... forget it. That way lies calm, the return of control, and constructive sanity.

Maggie came in, wearing an air of indecision, unusual for her, and with a sheaf of paper in her hand.

'What's up?' I asked her. 'Has an Order for Bankruptcy finally arrived?'

'I'm very sorry,' she said, 'as I know how you like to plan your day. But these got missed when I brought your tray in this morning. I'm afraid they're rather urgent.'

I took the sheaf from her. Late deliveries, waiting for my decision on substitutes for wine out of stock. Today, the prospect of working late didn't seem to matter, not at all.

'Don't worry,' I said cheerfully, 'I'll have them ready for you by tomorrow morning. It's what I'm here for, isn't it?'

'Oh!' Maggie said, blinking. 'Well. Not quite what I expected to hear, I must admit. I thought you were looking a bit peaky, last week – the break must have done you good.'

'It did, Maggie, it did. Helped me to get things in perspective. It can get a little claustrophobic here, living and working in the same place.'

'I can imagine,' she said. 'And all this bother with the police ...'

'That'll be sorted out, soon. Priestly sounded quite reasonable when I rang him earlier. I think they're realising it's a waste of time snooping about this house.'

'Well, I hope so,' she said doubtfully. 'But you know, the VAT inspector is always at his most soft-soapy when he thinks he's found an irregularity and is trying to catch us out.'

After she'd gone, I thought about that. She was right, of course. I stared out of the window into the deepening dusk. Then I got up, flung the curtains across with a gesture that threatened to rip them from their tracks, and went back to my desk.

Work, work was what I had to do.

And I did. It was nearly seven before I'd finished, and put the completed lists in the out tray for Maggie to collect in the morning. Not exactly hard labour by the standards of the self-employed, but my back was aching. Unusual, as I've got a chair which . . .

Ah yes, of course! Not the chair, but the effect of spending all night tied to a post in a Bavarian farmhouse – when was it? – only two nights ago. A change of scene, an afternoon of routine work, and Germany was already taking on distance in time and space. What was going on there, now? And what should I be doing about Krantz? I had to talk to Barbara, for a start. Perhaps she would be at home by now. I reached for the phone.

'She's not back yet,' Hugo said. He managed to make even that sound like a complaint. Why didn't Barbara throw him out into the world to start real life? Perhaps she'd tried, and he refused: kids are getting harder to get rid of, I've noticed. Sometimes the parents have to move out, instead.

'When does she usually get back?' I asked.

'About now. Hang on – I think she's coming in now. Yup.'

'Hello?' came Barbara's soft voice. It conjured up a picture of her, small and fragile.

'Thought I'd let you know I'm back,' I said.

'Oh, William! – how was it? Did you see him?'

'I certainly did. But it's a long story. I need to talk to you – can we meet somewhere tomorrow? Lunch, perhaps?'

'Just a minute,' Barbara said. I heard her instructing Hugo to go into the kitchen and put something into the oven. Then she came on the line again, sounding quieter than before. 'I've got to work in the morning,' she said, 'and in the afternoon, it's Jonathan's funeral. I don't suppose you want to come to that?'

'Oh yes, so it is. Of course I'll come, yes. Any chance of lunch before? Drinks are needed on these occasions – it's one of the few things where I see eye to eye with the Irish.'

'I'm afraid not. I'll have to go straight from work. But if you're going too, we can make arrangements at the, the place. It's at two o'clock.'

'I'll be there,' I said. 'Which place is it?'

She gave me the address, a crematorium in North London.

'I know it. And now, I expect Hugo is anxious to be fed.'

'Well,' she said seriously, 'as a matter of fact . . .'

'Goodbye, Barbara.'

'Goodbye, William.'

We had an early supper in the kitchen, instead of one of the ceremonial dining-room dinners which Claudine and I like to indulge in, as I've described before, to round off the day. Not tonight the gleam of candlelight on polished mahogany, the glitter of silver cutlery ready to hand, the glow of wine in tall polished glasses. We sat, instead, on kitchen chairs at the scrubbed pine table, round a big brown bowl of macaroni cheese – all of us including Julian, who normally avoids family supper as a waste of time and exists mainly on sandwiches eaten in his room over the garage. His unexpected and watchful presence was unsettling: he hardly spoke at all, but his eyes moved between Claudine and myself, recording all that was said and done. The girls, too, were unusually quiet: I found myself hoping for one or other of them to shatter our solemnity with chirpy comment, an argument however abrasive, anything – but they seemed struck dumb for once, and would not be provoked. I couldn't get much response from the macaroni cheese either – like all Claudine's preparations, it looked as perfect as a cookery book illustration, but it's food for hearty, happy eaters, and I wasn't in that kind of mood. Tonight I might have managed something small and delicate, but not this dish of slimy white worms, an unintended symbolism, I was sure, but impossible to forget once the thought had occurred. In spite of which, some of the stuff, at least, had to be eaten.

'I think I'll get some wine to go with this. Any preference?'

Claudine shook her head. She wasn't making much progress, either, I noticed. I left the kitchen, went down to the cellar, and

186

brought back a bottle of Bourg, plain but solid, the only claret that isn't wasted on strong cheese. Claudine accepted a glass, Julian refused. I managed to start a conversation with him on 'Architecture: Trade or Profession?' Claudine and the girls listened, or appeared to. The conversation fizzled as we found ourselves in agreement – there's no difference any longer between trades and professions, according to us. If there ever was. Supper came to an end. The girls offered to wash up. I watched them set about it with a dull despair settling at the bottom of my heart: if even the girls could feel the rocking of the boat, we must be at least halfway sunk.

'I wanted so much to avoid this, but I don't think it's possible any longer. Priestly isn't going to leave us alone until he's got every last detail. I'm going to have to ask you what went on at that last interview with the police, what there really was between you and Jonathan?'

Claudine lay on her back, her profile in silhouette against the shaded bedside light, her bare arms folded on top of the duvet across the mound made by her breasts. It was warm in our bedroom; rain pattered lightly on the skylight, and I listened to the swish and grumble of traffic in the street below, waiting for her to say something.

'Whatever it was, I've made up my mind to bear it – you must know that? We've got a good thing going, we understand each other, don't you agree? Before this happened, before Jonathan got himself killed, we were fine – weren't we? I don't believe you were unhappy, not seriously, not enough to want to break us up. Were you?'

I watched her profile, waited some more. It couldn't be that bad, not possibly. She must be wrestling with her inhibitions, the built-in instinct of the good bourgeoise to keep up appearances, show the world a smiling face, happy and confident, to the bitter end and beyond.

'Come on, darling! Don't think – just talk. It's overdue, and time to put our cards on the table. Would some brandy help? Let's get pissed and both let our hair down.'

Would she? – could she? Could I? If we were really in for True Confessions, I'd find it hard to avoid editing mine in places.

But I need only say enough to balance whatever she told me had gone on with Jonathan: then, after declarations of mutual forgiveness, we could clear the board and start again. So I hoped.

'I cannot,' she said.

I reared up, turned on my elbow, looked down at her. Her eyes were open, turned to the ceiling, brimming wet. She isn't given to crying, but now large tears were chasing one another down her cheeks.

Oh God. It *was* serious, then. And I'd been too self-absorbed, too insensitive, too *thick* to notice the signs. Because signs there must have been.

But *had* there? And what could explain her willingness, no, her enthusiasm for our reunion, our evening of solidarity and rediscovered empathy, the evening Krantz called and threatened me? Was that illusion? – could she have simulated that? How could she, how did she . . .?

'Claudine,' I began. Words stuck in my throat. What could I say that I hadn't already.

In silence, I lay down beside her, my arm across hers, my mouth close to her ear, breathing her familiar scent. 'Tell me,' I whispered to her ear, 'tell me, tell me, *tell me* . . .'

I felt, rather than heard her sigh. Then she told me what I had to know.

She spoke in a flat, faraway voice: it came from above, addressed to the ceiling, while I lay with my face against the side of her neck. I listened, not moving, not wanting to do anything to disrupt the flow, my arm tight round her as if to squeeze the words out. I tried to concentrate on the facts – dates, times, places, who said what and when – though images kept forming to distract me.

Factually, then, she had found Jonathan entertaining, attractive, a good companion – well, I knew all that. She had been out with him often while our house was being altered – I knew that too. But also while I was away – lunches and afternoons, locations and activities unspecified. For her, she said, it had been light-hearted, fun and flattery. As, she said significantly, these things should be.

She meant, I'm sure, to remind me of Ginny, my regular

188

girlfriend of many years, now back with her ex-husband and safely out of reach, but with whom things tended to get out of hand, although I never actually ... but this isn't the place to recount all that ... I shall never understand how she was able to take up again with Evan, a barrister and pontificating prune, a man totally incapable of appreciating ... no, not the place to recount all that.

Where was I? – oh, yes, light-hearted fun and flattery. I expect Jonathan was good at that. Maybe I'd been neglectful, though Claudine made no accusations, no excuses – she didn't need to. It's fair to say about our relationship (awful word) that it was based on positive impulses, constructive even, not on the baleful and negative compulsions of tit for tat. On the whole, of course. Fun and flattery. In restaurants and at his flat. At the table and in bed. She didn't say that, she didn't need to, I assumed it, because why not, if he could. It's a big word, bed, but not in itself, only because of what it can lead to. In this case, nothing – or rather, almost nothing, a puff of new ash from a chimney in North London tomorrow.

But would it have led to anything, otherwise? I listened to Claudine's faraway voice telling me that no, it wouldn't. Here is what she said, as it's important: *Cela n'était pas grand chose, je t'assure, William, je me suis amusée, c'est tout* ... Just what I'd assumed, of course. Then I heard: *Pour moi, c'était comme ça, mais* ...

Oh, I didn't like this twist in the telling. I didn't like that *mais* ... Complications were coming, I knew it. This was the crux of our problem, this was what the police were after. For Claudine, it was afternoon amusement, but for Jonathan ...

I listened to her telling me that Jonathan had planned for them to go off together.

Quiet as her voice was, her words sounded in my head with the roar of a falling building, redundant and dynamited, spurts of dust round the base followed by an accelerating landslide of brickwork, collapsing into rubble.

'You *agreed*?'

'Ah *non*! listen to me , . .'

'But you told the police this?'

'Not at first. But when they came back, *they knew* . . .'

189

'How could they know?'

'I cannot understand it. But *listen* . . .'

'They must have found something at his flat – a letter, plane tickets. Where were you going to go?'

'William! *Je t'ai dit, ç'est pas vrai* . . .'

'You must have given him some encouragement.'

'*Non! Rien de tout! C'était lui* . . .'

'Well. What were they then, these plans?'

'I . . . they were not . . . I did not think he was serious. I thought it was a game, he made me laugh with it.'

'A game?'

'Yes!'

'Did you explain to the police that it was only a game?'

'Yes. But I don't think they understood.'

'I'm afraid they wouldn't,' I said. 'I'm afraid you'd have done better with a blank denial. It sounds like an excuse, calling what happened a game.'

Silence. Then she said stiffly: 'You do not believe me.'

'Oh yes,' I said quickly, 'I do. Of course I do.'

Well, I wanted to. That's what I meant.

'I *thought* it was not a good idea to tell you of this,' she said.

'Oh, but you're wrong, darling. I'm glad you did.'

An hour or so later, an hour of darkness, silence and whirling thoughts, I wasn't so sure. I got quietly out of bed.

'Where are you going?' Claudine's voice arrested me.

'Can't sleep. Thought I'd go down and read for a bit. Sorry if I woke you.' I groped for my dressing gown.

'You didn't,' she said.

CHAPTER 17

Insufficient Understanding

*The sexual frigidity of women . . . is a phenomenon
that is still insufficiently understood.*

SIGMUND FREUD

So it was a dreary sleepless night for both of us. I must have slept a little, though, because when morning arrived I found the bed empty, and Claudine already gone. I stretched out and made the most of a few minutes of solitude, feeling more grateful than deprived. Sharing a bed with someone you're at odds with is like pressing on a bruise: it hadn't happened to us before, not like this, and I was hating it. The trouble is, whoever suggests sleeping apart for a while is making a move that may seem more divisive than restorative. I didn't want to take that risk, not yet – but another night or two like this one and I'd have to, unless Claudine cracked first. Oh Jesus! – the rot was really setting in.

I found her in the kitchen, busying herself with breakfast. Try as I might, I couldn't give her the usual squeeze, or think of anything to say that mightn't seem either trite or provocative. We were confined to basic civilities, as though we'd just met, this morning at this table, instead of thirteen years ago. I stood it as long as I could, and then took my coffee to the office with the excuse of work.

Just after nine, the telephone rang. Maggie had taken the call in the outer office and was putting it through.

'Oh – you *are* there,' she said, 'Claudine said you were. There's a call for you, from Germany. It's not a good line, but I'll put it through.'

From Germany! Would it be Ludwig? – or even, perhaps . . . 'Thanks, Maggie. I'll take it.'

I waited. A distant voice sounded; then there was a click as Maggie put her extension down, and I could hear better.

'Hello? I wish to speak to Mr Warner . . . hello?'

'Eva!' I said.

'Is this Mr Warner?'

'Yes – it's me, William. Speak up – the line's not good.'

'Oh. Yes, I will . . . can you hear me now?'

'Yes, I can hear you. How are you, Eva? Has anything happened?'

'Happened? No. I call you because I have to ask something. It is about my father, and . . . are you there?'

'Yes! Go on – what is it?'

'I want to say I am sorry, you know, for what happened. I think you were right when you wanted to talk to my father and I did not agree. Now I am afraid there will be more trouble for him. I have to ask you, please, if you have told the police what I told you?'

'About the courier work?'

'Please?'

'The *Fuhrwesen*.'

'*Ja, ja.* The *Fuhrwesen*. Have you told about that?'

'No.'

'Oh! I am so happy – that is very good. You are very kind.'

'Well, I . . .'

'You see, I should not have told you. If my father knew, he would be very angry with me. And also, I think, with you.'

'Listen, Eva, that's not . . .'

'Yes, but you see, if the police do not come, I think he will stop the *Fuhrwesen*. It is now too dangerous. So you see, you do not need to tell the police.'

'Are you sure? That he'll stop, I mean?'

'*Ja, ja.* I think so. And I have to ask you, if you see my father, not to say what you know. This will be better.'

'Eva, I hope you're right. But what will he live on?'

'Please?'

'What about money? I'm afraid that . . .'

Maggie's tap sounded on my door, and she put her head in. 'I'll just give you these,' she whispered, coming to the desk.

'Thank you, Maggie. Er yes, I'm afraid it may be difficult, but I'll do my best for you. Send me your price list, and we'll see. *Auf Wiederhören!*'

192

I put the phone down, hoping she wouldn't ring back. A strange experience, that, hearing her voice in these surroundings – our two worlds had seemed so far apart.

'No good?' Maggie said.

'I don't think so, Maggie. No, I think that's the end of it.'

'You must have had high hopes,' she said. 'You look really disappointed.'

I drove alone to the crematorium, thankful that Claudine had decided not to come – though I never expected she would – and relieved to have a little more time on my own. Vivaldi's *Four Seasons* was playing on the car radio; although hackneyed from constant misuse as boutique background music, it's a fine piece – economic, elegant, and with an elegaic quality that manages to be moving but not sentimental. Today, it exactly suited my mood. The timing was right, too – it finished just as I arrived.

It was raining again, of course, but on this occasion I didn't mind, it was an appropriate decision on the part of whoever stage-manages our cosmos. Earth to earth, dust to dust, mud to mud. Rain dripped from trees, roofs, umbrellas – the world weeping for Jonathan, maybe.

Nobody else was, much. Jonathan had perhaps spread his courtly charm too widely and too thin to have inspired deep and long-lasting affection. Or perhaps it was just that the functional atmosphere of the place discouraged emotion. Barbara must have decided to get the job done with a minimum of fuss as we were barely a quorum of mourners, a mere fifteen or so. There was a handful of relations, all elderly – Jonathan had had no children. There were a few male friends such as myself – I had hoped for a gaggle or flurry of competing mistresses, I must admit, but no such diversion was provided. And there was Superintendent Priestly, lurking in the background in the role of official vulture. We all exchanged glances with an air of careful solemnity, of best behaviour.

We could have managed a few sniffles, I'm sure, if it had been a proper funeral, if we had been gathered at a graveside, watching the long box slide down into the other world, listening to the dead leaves swirl with a dry clatter like bones, feeling the sodden grass through our polished shoes. That spectacle brings on the tears all right, some for the dear departed and rather more for oneself. That reminder is what funerals are for. But Jonathan's had none of that: it was the sanitised sort, free of creaking ropes and wriggling worms.

We filed through glass swing doors out of the rain, shaking and shutting umbrellas in a white-walled lobby that might have led to a canteen but for the sandblasted saints on the inner doors. We filed on, into the centrally heated Chapel of Remembrance, where a few brown fibreglass chairs had been unstacked for the occasion from piles of spares at the rear. Practical, yes, but chilling to the spirit and the bum.

So, where is Jonathan, who should be the focus of our attention? I look about me, filled with irreligious gloom as the furnishings come into focus, vestigial symbols of the C of E, gutless and suburban. Jonathan is over there, displayed on a dais; well, his box is, and we all presume he's inside. Too good a box, surely, to go into the fiery furnace – must be rented, is already booked for the next performance. After you, sir. No, no, *you* go first.

It's not a struggle, holding back the tears – no, the problem is how not to laugh. Especially when treacly mood music begins to seep from behind the scenes, electronic organ sounds, Bach-flavoured. It occurs to me that when I last heard an organ like that it was playing 'The Teddy Bears' Picnic', and my shoulders begin to shake. My neighbours glance at me, think I'm suffering. Well, I am, but not from sorrow. Perhaps if I blow my nose loudly it might relieve the pressure. Hoo, hoooo.

I am the resurrection and the life, saith the Lord: he that believeth in me, though he were dead, yet shall he live.

Here we go, then. And somebody's persuaded them to use the King James Bible. Praise be.

I caught up with Barbara on the path to the car park. She was with Hugo and Bill Charrington.

'Well, that's that, then,' I said.

Charrington turned his bearded face towards me. 'Ah. Hello, there,' he said without much warmth. I knew how he felt, because I was feeling it, too. Likeable enough, but not here and now. This was going to need careful handling.

'William, I do thank you for coming,' Barbara said in her quiet voice. So quiet you had to bend towards her to hear it. 'I'm afraid it wasn't much of a send-off. Poor Jonathan, I didn't know what else to do.'

'Not much choice, is there?' I said. 'I think people would boycott these places if there was. You did all you could, Barbara. Tell me, how did you get here?'

'Taxi,' she said, smiling. 'Are you going to offer me a lift back? Bill said he would, but it's more out of his way. And Hugo's started working for him – did you know? Just a trial period, to see how he likes it. Aren't you, darling?'

Hugo ignored this, but I thought it was very good news indeed. 'What are you working at, then?' I asked him, trying not to sound too pleased.

'Oh, surveys,' Hugo said.

'Helping me measure the old buildings down there in Dockland,' Charrington rumbled. 'As good a way to get to know the trade as any. We'll need to have a meeting at your place, William, to sort out that gable end and who's going to pay for it. Best if you and that builder chap would both come, to get it all agreed at one go. Unless you want to keep out of it?'

'No, I don't,' I said, 'not at all. The sooner we can get back on good terms, the better.'

'Manage tomorrow?'

'Afternoon, yes.'

'Right-oh. I'll fix it, and give you a ring. Bye now.' He and Hugo climbed into a red Volvo estate with survey poles in the back. Barbara stood, watching them go; she waved at Hugo, who lifted a hand in farewell. Then they were gone. And not a peep of protest from Charrington – too sensible for that, once Barbara had made her choice clear.

'Mine's over there,' I said, steering her towards the Citroën.

'Well then?' Barbara said, as soon as we were settled in the car.

'About Ludwig?'

'Yes! – I can't wait to hear all about it!' She sat half-turned in her seat, green eyes on my face. I engaged gear, got us out of the car park and on to the road. The traffic was heavy, but fast moving.

195

'You're sure you want to hear about him, Barbara? I mean, you're not too upset by all that.'

'The funeral? No – maybe I should be, but I didn't feel it had anything to do with Jonathan, did you? I feel fine, glad that it's all over, in fact. Oh dear, I'm afraid you'll be disappointed in me.' She put her hand on my arm for a moment. I took a quick glance at her. Women have a special look when they've made a certain decision, and I thought I saw it there. My pulse rate rose a little. Tuesday, goodnewsday.

I told her about Ludwig – the defunct studio, the strange white room where he lived, and about the two gangsters – no less – who'd tied me up for the night, thinking that I was after information to sell to a rival organisation. 'His daughter helped me to escape – do you know her?'

'I've heard of her,' Barbara said, sounding as if she was wondering whether to believe all this. 'Isn't she rather pretty?'

'In a lumpy, German sort of way,' I admitted. 'Then we were chased through a forest by these two thugs, being shot at. Ludwig turned up then, and rescued us. He shot one of the thugs; not fatally, but through the chest. I don't know if he survived – we let his partner drive him away.'

'I think you're . . . Do you promise me you haven't made all this up?' Barbara said after a stunned silence,

'I promise.'

'Really?'

'I'll show you the bruises.'

'Oh! Well, then . . .'

'Barbara, I know it sounds fantastic, but things like this are happening all the time. Is it any odder than Jonathan getting shot?'

'But what was Ludwig doing with these people?'

'I don't know exactly,' I said, remembering Eva's telephone call – some reason would have to be given, couldn't be avoided. 'But I think, from what I overheard when I was tied up, that Ludwig had been delivering illegal cargoes to Amsterdam and other places.'

'What things?'

'I assume drugs – isn't that the usual trade? I believe it's easier to make big profits on drugs in Amsterdam as the laws are not so strict. But he could have been delivering stolen cars, guns, gold, anything. It doesn't matter to us – the point is, it's illegal, and got him into bad trouble. The police caught one of the others involved, and that's scared him into giving it up. Permanently, according to his daughter.'

'Oh my God,' Barbara said faintly.

'Well, it's not all bad, Barbara, is it? He seems to have given it up.'

'Yes,' she said, 'but I feel as if I've just had an albatross hung round my neck. Suppose he does it again, and gets caught! For *drug smuggling*! That's just about the worst kind of publicity Nature Store could get – a connection like that. Think what the papers would do with it!'

'Turn on more, with Nature Store,' I suggested.

'Oh, William! Don't! Honestly, I'm not joking. It could destroy everything I've built up.'

'But, Barbara – he's your ex twice removed.'

'And just after Jonathan's death, too. They're calling it "The Cassell Killing". That's bad enough, but this about Ludwig could be far, far worse. I think it would be the end, I really do.'

'Shoppers aren't that easily put off, surely?'

'It's not the shoppers, it's the *shareholders*. We could be wiped out overnight. We're very fully stretched right now, with a whole string of new shops opening.'

I took my left hand from the wheel, and reached for hers. 'Barbara,' I said, 'you're worrying too much, I'm sure of it. As long as any trouble he causes takes place in Germany, it can't affect you here much, if at all. So what you've got to do is to make sure he stays there. He's short of money – you could pay him an allowance, perhaps, on that condition. Or you could threaten to shop him – better still, I could do that for you, so he won't realise it's the last thing you really want to do. Between us, I'm sure we'll find a way to keep him in Germany, and out of trouble. And his daughter will help – she's a good-hearted kid.'

Barbara made no reply, so I looked round at her again. The green eyes were on me, at full glow. I had to tear mine away, back to the road, before I ran down a whole bus queue without noticing.

'I do believe you're right,' she said at last. 'Yes, I think you are. Oh, William, I can't thank you enough. If you hadn't found all this out, the whole thing could have blown up without warning. Now, at least, I've got a chance to prevent it. I can't get over how kind you are, to go to all this trouble.'

Definitely my day, today, with ladies falling over each other with gratitude. Surely, this time . . .

'No trouble,' I said. 'I'd do a lot more than that for you, Barbara, just let me know. But right now, I'd better have my hand back – Marble Arch is coming up.'

'Oh!' she said, 'sorry.' We drove the last ten minutes in silence, but it was the right sort of silence, with a song in it. That's how it seemed. Well, a *hum* at least, if cynics will swallow that.

Barbara's bedroom was at the back of her house, facing away from the square. As in her living-room, she'd gone to town with fabrics, including masses of net curtain, gathered to each side of the wide sash window just far enough to leave a glimpse of the trees in her garden. She didn't seem to mind about this gap: maybe she knew that nobody could see in, or maybe she liked justice to be seen to be done. There are a few of those, I'm told, though I haven't encountered one myself.

Justice, in fact, had been abrupt, premature, and inadequate the first time round. Too much stress and unfulfilled excitement lately. But it was going better, now. Through the window, a few last handfuls of tattered leaves still clung to the nearest tree; rain drummed softly on the glass and slid down the panes, out of sight. Barbara's body lay stretched out beneath me, warm where we touched, slim but not skinny, just as I had imagined.

'You're beautiful, Barbara.'

'Am I?'

'You know you are . . .'

I bent my head to kiss her. She kept her eyes closed, her head slightly turned to one side, a cat-like smile on her lips. Her way was receptive, submissive – she moved only as I moved, shook only as I made her shake, stopped when I stopped. But she was beautiful.

'Will you get married again? Have you thought of that?'

'Married? I don't know . . .' she murmured, smiling more.

'Could you live alone?'

'William . . . all these questions . . .'

'I want to know about you.'

'Now?'

'Now is the best time.'

'Oh, I don't know.'

'You must know. How do you feel . . . about this, for instance?'

'This? Well . . . I like it.'

'Like it?'

'Yes. Of course.'

'Should I go slower? Faster? Do something else?'

'Oh William . . . this is fine.'

'I like to know, you see.' *And I can't tell. So I have to ask.*

'You're sweet.'

'As long as you're happy.'

How long have I been doing this? A clock by the bedside says ten to five, and it's almost dark outside. Time to finish it.

Barbara's body shakes as I use more force, more speed, trying to carry her with me. I see her lips part – will she cry out? – no, it's only an adjustment to her smile. I have to repeat to myself: she's beautiful, beautiful . . .

Well, it worked – that's over. I don't like to collapse on her, it wouldn't feel cosy, just brutish. I roll to one side, instead.

Oh, Barbara. Was it me? Or you? Or maybe us?

'You're sweet,' she says again, still smiling. She seems quite happy. Is that all she wants, or expects?

'You have first go in the bathroom,' she says in her soft, her everyday voice.

I go.

What had I expected, anyway? I asked myself a little later, as I sat alone on the bed, gloomily struggling into my socks. Had I really hoped that having a fling with Barbara was going to be any kind of compensation for falling out with Claudine, light of my life and queen of my hive? Had I been hoping that Barbara might turn out to be more than a fling – that I had found a new planet to orbit, serene and life-supporting, ready to replace the world which seemed to be crumbling under my feet. Was I ready to commit that degree of treachery, be that kind of rat?

Barbara emerged from the bathroom, dressed and smiling. I bent to conclude the battle with socks and shoelaces designed, as they must have been, by moralists intent on punishing men like me.

'Shall we go down?' said my partner in crime.

As we reached the bottom of the stairs, the doorbell rang.

'Hugo's back early,' I said, making a quick check of my attire. The suavest of manners is useless in face of a misbuttoned shirt or unzipped fly.

'It can't be Hugo – he has his own key,' Barbara said, making for the door. She opened it a little way, cautiously.

Through the gap I could see dark clothing. At the same moment I heard, in retrospect, Eva's voice saying, 'When you see him . . .', the significance of which I'd missed completely.

'It's Ludwig,' Barbara said, turning her head to me.

'Tell him to stop turning up on doorsteps like this,' I said. 'This is the third time –'

'But we want to talk to him, don't we?' Barbara said.

'Do we?'

'Actually,' Barbara said with a crispness to her voice, 'you said *you* would.'

Oh, but that was years ago, before . . . before I realised . . .

'Of course, Barbara – so I did.'

She opened the door wide. Ludwig stood there: his blue gaze focussed on me like a death ray; in a moment the front of my jacket over my heart would begin to smoulder and then burst into flames. I had to assume command of the situation, or try to.

'Come in, Ludwig,' I said, 'nice to see you again. Let's all go into the sitting-room: there are things I have to say to you.'

To my surprise, he came. He saw. And we conquered.

CHAPTER 18

Stable Position

With the thesis that the ego is the sole seat of
anxiety – that the ego alone can produce and feel
anxiety – we have established a new and stable
position.

SIGMUND FREUD

If hell exists, it's more likely to be a place of freezing cold than
roaring flames. That's always been my opinion, and another
night of sinking temperature in Church Street did nothing but
confirm it. Nobody can be as brittle and icy as the French when
they're feeling out of sympathy with you; Claudine, I was discovering for the first time in our life together, was not the exception I had supposed. She produced breakfast, she got the
girls off to school, and she settled down to the October trading
account, all with perfect correctitude and frozen features. It was
as chilly in the house as though the heating had broken down.
I knew there was no point in another discussion, not yet; I had
to get out, and left at midday for the warehouse, intending to
get a pub lunch before the afternoon meeting with Bill Charrington and Ron Green.

Pete was at the warehouse, and it was a relief to see his
cheerful, crafty face after the graveyard gloom of Church Street.
He took one look at me.

'Cheer up, guv – it may never 'appen.'

'It already has,' I said.

'What's that, then? If you don't mind my askin'.'

I found I didn't mind, not at all. In fact, just at present,
wading as I was in a mire of suspicion and conflicting emotions,
Pete's essential practicality was just what I needed. On impulse,
I said: 'Grab a bottle of red from the samples, and we'll split it
in the office. It'd do me good to talk.

He shot me another glance, and nodded. I went to the office
and he joined me there, putting an opened bottle of Crozes-

Hermitage on the table. Just like him, I thought – a good bottle to take advantage of the opportunity, but not so good that I would feel exploited. Two glasses had also appeared. I poured us each a generous dollop.

'Cheers!'

'How's it going with Miss Mullarkey?' I asked. She must have a first name, I supposed, but it couldn't possibly suit her as well.

'Miss Mullarkey and me's all right,' Pete said, 'definitely. Goin' from strength to strength, you might say.'

'Good,' I said. 'I'm glad to hear that.' I took a large mouthful of wine, rolled it round, swallowed it slowly. Habit mostly, but also, when it came to the point, I didn't know where to start.

'Things not so good up your way?' Pete prompted.

'No. Claudine and I . . .' I took another swallow of wine. 'Look, I might as well put you in the picture. I've got to talk to someone, and I may need your help again. It's like this . . .'

Ten minutes later, Pete had the outline. There was silence while he digested it. Then he said: 'Don't really think she meant to go off with 'im, do you?'

'No, I suppose not. But . . .'

'*Suppose*! You're not sure then?'

'I didn't think so, I never imagined she would. It's just that, since I tackled her about it, she's been like ice – cut herself off completely. Of course, she could just be feeling guilty – she didn't want to talk about herself and Jonathan, tried her hardest not to. It's against all her instincts to admit to anything like that, anything that might rock the boat. I don't think the police understand, but it's the way we live, and it's worked for us both up to now, as I've told Priestly already.'

'Till the rozzers stirred it all up.'

'Yup. Until then. They think I knew about Jonathan, and thought him enough of a threat to have him knocked off. I'm the only one who can be sure I didn't.'

'I believe you,' Pete said.

'Thanks. But why?'

'Not the type, are you? I mean, you might 'ave flown off the handle an' dotted 'im one, but to have 'im nobbled like that, at

202

second hand – no, not your style, is it? The Law must know that, else you'd be inside already.'

'Maggie said something like that.'

'Stands out a mile, dunnit? It's all the wrong way round, that's what I think. Miss Mullarkey thinks so, too.'

'How do you mean?'

'Well. That Jonathan, from what I've heard, 'e's just the type to pay other people to do 'is dirty work for 'im. By rights, it oughter have been 'im having you knocked off – the other way round, see?'

The wine in my mouth seemed suddenly to taste sour. 'Oh no,' I said quickly when I'd choked it down, 'don't say that – you see what that could mean, don't you? That Claudine must have let him think that she'd go . . .' Or worse, *that she knew it was going to happen* . . .

Wild ideas were flaring in my brain. It wasn't possible that she could have been party to *that*. Was it? Almost at once I pulled myself together, realised it wasn't possible, of course not. Was I getting so off balance that I'd forgotten where she was, and *how* she was, when the shooting happened? Impossible to stage-manage that, to have that degree of self-control. To choose to watch your partner of many years blown to shreds before your eyes, oh no, not possible, no alibi could be worth that.

'I'm sorry, Pete.' He'd been watching my face. 'Not been sleeping well. Thoughts getting a little wild. You were saying?'

'Sure you're all right?'

'Yes. Thanks. Nothing a glass of wine won't cure. More for you?'

'Why not.' I poured us both some.

'You were saying . . .?' I reminded him.

'Ah. Well. Hardly like to mention it, with you gettin' so upset an' all.'

'I'm all right now. What was it?'

'Well. I reckon it could have bin 'im, Mr Cassell, what organised the shooting.'

'But –'

'Doesn't mean your missus 'ad anythink to do with it, not at all. Could just have been Mr Cassell, on 'is own. Miss Mullarkey says, if you look for a one-word clue to murder, she'd pick

203

"obsession". That's what it takes to drive a man to murder – an obsession of one sort or another. 'Course, it's not always easy to spot, but once you have, there's your man. I reckon Mr Cassell could have been obsessed with your Claudine.'

I couldn't see it, and said so. 'Jonathan wasn't an obsessive type – and he never had much trouble getting the women he wanted. Why should he get obsessed with Claudine?'

'That's just the point, see? If he wanted to take her away, and she wouldn't go . . . well, that might have done it. Not used to setbacks, was 'e? Might have taken it hard. Got obsessed, like I said.'

I liked the sound of it better than what had gone before. Claudine refusing to go, telling Jonathan what she'd told me, that all she wanted was to be entertained, not run away with. Such as we both understood.

But, I belatedly realised, the theory had no foundation anyway. Because, according to the information already collected by Pete on that Sunday morning immediately after the shooting, the word was that the 'wrong man' had been shot – this based on the newspaper reports that listed me as the victim. *I* was the 'wrong man', so there'd been no doubt that Jonathan was the 'right man', the intended victim.

'Ah,' Pete said. 'Well, we could've been wrong about that.'

'But how? The gunman saw Jonathan's face – he stepped right up and fired his second barrel right into it. He must have known, or thought he knew, who he was shooting. It must have been a shock when he saw in the paper that he'd shot, not Jonathan Cassell as intended, but William Warner. He wouldn't have shot his own employer, would he?'

Pete said nothing, but drank some wine, watching my face. I went on trying to work it out for myself, as he seemed to expect this. Eventually the penny dropped.

'Oh,' I said.

'I see you got it,' Pete said. 'Simple really. If you're a villain paid to knock off a geezer, an' when you step up to your target to finish 'im off you find you've jus' shot your employer in the dinner pail, it's a bit late to say sorry, innit?'

'So you go ahead and finish him off, because you've got your identity to conceal,' I said slowly.

'Yeah. Won't do your professional reputation no good, but you're not goin' to get complaints, are you?' Pete said, downing the last of his wine.

I wasn't hungry, but Pete insisted on giving me a cheese sandwich from his lunch box, and we sat in the office, chewing cheese and finishing the Crozes-Hermitage while following this new line of thought. If I had been the target, and Jonathan the gunmen's employer, was I still at risk? No, I decided, because with their employer dead the gunmen would have nothing to gain by a new attempt on me. No – the worst of this new theory was that it would be more difficult to clear up: with the paymaster dead, the evidence could only be got from the gunmen themselves and, even if caught, they would almost certainly be unreliable, saying whatever might spread the blame, plunging us all deeper into a fog of uncertainty. There might never be outside confirmation of how far Claudine had been involved with Jonathan, and although I was more than ready to believe her version, she herself might find the situation impossible to live with. It would be better, far better, if Jonathan had been the target, killed for some reason which had nothing to do with either Claudine or myself. And it was still possible – I could hope for that. What progress were the police making? I must insist on their telling me. Was Priestly still interested in me, or was that a false impression? He'd do better to concentrate on the other end of the puzzle – find the gunmen. What were the chances of that?

'You never can tell,' Pete said. 'But the Law always know more than they let on: they 'as their little ways, and they can surprise you.' He didn't sound very hopeful.

'It's got to be sorted out,' I said, 'and I don't mind telling you, if I can see anything useful I can do, I'll do it.'

'Now,' Pete said reprovingly, 'now. You don't want to go stirring up trouble, not with these sort of fellers. You could get fed to the pigs yourself if they got wind of it. Leave it to the Law – they're fireproof.'

I said nothing. He was right – I knew that. But all the same . . .

'Ah well. Don't say I didn't warn you,' Pete said, his eyes on my face.

'I won't.'

'And wished you the best of luck. You'll need it.'

'Uh-huh,' I acknowledged, already regretting my outbreak of mulishness, and wanting to forget it. Patience was what I needed, must learn to practise. Meanwhile . . . What time was it? Two o'clock . . .

'The architect should be here soon,' I said. It would be good to have a change of subject, to one more constructive, less frustrating. 'And Ron Green. If he consents to turn up.'

'Your architect's here already,' said a voice from the doorway. 'And the builder said he'd come. Time will tell – not too much of it, I hope. I must get back early today – letters to get in the post.'

I had turned round with a start, having not heard him come up, and now saw a strange, a new, a beardless Bill Charrington. I wouldn't have recognised him with his bushy whiskers all gone – they'd been so much in character with him.

'Bill!' I said. 'Why?'

'Time for a change,' he said shyly. 'And it was going grey at the edges. Didn't fancy the slow change into Father Christmas.'

I guessed the main reason was otherwise and began with a B, but didn't suggest it. We walked to the front of the warehouse, talking, while Pete went back to work sorting cases of wine for delivery. As we reached the pass door, a Transit van drew up outside.

'That should be the builder,' Charrington said. We stepped through the pass door, Charrington first. I braced myself for the first meeting with Ron since his drunken telephone call. Had he mellowed, had he accepted that I'd called the lawyers off and was trying to solve the problem of our cracked gable wall amicably? Or had he come simply to hurl abuse?

'Hello,' I said, holding my hand out. 'Glad you could come. Mr Charrington here is going to tell us what needs doing, and then we'll talk about the cost and how to meet it. With the lawyers out of the way, it shouldn't take long.'

Ron Green brushed his palms together to remove some of the cement dust which caked them, and then grasped my hand. He looked a wary but chastened man. Behind Ron was a sullen dark-haired youth in jeans and a black T-shirt with a white

206

death's head on it. 'My eldest, Gary,' Ron said with a sideways jerk of his head.

I nodded at Gary, who looked away. 'Well, we're in your hands, then, Bill,' I said to Charrington.

We all trooped to the back of the building where the cracked gable wall was, and the meeting got under way.

'Well, that went all right. Many thanks, Bill.'

'Don't mention it,' he said. 'All in the day's work, things like this. Didn't give any trouble, did he? Mind you, I don't think he should, as you're paying for all the materials – he's only got to do the work, not find any money.'

'You think I've been soft?'

Charrington shrugged. 'I think he's a lucky man. But knows it. You wanted peace, and you've got it – at a price.'

I waved him in through the office door ahead of me. 'There's something to be said for having a legal eagle screeching in the background,' I said. 'Scared poor Ron out of his skin, practically. If the case had gone on, he could have lost his yard, his house, the lot. Savage stuff.'

'Who's your lawyer?' Charrington asked, dropping into a chair.

'You know him. Or at least he says he knows you. Paul Simpson.'

'Simpson! Yes, I know him all right. Never met him, but had dealings.' He put his briefcase on the table, paused, and then put out a hand to straighten it. I've noticed Julian do that: architects like things to line up.

'Tell me more,' I said curiously.

'About Simpson?' Without his beard, Charrington's face looked less all-weathering, more thoughtful. It was more lined than I would have guessed. Would Barbara like that? I wondered. 'I shouldn't say this, but you might soon find yourself looking for a new lawyer,' Charrington said.

'I was thinking of changing,' I said. 'Simpson seems to be turning into some kind of middle-aged swinger, all transatlantic chat and Italian suiting. I don't think I can stand it. But you've never met him?'

'No,' Charrington said, 'but I can believe that. No, what I
207

know of Mr Simpson is from the other side of the fence. He was handling a claim against us.'

'You and Jonathan?'

'Jonathan and myself, as partners, that's right. A leaking roof on an office block Jonathan designed, as a matter of fact. Small leak, but over the computer room. Bad luck, was that.'

'Expensive damage?'

'You can say that again. And Simpson made the most of it.'

'But you're insured?'

'Oh yes. But we wanted to fight it – it was the contractor's fault, not ours – to keep our record clean and our premiums down. Insurance already costs us as much as rent, and this would have jacked our annual premium up to a new level – permanently. However – underwriters wanted to settle.'

'Why was that?'

'Simpson.'

'He scared them?'

'That was stage one, yes. It's the American system catching on here – anything goes wrong, anything at all, and folks are reaching for their lawyers. Half the professional negligence cases brought since 1950 have happened in the last five years. Think what that means to us poor bloody architects! We're getting afraid to go out of doors, it's that bad. Insurers are scared stiff by it. Stage two was – we think – he offered to do a deal.'

'That's what it's all about though, isn't it? Getting the best deal for the client?'

'Not for his client. For himself.'

Charrington gave a grim little chuckle. Life's like that, it seemed to imply. I knew there were bent lawyers, of course, I just hadn't figured Simpson to be one. Like accidents, they were something that happened to other people. But after a moment's thought I could accept that what Charrington had said made perfect sense. More than that, it *explained* the new swinging Simpson, the re-styling and the go-getting. He must be in the grip of some inner compulsion – inferiority complex or identity crisis or whatever – as crippling as cancer though visible only in its symptoms. I should consult Miss Mullarkey again.

'I can believe it,' I said. 'What will happen to him, do you suppose? If he's started taking backhanders, it must be only a matter of time before he gets caught. Though sometimes you read about people who've got away with it for years, against all odds. You'd have to think you would, if you were doing it.'

Charrington stood up. 'I'd best be going,' he said, 'if that's all you need of me for today. I'll confirm what we agreed with your builder in writing, to avoid misunderstandings. And I take it, from what you've just said, that Simpson is now out of it. We don't want him upsetting the applecart.'

'I'll make sure of it,' I said. 'Tell me – did you get anything definite on backhanded dealings?'

'He's still your lawyer,' Charrington said.

'Oh, come on,' I said. The implications were beginning to take shape. It was like seeing an old puzzle from a new viewpoint. 'You know what I'm getting at, don't you? It must have occurred to you, as well.'

Charrington gave his grim little chuckle again. 'Ask him yourself,' he suggested gently, 'why don't you? I'd be interested to hear what he says.'

'You're bluffing him?'

'I didn't say that.'

'But you haven't shown him any evidence?'

'I haven't. And I must be going now. Goodbye, William.'

'But Jonathan did?'

Charrington shook his head. 'Ask him. Not me.'

He was going through the door. I leapt to my feet. 'Wait! Bill – you've got to tell me this. *Was the claim withdrawn?*'

'Oh yes,' he said, 'it was. Goodbye now.'

I stood in the office doorway, looking but not seeing Charrington walk away, ker-lap, ker-lap, through the warehouse to the pass door and out into the street. I hardly noticed the crashing of crates and the clink of bottles as Pete went about his common round, his daily task. It was a new angle, this, and looking good.

Jonathan had persuaded Simpson that he had evidence which, if reported to the authorities, would get him struck off, stripped of his professional qualification. Simpson had believed this, and dropped the claim against Jonathan. End of story.

But was it? Suppose Jonathan had turned the tables on

209

Simpson, and wanted cash in return for silence? Or suppose Simpson decided he couldn't live with Jonathan's threat hanging over his head? No – in that case, he'd have had to do away with Charrington as well. Unless he was persuaded that only Jonathan knew the evidence. Which might have been the case if Jonathan was already getting paid to keep quiet.

Too many questions.

It was easy enough to see why Charrington didn't want to tell me any more. He didn't believe that Simpson had got Jonathan shot, and didn't want to disturb the status quo – claim dropped and Simpson in check. Would the claimants take their case to another lawyer? Not if Simpson had provided them with learned counsel's opinion that it should be dropped – possible to secure such an opinion with selective evidence, as counsel are guided by what instructing solicitors tell them are the facts of the case.

But Charrington, for all his confident manner, could be wrong. He hadn't met Simpson – I had, and now I thought I recognised signs of desperation, of growing imbalance, of a man near the end of his tether. There were loose ends, it didn't quite add up – but why should it? – who knows what goes on inside the head of a man like that, except the man himself?

Still too many questions.

I don't think I can bear simply to feed them into the police machine, to sit there in suspense while Cooper fills his notebook and Priestly stares out of the window in silence. I'll tell them everything, if Charrington agrees, tomorrow.

Meanwhile . . .

This must mean something, I felt sure, looking out at the glittering wet streets through the Citroën's wide windscreen. The single wiper swept back and forth, leaving greasy smears which caught the lights of other cars, silver crescents glowing with red and amber jewels. It must mean something that he wanted me to come after office hours, so that we could talk undisturbed. I could hear again the change in his voice, from artificial bonhomie to conspiratorial hush as I told him that it was urgent, that I had to see him this evening, no, tomorrow wouldn't do. I didn't tell him what it was about, but I did say I'd just had a meeting at my warehouse with Charrington, with the intention of softening him up. Was that foolhardy, if I thought he could be behind the shooting of Jonathan? I reckoned not, because if a trap was to be arranged for me it would surely be sprung as I left, after Simpson had heard all I had to say, rather than on the way in. But I was feeling reckless – yes, I admit it. I was tired of indecision, and in military mood. There comes a time when you have to stop peering out of your foxhole, get out there, and gain some ground. This was it.

There'd been time to go back to Church Street, collect the old Webley from the deed box, and reload it with shot cartridges. I could feel it as I drove, heavy and uncomfortable against my midriff, tucked into my belt under my jacket. That was one advantage Jonathan didn't have: the other was to be fore-warned. *I* would be watching every street corner, every door-way, every car – and especially every motorcycle.

Simpson's office occupied the top two floors of a house in a side street just off the Tottenham Court Road. I drove past it once, at normal speed, looking for anything that might spell trouble – a parked van, hangers-about – but saw nothing to cause misgiving. I went round the block, passed the office again. Still nothing. I parked round the next corner, in Charlotte Street, outside a brightly lit Italian restaurant. I got out and, under my umbrella, inspected the menu. In the window, I studied the reflection of the street behind me. There were a number of passers-by, all hurrying to get to their destinations and out of the rain. Few carried umbrellas – they must be going out of fashion.

All right. Let's go. Slim precautions, but they'll have to do. I walked rapidly round the corner towards Simpson's office, looking about me but without turning my head. Mustn't look like a target, even if I feel like one. Here's the door.

Push hard, Simpson had said – it'll be unlocked. I did, and it was. There was a light on in the communal hall, and I took a rapid look round the edge of the door, still holding it as a shield of sorts in case anyone inside tried to pull it open and outline me in the doorway. They didn't, and the hall was empty. I made a mental note of the layout, the position of doors, and the turn of the stairs. Then I closed the door and switched off all lights in the hall and stairwell.

After a few seconds, I could see again by the street lighting which came through the fanlight over the entrance door. I moved towards the stairs, reached the bottom, stopped and listened. There was no sound from above. I put my umbrella on the floor, and took out the Webley. Then I started up the stairs, slowly. The stairs were narrow, linoleum-covered, with winders from one flight to the next. The first landing was in darkness. This, I thought, is the place: standing there, you'd only have to wait until the target's head appears, coming round the winders on to the second flight of stairs, lit by the street lighting filtering in below, while up on the landing, you're in darkness . . .

But then, *I'd* turned the light out. With it on, you'd be instantly spotted, and the target would have a clear escape route to the door. So . . .

As I turned the corner of the next flight of stairs I could see a narrow crack of light under a door on the next landing. Simpson's office. He was there, then. Of course, leaving the light on could be a ploy to make me think just that, while he waited in ambush for me somewhere else, outside the office. But where could he hide? The next landing, I knew, was very small, having been partitioned so that the top flight of stairs which led off it was included in Simpson's domain – you had to go into his reception area to get to it. And I was in sight of his door, now. There were no more corners, just the small, plain square landing in front of the door. There was nowhere for him to hide. It looked perfectly safe . . .

I found that I had come to a halt, while still at the turn of the stairs before the last half-flight. *What's this, then?*

Nowhere to hide! Left Brain was quavering.

I *know* that, for Chrissake! So, it's *safe* . . .

Nowhere for *us* to hide, if he opens that door and starts shooting as we walk up to it! Left Brain almost screamed.

I shrank against the wall. True enough. Better think about this before going further. Simpson could be waiting on the other side of that door, gun in hand. Of course, he wouldn't know I'd got one as well; I could get a shot off as soon as I saw the door open; that would keep him back while I retreated down the stairs at speed or, more likely, slithered. Yes.

On the other hand, he might simply be opening the door to let me in. No gun. Embarrassing, to say the least, if I shot at him in those circumstances. No, I couldn't shoot until I saw he had a gun, and by the time I saw that he might already be pulling the trigger. I begin to see why the police sometimes get a little trigger-happy in house searches. The walls box you in, you feel trapped.

A warning shot, perhaps? Let him know I'm armed, will stand no nonsense. *Come on out with your hands up?* Well – hardly. I think he's bent, but I don't know that he's violent. All I'm doing is taking precautions, since somebody did actually shoot Jonathan. In any case, a warning shot with the old Webley would make one hell of a din, bring half the street running. It isn't on.

Nothing for it, then, but to advance. As silently as possible, gun ready. Keeping close to the wall, where the stairs are better supported and less likely to creak.

Or go home, Left Brain wailed.

Shut up. Halfway there already.

A strong, distantly familiar odour came to my nostrils. I sniffed professionally, searched my memory. O–Cedar floor polish, vintage 1969 or thereabouts, last encountered in my father's country house in Devon. A feeling of unease came with it.

Cleaners' cupboard! – Left Brain was at it again.

With Simpson lurking in it? No – there's only one door on this landing.

Sure?

I ran the tape of my last visit here. My memory for visual images is good. Yes, I'm sure.

Well . . . all right, then.

A stair creaked – could Simpson hear that? I paused, listened. Nothing. I moved on and up. The remaining two stairs were solid and silent. I was on the landing.

Directly ahead, the crack of light under the door showed me the way. Still no sound from inside the office. And no telltale shadows across the crack of light to show that Simpson was standing there, ready to throw the door open.

I stood at the hinge side of the door, and reached across for the bell push. Not a bell but a buzzer – I heard it through the door. I waited, Webley at the ready, muzzle pointed to the ceiling.

He's taking his time. I pressed the bell push again.

No footsteps. Still no sound of any sort. Except the hum of distant traffic.

I groped for the door handle, grasped it, and turned it slowly and carefully. When it was turned as far as it would go, I very gently put pressure on the door. If it opened, it could mean that Simpson had planned to spring his trap as soon as I stepped inside. He could be sitting, waiting, gun on lap. In fact, thinking about it some more, it was the most likely moment for him to make his move.

But the door resisted my gentle pressure. I pushed harder. It was definitely locked.

I took a moment to wipe my sweating palms on the seat of my trousers. What next?

It would be an unbearable anticlimax to give up and go home now. An appalling, unacceptable waste of effort and adrenalin. I'd taken risks, wanted answers in recompense.

I bent down, and called through the letterbox.

'Simpson! Are you there? Open the door!'

Through the letterbox I could see grey carpet squares, the bottom of a filing cabinet and one leg of the receptionist's desk, black steel and functional.

I straightened up, found the landing light switch, and blinked in the sudden light. My attention focussed on the lock. It was a Yale cylinder lock, nothing fancy – this was normally an internal door, and the high security stuff would be on the front door. Maybe I could . . . Inside, there would be Simpson's files . . .

I moved to the top of the stairs, and listened. The lower floors were also occupied by office users – I couldn't remember what they were, and hadn't been able to see the names on the way up. In any case, there had been no lights showing under the other doors, and nothing to indicate that anyone else was working late.

What were the options? The door itself was flush, solid, with no glass panel I could tap out a corner of. Shooting the lock off would be fun, but impossibly noisy. I could try a heavy kick, but didn't really want to do that much damage.

Ah! Now is the time to try the credit card trick, often heard about but never attempted. I stuck the Webley back in my belt, and took out my wallet. Come on then, Barclaycard. Into the gap between door and frame, opposite the lock. Go on, then. Push harder. Get in there – what's the matter with you?

It wasn't working. The trouble was, I had to negotiate the card round a right-angle bend, behind the doorstop (which the door closes against) and then between the door and the frame. How professionals manage it I don't know, but I have to report that, for all but the most ill-fitting of doors, a Barclaycard is too stiff.

It wasn't going to work, I could see that. I opened my wallet to put Barclaycard away, his virtue intact.

Then, with the wallet still open, I saw another candidate for the job. I belong, of course, to the International Exhibition Co-Operative Wine Society. Their membership card, looking in its leatherette binding, gold embossed, rather like a miniature British passport, might just . . .

The Yale yielded. The door opened. I stowed away the Wine Society card, took out the Webley again and went cautiously in. I saw nothing but office furniture. Then I turned round.

Simpson was there, after all. But I could see why he hadn't answered the door. It was the Gucci shoes with the gold buckles I caught sight of first, as they came into view at eye level, over the flight of stairs to the top floor of Simpson's office.

'Jesus!' I said out loud.

I stood beside the shoes, and forced myself to look up. He'd put a board across the banisters at the top, and tied one end of a doubled electric flex round it. The other end was round his neck. He'd taken off the Italian jacket to do it, but the trousers bore evidence of the terrors he must have suffered. A stepladder lay on its side where he had kicked it away.

'You poor sod.'

I moved back, away from the dangling figure.

From swinging Simpson.

CHAPTER 19

Relentless Fate

There are people in whose lives the same reactions
are perpetually being repeated unconnected, to their
own detriment, or others, who seem to be pursued
by a relentless fate, though closer investigation
teaches us that they are unwittingly bringing this
fate on themselves.

SIGMUND FREUD

The police said they'd have a car round as soon as possible. 'Be
a few minutes, sir. A lot of calls at the moment.'

'That's all right. I'll wait here for them. And you'll let Superintendent Priestly know?'

'Who, sir?'

'Superintendent Priestly – Chelsea CID. This has a bearing
on the shooting of Jonathan Cassell.'

'What's that sir? Someone's been shot?'

'Superintendent Priestly's looking into it. It was in Chelsea,
about two weeks ago. There could be a connection. Will you
please let him know?'

'I'll see if he can be contacted, sir. Superintendent Priestly,
you say?'

'At Chelsea CID,' I repeated.

'At Chelsea. Right, sir, got that.'

And about time too. Still, it must be difficult: mislaid moggies
one minute, suicide or murder the next. I'd be able to explain
the situation better when the car turned up.

I sat back on the receptionist's chair to ease the pressure of
the Webley in my belt. *The Webley!* – Christ, I'd have to get rid
of that before the police turned up, Priestly would . . .

I couldn't hide it in this office – they might decide to turn the
place inside out. No, I'd have to put it back under the seat in
the car. And be quick about it – the police were already on the
way.

I ran down the stairs to the front door. Outside, the rain had settled into a steady drizzle – I was going to get wet without my umbrella. Where was it? I had it when I arrived, but not when I broke into Simpson's office. Ah yes – I'd left it at the bottom of the stairs, to free my hands for action. I collected it, returned to the front door, and stepped out, holding the umbrella up for shelter while I pulled the door to behind me, closed but not locked.

A glance up and down the street showed that the police car was not yet in sight. I ran down the half-dozen steps to the pavement, turned right, and began walking briskly towards Charlotte Street and the Citroën. Well, it wasn't certain, but there was a good chance that all this would soon be over, that I would be able to live a normal life again, the simple pleasures of bed and board, relations with Claudine restored and business booming. We'd be able to laugh about it all – 'Do you remember? – wasn't it ridiculous?' It would be good to leave Maggie in charge for a couple of weeks and go off somewhere, just Claudine and myself, no kids, nobody but ourselves, get right away from claustrophobic London, police, rain, motives and mistrust, poisonous introspection and the atmosphere of abnormality. Oh yes, that'd be wonderful! Where should we go? Not France, certainly not Germany. Italy, perhaps – we could rent a villa in Tuscany and let that calm and light-hearted landscape work its magic on us, seep into our souls. Yes – let it be Italy. And let poor Simpson be the one we're all looking for, let Priestly find the evidence in his files, let there be a visit or telephone call tomorrow to say, Yes, it's all there, no doubt about it. We've still got the gunmen to find, of course, but that doesn't concern *you*, Mr Warner, it's all over as far as *you're* concerned, we were only doing our duty of course. Of course, I'll reply, quite understand, my dear and most respected superintendent. And the best of luck – goodbye, goodbye!

Oh yes. Wouldn't it be wonderful.

I turned the corner into Charlotte Street. No police car in sight from here. They could be coming the other way, from the Tottenham Court Road direction, of course. But once I've got the gun back into the Citroën I can always say I thought I'd left the car unlocked, dashed out to check, something like that. The main thing is not to have the gun on me. Well, here's the

Citroën. My keys are in my trouser pocket, the left one as usual. I'd better hold my coat across with my right hand, or the gun will be exposed. I'll have to put the umbrella down for this – not enough hands. Still pouring with rain. I wouldn't like to be setting out on a motorbike in this weather, not even in the best of gear, like the bloke over there. The rain drives through the slightest gap, in under the helmet, soaking the scarf until you feel an icy trickle down the back of the neck. Bloody fool is starting up, and his leather jacket's still half open, he'll get . . .

Why is his jacket half open?

And what's that he's got just inside it, making a long awkward bulge in it, as he wheels quite slowly in my direction, engine just ticking over . . .?

Yes! It could be, I think it is, I think I'll just . . .

NOW!

It was a visit to Italy, sort of. But not the sort I'd intended. Much too hurried, and not at all relaxing.

The Italian restaurant I'd parked in front of. Full of somnolent diners, confiding to each other dreams of romance and finance. No shortage of dreams or dreamers, tonight.

'So sorry. All tables are taken.'

Outside, the motorcyclist had stopped, irresolute. I could be making a mistake. But his jacket was still open, letting in the rain. No way was I going back outside. Various scenarios were possible, including giving the head waiter a glimpse of my gun – maybe he'd jump to conclusions.

'Luigi sent me,' I could mutter. 'The payment is late.'

'No! No!' he would plead, 'business is bad – I give you half now, the rest next week? I swear it . . .'

'Luigi says – *now!*'

'*Aie, mama mia . . .*'

No, I couldn't risk it. Having a gun in your belt does prompt these ideas, I'm afraid. But it wasn't necessary.

'Once,' I said, 'I had here the most marvellous *Zuppa di pesche*. With chilled white Sicilian wine – Corvo, I think it was called. Mmmm – delicious! Do you still have it?'

'*Zuppa di pesche?* Ah yes, ees very good, ees delicious as you say. But ees off.'

'Tomorrow, perhaps?'

'Perhaps.'

The motorcyclist had not moved. His black visored helmet, glinting with rain, reminded me of a Japanese warlord. Except that the mad eyes were concealed. It turned towards me, briefly, and then away.

'You wish to book a table for tomorrow?' the waiter prompted.

'Er – I'll telephone in the morning,' I said. 'But perhaps you've got a menu I could take away?'

'Ah no, sorry. Ees different every day. You telephone, and we tell you. So sorry.'

He wasn't a Japanese warlord, though. Just a solitary stupid burk with a sawn-off shotgun. Who deserves two fingers.

I turned towards the street, behind the plate-glass door. The lobby I was standing in was lit from above, me with it. The glass was thick enough to stop shot, except at close range. Nobody else was out there, just the motorcyclist, now with the visored helmet turned directly towards me. He showed no sign of getting off, and the engine was still throbbing.

All right, then – two fingers it is. With my back to the waiter, I made the most of my six foot two, stared straight at the visored helmet, and drew my jacket open far enough to show the Webley. Then I let the jacket fall back, put my right hand inside on the butt of the gun, and reached for the door handle with my left.

'Good night, *signor*, good night. Tomorrow, perhaps,' the waiter said from behind. Outside, there was a crackle of exhaust as the motorcycle took off.

'Certainly,' I said with relief. A tomorrow now seemed more likely.

I crossed the pavement to the car, and slid the Webley back under the seat. Then I got out again, locked the car, and began the return walk back to Simpson's office. Not more than three or four minutes had been wasted by the motorcyclist. I might still get there before the police but, if not, at least I was rid of the gun. The motorcyclist wouldn't know that, though; I must have frightened him off for the time being.

So Simpson *had* laid on a reception for me. And then changed his mind, decided he couldn't escape detection and ruin, and strung himself up. Nothing much had changed, except my feelings towards him. I had felt some sympathy, but no longer, not now he'd nearly succeeded in taking me with him. The police would have to catch these motorcycling maniacs before I could feel safe again. Although, once they heard that Simpson was dead, they'd have no reason to complete their contract, every reason to pack it in.

I turned the corner out of Charlotte Street again. Simpson's office was only a hundred yards away, and still no police car in sight. They were taking a long time in coming, but perhaps suicide didn't rate top priority. This street was quieter, with a few restaurants and small shops, but offices predominated. At this time of the evening there was little traffic.

Which is why I heard him coming.

Yes – it was his exhaust that gave him away. There used to be a water-cooled bike that was almost silent, but it wasn't popular – too complicated, some said, but I was convinced that the reason it flopped was that bikers like to ride on a wave of sound. This one did. Luckily for me.

I looked round, and saw him coming. Must have waited at the next corner, and watched me as I walked back. An opportunity too good to miss. Crazy, though, if he'd seen the gun, knew I was armed. Perhaps through the visor and the glass door he hadn't seen it, perhaps it was just coincidence that he'd driven off at that moment, having decided to follow me and watch for a better opportunity. Or perhaps he *was* a maniac, a lethal hooligan, excited by the prospect of a duel, pistol versus shotgun.

In which case he was luckier than he knew.

There was no cover. The houses had no front gardens: some had doors straight on to the pavement, a few had basements with walled areas leading down to them but, once down, I'd be trapped, with nothing to do but wait for the helmeted head to appear above, outlined against the sky behind the double barrels of his weapon, the last sight I'd see. Nothing to do, then, but run.

I ran. Whatever the world record is for the hundred metres, I broke it that night. Or rather, I was on the way to breaking it when the police car appeared at the far end of the street.

Now I could jump for it, take shelter in the first basement area I came to, because he couldn't follow me there. He had seconds only to shoot and get away before the police arrived.

I jumped. Damp, crumbling brickwork rasped my trousers as I slid into safety. I didn't look out, but heard the motorcycle keep on past, mission abandoned. He was cool about it, and didn't accelerate.

There were concrete steps leading back to street level. I hurled myself up them, and sprinted the last few yards to Simpson's office, outside which the police car was just pulling up. There were two uniformed officers in the front. Panting, I tore open a rear door, and fell in, on to the back seat.

'I'll explain as we go,' I gasped, 'but spin this thing round and get after that motorcycle – if you can't catch him, then at least try to get close enough to see the number. I think he's got a sawn-off shotgun, and . . .'

'Now, hold on,' the officer in the passenger seat said, as both of them turned to stare at me. 'What's all this about, then? You can't just . . .'

'For God's sake! Just *do* it! – *please*. I'll explain as we go.' I looked out of the back window. The motorcyclist had nearly reached the far end of the street, and was about to turn left into Tottenham Court Road. He seemed in no hurry, was hardly more than ambling along. One of his twin rear lights wasn't working. The number was – it was just too far to see the goddam number.

'You can still do it,' I urged. 'He's going slow on purpose, so as not to look suspicious – catch him up, and see what he does then. Oh, come *on!*'

'Can't do that, sir. We're already on a call,' the same officer said.

'I know, a suicide, I'm the one that rang you, it's all connected,' I almost shouted. Through the rear window, the motorcyclist disappeared round the corner.

'Just take a look then, shall we?' the driver said to his companion.

'All right. But you, sir – you'd better have your story ready.'

'And you'd better get ready to explain why you blew the only chance there's been to identify one of the Cassell gunmen,' I said bitterly. But it was drowned in the din as the driver started the motor and revved it for take-off.

I think if it had only been up to the driver, we might have succeeded. He had the Ford Escort round and going up the street like a rocket. But when we reached the Tottenham Court Road end, there was no sign of the motorcycle. We spun left and shot up as far as Warren Street tube station, siren going and blue lamp flashing: traffic parted ahead of us like twin tidal waves. But it was too late. The bike had gone. The lamp and siren were switched off, and we cruised back to Simpson's office at normal speed, while I tried to explain what I thought was going on. It didn't sound too good. Leading the way in and up the stairs, I reflected that the next disaster could be to find that someone had been in, and removed the body.

But they hadn't. Simpson still swung from his halter of twisted flex, his face, far above us, twisted upwards as though he'd found something of compelling interest to study on the ceiling. His palms, I hadn't noticed before, were streaked with congealing blood. The smell, which I had noticed, seemed stronger.

'Shat himself, poor bugger,' the driver said.

'Often do.'

'Seen one before, have you?'

'Look,' I said, 'I'll be in his office, through there, if you want me. Do you know if Superintendent Priestly is coming?'

'No, sir. Where's he from, then?'

'Chelsea CID. He's in charge of this case – or at least, of the Cassell case, which this is a part of, as I've explained. I told them to contact him, when I rang to report this.'

'Ah. Well, I expect they'll have done that, sir.'

'Better get on the blower. Check it with control,' the driver said.

'Me?'

'Why not.'

'Four flights of stairs is why not.' But he went, all the same.

'He's a bit knackered. Up most of last night,' the driver said.

'That explains it.'

I went into Simpson's office. In the framed photograph on his desk, Maryanne was still poised on her skis, still blonde, still smiling, but holding the arm of a corpse. Somebody would have to tell her. Bags not me. I sank into the chair I'd been in so recently, on that last visit. It was good to sit down, I realised. I was feeling a bit shaky, to be honest. Finding Simpson like that, and then feeling sure I was going to get shot at, sprinting down the street, jumping into cover, running up steps, thrown about in the back of a racing police car – it was enough for one evening.

And it wasn't over yet. There was bound to be a long session with Priestly. I'd told Claudine I was seeing Simpson, not to expect me back until late, that I'd find my own supper. Suited her well enough, I could see that. Acknowledged with a nod and an *'entendu'*. In spite of which, or because of which, I'd better give her a ring now, be extra attentive, if I want to start winning her round. It isn't fair, but women aren't interested in rights and wrongs; what they value most is effort. You've got to be on the short list to start with, of course. And I wasn't sure of that, not now, not any more.

Mind you, I had some high cards to play. It would take a Lady Macbeth to react impassively to these.

'Ah, *mon dieu!*'

'With twisted electric flex,' I said, rubbing it in a bit. 'All he could find, I suppose.'

'Oh, *le pauvre*, oh oh. *Et c'est toi qui l'as trouvé?*'

'Yes. I, er, the door was open, I went in, and there he was. I rang the police – they're here now. I'll have to stay and make a statement. So I'll be back late. There's more, but I won't go into that now.' Both policemen were standing nearby, or I would have been tempted to elaborate.

'See you later, darling. Don't wait up for me.' *But perhaps she'd insist?*

'All right,' she said, ringing off. *No, she wouldn't.*

I put the telephone down. There'd been sympathy for Simpson, but a lot less than I'd hoped for me.

'Well? When's Priestly going to get here?' I said. 'If he's not coming . . .'

'Superintendent Priestly's on his way now, sir.'

'Oh,' I said, 'well then. Good. I hope he gets here soon. Not exactly the Flying Squad, is it?'

'It wouldn't be, sir. Not for a suicide. Not going anywhere, this gentleman, is he, sir?'

'No.' From where I sat at the reception desk, I could see Simpson's shoes, turning slowly in mid-air, the gold buckles glinting as the light caught them. 'I'm a bit edgy – it's all been a bit much . . .'

'That's all right, sir. Why don't you go back into that office, wait for the Superintendent there?'

'Yes. Thanks – I think I will.'

In due course – that lugubrious phrase, so well suited to Priestly, whose whole life, I had no doubt, had been conducted at a steady pace which must have ensured the missing of innumerable boats – in due course, he came. With him came a photographer, and a plain clothes officer I hadn't seen before. I stayed in Simpson's office and, after a tour of Simpson, they came to me there. I got up to receive them.

'Good evening,' I said. 'If that's the right way to describe it.'

'Sergeant Thomas,' the new man said. He had a dark, humorous face. 'Better for some than others,' he added. I could hear the Welsh in it.

'You found him, Mr Warner, I understand?' Priestly said.

'Shall we sit down?' I suggested. We arranged ourselves round Simpson's desk; I gestured Priestly into the boss's chair. 'Yes. I asked for a meeting – I'd better begin at the beginning.'

It took some time. I gave Priestly the whole story, including what Charrington had told me about Simpson's suspected double-dealings over negligence claims. I had to, whether Charrington liked it or not, if the police were going to make any sense of what had happened – and they would have got there in the end, anyway. I didn't suppose Charrington would have expected me to do otherwise.

'You say you found the door open?' Priestly asked.

'Pushed shut, but on the latch,' I said glibly. 'Like the one downstairs.' Well, that *had* been. And I'd put the office door on the latch when going out to dump the Webley.

'You went out, sir, before the patrol car got here?'

'Yes. It seemed to be a long time in coming, and I went out to see if there was any sign of it.' A better story than going to check my car was locked. 'Then, when I got to Charlotte Street, I saw the motorcyclist I've told you about.'

'That was when you'd walked on, and were near your car?' Priestly said.

'Yes.' *He may be slow, but he's no fool.* 'I thought, as I'd got that far, I'd just check the car – can't be too careful, these days.'

'I see.' He went into one of his silences. I looked at Thomas, but he kept his eyes on his notebook. Eventually Priestly said: 'Just tell me again, sir, why you thought this motorcyclist had a gun.'

'Yes.' I thought about it. 'Well, for a start, his jacket was half open, although it was raining quite hard – a heavy drizzle. He must have been getting wet. Then, he was quite clearly hanging about, waiting. He kept the engine running. It was odd – suspicious behaviour you could certainly have called it.'

'Waiting for someone to come out of the Italian restaurant, perhaps? A girlfriend, one of the waiters coming off duty?'

Was that possible? 'No, I don't think so. Surely, in that case, he would have parked the bike and waited inside, not sat out there in the rain with his engine running.'

'I see.'

'And then, of course, he drove off alone. Then reappeared, behind me, when I was walking back to this office.' Yes, I'd been sure all right; I wouldn't forget that sprint, not ever. 'It wasn't any one thing but the whole episode, taken together, that convinced me.' Yes, that was it.

'Convinced enough to do that to your trousers,' Thomas put in.

I looked down. Mossy brickwork had visibly taken its toll.

'So I see,' Priestly said.

There was another silence. Something else had convinced me, too – what was it? Through the open door came another series of flashes like summer lightning. 'That's it, then,' a muffled voice said. The photographer appeared in the doorway, and nodded at Priestly. 'Be with you in a moment,' Priestly said. 'But you can take him down, now. Gently, mind. I'll want another look before he goes.'

'The visor!' I said. 'I knew there was something else. He kept his visor down all the time I could see him. Reminded me of a Japanese medieval warrior.'

'Give them a hand, Thomas,' Priestly said. 'Get the contents of his pockets out, check them over, the usual. And find where that flex came from.'

'Right, sir.'

Stumbling feet, grunts and muttered instructions from outside the door. They were being remarkably thorough, surely, for a . . .

'I suppose it *was* suicide?'

Priestly looked at me. 'What makes you say that, Mr Warner?'

'All this trouble. Is it usual?'

'There'll have to be an inquest.'

'Oh, yes. But then . . . I suppose you noticed his hands?'

'I did, sir.' Priestly's gaze was still on me.

'Streaked with cuts . . . as if he'd struggled . . .'

'Probably did, Mr Warner. He probably changed his mind, wouldn't you think? But then, the flex was too thin to get a grip on. He wouldn't have had a chance.'

I passed two ambulancemen with a stretcher on the lower landing. And in the street, a car with a printed notice on the windscreen – 'DOCTOR ON CALL' – was just pulling up behind Priestly's Rover. No real need to help with directions, but I paused by the driver's window. He wound it down.

'It's that one,' I said, 'top floor.'

'Ah. Thank you.'

He began to wind the window up again, but I put a finger on it, and he stopped.

'I'd very much like to know this,' I said. 'People who

226

decide to hang themselves – don't they usually contrive to tie their own hands together, first. So they can't change their minds?'

'I'm sorry, I can't . . .'

'I found him,' I said.

'Oh. Well, in that case . . . it all depends how much time they've had to think about it. If it's been carefully planned, you'd be more likely to find the hands tied. What happened here?'

'They weren't tied. Looks as if he had second thoughts.'

'I see. Well, could have been a snap decision, then. But you can't really . . . I'm afraid I must get on.'

'Yes. Thanks. Good night.'

I walked on down the street. The rain had stopped, leaving the pavement shimmering with city lights. Priestly hadn't offered me protection, merely suggested that I went straight home and stayed there. So much for my credibility. No doubt I could have insisted on going home in a police car – he could hardly have refused – but what about tomorrow, and the day after, and all the days after that? I preferred to take precautions, but look after myself.

What progress were the police making, anyway? Priestly wasn't saying. The pair in the panda had missed the chance of catching or at least identifying the motorcyclist. All we knew was that he had one rear light out. Probably a dud bulb, which he'd find and replace tomorrow. I'd told Priestly that, and Thomas had noted it but, as far as I knew, they'd done nothing about it. They could have put out a call, I thought – all right, it was a slim chance, but the only one we'd got. One of their cars might have struck lucky.

I reached the Citroën, and was able to relax a little. Much more of this, and I'll grow eyes in the back of my head. I reached under the seat to check that the gun was within easy reach. Cars feel safe, but you don't have to think for more than a moment to realise that's an illusion, that you can't rely on speeding away from trouble. The First World War started after the Archduke Ferdinand was killed in his car; after that, we've had a string of automobile assassinations from Mafia gangsters to J. F. Kennedy, and beyond. The car identifies you, that's the first problem. Then, you can get stuck in traffic, a fixed target in a glass box.

All right. Do I drive – or take a bus, tube, or taxi?

CHAPTER 20

Sticking Point

> It is tempting at this point to go more deeply into
> the castration complex, but I will stick to our
> subject.
>
> SIGMUND FREUD

I drove, of course. Partly inertia, partly bloody-mindedness. Once back behind the wheel, the familar controls ready to hand and waiting to be used, the gun only inches away under the seat – well, illusion or not, it felt good. I wasn't going to give this up for a seat on public transport, whatever the theoretical reduction of risk.

It was just after nine, and London nightlife was in full swing. I drove north, up to the relative calm of the Marylebone Road, and turned left, heading for home.

It could all be over, quite soon. The police hadn't kept me for long, and it was likely that Priestly would, at this moment, be searching Simpson's office for the evidence that would link him with the killing of Jonathan. And when the news of Simpson's suicide got out tomorrow, then, with their paymaster dead, there'd be no point in the gunmen coming after me again. That was what Pete and I had agreed when we thought that Jonathan was the paymaster, and the same applied to Simpson.

There was a flaw in the reasoning, of course. Why, having set the trap for me, did Simpson then give up the struggle and hang himself? But that wasn't hard to explain, by imagining his state of mind at the time. He set up the trap, but couldn't be sure that something might not go wrong – as, in fact, it did. You could imagine him pacing about the office, working himself into a frenzy of anxiety as the minutes dragged by, as the time of the meeting got nearer and nearer. It was all too much for him: he'd been living on his nerves for too long – and he finally cracked. A snap decision, as the police doctor had (rather

unfortunately) put it. Then, evidently, another change of mind –
but too late. His only consolation might have been that I was
going to cop it, as well – and that he wouldn't be around to
pick up the bill. Half in advance, I've heard, is usual.

I turned into the top of Church Street, and glanced at the car
clock. Not yet half-past nine. Claudine might not yet be in bed.
I could do with a drink, but home wasn't the place for it, not at
present. Somewhere soothing was what I wanted. I drove past
my house, feeling like an outcast – usually, I'm only too glad to
get home. At the bottom of Church Street, I turned right into
Kensington High Street. A shortage of pubs, there. Plenty of big
bustling hotels, but that wasn't what I wanted, either. Now,
down in Edwardes Square, there's the Scarsdale ...

Whisky should do the trick. I had a double Laphroaig and
water, tasting like a fiery bog. Some say you shouldn't water
malt whisky, but they often do in Islay. I had another one,
without water, to check the difference. The taste of peat was
almost too much. Then I went to have a pee.

It's popular with Sloanes, the Scarsdale, and the green wellie
brigade were there in force that night. Even the graffiti tends
that way. On the wall above the urinal a neat pencilled notice
caught my eye: 'Nigel Deeply Admires Fiona Barker-Harlowe.'
The pure simplicity of this message was somewhat spoilt by the
advice which other, cruder souls had thought it necessary to add
all round it, but I was glad to see that romance still had her
devotees. Even if, for me, the whole idea had become ...

Well, no. Let's admit it. That's why I'm here, isn't it? In
Edwardes Square, barely three minutes walk from ...

'Oh! William!' Barbara said.

After what had happened yesterday, I'd rather intended to
give her a ring, suggest lunch in a few days' time, next week
maybe, and steer the whole thing in the direction of Just Good
Friends. Back off, in other words. It hadn't seemed to me that
the essential chemistry was there. But this evening, and especially now as I saw Barbara standing there above me, in her
doorway, her slim body and pale hair outlined by the hall light
– now I thought I'd been altogether too hasty, too quick to
jump to conclusions. I shouldn't have expected so much so soon;

I should give her, give *us* time to relax together, and see what might evolve.

'Barbara,' I said, 'I'm sorry to turn up like this. I've been meaning to get in touch all day, but things have been happening. I think, when you hear, you'll understand.'

'I see,' she said. 'Yes. Well, um, you'd better come in.'

Not the most ecstatic of welcomes, I recognised. The reason became apparent as she led me into the little sitting-room.

'Well!' I said in the hearty voice that seems to force itself to the surface on these occasions, 'Hello, Bill!'

Charrington stood with his back to the fireplace, facing the door by which I'd come in. He looked burlier than ever in this draperied boudoir. So I'd guessed right about the reason for his shaving off his beard. How far had that got him with Barbara? I wondered. Had I arrived just in time to wreck his plans for that evening? He was putting his best face on it, but there was an uneasiness in his eyes.

'Hello, William,' he said quietly. 'We meet again, then.'

'Right,' I said, 'right. How's Shirley?'

'Fine. How's Claudine?'

'I think there's a bottle of whisky in the kitchen,' Barbara said, sounding nervous. 'I'll just get it. If that's what you'd both like.'

'Fine,' I said. Charrington nodded.

She left the room. 'Listen, Bill,' I said quickly, 'I went to see Simpson this evening. He's dead – hanged himself.'

Charrington stared at me. Then he said: '*Dead?* You're sure?'

'Of course – I found him. I called the police, had to stay to make a statement.' I began to tell him the details. Then Barbara came back with a bottle of whisky, a glass jug of water, and two glasses on a tray.

'I forgot to ask if you wanted ice,' she said.

'William has just found his solicitor dead,' Charrington told her. 'Hanged himself. William's just come from there.'

'After a couple of whiskies at the Scarsdale to pick myself up,' I put in.

'William! How awful!' Barbara said, her eyes wide.

'Not that awful,' Charrington said bluntly. 'Man was a bloody menace, to be frank.'

'There's more,' I said, taking a glass from Barbara. 'Just a drop of water, thanks, that'll do. What d'you make of this – in the street outside Simpson's office, I got chased by a motorcyclist who, I'm sure, had a gun ready just inside his jacket.'

'Oh my God,' Barbara said in her small voice.

'Sit down, Barbara,' Charrington said, 'here.' He patted a cushion at one end of the big sofa.

'No, I'm all right,' Barbara said. 'Well, perhaps we should all sit down. William – tell us about it.'

'Are you sure he had a gun?' Charrington asked.

'Ninety per cent,' I said. 'Ninety-nine, at the time. Look what I did to my trousers.'

I told them the whole story.

'You certainly make it sound convincing,' Barbara said. 'Did you – oh, hold on a moment. I think I heard Hugo coming downstairs.'

She got up and went out into the passage.

'I don't know that the police were all that convinced,' I said. 'I got off on the wrong foot with Superintendent Priestly from the start, and he's not a forgiving type.'

'I can imagine,' Charrington said. There was a pause while we listened to Barbara and Hugo out in the passage. 'I don't mind if you're really starving,' she was telling him, 'but do make sure you put the butter back in the fridge. And do wear your slippers – I can't bear all this squalid padding about in your bare feet.' She came back into the sitting-room and took her place on the sofa again. I wondered if Charrington felt as I did about Hugo. He'd be a very painful thorn in the side of anyone who took up with Barbara. Maybe I'd be wise to settle for Just Good Friends, after all, and leave the field to our Bill.

'Did I miss anything?' Barbara asked.

'No,' I said, 'I think that's it.'

'Oh, I know,' she said, 'I was just going to ask if you were able to tell the police anything about this motorcyclist, to help them find him?'

'Apart from colour, they all look much the same to me,' I said. 'The rider's helmet and his jacket were black, or very dark. It was a big bike, with a rasping exhaust – multi-cylinder, four probably, but those are common enough. And after he'd gone past I was trying to read the number plate and noticed that the right side was brighter than the left – must have had twin rear light bulbs and one was dud. Which he'll replace first thing tomorrow.'

No, it wasn't much. If only the police car had been quicker off the mark . . . but it hadn't. That was that.

There was silence for a while. Then Charrington said: 'So, William, you think Simpson had Jonathan shot, do you? Oh – I'm sorry, Barbara, I was forgetting –'

'Don't mind me,' she said. 'I've had plenty of time to get used to the idea. I just want the whole thing cleared up, over, and done with so that we can all get on with our lives again.'

'My feelings exactly,' I said. 'As far as I'm concerned, relations with Claudine are at an all-time low because of endless police muckraking. Things are so bad we're hardly on speaking terms now. If they're making any progress, they're not giving any sign of it. I've got to the stage when I'd jump at any chance to clear this thing up, as I did this evening. Maybe it almost got me shot, but I can tell you, I'd do it again, and more.'

'Poor William!' Barbara said softly. 'I'm sorry . . .'

'Must be rough,' Charrington conceded.

'Yup. Can't deny that it is.'

'If only there was something I could do to help,' Barbara said with a sigh.

I looked along the sofa at her. It was the sort of thing people often say when help is safely out of their reach. But perhaps she meant it, or at least had wanted to make a gesture of support.

'Thank you, Barbara,' I said. 'If you really mean it –'

'Oh – I do.' She looked back along the sofa, past the intervening bulk of Charrington, all anxious enquiry.

'Give me another shot of whisky, then,' I said, passing along my glass.

Charrington managed a dry chuckle. Barbara said: 'Oh well – I can certainly manage that,' and passed back the refilled glass with a serious expression – jokes, I'd noticed before, seemed to pass her by. Not that it rated much appreciation, I grant that, except as an attempt to lighten the atmosphere. Nobody else said anything. I decided I'd better drink up and go home.

Then Charrington said: 'Do you mind if I speak frankly?' He was looking at me.

'I'll try to bear it bravely,' I said.

'Right. If I were you, I'd go home and sit tight. Not try to do what the police are there for. What they're trained and paid for, as well. I understand your reasons, but I think you're on a hiding to nothing, and you'll maybe queer their pitch into the bargain. If you're right in what you told us, about that motorcyclist having a shotgun, it makes no sense to go out looking for him again – next time you'll likely get your head blown off, same as Jonathan. Makes no sense, does that.'

He was still looking at me. I saw he meant it, felt it strongly.

'What's more, I haven't got so many clients I can afford to lose one,' he added. 'Enlightened self-interest, they call it.' His face wore a slight smile now. Oh yes, we both understood one of the reasons he wanted me to stay at home. It would prevent more wasted evenings like this one. But his explicit reason, I thought, was sincerely meant.

'What do you think, Barbara?' he asked.

Barbara's response was immediate. 'He's right, William,' she said, leaning towards me earnestly. 'He's right. If Claudine knows what happened tonight . . . she does know, I suppose?'

'Not all of it. I haven't been back yet,' I admitted.

'Well, when she does, surely she'd agree with Bill, too? However badly you're getting on at present, I'm sure she wouldn't want you to take the kind of risks you've been describing – would she?'

They were both watching me now, as I tipped a large slug of whisky back. Fire in the throat, then fire in the belly. Not a good boy. Godammit, they were sounding like my parents. The voice of the superego, and you *know* it makes sense.

'You're, right, absolutely right,' I said unsteadily, 'in one way. I could, maybe I should, go home and sit tight. I could try to ignore the slow collapse of my marriage while Priestly and his sleepwalkers drift about their business, turning up every two or three days to throw a little more fuel on the flames. I could sit tight in my office, fiddling with bits of paper, and feeling more and more isolated. I could pretend not to notice that our once glorious meals have sunk to the level of packet soups and jacket potatoes – and if that sounds trivial, I can assure you it isn't: it's symbolic of the collapse of my household brought about by the pestilent Priestly. Compared to which a skinful of shotgun pellets is a minor irritation. And to avoid which I shall swim seas, move mountains, and slay as many dragons as get in my way. I think I'm pissed.'

Charrington's face resembled a *gros pain*, one of those big round loaves Claudine and I buy from the local baker when we're at our house in France. But they don't ripple, not like this. I leant back against the cushions and shut my eyes for a moment.

I've usually got a good head for drink – have to, in my job. You soon learn to spit the stuff out at tastings, of course, and not to swallow more than you can hold. But tonight, I'd been careless, put down too much spirit on top of an empty stomach. Hadn't eaten more than Pete's cheese sandwich all day. It was time to go home, raid the larder, go to bed.

'. . . that it was Simpson,' a voice was saying. 'But the police will make their own minds up about that.'

I opened my eyes. Bill and Barbara had their heads together, and she was nodding to what he'd just said. She saw me looking, and said: 'What do you think, William?'

'I don't know what I think, not any more. I hope the police can prove it was Simpson – that would tidy the whole thing up nicely. But I'm afraid they're going to be reluctant to give up the idea that it was me – stronger motive, you see. Not only that Jonathan was after Claudine, but because she'd have taken a lot of money with her, wrecked my business maybe. You know what woman are getting away with in divorce settlements these days.'

It seemed they could find nothing to say to this. A huge yawn escaped me; I shut my eyes again. No, this won't do. With an effort, I sat upright.

'Must go home, now. At least Claudine will have gone to bed, and I won't have to meet with a whole lot more questions to which I don't know the answers. I've really had it, for today.'

I stood up. The room tilted briefly, and then settled into the horizontal, or near enough.

'William – I am so sorry,' Barbara said again.

'You've been very kind and supportive, both of you,' I said. 'Coming here was like stepping into an oasis of calm – I really appreciate that.' Another yawn emerged. 'Sorry.'

'Are you sure you're all right to drive?' Charrington said. 'I could run you home – no trouble.'

'I think I'll be all right. More tired than sloshed – let's see what the night air can do for me.'

We all got up. Charrington took charge, and saw me to the door. Well, he would, wouldn't he – there was still some of his evening with Barbara left to salvage. And, if what I remembered of my drunken speech was accurate, I'd queered my pitch with Barbara. I'd more or less told her that what happened yesterday had been on the rebound. Charrington had the field to himself, now.

We stood together on the doorstep, looking out.

'What do you think?' he said.

'Oh, not again, Bill,' I said. 'No, I've really had enough of it all . . .'

'I didn't mean that,' he said. 'I meant, can you drive, or shall I . . .' Now that I was almost out, his reluctance was palpable. I laughed. A good loser, you see. When there's no alternative in sight.

'Get back in there, Bill,' I said. 'And the best of luck.'

CHAPTER 21

Mother and Son

A mother is only brought unlimited satisfaction by
her relation to a son; this is altogether the most
perfect, the most free from ambivalence of all human
relationships.

SIGMUND FREUD

I'd rather be summoned by an honest old-fashioned bell than
by the simpering chirrup which is all that the modern telephone
can manage. If it's meant to be user-friendly, its charm is lost
on me. Especially at seven in the morning.

I groaned, and groped for the thing on the bedside table. On
the other side of the bed, far far away, Claudine stirred and
subsided again. The days are not so good I want them prolonged
by early calls. It had better be essential.

'Yes?'

'William? – is that you?'

'I think so.'

'Oh, William – I'm so sorry if I've woken you, but it's Hugo.
He's gone.'

It was Barbara, sounding more distraught than I'd imagined
her capable of.

'Gone?'

'He's not in his room. A bag and some clothes are missing.
I've started to ring up people who might know something about
it, about where he's gone. He didn't say anything to me last
night, and it's not like him to go off without a word.'

'Barbara, I'm sorry – I haven't seen him, I don't know what
to suggest. Except the police, of course, if you're that worried.'

'Well, I am worried, yes. He's never done anything like this
before. I'll have to tell them, if I can't locate him.'

'Perhaps he's had a night on the tiles.'

'Hugo? It's most unlikely – he hasn't actually got around to
girls. And anyway, he'd just have stayed out, wouldn't he? –

237

not come back in and then gone out again without telling me.'

'True.'

'I did just think he might have gone to the cottage – he's been there on his own before – but I've rung, and there's no reply.'

'Perhaps he's there but not answering.'

'Yes, perhaps,' Barbara said. 'I don't know what to do, now. I'm stuck without a car, you see. I suppose I could hire one. But I feel I ought to stay here, in case he turns up.'

There was a pause. I began to realise that this script had already been written. Perhaps I ought to go – Barbara did sound very worried about her Hugo.

'Have you rung Bill?'

'No, not yet,' Barbara said. 'I thought I'd ring you first.'

Impossible not to feel a tickle of pleasure at that . . .

'You're always so understanding.'

Oh, now! Trouble is, it can be obvious – and still work . . . But –

'Get the police to call?' I suggested.

'Well, yes, I could. But if he's there, he'd terribly resent that. And if he isn't, I'd feel awful for wasting their time.'

Ah well. Nothing for it, then . . .

'I tell you what – why don't *I* go?' I said brightly. So. A good deed that would get me out of the house for a while, a day in the country, a day of problems shelved and out of sight . . .

'Oh, William – would you really? I'd be so grateful. It's in the New Forest: I'll give you the address. Ready?'

I reached for the bedside notepad. 'Ready.'

Only after she'd rung off did I realise there was a better motive than my sympathetic nature for Barbara to ring me before Bill Charrington. It was called Shirley.

I had my own wife to square, of course. But, as Barbara must have calculated, one less likely to make a drama out of it than Bill's droopy and tearful Shirley. Claudine heard me in silence.

'Why must you go?' she asked when I'd finished.

'Barbara doesn't want to send the police round. I know what she means – he's a strange, moody boy, and easily upset.'

'He does not mind to upset his mother,' she pointed out.

238

'Apparently not. But that's the way they are together – she seems to dote on him, though I can't see why.'

Claudine shrugged, a gesture so essential to the French that they've developed a horizontal version of it for use in bed. Then she said: 'William –'

'Yes?'

Something in her voice impelled me to walk round the bed to her side. But all she said was: '*Bonne chance, hein.*'

Thank you, darling,' I said. Well, it was better than nothing.

It was a grey, dank day, with dead leaves and broken twigs littering the pavements from the recent storms. I left London by the old Twickenham road to avoid the heavy commuter traffic which would already be building up on the motorway. I kept watch on all motorcycles, and for any other signs of trouble, but I felt safe – nobody knew where I was going except Barbara, and Claudine, of course. Others might be told later, but by then I'd be well away from London, position unknown. And by the time I got back, the police might have turned up the link between Simpson and the gunmen, and might be waiting with reassurances and even, it was possible, apologies. Meanwhile, I had this little errand to do for Barbara. For which she'd chosen me instead of Bill. Perhaps things hadn't gone too well last night. It would take a far holier nature than mine to hope that it had. Had Shirley found out, and clapped on the handcuffs? In the police car, they kept their handcuffs hooked over the gear lever, I'd noticed, within easy reach of either side. And Southampton coming up.

The Cassell cottage was near Burley, about twenty minutes' drive from the end of the motorway. I'd never been there before, but Barbara's instructions were detailed and precise. The New Forest is a misnomer, really – there are wooded bits, but much of the area is sandy heath, with clumps of pines and a lot of heather and gorse. It's the sort of territory favoured eleswhere by the military, since I suppose it has little agricultural value, and won't support much except wild ponies and butterflies. Past a filling station, she said – and here it is. Up a long hill, with distant views towards Bournemouth – and there they are. Left at the next crossroads, and the drive is two hundred yards further on, on the right.

And here it is.

I slowed down, and pulled in to the side of the road just before the drive. It was unmarked, but looked well used; a dirt surface, much pitted and patched. Through a rough belt of scrubby pines and large overgrown bushes, I could see three or maybe four houses; low, rambling, cottage-style buildings with tile-hung gables and dormer windows in their red-tiled roofs. Theirs, Barbara had said, was the last one, at the far end of the track.

Yes, this must be the place. I moved off again, and steered the Citroën along the track, trying to avoid the worst of the potholes. It was ten o'clock now, time for all but the most dilatory of households to be stirring, but there was nobody about. From the look of them, these, like Barbara's, were all second homes, holiday cottages, and the place only came to life at weekends and in the summer. Only one car could be seen, a black Golf GTi, parked at the side of the track outside the first house; I looked past it, up a brick paved garden path, and noted bedroom curtains still drawn. Someone making good use of the parental cottage, I guessed. Perhaps it was Nigel and Fiona from the Scarsdale. It was the classic green wellie car, anyway.

The track widened outside the last cottage to allow space for turning. If Hugo had been here, I'd have seen Barbara's car parked by the hedge outside the cottage, surely. Like the other cottages, there was no drive, only a small white painted wooden gate in the hedge with a footpath beyond. Still, having got here, I'd better take a look.

I stopped the car beside the hedge, just before the gate, and got out, avoiding the puddles which lay ready to trap the unwary. The gate needed lifting before it would open, and I didn't bother to shut it after me. The path was of red brick, pitted by frost and slippery with moss; neglected herbaceous borders dripped on it from both sides. Barbara's interests didn't extend to gardening, and I didn't imagine that Jonathan would have done much, either, except under protest. I sympathised: weekend cottages are nothing but work unless you decide to let the place run wild – romantic, let's call it. I walked up the path, watched by blank, uncurtained windows.

Well, here's the front door, under a little tiled porch. Green painted wide boards with a small brass knocker. So small, it hardly makes any noise at all. I try again using my knuckles.

'Hugo? Are you there?'

Silly question – of course he isn't. But I wait a while, turning to look down the garden, then up at the grey and seamless sky. Should you call it sky, when all you can see is cloud? The air is still and damp, making a faint prickle on the skin that might be the beginnings of rain, as yet invisible.

'Hugo?'

I knock again, wait some more. But still no reply. Well, I've done what she asked. I'd better drive back into Burley, find a call box, and tell her he isn't here. Perhaps he's turned up there meanwhile; is sitting in the kitchen drinking coffee and moodily listening to an earful from Barbara.

I started down the garden path. Then it occurred to me that, having come all this way, I'd better do a little more to justify all this expenditure of time and effort, not to mention petrol. Look in the windows, go round to the back and see if there are any signs that anyone's been here recently, futile probably, but I'd regret it on the way back if I left without.

There were two ground-floor windows at the front. Cupping my eyes with my hands to reduce reflection, I peered in through the leaded panes. I saw a small pine dining table and chairs in one room, a small chintz-covered sofa and pine bookcase in the other, together with sundry bits and pieces of furniture of the useful but characterless sort that often ends up in weekend cottages. I saw no bags, clothes, or any personal belongings; nothing to suggest that anyone was in occupation. Still on duty bent, I trudged conscientiously round to the side of the house. As I turned the corner, following a continuation of the brick path, I received a sudden jolt in the solar plexus.

Not physical. Nobody was waiting there to sock it to me. It was an inanimate object that stopped me in my tracks, muscles tensed and pulse rate soaring. The type of object I had recently learned to associate with all that was wicked in our world.

A motorcycle.

Instinctively, I stepped back a pace, to bring the corner of the cottage within easy reach in case I should need to retreat round it.

It was a big bike, a four-cylinder job, massive and powerful. It looked in good condition, either very well maintained or nearly new. It was the general shape of the machine that had chased me down the street outside Simpson's office. The sort of machine that shouldn't be here.

Near the motorcycle was a side door – the kitchen door, probably. I should try that before I went. But I didn't feel like knocking on any more doors, not now. It would be best to go and ring Barbara first, see if she knew anything about this.

Of course, motorcycles like this aren't exactly rare. There are plenty of them about, in fact. It's probably not the one I'm thinking about, but is here for some perfectly innocent reason. Most likely.

There's one thing I could try, though, to test this coincidence. Switch on the lights.

I moved forward quietly, found the switch, turned it.

Then I stepped back, to look at the rear light.

Even that could have been coincidence, I told myself as I reached the Citroën. I hadn't exactly run down the garden path, but hadn't wasted any time getting out of there. Keeping my ears tuned to the creak of a bedroom window being opened, or footsteps on the brick paving behind me. Which hadn't happened. But if so, a coincidence that I was going to treat with extreme caution. How many bikes would be driving round, just now, with one of the twin rear light bulbs defunct? And how many of those would come within my orbit in the space of twelve hours?

The effect was much less in daylight, of course, but it had been possible to see the distinct difference in light intensity between one side of the red lampholder and the other, and to see the lopsided lighting of the number plate that had first caught my eye.

And it was the left-hand bulb that had gone, too. The same as last night. That, surely, stretched coincidence to the limit.

Hugo?

I started the engine, glancing out of the side window at the cottage as I did so. Was that a face at the dormer window? A pale oval, not moving. It could be.

My breath was condensing on the clammy glass of the telephone box, obscuring the view down the village street.

'I'm in Burley, Barbara. In a call box. No, I haven't seen him yet, or I may have, I'm not sure. Now hold on – listen, let me explain. Yes, I've been to the cottage, I've just come from there. Barbara – please listen. How did he . . . How would he have got here?'

'Oh, William – on his motorbike, of course,' Barbara said impatiently.

'You didn't tell me that. I didn't know he had one.'

'You didn't ask. I thought you knew.'

'I thought he'd taken your car. You *said* he had – I'm sure of it.'

'I couldn't have done – it's in the garage, being serviced or something.'

'Well, anyway . . . I suppose I jumped to conclusions. It was early . . . Listen, Barbara – what sort of motorbike is it?'

'What sort? Does it matter?'

'Yes.' *And how. . .*

'Well, it's, I don't know, a big red Japanese thing. They're supposed to be safer, aren't they, the big ones? William! – has he had an accident?'

'No, Barbara, no, don't worry, it's not that.' *What should I say?*

'What is it, then? Something's happened, hasn't it?'

I'll just have to tell her – there's no choice.

'Barbara,' I said carefully. 'It could be, probably is, a coincidence. But there's a motorbike outside your cottage now and, from what you say, it could be Hugo's. But it's got a dud rear lamp bulb, just like the bike I was chased by last night.'

The telephone seemed to have gone dead. 'Did you hear that?' I asked.

'Yes,' Barbara said. She sounded distant, as though she wasn't holding the telephone properly. I could hear a faint murmuring, as if she was talking to herself. Then her voice came on again, louder, and quite firm.

243

'As you say, it's coincidence of course. You're not suggesting that it was Hugo on that motorbike last night, are you?'

'Well, no, I don't know . . . it is *odd*, you must admit.'

'William! Do you realise what you're saying? Are you feeling all right?'

'Someone could have borrowed it, perhaps?' I persisted. Why did everybody want to deny what had happened, want to make me feel at fault? I hadn't imagined last night, there had been a gun inside that jacket, I was sure of it . . .

'Listen!' A thought had just surfaced. 'Barbara – do you know if Ludwig went off to Germany as he promised he would when we confronted him the other night? Have you seen him since?' After I'd got him to agree, I'd thought it tactful to withdraw, leaving Barbara to talk about the allowance – danegeld, really – that she would pay, on condition he stayed away.

'As far as I know, Ludwig went back to Germany, and I haven't seen him since,' Barbara said in the tones of someone who is being carefully patient.

'But he might not have – he could still be around.'

Barbara sighed. 'William,' she said, 'please. As you're there. Would you please go back to the cottage and see if you can find Hugo? I would be most grateful. And then ring me back. You can do it from the cottage.'

Well, that's it – I've got to say yes or no.

'Barbara, I will, but I think I'm going to have to . . .'

The pips went. We were cut off.

I held the telephone, swearing. I'd just been going to tell her that I would have to tell the police about the motorcycle, before I went back to the cottage, perhaps with a police escort. Well, too bad. She was asking a lot of me – I didn't think she realised how much. I wouldn't bother to ring her back – I'd just get on and do it.

I stepped out of the telephone box. All I wanted, really, was to find the local bobby, a uniformed witness and deterrent, just in case Barbara was wrong. I didn't know much about Hugo, but from what I'd seen he struck me as definitely odd, a bit of a weirdo. Barbara must think so too, or she wouldn't be so protective towards him. And, I wasn't forgetting, he was Ludwig's son. That must be a heavy burden for any lad to drag around.

Yes, it was time to step into the background, and let the Law take a turn. Do what they're paid for, as Charrington had put it.

The traditional village policeman, he was. I'd expected him to come out of the police house with the old push-bike, and to have to persuade him to take a lift with me rather than come puffing on behind. But times change when you're not looking – they have cars now, it seems, and he followed me in that, reminding me, whenever I checked in the mirror to see he was still there, of the occasions when I've been pinched for speeding, the guilty shock it gives you to see all that white paint and blue stripes close on your tail.

Too obtrusive for the occasion, I felt. If Hugo were there, and I was wrong about the motorcycle, I wanted the reunion to go off with as little fuss as possible. Not to have police cars drawing up outside.

I pulled up just inside the beginning of the track, and the police car stopped behind me. I got out, and went back to explain what I thought. He wound his window down, and listened.

'All right, sir. If you think that'd be better. Don't want to set the neighbours talking, do we now?'

He got out, a large man of about my age, cast in the uncle mould. I waited while he put his helmet on, and we set off down the track on foot.

'This is probably a complete waste of time,' I said, 'but if he is there, and feeling troublesome, the sight of a policeman should make him think twice.'

'That's what we're here for, sir. To make our presence felt, as you might say.' We skirted a large pothole. 'What sort of trouble did you have in mind, sir?'

'Probably none at all. Just a precaution,' I said, uncertain how to express it. Now that I had secured the help of a real policeman, and not just a shadowy representative of the Force, I was beginning to feel responsible for him. 'I must warn you,' I said, 'that he's a nervous, unpredictable sort of lad. It's not impossible that he may, for instance, have a gun in there.'

245

He stopped. I stopped, too. He looked at me, frowning. As well he might.

'What sort of gun, sir?'

'I don't know. But I think a cautious approach would be best.'

'What makes you say that, sir?'

'Unstable family background,' I said. 'And ... other things too complicated to explain.' Oh no! I realised suddenly – this is madness! 'Look – wouldn't it be better to call up reinforcements? You've got people trained to handle this sort of thing, haven't you? Flak jackets, protective shields. Tear gas perhaps.'

He was still looking at me, still frowning. 'Flak jackets?' he said slowly. 'Reinforcements? Are you being serious, sir?'

I swallowed. It was Hugo in there, Barbara's teenage son – shambling, unaggressive, harmless – surely. But what was embarrassment, when weighed against what just *might* happen . . .?

'Yes,' I said. 'What do you think?'

'I think,' he said, stepping out decisively, 'that I'd best see if this young lad is there, and just what all this is about. Is this the house?'

'Yes,' I said. 'But I do urge you . . .'

'Better leave it to me, sir, thank you. I can handle it.'

We arrived at the gate. The cottage looked the same as when I'd left it: windows still shut, no sign of life. Except, perhaps, for that pale oval at the dormer window. It hadn't moved, was still in the same position. A mirror, or ornament on the windowsill, perhaps.

'I'll come with you,' I said. 'If he's there, I'll be able to –'

'No sir, thank you. You stay here, if you please. What was his name again?'

'Hugo,' I said. 'Hugo Cassell – no, Krantz.'

'Well, then. Let's see what Master Krantz has to say for himself.'

He opened the gate, all constabulary dignity. I began to feel I'd done the right thing. Only a hardened criminal or complete nutter would commit any kind of outrage against . . .

The pale oval behind the dormer window moved suddenly. There was a crash and tinkle of breaking glass.

246

'Look out!' I shouted.

There was just time to be aware of a long shotgun barrel being poked through the broken window before I hurled myself into cover behind the hedge. The ground came up and hit me, cold, wet – but welcome.

I heard the blast, followed at once by a second. And a nearby curse.

'Run for it *now*!' I called urgently. 'Before he can reload.'

The constable joined me behind the hedge. He was wincing.

'Are you hit?' I said anxiously.

'Not much,' he said, breathing heavily. 'One or two in the arm, think that's all. Bloody well stings, I don't mind telling you. That little bugger . . .!'

'Let's get out of here. This hedge isn't much protection,' I suggested. I'd hardly finished speaking before two more shots sounded, and the hedge crackled as if on fire. We got up and ran for it.

A hundred yards down the track, we slowed up. We'd be safe enough at that range.

'I'm very sorry,' I said, 'I should have been more emphatic. I didn't believe he really would, you see. Not Hugo.'

The constable didn't answer me. He was getting into the police car, reaching for the radio.

'Little bugger,' he said grimly, looking like an uncle no more.

CHAPTER 22

Infantile Behaviour

Many people are unable to surmount the fear of loss
of love; they never become sufficiently independent of
other people's love and in this respect carry on their
behaviour as infants.

SIGMUND FREUD

The constable and I sat in the police car while he reported
what had happened. His voice as he spoke into the handset
was tightly under control, but I could see that he was a lot
more shaken than he cared to admit. I felt quite shaky myself,
though in my case it was not so much the fact of being shot
at (and missed) but the shock of seeing the barrels poked
through the shattered window and hearing the double blast –
so forcefully reminiscent of what had happened on the pavement outside Les Trois Pigeons. As an *aide memoire*, the made-
leine biscuits dipped in tea which Proust fans are always going
on about are a mere tickle in the brain compared to the
double blast of a shotgun, believe me. You don't forget that,
not ever, especially if you happen to be in line with the business end when you hear it.

'Control says to wait here, and reinforcements will be out
shortly,' the constable said. 'You too, sir.'

'Of course. And would you tell them that Superintendent
Priestly of Chelsea CID ought to be informed about this. He
may want to come down.' And I'll have to tell Barbara what's
happened. Perhaps not quite yet, but soon, when more police
arrive. Perhaps Hugo will come out, and I'll have better news
for her. Or, God forbid, *worse* . . . The constable had finished on
the radio.

I said: 'How are you? Shall I have a look at it for you?'

'It stings, that does. Stings like hell.' He rubbed his uniformed
arm, inspecting it for damage. Two or three tiny punctures were
visible where pellets had penetrated.

'If you'd like to take your jacket off?' I suggested.

He nodded. 'Best see what the damage is. But I must keep a look-out for the lad. I've collected enough of these for one day.'

We got out of the car. We were well out of range of the cottage, but Hugo hadn't been seen since firing off the gun. I helped the constable off with his jacket, and rolled up his sleeve. He winced. 'Ouch!'

'Sorry.'

'Three, is it? Not bleeding much, are they?'

'No. That's lucky.'

'There's a First Aid tin in the car, sir. If you wouldn't mind . . .'

I applied Elastoplast, helped him on with his jacket again, and we got back into the car. We both stared through the windscreen at the cottage, partly obscured by trees from where the car was now parked, but we could see the upper windows and the garden gate. No sign of Hugo. Of course, there might be a back way out. But not, I thought, that he could ride the bike over. For that he'd have to come this way . . .

'How long before more police get here, do you think?'

'A few minutes sir, not long.' The constable's voice had steadied. He looked less thunderous, almost good-humoured. Of course, if you come through a drama like this with only a scratch or two it does ensure you a good audience and some free drinks at the pub. I was thankful for that, it could have been much worse . . . I'd thought the sight of a police uniform would be protection enough while we found out what was going on, and I really hadn't believed Hugo would actually start shooting, for God's sake, a home-loving mother's boy like that, it didn't make any sense, not at all. *Could* the bike outside the cottage be the one that had chased me on the night of Simpson's suicide – was that possible? With *Hugo* on it? Is that what this meant? But *why?*

'Well, sir,' the constable said, 'while we're waiting, suppose you tell me what it's all about.'

'I wish I knew,' I said. 'It's because it's all so complicated that I didn't tell you more before we went up to the cottage. I didn't know how to begin, quite honestly. And I still can't

249

believe that young Hugo, in there, is *really* involved – not in *murder* . . .'

He turned to stare at me. 'What murder? Are you telling me sir, that you –'

'Otherwise,' I said, 'I would never have asked you to go up to the cottage. Of course I wouldn't.'

'Hold on sir. *What murder?*'

'It's the Cassell murder,' I said, 'the shooting in Chelsea. Of course, what I keep forgetting is that Hugo is not only Barbara's son, but also Ludwig's. That does make a difference, perhaps *all* the difference, because Ludwig is a *total* nutter – I know that, I've seen him in action. Yes, I'm afraid I forgot to take that fully into account. The Ludwig factor, I mean.'

I was aware of heavy breathing at my side. 'Perhaps, sir,' the constable said, 'on second thoughts, you'd better keep all this for CID. They'll be along any minute now.'

And shortly afterwards, the first car arrived, bringing a uniformed inspector, a sergeant, and two constables. Evidently, after what had happened, the police intended to make their presence felt. After I'd outlined the situation, I persuaded the inspector to allow me to drive down to the village with one of the constables so that I could telephone Barbara.

'William! Oh good – I was beginning to think you'd never ring. Is he there?'

'Yes, Barbara. He's there.'

'Oh, what a relief! I thought he must be, of course, when you told me you'd seen his motorbike outside the cottage, but you can never be sure with Hugo. What on earth got into him? – did he say?'

'No – not yet. Listen, Barbara –'

'He hasn't? Oh well, the main thing is, he's found! I'm so grateful to you, William, for –'

'Barbara – listen! He's there, but he's refusing to come out.'

'*Refusing?* What do you mean?'

'Well. You know what I told you when I rang earlier, about the motorbike? That it had a dud rear light like the one outside Simpson's office?'

'William, you're not going to start on that again, are you? I told you – it can't possibly be anything to do with Hugo. You really are being very strange about this.'

'Just listen, Barbara, *please!* Nobody seems to be prepared to take it seriously, but I'm *sure* that motorcyclist had a gun in his jacket, the one that chased me. And he certainly had a rear light missing.'

'I know you don't like the poor boy,' Barbara said, 'but this is unbelievable. I can't think why you want to –'

'Barbara,' I said, trying to hold on to my patience, 'because of what I just said, I decided to go back to the cottage with a policeman. I've got nothing against Hugo – or I hadn't before this – but I was suspicious and, quite frankly, nervous.'

'Of Hugo? That's ridiculous!'

'Barbara, I'm afraid he stuck a gun out of the window and peppered the policeman.'

There was silence. Then: 'Oh, my God . . .' Barbara said faintly.

I waited for a decent interval, and then asked: 'Did you know there was a shotgun in the cottage?'

'No. But wait . . . Jonathan used to have one . . . it could have been there . . .'

'I don't suppose you know how many cartridges there might be?'

'Jonathan used to keep a sort of belt thing with some cartridges in it. I think I saw that not so long ago.'

'Would it have been full? Half full? Did he keep any spare boxes of cartridges, can you remember?'

'I don't remember any boxes. He never used the gun much. Just the odd shot at a pigeon in the garden. The belt might have been half full – I'm sure there were usually gaps in it. It used to hang in the wardrobe – that's why I noticed. Was the policeman . . . Is he . . .?'

'A few pellets in the arm, at quite long range. No serious damage, except to dignity. The problem is, what happens next?'

'I'll come straight down.'

'If you can bear not to, Barbara, wait until I ring you again. The police have got it all under control, and there's a good chance Hugo will see sense and come out.'

'Oh, I don't know if I can.'

'It would be better, believe me. By the time you've hired a car, it may be all over. I'll ring you in half an hour.'

Another silence.

'I feel for you,' I said. 'But don't worry too much. He's just a silly lad, with teenage trouble. How old is he?'

'Eighteen,' she said. 'Nineteen next February. All right. I'll wait for you to ring.'

There was no more to be said. As I put the phone down, I hoped for her sake that my words of comfort would turn out to be true. The trouble was, of course, that a silly lad can pull a trigger as well as the rest of us.

I called Claudine, then, to say what had happened, and that I didn't know when I'd be back. That took some time because she'd been asleep when I got in last night, and so hadn't heard about the motorcyclist, half-open jacket, the dud rear light, etcetera, etcetera. Perhaps because I'd now had to repeat it so often, so that it now sounded a tired old tale, she didn't react nearly as much as she had when I'd rung her from Simpson's office to tell her about his suicide. In fact, she sounded more bemused than alarmed by it all, though very heartwrung on behalf of Barbara – that was the aspect that stirred her most, rather than the fact of her husband having survived two dramas within a few hours. She asked me to give messages of sympathy and support to Barbara – Mothers of the World Unite! was the general theme.

'Yes,' I said, 'I'll do that. Let's hope he doesn't shoot anybody else, meanwhile. Me, for instance.'

'Why should he do that?' Claudine asked. 'The poor boy.'

'The "poor boy" came near to shooting me, last night,' I said. 'Or so I believe.'

'Oh, William!' she said. 'You must be mistaken!'

'Do I have to come home full of bullet holes before anyone will take any notice of what I keep saying?' I complained.

'You are not hurt. It is the poor Hugo we must think of now,' she said reprovingly.

No doubt about it. The adult male must learn to look after himself. No one else is going to.

*

Back at the scene of Hugo's crime I saw that more police had arrived, including some volunteer reinforcements with eager expressions who were having to be sent back to their regular duties, with crisp instructions to stay there. The police in action were at once more haphazard and more human than I had imagined they would be: the younger ones were frankly keen to get in on the act.

'Suppose he makes a break for it, sarge – wouldn't it be better if –?'

'Be off with you, lads. You'll be called if needed.'

There was a visible stiffening of discipline when a car bearing a uniformed Chief Superintendent came down the lane and pulled up behind the three others already parked at a discreet distance from the cottage. I was called over to say my piece about Hugo and the motorcycle once again. To me, it sounded less convincing with each re-telling. But the Chief Superintendent's attitude to what I told him was quite matter-of-fact: he had, I discovered, already been in touch with Priestly, so it seemed that I still kept some credibility with Chelsea CID.

Meanwhile, a pair of police marksmen had arrived, burly in bulletproof jackets. They were only armed with revolvers, which seemed to me of limited use in this situation, if it should be necessary to get into the house.

'They're here to protect our men, Mr Warner,' the Chief Superintendent said, 'not to confront this young fellow directly. We want to get him out of there in one piece, if possible – that's our aim. It might take some time, but we won't rush it, just take it nice and easy. He can do no harm, meanwhile.'

'Except, perhaps, to himself,' I said.

'That's right, sir, quite right. But we'll hope not. We'll be trying to make contact quite soon, to get him talking. And then, later on, we'll let him hear from his mother. Patience and good timing, that's the ticket.'

Poor Barbara, I thought. She'd have to see and endure this, now. I glanced along the track to where one of the police marksmen had taken up position behind the hedge, near the gate. The other had disappeared, probably to cover the back of the cottage. Looking round, I could see several more blue uniforms crouched behind trees and bushes, all intent on the cottage like terriers at a rabbit hole.

'Well,' I said reluctantly. 'I'd better go and telephone his mother again, then – she's waiting to hear what the situation is. When will you be wanting her?'

'Thank you, sir,' the Chief Superintendent said, 'but that's all taken care of. Chelsea CID are picking her up. They'll be here in an hour or so.'

Perhaps Hugo would see sense and come out before she arrived. I hoped so.

I waited behind the line of police cars for an hour, watching the cottage, hearing the intermittent muttering of police radios. No sign of Hugo. Then I walked back along the lane to the Citroën, to wait for the arrival of Priestly with Barbara. At the point where the track turned off the main road, a constable had been stationed to prevent reporters and sightseers from coming in. Half a dozen cars had already been stopped. As I approached, the constable was talking through the driver's window of a Ford Transit van loaded with television equipment.

'No, sir. No one goes past this point. That's final.'

The driver of the van saw me, and said something to his passenger, who nodded, jumped out, and came up to me.

'Excuse me! You look as if you know what's going on here. Do you mind saying a few words? Over there will do nicely – I'll just tell the cameraman –'

'Sorry. No comment.'

'Oh, come on, sir, just a word or two –' Behind him, I saw car doors opening, eager figures emerging with cameras at the ready . . .

'No comment.' I dived into the Citroën, and slammed the door quickly. Vultures! I avoided his eye, and after a few moments he turned away and went back to the van. But it didn't drive off. No good waiting for Barbara here. I started the car, moved it down the track, out of their field of view, and sat, waiting.

Ten minutes later the grey Rover appeared, with Priestly himself at the wheel, Barbara beside him, and Cooper in the back. I had got out of the Citroën the moment I saw them coming, and Priestly pulled up alongside. I opened the door for Barbara to get out. She looked nervously down the track where the blue uniforms were grouped beside the line of police cars.

'Oh, William . . .'

'Nothing's happened, but it's all right,' I said, putting an arm round her shoulders for a reassuring squeeze.

'He hasn't come out?'

'No. Not yet. But I expect he will now you're here. Hello, superintendent, Sergeant Cooper. You made good time.'

'Hello, sir. Now, I'm going for a quick word with the police officer in charge here. Perhaps you would bring Mrs Cassell along in a couple of minutes?'

'All right. We'll be there.'

Priestly and Cooper strode off down the track. 'Might as well sit in the car,' I said, reaching for the door handle.

'No, I'm all right,' Barbara said. 'You're being very nice about this, William – I'm so grateful. I'm sorry I got angry with you about Hugo.' She tried to smile. For someone normally of such composure, it was a pitiful effort.

'Maternal instinct,' I said. 'Entirely understandable.'

'I couldn't accept it, you see. He really did fire off a gun at a policeman? You saw it yourself?' She couldn't look at me; was trying to hide her misery in profile.

'I'm afraid so. Fortunately, it was at a fair distance – more of a gesture than anything more serious. If he'd wanted to do real damage he could have waited until the bobby came closer.'

'But . . . but he hit him?' She was hating the words.

'Three pellets, that's all. I'm sure of that, because I bandaged him up. He was cursing but he'll be fine when they've got the pellets out. But of course the police don't like their officers being shot at, and they are taking it seriously, I'm bound to say that.' I watched her face, anxiously. Best to be factual, surely . . .

'What can have got into Hugo?' Barbara said in an uncertain voice, looking in her handbag. 'Damn – I haven't got a handkerchief. Oh yes, here it is. Sorry, I must get this over before I have to talk to the police again.' She dabbed her eyes, blew her nose. 'Oh God. I'll be all right in a minute. Take no notice.'

'Take your time,' I said.

Down the track, Priestly and the Chief Superintendent could

be seen in earnest consultation. I waited. Two minutes must be up, now. Yes, Priestly had turned his head this way, and was beckoning.

'Better?'

'Yes. I'm all right now.'

'Shall we go, then?'

We walked together down the track to the Chief Superintendent's car, where he was still conferring with Priestly. They looked up as we came near.

'This is Mrs Cassell,' I said to the Chief Superintendent. He greeted her with careful courtesy, like that offered to the bereaved. Barbara looked about her, at the cottage and at the crouching policemen.

'Has that man got a gun?' she said sharply.

'Only a precaution, Mrs Cassell,' the Chief Superintendent said. 'There's no intention to approach the house. We're going to wait for your son to come out, that's our policy. Shall I explain?'

'Yes,' Barbara said, 'I think you'd better.' There was a short but embarrassing silence until she added in a contrite tone: 'I'm sorry, I didn't mean to sound like that.'

'That's all right,' he said. 'I understand how you must feel.'

I felt a hand on my arm. It was Priestly. 'I'd like a word with you, Mr Warner, while the Chief Superintendent is explaining the situation to Mrs Cassell. In my car, perhaps.'

I looked across at Barbara. Well, we'd only be a few yards away. I followed Priestly to his car.

We settled ourselves into the Rover. 'Well, Mr Warner. What have you got for us this time?' Priestly said. Neither his face nor the tone of his voice indicated an attempt at jocularity. I decided it would be safest to take his words at face value.

'From the beginning?' I asked.

'If you please, sir.'

Barbara's early morning telephone call already seemed a long time ago. I started with that, and worked on through the day's events. It took some minutes to cover everything, but eventually I felt I had. My style of recitation must have been improving, as Priestly asked hardly any questions, and even nodded appreciatively once or twice.

'Thank you,' he said. 'A very clear statement, if I may say so.'

'I've had plenty of practice,' I said. We were sitting in the back of the Rover, with Cooper in the front taking notes.

'You missed it all, last night, Sergeant Cooper,' I said.

'I did, sir. On other duties, I was. But I've heard all about it.' He turned his head round to give me what seemed quite a companionable smile.

'Fortunately,' I said, 'there's a police witness to what happened this morning. Proof that not all of what I tell you is imaginary.'

'Now, Mr Warner,' Priestly said, 'that's not quite fair, is it?'

'If you believed me,' I said, 'why did you let me go off home without even offering protection? That motorcyclist could still have been around, couldn't he?'

Priestly and Cooper exchanged glances. 'All right,' Priestly said at last. 'Go on, Cooper. Tell him.'

Cooper turned over some pages of his notebook. 'Here we are, then,' he said. '8.55. Left Mr Simpson's office. Turned right, walked up to Charlotte Street where grey Citroën CX, registration number MLD 104X was parked. Proceeded to drive up Charlotte Street, and continued in that direction until the Marylebone Road, there turning left and continuing westwards across the Edgware Road and into Sussex Gardens. Turned right at the Bayswater Road, continued to Notting Hill Gate. Turned left into Church Street, and slowed by William Warner Wines Ltd, appearing to be about to turn off, but then continued down to High Street Kensington, turned right, proceeded westwards until the turning into Edwardes Square. Parked on the double yellow lines at the north side of Edwardes Square, and proceeded on foot to the Scarsdale Arms public house, where observation was maintained from outside.'

'Very proper,' I said. 'If true.'

'Entered there at 9.37 p.m. Came out at four minutes past ten, and walked to the west side of Edwardes Square. Knocked at the door of number twenty three, and was admitted by a lady, later identified as Mrs Barbara Cassell, and the owner of that property. Watch was maintained until the subject came out at 11.42, and drove himself to his own shop and residence in Church Street. A further watch –'

'That'll do, Cooper,' Priestly interrupted. He shot me a brief glance, and then switched his gaze to between the front seats, through the windscreen, on which a few drops of rain were beginning to appear. 'We could do without that,' he said, apparently to himself.

'I owe you an apology,' I said.

Priestly shook his head. 'No need,' he said mildly, 'no need.'

'Of course,' I said, 'it wasn't just protection, was it?'

'It's our job to know what's going on, Mr Warner. And to use our meagre manpower to best effect. I'm not going to discuss the how, why and when. That's for us to decide. But we're not being idle, I wanted you to know that. Far from it – we're overworked and needing all the help we can get. Information, of course – not on the ground. Now, is there anything you can tell me that you haven't already?'

This was a new Priestly – or my perception of him had changed. Perhaps I'd been ... but this wasn't the time to go into it.

'About what, specifically?' I asked.

'We might make use of the time we're having to spend here by clearing up a few loose ends,' he said. 'Remind me, Cooper.'

'Cash withdrawal from bank account,' Cooper said, after a brief search in his notebook.

'Ah yes,' Priestly said. 'Have you turned up those invoices, Mr Warner?'

'No,' I said. Priestly waited. Well, I thought, he *has* to clear it up. 'And I'm afraid I'm not going to be able to.'

'Why's that?'

'You've probably guessed it. Cash payments to French workmen, under-the-counter, tax free. I can't prove it, and they won't admit it. But it's true, all the same.'

'Tut, tut, Mr Warner,' Priestly said. 'But it's the French government who are losing out. Cross that off, Cooper. What's next?'

'Krantz,' Cooper read out.

'Krantz? Ah, of course – that's not the young man that's keeping us all in suspense here, but his father, Mr Ludwig Krantz. German police say they've been keeping an eye on him for some time, suspected trafficking in various goods, drugs included. You didn't happen to hear anything about that, did you, sir? On your business trip to Germany?'

He was still looking ahead, through the windscreen. 'Yes,' I said.

'You did? May we hear about it, sir?'

'His daughter told me,' I said. 'I understand he was some kind of courier. But that he's given it up, now.'

'His daughter. That would be – have you got it, Cooper?'

'Eva Krantz,' Cooper said.

'Miss Eva Krantz. Or perhaps I should say *Fräulein*. Have you anything to add to that, Mr Warner?'

'She's doing her best for her father,' I said, 'trying to keep him out of any further trouble. I didn't want to make it more difficult for her.'

'Well, we'll leave it there for the moment. A matter for the German police, that one. Unless he starts peddling his wares over here, of course.'

'Mrs Cassell – his first wife – is paying him an allowance to stay in Germany,' I said. 'So I don't think there's much chance of that.'

'Is she now? Very generous of her.'

'She doesn't want the risk of bad publicity.'

'Because of her business? That explains it, then. But will he stick to his side of the bargain? That's a question, isn't it? When did you last see Mr Krantz senior, sir?'

I thought for a moment. 'At Mrs Cassell's house, on Tuesday evening. That was when the agreement was made.'

'Tuesday evening. Cooper?'

'Mr Krantz left the house at 6.15 p.m.,' Cooper said. 'Approximately one hour after Mr Warner. Stayed the night in a bed-and-breakfast in Earl's Court, and was on the 10.15 flight from Heathrow to Munich the next morning. German police were notified, and confirmed his arrival.'

Had police binoculars been trained on Barbara's bedroom that afternoon? I wondered. I looked at Cooper, but his eyes were on his notebook.

'So he's still there?' I asked.

'We understand so, Mr Warner, yes,' Priestly said. 'Good. That ties up very nicely.'

'Do you know if Krantz was in London the night Jonathan Cassell was killed?' I asked.

'Not yet, sir. But we're working on it. Now, that would be interesting, wouldn't it? Two people on that motorcycle, the driver and the pillion passenger who wielded the shotgun. Not like last night's solo effort, as you've described it, Mr Warner.'

Did that mean he now believed me, or not? Priestly's expression gave nothing away. Neither, perhaps. He noted what he was told, waited on events to prove or disprove the truth of it. Events like the one we were waiting for now.

'Thank you, Mr Warner. Perhaps you'd like to return to your own car,' Priestly said, in polite dismissal.

I found Barbara in the Citroën, propped in the passenger seat with her left hand to her forehead, shielding her eyes. I eased myself into the driver's seat beside her. 'All right?'

Barbara heaved a sigh, shook her head from side to side, slowly, miserably.

'What is it?' I asked, gently.

She didn't look up. 'We've got to wait, he said.'

'Who?'

'The one in charge.'

'The Chief Superintendent? What did he mean – wait?'

'To try to make contact. He says it's better to let Hugo stew for a while, to soften him up. That's not how he put it, but it's what he meant.' She shook her head again, not wanting to accept the idea, but not knowing what she could do about it.

'He could be right, I suppose. They must have training in how to deal with this sort of thing. How long does he want to leave it?'

'Until four o'clock.'

'Not until then?' I looked at the car clock. 'But that's four hours away! It'll be starting to get dark . . .' Maybe that's what they're waiting for, I thought. Then, if Hugo doesn't respond, they could move in as the light fails and settle the matter. There must be a limit to the time they're prepared to spend on this, however reassuring the Chief Superintendent might sound about taking it nice and easy . . .

'Four hours, yes. And, oh, William – think what it must be like for Hugo, trapped in there . . .'

She saw it, of course, entirely from Hugo's point of view. I sympathised with that, but she was sounding a bit like those mothers who, as their drug-peddling gun-toting sons are being led away in handcuffs, wail indignantly, 'But he was always such a *good* boy . . .'

'Well, you know, he isn't *trapped*, is he? He can come out any time he wants. I mean, I'm terribly sorry for Hugo; he's got himself into a very unpleasant situation, but he can get out of it easily enough. Can't he? It's not so bad, if you look at it like that.'

Silence. Then Barbara said wearily: 'I suppose so. I suppose you're right. I can't think clearly about it, I can only think what he must be going through at this moment. I want it cut short, not dragged out.'

'If you feel that strongly about it, you could insist on trying to make contact earlier. You are his mother, after all.'

Barbara didn't reply. I sensed that she didn't really want to go against what the police advised. And, in any case, I remembered, a crime had been committed – the police were in charge, whatever Barbara might want.

'Do you want me to try persuading them?' I asked.

Still silence. Then Barbara sighed again. 'It's going to be the longest four hours of my life,' she said with resignation.

Three hours and fifty-five minutes now. That doesn't sound any shorter, almost the reverse. How will we get through it?

The police are certainly aware how hard the waiting is for Barbara. The Chief Superintendent comes up, and asks if he might sit in with us for a minute or two, ostensibly to explain the plan to me, but also, I've no doubt, to reinforce what he'd already told Barbara. Putting the lad in receptive mood – that's his way of describing the process. He must feel the need to justify the long wait, quoting cases where the plan has proved successful, just as the police psychiatrists who had originally worked it all out had predicted. I'm reminded of surgeons I've encountered, and their professional air of optimism – it's all going to be fine, quite a routine little operation, nothing to worry about, splendid! Makes you wonder why the hospital bothers to have a mortuary. Fortunately, we're distracted from such negative thoughts by a constable bringing sandwiches and a Thermos flask of coffee, and the Chief Superintendent leaves us to it.

Barbara says she can't eat, but will have some coffee. I hand her the plastic cup, half full of hot but strange smelling liquid, and while she sips at that, staring out of the window at nothing in particular, I eat all the sandwiches, trying not to look as if I'm enjoying them because it would be heartless, but actually very glad to get my teeth into some food – the first since a rushed and inadequate breakfast. Not really heartless: the plan *will* work, Hugo *will* come out, there *will* be questions but no shooting, and we *will* all then go home, with the possible exception of Hugo for whom a night in the cells might well be a salutary experience. Are there any more sandwiches? I wonder. I ought to bully Barbara to eat some for the effect on morale.

Three hours to go. We can't even go for a walk, with the cottage siege in one direction, and a siege of reporters in the other. How do news photographers and reporters stand it? Hours of waiting, poised for action, for a brief glimpse of something or someone, all to pad out a newspaper that will be glanced at for one day and forgotten the next. This waiting would be bad enough even if Hugo wasn't involved: it's certainly not something I'd choose to spend my life doing for the benefit of a newspaper. Perhaps, if I reclined the seat, I could sleep for a while. Perhaps I can persuade Barbara to try it, or at least pretend.

Surprisingly, she will. We lie back, side by side, staring at the silver grey fabric that lines the car roof, as grey as the clouds that line our English sky, seemingly become permanent. How does it go? – 'The glass is falling hour by hour, the glass will fall for ever/But if you break the bloody glass you won't hold up the weather ...' Why on earth did my mind choose to retain that? Or, 'The great, *grey*-green, greasy Limpopo river, all set about with fever trees ...' Or 'A policeman's lot is not a happy one ...'? Continue, scoring ten points for maximum relevance ...

Or perhaps not. Concentration already wavering ...

262

Will try to sleep.

Rat-a-tat! Rat-a-tat!

I woke with a jerk. Jesus! – shooting's started. No, it's a constable rapping on the window.

I pressed the button to open it. Nothing happened. Always do that – always forget you have to switch the ignition on before the electric windows will work. 'Yes?'

'Chief Superintendent would like you to step along, sir.'

'Right.' I rubbed my eyes. 'What time is it?'

'Just coming up to four o'clock, sir.'

Zero hour! 'I'm coming,' I told him. I turned to Barbara. The passenger seat was empty.

'Mrs Cassell's already with the Chief Superintendent,' the constable said.

I yanked the door latch and scrambled out of the car. Left me sleeping! How useless can you be?

I followed the constable along the track. Dusk was beginning to soften the outline of hedges and buildings. We passed a engineer standing at the bottom of a telegraph pole on which a temporary wire had been rigged from a looped connection at the top. Then we arrived at the line of police cars.

Barbara was there, with Priestly and the Chief Superintendent. They were all intent on the cottage, which was partly obscured by trees, but you could see the upstairs windows clearly enough. Range, sixty or seventy yards, I reckoned. I tried to remember shotgun statistics: with full choke, spread of shot at thirty-five yards about two foot six inches. Beyond that, an increasingly dispersed pattern . . . Of course, we could duck for cover behind the cars.

'Take a look, Mr Warner,' the Chief Superintendent said, passing me a pair of binoculars. I rested them on top of his car, adjusted the knurled focussing wheel, swung from one dormer window to the other, hesitated, then felt for the focussing wheel again. *Was it?*

'See him?'

'Yes.'

It was Hugo all right: his thin features behind the glass appeared ghostly in the fading light. It was like a picture of a soul in torment. He must be able to see glimpses of the blue uniforms surrounding him. Was meant to, perhaps.

'Are you going to make a move, now?' I asked, passing back the binoculars. 'He's had long enough to think it over, surely.'

'Yes, we'll get on with it,' the Chief Superintendent said with decision. 'Now, Mrs Cassell, there's a direct telephone line rigged to the cottage telephone. The handset's in the car here, if you'd care to sit inside . . . that's right. Now, I'm going to use a loud-hailer to tell your son that you're here, and would like to talk to him, and we'll see what happens. It doesn't matter what you say, just try to talk to him much as you would normally – the first point is simply to establish contact, no more. Do you feel up to that?'

'I suppose so,' Barbara said. She looked up at me, her face showing her nervousness.

'You'll do just fine, Barbara,' I encouraged her. 'Sure you will.'

She nodded and tried to smile. 'All right,' she said.

The Chief Superintendent sensibly didn't waste time, but took the loud-hailer from a waiting sergeant and strode off with it. We watched him take up his position some twenty yards away, in the shelter of the hedge.

Priestly leant towards me and said quietly: 'I suggest you get in with Mrs Cassell, Mr Warner.'

'Oh, right.' I joined Barbara on the back seat.

Priestly leant in and pointed to a speaker box propped behind the steering wheel. 'We'll be able to hear his replies on that,' he said. It gave confidence, that they'd taken some trouble with equipment.

I glanced at Barbara. She was holding the telephone handset as one might a scorpion. 'Soon be over now,' I said. She nodded but said nothing.

We waited a few moments in silence. Then we heard a screech from the loud-hailer, followed by the Chief Superintendent's amplified voice, eerie in the gathering gloom.

'Hugo. Hugo Krantz. Can you hear me, Hugo? Your mother is here, and she'd like to talk to you. Pick up the telephone in the house, Hugo, and your mother will be on the line. You have nothing to fear. Just pick up the telephone and talk to her – she's come all the way down from London and wants to talk to you. Will you do that, Hugo? Your mother is waiting to talk to you now.'

We all watched the Chief Superintendent lower the loud-hailer. We waited. Nothing.

He lifted it again, and tried a second time to persuade Hugo to the telephone. Not easy, I realised, to be persuasive at a fairground level of decibels.

Then Barbara was waving her free hand, beckoning.

'Hello?' she said into the telephone. 'Hello? Hugo, darling – is that you?'

A brief but agonising pause. We all held our breath. Then the loudspeaker cleared its throat.

'Uh, yeah, it's me.'

'Hugo! Oh, darling, I'm so glad –'

'Go home, Mum,' the loudspeaker said. '*Go home.* You shouldn't have come.'

'But listen! – darling! It's all right. You can come out now – there's nothing to be afraid of. It'll be all right, I promise you.'

There was no reply.

'Hugo? Don't leave the telephone – just stay there and talk to me if you don't want to come out yet. Hugo?'

The Chief Superintendent had rejoined us, and was listening. 'That's very good, Mrs Cassell,' he whispered into the car. 'You're doing very well. Just keep it going if you can.'

Barbara nodded. She was listening intently. She put her hand over the mouthpiece for a moment and said despairingly: 'I think he's gone ... no, wait.' She spoke into the telephone again. 'Hugo, please believe me. It *will* be all right, I can promise you that.'

Still silence, while we waited again. Then there was a sigh from the loudspeaker, and Hugo's uncertain voice said: 'You don't understand. I can't do that, can I?'

'What don't I understand?' Barbara said. She looked at us, and I saw she was having a hard struggle to control herself. 'Why can't you? Oh, Hugo! Listen ...'

'Because ... Are the police listening to this? They are, aren't they?'

'Yes,' Barbara said, 'but you needn't worry – they're very nice and understanding, and –'

265

'Because,' the loudspeaker said, 'it was me that shot Jonathan. Sorry, Mum, but he had it coming. Someone had to do it.'

Barbara let the telephone droop away from her face. A low wail escaped her; she was staring at nothing, and her shoulders began to shake.

'Better let me take it, madam,' the Chief Superintendent said quickly, leaning forward. 'Hello, Mr Krantz? My name is Hall – I'm in charge out here. Now, sir, it's quite correct what your mother's just told you. There's nothing to be afraid of. Just come out quietly, Mr Krantz, and we'll have a talk about whatever is on your mind. Come out now, sir, please. No point in staying in there all night, is there?'

Barbara had got out of the car, and now stood beside it with her hands to her face. I felt racked for her. First Jonathan, and now, much much worse, this . . . I put my arm round her, and she allowed herself to be led away from the car and the maleficent loudspeaker.

'Come and sit in my car,' I suggested. It was better to get her away, out of earshot.

'It isn't true,' she said. 'It isn't true . . .'

'Barbara, of course it isn't. Don't worry, the police will work it out. Here. Shall I sit with you?'

'Thank you,' she said, 'but no – I've got to be on my own for a few minutes. I . . . don't know what to make of this.'

'I'll come back in a little while, see how you are,' I said.

She didn't reply. I shut the car door as gently as I could, and went back to the police car. They were all bent round the loudspeaker, their faces solemn.

'. . . insulting,' Hugo's voice was saying. 'Nobody was going to treat my mother like that. Used to hear him boasting about it to her, when he'd been with some other woman. It was disgusting . . . *disgusting*. Then there was the money side of it. After all the work she'd done! She'd built it up – all he'd done was help her. He was a real bastard. I'm not sorry, he deserved all he got.'

Priestly nudged the Chief Superintendent's arm, and got a nod of assent. He took up the handset, and said quietly: 'But there were two men on that motorcycle, Mr Krantz. If one was you, who was the other?'

'A man I met,' the loudspeaker said. 'I'm not telling you where. He only drove, anyway. I did the shooting.'

'With the gun you've got in there?' Priestly asked silkily.

'Course not. Another one, with sawn-off barrels, not like this.'

'Where is it now?'

'Threw it in the river. After last night, of course.'

So it had been Hugo after me last night . . .

'What do you have against Mr Warner?' Priestly asked.

'He's another one like Jonathan. Oh yes. I've seen him smarming around my mother. But mainly, he was getting too close. It's because of him I came down here, to decide what to do next.'

Thank God Barbara wasn't listening to this . . .

The Chief Superintendent had taken back the handset. 'Well now, Mr Krantz,' he said, 'now you've told us all this, there really isn't any point in staying in there any longer, is there? I repeat that no harm will come to you if you come out now. Don't you think this has gone on long enough? If you really care about your mother, as you've told us, and I'm sure you do, give her the pleasure of seeing you out here, safe and sound. Come on, Mr Krantz – let's be sensible, now. Come on out.'

We listened to the loudspeaker: a kind of silence, but I thought I could hear breathing. Then it said: 'Oh no. No, it's not as easy as that.'

'What do you mean, sir?'

There was a click.

'Damn! He's put the receiver down,' the Chief Superintendent said tersely. 'And I didn't like the sound of that, did you? Could be going to do something stupid. Sergeant! – tell those men to keep alert.'

'Shall I fetch Mrs Cassell?' I offered.

'No. Nothing more she can do, in my opinion. It's up to us, now. We may have to rush the place, try to stop him turning the gun on himself. It's getting dark – that'll help.'

'I asked Mrs Cassell how many cartridges he'd got. She thinks she remembers a cartridge belt about half full. She doesn't remember seeing any spare boxes. It was her husband's gun, and he didn't use it much,' I said.

'Ah, thank you! If only people would turn these things in when they've got no further use for them ... half a belt, that's about a dozen. Might as well be a hundred – I'm not risking my men against ... yes? – what is it?'

'Wilson would like to know if you've any special instructions, sir?' the sergeant asked.

'Instructions? Tell him to stay put, fire only if the lad tries to break through with the gun. *With the gun* – got that? Can't have him going on the rampage with a gun. Without it, he won't be such a – *what's that?*'

Two shotgun blasts had sounded from the house, followed by shouts, and what might have been a scream from Barbara. We all strained our eyes, peering through the dusk for signs of movement. The sergeant hurried off, spoke briefly to the marksman who was still in position by the gate, and came panting back.

'Nobody hurt, sir. But he's out of the house, round at the side, out of sight. Let off two shots as he came out. Not aimed, Wilson says.'

'Next ones may be. He's probably reloading,' the Superintendent muttered. Then he raised his voice. 'Watch yourselves, lads! I don't like the feel of this.'

He was right. Through the distant hedge I could just see a lean, shadowy figure, hardly more than a blur of movement in the twilight, come charging down the garden path towards the gate. Son of Ludwig, inheritor of the murderous moods I'd witnessed in his father.

There was a chorus of cries, including my own heartfelt warning. Above them all, the Chief Superintendent's command carried like a cannon's roar.

'WILSON!'

I saw the marksman raise his revolver, clasped in both hands, take careful aim through the garden gate.

And fire.

I remember the sounds, first of all – Barbara screaming again, the shouts of men and the pounding of many feet, the howl of the loud-hailer as the Chief Superintendent issued orders. Then I can recall images – blue uniforms emerging at the double from hiding places around the cottage as we all converged on the white garden gate at the centre of the scene; the flying figure of Barbara just ahead of me as we reached the gate and poured into the tiny garden; the white face of the police marksman standing back to let us pass, and the dark shape of his target lying face down across the brick path, motionless.

'Don't move him, madam! Ambulance is on the way.' Barbara had thrown herself down beside her son, and was trying to see his face. 'You sir – can you keep her back?' I got down, took her by the shoulders. 'Come on, Barbara. They're right, you know. Best not touch him yet.'

I felt her shudder. She flung her head up, glared at the blue wall of police uniforms. Her face was unrecognisable. 'I could kill *you*!' she hissed, 'I could kill you *all!*' Nobody said a word. I held her shoulders still, kept a pressure on; it seemed better than words.

'Ambulance is here,' a voice shouted from outside the garden. I looked up. So soon? – it must have been in waiting, laid on for four o'clock. The ambulance came into view, jolting on the rough track, and reversed up to the gate. The rear doors were swung open and a folded stretcher passed out. Two attendants came running up the path with it, and laid it out beside Hugo. One of them reached for his pulse, felt it, nodded, and they began to ease him on to the stretcher, turning him as they did so. Hugo made a feeble sound of protest. 'All right, lad,' one said, 'all right. We've got you, just relax.'

They might need to check the wound before carrying him away, I realised. It was time to get Barbara away. 'Come on, now,' I urged her, 'we must give them some room.' She allowed me to pull her to her feet, and I managed to block her view of the stretcher for a few moments. Then it was being lifted. We followed it down the path, and saw it loaded into the ambulance. The doors were closed.

Priestly appeared at my elbow. 'May I suggest that Mrs Cassell comes with me to the hospital?' he said, 'I have to go there myself, of course. I'll be in touch with you tomorrow, Mr Warner. You'll be going straight back to Church Street, I assume?'

I looked at Barbara. Surely I should take her? She looked dazed now, hardly aware of us.

'Is that all right with you, Mrs Cassell?' Priestly persisted. He had brought her down this morning, I remembered. And I knew, after today's talk, that he was more sympathetic than I had supposed. She'd probably be all right. But she must decide.

'Barbara?'

The ambulance was leaving. Her eyes followed it as it began to bump slowly along the track.

'It's all right with me,' she said in a small, flat voice. 'Can we go now?'

I watched them walk together to the Rover, policeman with murderer's mother. Well, that's how it was. Poor, poor Barbara.

CHAPTER 23

Time of Truth

This correspondence with the real external world
we call 'truth'.

SIGMUND FREUD

'The poor boy!' Claudine said again.

'I suppose there is an age at which homicide stops being
rather naughty and becomes properly reprehensible,' I said. 'But
I suspect you put it rather higher than I do. I think if you're old
enough to vote, you're old enough to refrain from shooting
people. *Tu n'es pas d'accord?*'

She turned her head on the pillow to look at me. Her dark
eyes surveyed my face with dispassion. It wasn't what I wanted,
but any look was better than the nothing – which had been my
lot lately.

'Of course,' I said, 'as far as Barbara is concerned, I've got no
shortage of sympathy. She didn't, of course, know what she
was letting herself in for when she took Ludwig's baby on board,
or that it would turn out to be a psychopath. Now that I've
encountered Ludwig a few times, I'm surprised that she ever
got entangled with him, but that's only being wise after the
event. Perhaps, when he was younger and being successful, his
essential craziness didn't show. And, of course, when she did
see it, she threw him out. But she could never do the same
with Hugo – she did the opposite thing, and over-protected
him.'

If the wine trade goes on collapsing, I thought, I should
maybe take up psychotherapy. With Miss Mullarkey's help, and
the experiences of the last couple of weeks, I'd already made a
good start.

'What does this mean – *psychopath*?' Claudine asked,
frowning.

'Well, it's, you know . . .'

'I do not know. Or I would not ask.'

It takes a little time to get hold of the terms, of course. 'Ah yes. I think this is right – someone who is insanely anti-social.'

'Someone who does not like to go to parties?'

'No, darling, no. More than that. Look, it's a little difficult to explain in just a few words. If you're interested, I'll buy you a book on it.'

'Thank you, *chéri*, but I think I am not.'

Did I hear right? 'You called me *chéri*!'

'We are married,' Claudine said drily. 'It is usual, no?'

'No! Not lately, that is. You've been like an iceberg.'

She sat up in bed with a jerk that brought her breasts flying into full view. 'And I haven't seen those for weeks,' I said. 'Well, days beyond count. I feel seriously deprived.'

She seemed struck speechless, but from the flexing of her features there were words on the way.

'*You*,' she said at last, in the sort of voice that turns people into salt, or stone, or maybe a small muddy puddle, '*you* are the one who has been like an iceberg. An *English* iceberg – *le plus froid du monde* . . .'

'Oh no, now hold on – when it comes to freezing politeness, the French hold the world record. It wasn't me, you must know that. It was you –'

'*Ah non – you*!'

'You, dammit . . .'

'*Absolument pas*! It was you!'

There was a pause, while we glared at each other. Then: 'Claudine,' I said, '*chérie*. What *are* we arguing about?'

I was up first in the morning, and on my way downstairs while Claudine was still at the bathroom mirror scrubbing off Forté Vital de Nuit.

'Come on, girls!' I called, knocking on their doors as I passed their bedrooms. Uselessly, because when I arrived in the kitchen they were already there before me, bent over bowls of Shredded Wheat. 'All that sugar,' I warned them. 'Your teeth will fall out and you'll be doomed to a life of miserable spinsterhood.'

'Papa,' Nichole said through her Shredded Wheat, 'lots of girls don't want to get married, you know. They like living on their own.'

'Nonsense, Nichole.'

'It's not nonsense, Papa. Is it, Sylvie?'

'You can have babies on your own,' Sylvie said. 'You just choose a man to *do* it, you know, and then . . .'

'Subversive nonsense,' I said firmly. My God! – if this were to spread . . . 'And anyway, it's very bad for babies to be brought up without a father. You'd miss . . . all sorts of things. The masculine point of view, and so on.'

'There'd be less washing-up,' Nichole said.

A dignified silence seemed the best course. I started to look for the coffee pot, but Nichole got there before me, and evidently knew what she was doing, so I stood back and let her get on with it while I loaded the pop-up toaster. A couple of slices of well-buttered toast with dark Cooper's Oxford on it and a large breakfast cup of milky coffee soon restored my day. Claudine arrived, looking cheerful.

'I am late,' she said, 'but I see you have coffee.'

'Nichole made it,' I explained.

'Good!'

'But it may be for the last time.'

'*Comment?*'

'I've been given the sack. Fathers are redundant, my daughters tell me.'

'Nichole! Sylvie! Your poor papa!'

'There – you see!' I said, making faces at them.

'Sometimes,' Claudine said, 'I think there are no fathers. Only mothers, little children, and bigger children.'

Maggie was pleased to see me.

'You're looking so much better,' she said.

'Better?'

'You've been like a thundercloud this last week or two,' she explained. 'So it's all over then? What a dreadful thing for poor Mrs Cassell, her son going off his head like that.'

'Terrible. I ought to call her at the hotel to see how she is, but Superintendent Priestly said he'd ring this morning, and I'm waiting for that.'

'Yes, of course. Claudine said it was touch and go.'

'He was hit in the stomach: the marksman aimed at his legs, he said, but it was all just a blur. But they rushed him into hospital in Bournemouth, saying they thought he had a fair chance. Well, Maggie, life – and work – must go on. What have you got for me?'

About ten, the telephone rang. Not Priestly, but Bill Charrington.

'What a dreadful thing to happen,' he said, echoing Maggie's words. I repeated what I'd already told her. 'I was going to ring you too, Bill, but you seem to know as much as I do.'

'It was in the papers,' he said. 'Siege of Burley, young man with shotgun holding police at bay, all that. Nothing about Barbara, yet. Lucky that Hugo's not got the same name – that may hold them at bay for a while.'

'Let's try to keep it that way,' I suggested. 'I'm afraid this will really knock Barbara for six – she was very close to Hugo.'

'She was that,' he agreed. 'Now, William – if you can possibly manage it, we ought to have a meeting at your warehouse before the weekend. The builder's starting to make excuses why he can't start before next month, and it's got to be jumped on. Next thing you know, we'll be into the frosty season, and have to put the whole thing off until the spring. We can't have that.'

'Before the weekend? But it's Friday – that means this afternoon.'

'So it does. Can you manage it?'

I thought for a moment. 'I suppose so. Two-thirty?'

'Make it later – I've got another job to visit. Four-thirty?'

'All right. Yes, no problem. See you then.'

I rang Pete to see if he could be there as well – he's supposed to be in charge of the warehouse, and I like to keep him in the picture. But also I wanted to know if there was any chance of his bringing Miss Mullarkey – I knew she'd be interested to hear the end of the story, and could perhaps clear up a few points of psychology that were beyond me.

'I'll give 'er a buzz,' Pete said. 'If you ask me, wild 'orses won't keep 'er away. See yer.'

*

Priestly rang an hour later.

'Could be worse, Mr Warner,' he said, 'could be worse. They've got the bullet out, and his chances have improved. Mrs Cassell's been allowed in for a few minutes; he recognised her, but was too groggy to say anything. She'll be going back this afternoon.'

'You checked the motorcycle, I suppose?'

He made a noise that might have been meant to indicate amusement. The ice did seem to be thawing today, in all directions. 'I thought you'd be asking that. Yes, we checked it. The rear lamp had only one bulb in it. We found the dud in his pocket – took it out to match it, but hadn't had time to buy a replacement. Yes, you were sharp there, Mr Warner, noticing that. But now, how do you think he knew you were getting close to him?'

'I've worked that out, superintendent. He must have heard me talking about it when I was at the house in Edwardes Square on Wednesday evening. Mrs Cassell found him at the bottom of the stairs, just outside the open door of the sitting-room where we were talking. I remember her telling him to wear his slippers and stop padding about in bare feet. He pretended he was hungry and on his way to the kitchen for a snack, but he could have heard all we were saying. Must have given him a fright, too – I was swearing never to give up the trail until Jonathan's killer had been found.'

'Were you, sir?'

'Yes. Well, I know you were doing all you could, but the trouble was that you seemed to have me listed as suspect number one, and your enquiries here were wrecking my marriage, as I explained.'

'I'm very sorry, sir. *My* trouble was, though, that you were not being entirely frank with me. It was that, I must point out, that made it necessary to apply a little pressure at times.'

'Well, you certainly did that,' I said. 'But you're right – it was my fault. I apologised yesterday, and I'd like to do so again, now, if that's any use. I meant to protect my wife and myself – not to make your job harder.'

'All right, sir. No harm done this time, but –'

'Yes, I know. But let's hope there isn't one. Goodbye, superintendent.

'Goodbye, Mr Warner.'

There was an air of finality about that. Probably the last I'd hear of the Pestilent Priestly. Quite human, when you got to know him better. As for myself – no, no, let's not have boring speculation about whether I'd do the same again. The same situation won't happen again, so it would be a complete waste of time.

After lunch, I got out the Citroën and set off for the warehouse. Everything was returning to normal, and I felt myself slipping comfortably back into the old routines. Even the car seat felt more comfortable: it wasn't really the seat, of course, but my own body relaxing after the alarums of the last two weeks, my spine freeing itself from tension, my tum returned to acid-free anonymity. Too much stress is certainly damaging, I thought. Any more of that, and I must have started ulcers. But now, instead of anxious speculation about Claudine, I could concentrate on business. Somebody said that there's no less harmful occupation than making money, if not taken to excess. Could be, could be.

I pulled up outside the warehouse, stepped in through the pass door, and could hear voices in the office. Oh good! – it sounded as though Miss Mullarkey had been able to come. I set off down the aisle of crates towards them, followed, as always, by the ghostly echo of my footsteps, ker-lap, ker-lap. Pete looked out of the office door to see who was coming.

'Hello, Pete. Sounds as though you've brought her.'

'Like I told you,' Pete said, 'couldn't keep 'er away.'

'Hello, Mr Warner,' Miss Mullarkey said.

It wasn't just indulgence, though I was looking forward to Miss Mullarkey's comments on Hugo's breakdown – what had happened was horrific, tragic, but I couldn't help being fascinated by just what caused someone to behave like that. No, there was also, I felt, a debt to be repaid, and that I could best repay it by completing this case history for her.

I was right about that, obviously.

'Oh yes! That's most interesting,' Miss Mullarkey almost sang, as I finished the tale. We were sitting, as before, on opposite sides of the table, our elbows almost touching, and Miss Mullarkey's spectacles flashing inches from my face.

'You've heard of things like this before?' I asked.

'Yes. But not, pardon the expression, from the horse's mouth. It makes all the difference, oh yes indeed. I would love to know even more, of course – what he was like as a child, for instance.'

'I didn't know them then. But I've heard Barbara say that he was always a good child: quiet, reserved, no trouble at all. That makes it all the more tragic, what happened.'

'Tragic, yes. But not surprising. You often read about the mothers of young men convicted of violent crime saying, "He was always such a *good* boy", don't you?'

'Yes. At one point, I almost expected to hear Barbara say that. But I don't see . . .'

'There is probably some genetic inheritance, as you've pointed out. But more important is the parental influence, or lack of it. The father is often absent or uninterested – a weak influence, as in this case. The mother may well be . . . I hesitate to suggest this about Mrs Cassell.'

'Go on – just between ourselves.'

Miss Mullarkey turned her head to glance at Pete, who was sitting to one side, listening.

'Oh, I see,' I said. 'Well, whatever Pete told you about Barbara and myself, it's all over now. It was a sort of mistake. Nothing in it.'

'Well,' Miss Mullarkey said doubtfully.

'Go on,' I urged.

'All right. The mother may well be rather cold, detached, incapable of giving the child the physical affection it needs in order to develop into a normal adult. Consequently . . .'

I was staring at Miss Mullarkey as though she were a witch. 'But . . .' I said, 'but . . . that's exactly what I found when I, er, when we . . . I slept with her, once. She seemed to me completely unresponsive. And *detached* – exactly that – from what was going on.'

'Exactly!' Miss Mullarkey said with satisfaction. 'Detached. So, you see, the child grows up without ever really being brought to life. Not only that, but the child's lack of self, his unde-mandingness, is reinforced by being equated with "goodness", and rewarded.'

'And then?'

'And then, when the child is fifteen or sixteen, perhaps, the mother starts to push the child towards outside interests, to break the apron strings. This terrifies the child, of course, be-cause he hasn't developed any character of his own, independ-ent of his mother.'

'So he struggles not to be pushed out.'

'Yes. He can't imagine life separate from his mother. He identi-fies with her interests, fights for what he thinks are her causes. And sometimes, as we see here, avenges her insults.'

'Jonathan. Telling Barbara about his other women. With a glint in the telling.'

'He probably overheard that. Many times, perhaps.'

'Padding about in bare feet . . .' I said, thoughtfully.

Miss Mullarkey smiled. No more to be said, her smile implied. But no more was needed – I could see it all, now.

Through the open door came the sound of approaching feet, ker-lap, ker-lap. I looked up. It was Bill Charrington.

'Well,' I said, 'thank you very much, Miss Mullarkey. I shall know to be wary of "good" children in future.'

'Thank *you*, Mr Warner,' she said, standing up. 'It was very kind of you to tell me the rest of it. I really appreciate that.'

'Here we are again, then,' Bill said from the doorway. 'Ready, William? The builder's outside.'

'I'm right with you,' I said. 'I suppose we'll have to be tough on our own, now, without Simpson looming behind us rattling writs. We may have misjudged him, you know. They're like quicksilver, these builders – always sliding off to other jobs. Simpson had his uses, I'm afraid.'

We went out, into the fray.

It didn't take too long, in the event. Charrington began by read-ing the riot act on builders who didn't know when they were well off, and told Ron Green in plain Yorkshire that if he didn't get his arse off the ground and his back into the job he'd find himself under attack from my new legal eagle (entirely fictitious) compared to whom Simpson was a twittering sparrow. Poor Ron buckled under this tirade, and went off muttering he'd be on site first thing on Monday morning. Shortly afterwards, Bill departed, grimly pleased at his success. I went back to the office to clear up loose ends, and was soon free to go myself.

'I'll be off then, Pete.'

'Cheer-oh, guv'nor.'

'Goodbye, Mr Warner,' Miss Mullarkey said, 'and thank you again.'

I walked back through the echoing warehouse and reached the pass door. Home James, and don't spare the horses – there may be crumpets for tea. Though, as it's the rush hour, I may get there too late. Never mind: surely, tonight, we'll have a proper candlelit, foodie's paradise of a dinner. I stepped out into the street, and climbed into the car.

It was dark, but the sky was clear. A minor miracle had happened – it hadn't rained all day. I fitted the key into the ignition. Somewhere behind me a motorcycle started up. It brought back memories – well, it would be some time before I got rid of those. I started the engine, and drove off slowly, over the familiar cobbles. A proper dinner – yes, I was looking forward to that.

The motorcycle was catching me up, fast. Got no sense, some of these lads – on cobbles you've a job keeping a motorcycle upright, and it pays to go easy on the throttle. Too fast.

On impulse, I pressed the button to slide my window down. Above the soft hum of the Citroën's engine, I could hear a rasp of motorcycle exhaust.

A rasp I could, just *could*, have heard before. Impossible, of course. That motorcycle is now in police custody. There must be dozens, hundreds even, still roaming the streets and sounding just like it.

I slid the window up again. Nothing to worry about, it just couldn't be. Left Brain said it was impossible. Right Brain said –

The car was in second gear. I slammed the accelerator down, felt the front wheels scrabbling for a grip on the cobbles. Then we were off, putting on speed fast, to get the hell out of there.

But not fast enough. A big bike can do nought to sixty in under six seconds – almost twice what I could manage in the

Citroën. The cobbles would slow him, but he was taking risks, big risks, and catching me up with ease. I slammed the gear lever up into third, glanced in the mirror. The headlamp was close behind now, moving out to pass me. My imagination was in overdrive – I could see him draw level, bring out the shotgun, use the first shot to shatter the window, and then, at point blank range . . .

We flashed past a street light. It was then I saw that the bike had two up. And that the passenger had already drawn out the gun, and was holding it ready . . .

I realised afterwards that I'd got the idea from reports of aerial combat in the Falklands war. When attacked from behind by the much faster Argentinian fighters, our Hawker Harriers used their vertical take-off jets to come almost to a dead stop, forcing the Argentinians to overshoot. After which, positions reversed, the hunter became the hunted.

Citroën brakes are power-assisted, light to the touch, but marvellously effective. My right foot went down on the button. The car's tyres clung to the road, throwing me against my seat belt. Out of the corner of my eye I saw the motorcycle flash past, caught unaware. There was just time to see an unevenly lit rear number plate before the stop light went on, then off again as the driver fought to control the machine on the greasy cobbles, in the glare of my headlights.

It was probably my only chance – they wouldn't let that happen again. Wing cannon or guided missiles would have been better, but even Citroëns don't come equipped with those. Believing that peace was restored, I'd put the Webley back in the deed box, at home. I had no other weapon than the car itself.

I threw the gear lever into second, and covered the intervening ten yards at full blast, front tyres shrieking. There was a bang and screech of metal as Citroën and motorcycle collided: the car's speed and weight caused the front end to bounce up and on to the bike before the two locked together and slid down the road with a hideous grinding of steel on cobblestones.

The car slewed, throwing me sideways to thump against the door, but my seatbelt prevented me from being thrown forward, or I would have gone through the windscreen. The din seemed to go on for a long time, but was probably about six or seven seconds. Then we came to a halt against the kerb. There was a hissing and a groaning to be heard. The hissing sounded mechanical, but the groaning was not.

I got out, ready to run for it. But there was no need. The car looked like a giant grey beetle with a red insect in its jaws. Its headlights still glared, but at such an angle that nearby telephone wires glinted in their light. Something clunked against my right foot: I looked down and could see the dull blue metal and polished wood of a shotgun lying on the cobbles, the barrels cruelly amputated. It was like a sign of surrender.

To hell with fingerprints – safety came first. I snatched it up, and broke it open. Both barrels were loaded. I snapped it shut again, and felt with my thumb for the safety catch. I'd learned a few things about overconfidence, lately.

The red beetle had black leather legs. Only two on this side. I shook one of them by the foot. It moved without resistance, limp and apparently lifeless. The rest of the body was under the car.

Keeping a firm grip on the shotgun, I ventured round to the other side. There was no sign of the second rider. My stomach did a quick flip and, heart thumping, I wheeled round, prepared for attack. There was no one in sight. I looked under the car again.

I could see part of a face, but the helmet surrounding it was crushed under the Citroën's sump. This, I calculated, was the owner of the legs sticking out from under the opposite side of the car. He seemed unlikely to be needing them any more.

Car headlights appeared on the road, approaching from the direction of the warehouse. The boss, coming to inspect his hireling's work? I took cover at the front of the car. Then I recognised the tall outline and indifferent lights of my own taxi. It stopped a few yards away, and Pete appeared.

'Wait!' I shouted. 'Keep away – there's one missing. There were two of them . . .'

'Counted 'im, 'ave you?' Pete called back.

I looked where he was pointing. The taxi's lights illuminated a helmeted figure lying against a high brick boundary wall where the collision had hurled him. I approached cautiously, the shotgun levelled. This time, the eyes that looked out of the helmet moved, and blinked.

I became aware of another figure coming up to us, and whirled round in near panic. My nerves, I realised, were strung to breaking point.

'Careful! It's Miss Mullarkey,' Peter warned. 'Told 'er to stay in the car, but she never listens.'

I lowered the gun, and breathed deeply. *Too close . . . get a grip on yourself . . .*

We gathered round the prostrate motorcyclist. His eyes had closed.

'Wake up, yer bleeder!' Peter exhorted him.

'I think he's badly hurt,' Miss Mullarkey said. But her opinions, I'd just discovered, were not always flawless. And, in fact, we all then saw his eyes open again.

"Orspital,' the figure whispered.

'Right, matey,' Pete said. 'But we got a few questions, first.'

'Me fuckin' leg's broke.'

'Yeah,' Pete said. 'And you're about to get the other one broke an' all, if you don't speak up. Who's your gaffer? Eh?'

'Come on, Pete,' I said, 'we'd better . . .'

'This 'ere's the big chance, guv,' he whispered fiercely. 'Can't miss it.' He bent down and put a hand on the leg nearest to him. The figure gave a gasp of pain. 'I'll ask you one more time,' Pete said, bending down to stare into the helmet. 'Give us the name! Last chance, now. *Give!*'

'Fuckin' . . . bastards . . .' He could hardly get it out.

'I'll go and telephone for an ambulance. And the police,' Miss Mullarkey said, starting to walk away.

'No! 'Ang on! – witness, aren't you?' Pete called. She came back, reluctantly.

'Right, mate. You 'eard the nice lady. You'll get your ambulance just as soon as you speak up,' Pete said, bending down again.

'Ah, Jesus . . .'

'Keep 'im out of it. *Who was it?*'

I could see the eyes in the helmet switch from side to side, looking for a way out. But there was none.

Then the lids drooped, flickered, and shut.

'Snuffed it!' Pete said quietly, straightening up.

But from pavement level a voice could be heard, not much more than a gasp now.

'What?' I said.

We all bent down to hear it.

'Geezer . . . by the name of . . . Cassell.'

Miss Mullarkey went off at a fast trot to the telephone. Pete and I stood guard, one at each end of the wreckage. Two cars came up, had to be manoeuvred past and help declined.

'All under control, thanks. Ambulance on the way.'

Then, at the far end of the street, a flashing blue light appeared.

'That was quick!' I called across to Pete. 'She can hardly have put the phone down.'

The police car approached at speed, and pulled up with a screech of tyres. Somebody jumped out and shouted my name.

'Over here,' I called back.

It was Priestly.

'Hello, superintendent! I must say, you got here in record time.'

He only glanced at me before making a rapid tour of the Citroën and its half-digested prey, returning with pursed lips and a weary expression.

'I've got two for you, this time,' I said to forestall him. 'And a sawn-off shotgun.' I offered it to him.

'Thank you,' he said, taking it.

'This one here's just given us the name we wanted. A "geezer called Cassell".'

'Cassell?'

'That's it. Someone's rung for an ambulance. I'm afraid we're going to need a breakdown truck as well – my car'll never be the same again.'

'Seems unlikely, sir.'

'How did you get here so fast?'

'Let's go and sit in the car, shall we, sir?'

I wouldn't mind sitting down, I thought – no, not at all. I followed him across the cobbles, and we settled into the back of his Rover. Cooper, who had completed his own tour of the wreckage, got into the front.

'Hello again, Sergeant Cooper.'

'Hello, sir.'

'While Cooper gets his notebook ready,' Priestly said, 'I'll answer your question, Mr Warner. I was already on my way, you see. And the reason for that was that I'd just got the results of the test on that bulb we found in young Mr Krantz's pocket.'

'The rear lamp bulb from his bike – that you said was dud?'

'I thought it was dud, of course, but as a matter of routine I had it tested. Nothing wrong with it at all.'

'Ah.'

'You see what that means, don't you, sir? That Master Hugo was having us all on. That someone else –'

'The bike under my car had half the rear light out. I saw that before the crash.'

Priestly shook his head. He wasn't disagreeing with me, but was annoyed with himself, I could see that.

'If I may make a suggestion – don't worry about it,' I said. 'I survived, even if my car didn't. And I've thought for some time that this affair was only ever going to get solved from the bottom up – by finding the gunmen. So – we have.'

Priestly sighed. 'Kind of you to put it that way, Mr Warner.'

'Let's just say it evens things up between us, superintendent.'

He nodded.

'So, now we've got the name. And I do feel the whole thing rounds off very neatly: there can seldom have been a more poetic piece of justice than Jonathan getting shot by his own gunmen.'

'Now, hold on, sir. Why would he –?'

'I had this worked out some time ago. After all, I had what you could call a pressing personal interest in knowing whether Jonathan or myself was the intended victim. It could have been a case of mistaken identity, as we were both dressed alike in dinner jackets, and are the same height and approximate appearance. Jonathan's mistake was to come out of the restaurant with Claudine – that made the gunmen think it was me. It was a stupid thing to do, but we'd all had a lot to drink, and I think he liked the idea of being off the scene when the shooting took place. It was his bad luck that they were careless.'

'But the gunman fired the second shot from close up, Mr

284

Warner. He must have known that he was shooting the wrong man.'

'That's the point I got stuck on for a long time. But Pete – that's him over there – explained it. He said, when you find you've shot your employer in the dinner pail, it's too late to apologise, you just have to go on and finish the job, to protect your identity.'

Priestly was silent. Then he sighed again.'Makes sense, I suppose,' he said.

'And that's what all the rest of it was about, it seems to me,' I said. 'Protecting their identity. These two come from round here – Eastenders, I bet you'll find. They heard about the enquiries I was making – the walls have ears in this part of the world, don't they? The gunman himself made one solo attempt on me, which failed. So this evening, they decided on a full-scale, two-man attack to finish it. And instead, lost the whole game.'

'And Mrs Warner –'

'A brief affair,' I said. 'We're together again now, and I'm convinced of that. She had no idea that Jonathan saw it all differently, expected to scoop her up and my business as well. I never realised he was such a cold-blooded bastard, and I'm sure Claudine didn't either. He was very good at laying on the charm.'

Lights were coming up behind us – the ambulance. 'See to it, Cooper,' Priestly said. Then he lapsed into one of his silences. I sat on, content this time to wait while he ruminated. After a couple of minutes, Cooper returned.

'Have to wait for the breakdown truck to get the one under the car out,' he said. 'Need lifting gear for that.'

'All right. Tell them to take the other one away, meanwhile,' Priestly said. 'I'll have some questions for him.'

'Afraid it's too late for that, sir,' Cooper said.

'Dead?'

Cooper nodded. There was enough streetlight coming into the car for me to see Priestly's lips moving. No, it wasn't his day.

'Who heard what he said?' he asked me.

'I did, of course. Also Pete, my warehouse manager, and Miss Mullarkey, a social worker.'

'Three. Could be worse,' Priestly murmured to himself.
'That should be enough to wrap it up, shouldn't it?' I asked.
'I'd like to think so,' he said.

CHAPTER 24

A Little More

'Stop a moment!' you will exclaim; 'we can't follow
you any further there!' You are quite right; I must
add a little more . . .

SIGMUND FREUD

I wanted to think so too, yes, indeed I did. Claudine wasn't too
happy about it, though. I broke the news as gently as I could,
only too aware of how she would feel on learning what had
lurked beneath Jonathan's courtly manner.

'This is true?' she exclaimed, her dark eyes searching my face
uncertainly, as though she half believed I might suddenly burst
out laughing and declare it a macabre joke.

'Three of us heard it,' I said. '"A geezer by the name of
Cassell". We can't all be mistaken. And as I've explained, my
darling, it does, I'm afraid, all add up. He thought he had you
hooked, you see. I don't think you Continentals realise, when
you're playing these social games you all understand, that us
literal Anglo-Saxons are inclined to misinterpret, and take you
seriously.'

We were sitting at the kitchen table. Claudine had her elbows
on it, and I saw her shoulders droop.

'*Ah, mon dieu*,' she said. Then she put her face in her
hands.

I went round to her – I seemed to be getting a lot of practice in
dishing out comfort, these days – and, pulling up a chair beside
her, put my arm round her shoulders. 'Don't,' I said, 'don't. You
couldn't possibly have guessed anything like this would happen.
It's like an accident, that's all – a conflict of events at the same
point in time, like crossing the road in front of a drunken driver.
And it's all over, finished. Let's have a brandy – no, better, some of
that Calvados I opened the other day.'

287

'C'est incroyable . . .'

'I'll get the Calva,' I said. 'Back in a second.'

It was obvious she was going to lie awake, worrying about it, so I persuaded her to take three of the pills. I slept well myself, apart from a dream in which I was walking endlessly through the echoing warehouse, my feet going ker-lap, ker-lap.

But in the morning, everything looked brighter, including the weather. No actual sun, but the clouds were the thinnest they'd been since the weekend Jonathan was shot. Heaven smiling on justice, perhaps. Or a chance distribution of isobars. I keep my options open.

'I suppose,' I said at breakfast, 'I'd better call on Barbara, and make sympathetic noises. Priestly said she was coming back home as Hugo is off the danger list. She's going to get him transferred to London as soon as the hospital will allow it.'

'I suppose that you should,' Claudine said without enthusiasm.

'And then,' I said, 'I doubt if we'll be seeing much of her, now this business is all over.'

Claudine took a sip of coffee. 'I never did see much of her,' she said carefully. 'But I think you should go, certainly.' And then that's it, she didn't have to add. We were wiping the slate clean, and it was fair enough, but how do women detect these things? If the State ever assumes absolute power, it's women who will run the Thought Police . . .

I made a telephone call first to make sure Barbara was at home and prepared to be visited, and then went out to find a taxi.

'Sweet of you to call,' Barbara said. She looked pale, with dark circles under her eyes, but paleness suited her. In Edwardian times she would have patrolled lawns under a parasol, refusing cucumber sandwiches.

'Telephones are hopelessly inadequate at a time like this,' I said. 'What's the news on Hugo – out of danger, I'm told?'

'Let's go into the sitting-room,' she said in her quiet voice, leading the way. The curtains were drawn back, but swathes of cream-coloured net across the big sash window reduced the daylight to a subdued softness, calm and controlled.

'He's going to be all right,' she said.

'Oh Barbara – I'm so glad. I can imagine what you've been through.'

Hard to believe, looking at her, that it was this same cool quality, so attractive to men, that had driven Hugo to such extremes – except that I myself had also felt the frustration it could cause when I had tried to get closer to her. That was partly why I'd wanted to see her again this morning – not just to offer sympathy, but to try again to understand what it was that had misled me and almost destroyed Hugo. Because, according to Miss Mullarkey, it made no difference to her theory that he had not actually shot Jonathan. It was enough that he had *claimed* he had done it – snatched at the opportunity to force his mother's attention to him, to become a hero in her eyes, as he saw it, no matter what the risk. It was no odder, Miss Mullarkey had pointed out, than any of the other false confessions to all kinds of crime including murder that the police had constantly to be on their guard against. Psychology, it seemed, could point to opposite conclusions with equal conviction. Perhaps I'd better stick with wine.

I gave Barbara an outline of what had happened yesterday evening, and we talked about Jonathan for a while, much on the same lines as last night's discussion with Claudine. Except that, on the whole, Claudine was the more upset. That was understandable, as Barbara had, after all, tired of his tricks and thrown him out. Conversation slowed, became a trickle. It was time to go.

Barbara came with me to the door. I opened it. For once there was no Ludwig on the doorstep, bearing guns or roses. Barbara touched my arm, and put up her cheek. I kissed her, lightly. This was it, *finis*. I'm sure we both knew that.

'Goodbye, Barbara.' She smiled, and nodded.

I walked down the short path, and turned at the gate to wave. She was still standing there, in her doorway, watching me. I went through the gate and, when I turned round to close it, the house door was already shut.

*

I suppose I could say that normal life was then resumed, and in the sense that I was able to go about without being shot at, or interviewed endlessly by the police, or avoiding reporters, or discovering suspended solicitors, yes, normality did return. But normality, alas, includes not only work, food, and making love but trying to find time for these activities between the insatiable demands of those who have clearly never heard of them but believe our time should be spent entirely in form-filling and record-keeping. I had to make more statements to the police. I had to attend three inquests (Jonathan's having been delayed at the request of the police while further enquiries were made). I was given notice that I would be required to attend a court hearing in the matter of the Burley siege as soon as the principal participant was well enough to appear.

And last but far from least, I had to persuade the insurance company to replace the Citroën, which was a complete write-off. I was sent accident report forms. I completed them with truth and detailed accuracy. In the space provided for a diagram of vehicles involved and their positions before and after the accident, together with any other relevant information, I drew in the Citroën, the motorcycle, the positions of the two motorcyclists, together with arrows and notes to show how the final entanglement had come about. I added the shotgun as a relevant factor. It wasn't my fault that the completed diagram looked more like the battle of Waterloo – Wellington *here*, Napoleon's artillery *here*, line of Blücher's advance *here*, and so on – than a road accident. An assessor came to see me, to query whether I hadn't, in fact, deliberately destroyed the vehicle? – in which case the incident, as I would understand, was not an 'accident' as such but came under clause 17 subsection (iii) of the policy, compensation being thus excluded.

'Oh?' I said. 'Well, I also have life insurance with your company. My feelings apart, wouldn't you rather meet a claim of £10,000 for a new car than pay out £100,000 following my death by shotgun?'

'Oh,' the assessor said earnestly, 'I'm afraid it doesn't work like that. But I'll suggest it's referred to Head Office for a decision.'

'What are the chances?'

'Well,' he said, 'I can't really say. It's not a frequent occurrence, you see.'

He wasn't joking, of course. Just checking the chart of statistical probability that fills his brainbox as well as his briefcase.

Barbara had gone out of my life and, when Ron Green had finished rebuilding our gable end, Bill Charrington faded out as well. Cities are like that, as everyone knows who has ever lived in one: you can live next door to people and never see them unless you make the effort. He'd never been a friend, anyway, just the sort of acquaintance you collect in the course of work. Christmas, that great watershed of the year, came and went, and if Claudine and I talked of the Jonathan episode, which we did less and less, it was now in terms of 'last year', which put it firmly in the past. She now seemed completely restored to her own elegant and efficient self, my beautiful dutiful wife once again – though I've got to admit the phrase didn't have quite the same meaning as it had before. I'd been brought to realise that her compliance in the role was both more voluntary and more precarious than I had supposed. And, although she didn't actually show any sign that the frightful menace of women's lib had gained a foothold in the house, I was sufficiently aware of my weakened position to take care of my defences – the washing-up machine was regularly serviced, as if my life depended on it. Which, in a way, it did.

By the time spring arrived, Jonathan was ancient history. Shocking to say, but easy to believe – happens all the time, and everyone knows it. There was hardly a trace of that time remaining – mere months had been enough to bury it. Except, occasionally, at night. Claudine slept well, hadn't had another headache or needed any pills since the evening I'd charged the motorcycle. I slept well, too, but still heard those echoing, ghostly footsteps walking through my dreams, ker-lap, ker-lap. Once or twice, I heard the collision again, shrieking tyres and grinding steel. But more often it was the footsteps. Eventually, I supposed, they'd go, walk away and disturb someone else's sleep. It didn't really matter.

*

Summer came then, and school holidays. The insurance company finally agreed to supply me with a new Citroën, almost identical to my faithful friend now departed, and we set off in it to spend a month at our French farmhouse – the two girls, Claudine and myself. Julian wasn't with us: he had gone with a party of students to Moscow to study underground stations – well, that's what he claimed, though I hoped for his sake it would be more fun than it sounded.

We rolled on to the overnight ferry at Southampton, bound for Le Havre. It was nearly 10 p.m., and all around us were cars similarly loaded with families and holiday equipment, heading south to the sun. It's a scene I prefer to ignore, but you can't shut your eyes for long as the queue ahead moves on and the people behind start hooting. So I stare moodily about, longing for the whole thing to be over, to hit the bunk and go to sleep.

There are always a few flash outfits among the family saloons and estate cars, and I spotted one about three cars ahead of us now – a red sports Triumph, hood down, with a blonde girl at the wheel. On her own, heading for summer adventures on golden sands and in throbbing discos. In the glare of the dockside floodlights her hair shone like a yellow beacon, and the moths of men in adjoining cars were responding to it by jumping out to polish their windscreens and shout irritably at their wives and children. I exchanged sardonic smiles with the driver of the car next to mine, a sensible-looking middle-aged man who might have been a doctor, with a nice- rather than good-looking grey-haired woman sitting beside him. I looked ahead again, wondering where I now fitted in the male spectrum between youthful enthusiasm and middle-aged resignation. There were sparks in there still, I realised, or the scene wouldn't have caught my attention in the first place. But this . . .? The girl turned her head for a moment, and the floodlights flashed off the dark glasses she had perched on her head, the lenses aimed skywards . . . dark glasses, ready for use in this darkest of nights . . .? No no, not for me, not any more. Then the queue of cars moved on into the bowels of the ship, and the blonde girl in her red car was sent somewhere out of sight.

There are both English and French boats on that run: you

can find yourself on either according to the mysterious workings of time, tide, and the National Union of Seamen. This one was French.

'Ah *bon!*' Claudine cried. It wasn't merely an outburst of nationalistic pride, but recognition of the fact that, on the French boats, it is fairly safe to have dinner on board. I gave the girls the cabin number and a fistful of gold, and left them happily assaulting the fruit machines. Us oldies headed for the restaurant.

We were early enough to get a corner table, and sat side-by-side studying the menu and watching the other tables fill up. I was on the outside, next to the entrance doors, and after a while became aware that the blonde girl of the red sports car had just come in, and was hesitating by my elbow. A waiter came forward, and showed her to the next table, where she chose a seat facing us.

'*Sole meunière*, I think,' Claudine said, 'with sauté potatoes and petits pois. They cannot go wrong with that, I 'ope.'

'Shrimp cocktail to start with?'

'I don't think so. Always they put too much vinegar in the sauce. I will have crudités.'

'Same here, then. And some St Véran.'

I looked up to catch the waiter's eye. The blonde girl was looking at her menu, the dark glasses still in place on the top of her bright blonde head. Well, it's a recognition symbol – junior jetset, real or chimerical. She's not all that junior, though – older than I'd supposed, over thirty certainly, but trim and tanned as though she's going *back* to a place in the sun rather than *out* to one. Simply dressed, jeans, and a big white loose knitted sweater which Claudine would probably identify. She's –

Seen me looking. It's the waiter I want. Where is he? Ah – here he comes. Are we decided. Yes, we'd like –

Stopped at her table. I've been staring at him for hours, and all she has to do is look up. Having collared him, she's now looking at me. Smiling ... well, we were here first, but I'm not going to make a thing of it. Smile back, gesture of indifference ...

Now she's getting up.

293

And coming over to our table, leaving the waiter standing.

Sudden panic – I *don't* know her, do I? Anyway, if I did, she surely wouldn't be so stupid, not in front of Claudine. Who has also looked up now . . .

'Don't recognise me, do you?' the girl said.

My God – she *is* stupid. But in fact, I don't recognise her, it's got to be a mistake . . .

'I'm *Shirley*!' the girl said, smiling even more. She stood by our table, confronting us, that's what it was, smile or not.

'Shirley?' I said. At my side, Claudine was stiffening by the second.

'Shirley Charrington!'

'Oh,' I said. 'Bill's Shirley. Yes, of course! So you are. Well, what a surprise! Do you know Claudine?'

'We've met,' Shirley said, 'but I don't expect you remember.'

'Oh, but I think so,' Claudine said in her bright, social voice.

'Why don't we . . .?' I began.

'Of course,' Claudine said. 'If you will sit with us, Shirley, that would be very nice.'

'Thank you,' Shirley said, 'Claudine.' She sat down. The waiter was still hovering. 'Well! This calls for some champagne. May I?'

'Let *us*,' I said. 'After all, we're two, and –'

'Oh no. I insist!' Shirley said.

'Champagne, madame?' the waiter said.

'What is it?'

'Moët et Chandon, madame.'

'Brut?'

'Yes, madame.'

'That will do,' Shirley said. She seemed to be enjoying herself.

I had to answer questions about us, first. Where we were going, how long for, how the children were, did we do this every year, did we always cross the Channel by this route? At last the inquisition ended.

'You don't blame me for not recognising you, I hope?' I said. 'You look quite different, you must know that. What's happened, if that's not too blunt a way of putting it?'

294

Shirley took a swig at her champagne, without loosing her smile. It was clear that she was relishing this moment.

'You know that Bill and I split up?'

'No, I didn't,' I said. 'I haven't seen him for some months. Not since he finished that job for me. I'm sorry to hear that.'

'You needn't be,' Shirley said. 'No, you needn't. Best thing that could have happened, I'll tell you that.'

'Oh, well, good . . .'

'He went off with that Barbara. Been going on for some time, that had, but I thought it best to take no notice. However, the time came when I'd had enough. So I told him I wanted out.'

'Was he upset?'

'No. I don't think I was ever what he wanted, not really, not since he moved to London anyway. Thought I couldn't keep up with him, you see. He was ambitious, he wanted to get into the big time, and I couldn't help him there. It was right for him to team up with Barbara.'

'So it all ended amicably? That's good. Where are you living?'

'I've got a nice little villa near Alicante,' Shirley said through a mouthful of bubbles. 'View of the sea, and its own swimming pool. I'll give you the address – you can pop in if you're ever passing. Stay the night. There's a spare double bedroom, with bathroom adjoining.'

'So kind . . .' Claudine murmured.

'Don't mention it, I'd be glad to see you. Not that there's any shortage of people down there, and all very friendly. Oh yes, I've met some really lovely people. Of both sexes.'

'Oh good,' I said. 'It's so important to –'

'Mind you, I'm quite choosy – I don't take to just anybody. They have to be just right for me. Like my boyfriend of the moment, for instance – he's a lovely lad. Estate agent. That's how he met me, of course. When I was buying the house. Love at first sight, he said. Are you having lobster salad?'

'Sole meunière. Well, you've left London far behind then, Shirley.'

'I think we should have another bottle ready, don't you? Oh, you've got something else. St Véran, I've seen that before. White burgundy, isn't it? Oh, you needn't look surprised, I'm catching up fast. I say, don't take offence, but I'll never forget your face that day you came to the office, and I said that about your off-licence. *Off-licence!* Oh dear, you didn't like *that* one little bit, did you! Oh, I know I shouldn't have said it, but I did think you were just a little bit – don't mind my saying this, will you? – a bit stuck-up. But I don't suppose you can help it, London's like that, the people aren't friendly like they are at home. Oh, I am enjoying this. Yes, I wouldn't mind a glass, thanks. Well, go on then, you might as well fill it right up while you're about it, a bit stingy, is that. That's more like it. Yes, as you were saying, I've left London far, far behind me, and I'm not sorry. I've got no regrets, none at all, I didn't like it when I was there and I've no wish to go back. But then, I've no need to, I'm quite comfortable now, it was all for the best, and for the first time in my life I can look back and say to myself, Shirley, you did all right. Yes, I'm quite satisfied.'

'You got a good settlement, then, obviously.'

'No complaints. Mind you, they can afford it. I'll say this for that Barbara, she's got a good head on her shoulders for all her little-girl ways that keep the men buzzing round her like flies round a jam jar; it takes a woman to see through that but the men can't or don't want to, though between you and me I don't think she's got much to offer except what's on the surface, if you know what I mean. That won't worry Bill – he's much the same himself, he likes his work, good at it too, but that's about as far as it goes, he was no good at anything else, I don't mind telling you, no good at all, it was once a month if I was lucky and even then it was me that had to make the running. I used to think it was my fault, well, I had no confidence in those days and no money to spend on myself, but I've found out since that it wasn't. And talking of that, excuse me if I leave you now and go along to the bar for a nightcap, there's someone said he was hoping to see me there and I don't see why not, I've a lot of living to make up.'

She reached for her bag and opened it.

'Don't do that,' I said, 'I'll take care of this. But just before you go, how's Hugo?'

'Working for his mother,' Shirley said. 'They got him off with a suspended sentence. Can do anything with money, can't you?

Yes, he's in her office, calls himself her personal assistant or some such. No thanks, I'll pay my share – I can afford it.'

She brought out two ten pound notes, and dropped them on the table. 'There you go. It's been really nice talking to you. *Hasta la vista!*'

Claudine and I watched her make with a swinging stride for the door, which a waiter rushed to hold open for her. With a nod to him, she vanished from view.

'*Ooh là,*' Claudine breathed. '*Quelle créature!* What was it, all that?'

'I think,' I said, 'we've just been bitten by an underdog. And that we're not the only ones.'

'But why?'

'I'm working on it,' I said. 'Tell you later. Meanwhile, let's have a couple of cognacs to help restore our confidence. That girl's left me feeling like a first-year physics student in the presence of Einstein.'

We had a cabin with two bunks, and when we'd recaptured the girls and stowed them safely away in an identical cabin next door, we got ready for bed. Claudine took the top bunk, as always, and I lay on the one underneath, alone with my thoughts.

My head hummed with them, and I couldn't decide where to start. In the centre of the cabin ceiling, the circular air vent added its insistent hiss to confuse me still further. I had the general lines roughed out, of course, but the details just wouldn't fall into place. After some minutes of lying there and trying to puzzle it out, my eyelids began to droop . . .

Ker-lap, ker-lap, ker-lap.

So loud, this time, that the familiar footsteps woke me up. The brown woodgrain of the cabin walls again replaced the white of the warehouse office. But this time, I woke knowing what the footsteps meant.

They were the sound you make, when walking through the warehouse. *Unless you deliberately creep through, walking on your toes . . .*

Just as *he* must have done, that day we had the first meeting with the builder, when he surprised me by appearing in the

297

office doorway without warning, just as I was telling Pete I had to look for the gunmen myself. *Charrington*...

Oh yes. That started it off.

He must have been alarmed at hearing that. He wasted no time in suggesting I went to see Simpson, hinting – no more than a hint, but it was enough – that Simpson had a motive to kill Jonathan, who had threatened to expose Simpson's illegal dealings on negligence claims. He must have telephoned Simpson, then, to find out if I had taken the bait and was going to a meeting: if so, a trap could be set for me, which might appear to be Simpson's doing.

But Simpson took fright and, thinking he faced exposure and ruin, hanged himself. I arrived, found him, but still fell into the trap – or nearly.

Then there was the Hugo episode. That was exactly as Miss Mullarkey had explained it – he was trying to protect his mother. Where we all made a mistake, though, was to assume that, because Hugo's claim to have killed Jonathan and tried to ambush me was a fabrication, his belief that his mother needed protection was equally misguided. In fact, he really *had* discovered what was going on. Barbara knew that, but didn't need to hide her distress because of what had happened to Hugo, though she must have been in a much worse state than anyone realised.

What exactly *had* been going on, then? And who had Jonathan killed – Charrington, or Barbara?

Both – it had to be both. Her money, his arrangements. Gunmen located during his frequent visits to the East End on his Dockland development work. Beard then shaved off to reduce the risk of recognition – it was only my idea that Barbara didn't like it. Both of them had reason to dislike Jonathan: Bill, because he was contributing less and less to the practice but still retained partnership rights; Barbara, because he had made her feel inadequate with complaints of her frigidity – I knew how much she must have hated that. But none of that was motive enough for murder – all it did was to pave the way. No, the central motive was the elimination of an estranged husband who, in divorce proceedings, would have been able to claim that Barbara's highly successful Nature Store shopping empire was a joint matrimonial asset, its success partly due to his design skill, a valuable contribution even if he could not claim to have been the dominant partner in the business. In a court action he would have been awarded a substantial part of it – or, a motive almost as forceful, *Barbara must have been afraid that he would.* The 'Darling of the Unlisted Securities Market' would have been stripped of her majority shareholding, and would have lost control of the company which had become the mainspring of her life.

Shareholdings can be checked. Priestly could do that, and . . .

And what? What would that prove?

No, hold on! First let's see how the rest of the story fits in. There's the last attempt on me outside the warehouse to explain. Arranged by Charrington, of course, after learning that Hugo was off the danger list and would soon be closely questioned by the police. That made a difficult situation! Although it would have been terrible for her, Barbara might have been able to bring herself to accept that Hugo, dead, could be left to take the blame for Jonathan's murder – a willing sacrifice. But Hugo alive! – that was a different matter. She would certainly have wanted his innocence established. But how could this be done without incriminating Charrington and herself?

Answer – bring back the shotgun team for a final attack on me. This would make it seem that I *had* been the intended victim all along, and that their employer was Jonathan, who'd been shot in error. It would be thought, not (of course!) that the gunmen were fulfilling their contract with a dead employer, but that they were worried I was on their trail – just what we had all assumed in the event. Even though the attack failed, it had just the effect Charrington wanted. Straight off the drawing board, you might say.

Anything else? Ah yes.

Shirley.

Well, whatever Shirley knew, or had pretended to know, she'd got just what she wanted, her own place in the sun, guaranteed for life provided she kept her demands within bounds. She wouldn't be rocking the boat. There was Jonathan's example to remind her of what could happen if she pushed her luck too far. A villa in Spain, even with private swimming pool, wasn't going too far, not at today's rate of exchange – you could buy two of those for the price of a London terrace house such as Charrington's. Relations, Shirley had indicated, were amicable – she'd even expressed admiration for Barbara's business acumen.

They must think they've got away with it, Barbara and Charrington. And when you think about it, who (apart from the police) had any personal interest in pressing for justice to be done? Jonathan had no children and few relations interested enough even to come to his funeral – I'd heard of none of them since. Simpson had effectively gambled and died in a disaster of his own making. If the gunmen had sorrowing family they were hardly likely to start protest-marching on behalf of their boys. Ludwig was getting an allowance which he wouldn't want to jeopardise. Hugo had got what he wanted, which was to stay close to mother. Who else was there?

Me, of course. I had a score to settle, indeed I did! But as things now stood, I was perfectly safe – Charrington thought I believed the official verdict that Jonathan was the villain, me the intended victim. Did I really, after all this time, want to stir up the whole hornets' nest again, and try for revenge by getting a conviction, with no proof in sight? Did I?

Perhaps, for once, consultation was essential.

'Claudine?'

'What is it, *chéri*?' Her voice, coming from the top bunk, was muffled and other-worldly.

'It wasn't Jonathan behind it all – I've just worked it out. Or I think I have.'

'Not Jonathan, no. Myself, I never believe this, *chéri*. He is not the type.'

'But then, the man I ran down said that Jonathan had hired him – so we thought. But now, I've thought of another explanation for what he said.'

'Yes?'

'The man was semi-conscious, darling – he hardly knew where he was or what was happening. He knew he had to get to hospital, and for that he had to give us a name. So he gave us the only one he knew – the name of the man he'd been hired to kill, a "geezer by the name of Cassell". When you think

300

about it, it isn't likely that a man hiring a gunman is going to say, "Good morning, my name's Smith – I'd like you to do a job for me." All he's going to do is hand over a photograph, some instructions, and half the money. No need to give his name.'

'Unless,' Claudine said sleepily, 'he wants to put the blame on someone else . . .'

Wham!

She didn't even pause before saying that! Didn't need to: a knowledge of the subtleties of human nature is built into all women. Men just have to learn the hard way.

'You mean,' I asked, 'that Bill Charrington could have used Barbara's name when hiring the gunmen, to make sure she was firmly involved? Bill being "the geezer", but Barbara the name?'

'But of course, *mon pauvre homme!* Would *you* trust her, the little Barbara?'

Memories rose up to mock me. No no, I'd never *exactly* trusted her . . . it was an *investigation*, wasn't it? . . . risks had to be taken . . . nothing venture, nothing gain . . .

'Look here, darling,' I said firmly, 'it's complicated enough already without that. Do you want to hear what really happened?'

'Of course I do, *chéri*,' said Claudine, soothingly.

'Well then . . .'

'But perhaps . . . I *am* rather sleepy, and it *is* all over now. Will it be all right to tell me in the morning?'

PRECINCT: SIBERIA

Tom Philbin

NINE SQUARE MILES OF SAVAGE NEW YORK STREETS

Siberia: the 53rd Precinct. Where the heaviest criminals hang out; where the most hardened cops are sent.

Detective Joe Lawless: tough, street-smart and ruthless, his battles with the brass have landed him in Siberia. Now he's out to nail a sadistic child-murderer before he kills again . . .

Police Officer Barbara Babalino: sent to Siberia for refusing the advances of her boss, she's out to rescue a young hooker. But the girl's pimp knows something that could destroy Barbara's life . . .

Detective Leo Grady: with five months before retirement and a flask of vodka in his pocket, he thinks he can take it easy. He can forget it. Nothing's easy in PRECINCT: SIBERIA

0 7474 0283 3   CRIME   £3.50

SUSPICIOUS DEATH

DOROTHY SIMPSON

ACCIDENT, SUICIDE ... OR MURDER?

The woman in the blue sequinned cocktail dress was dragged from her watery grave beneath a bridge. A highly suspicious death – and Inspector Thanet is called in to investigate.

The more he learns about the late Marcia Salden, mistress of Telford Green Manor, the less likely a candidate she seemed for suicide. A successful self-made woman with a thriving business, she had everything she wanted, including the mansion she had coveted since childhood. She also had a knack for stirring up trouble . . .

As Inspector Thanet attempts to unravel the complex sequence of events surrounding her death, he discovers that if Mrs Salden hadn't managed to get herself murdered, it wasn't for want of trying . . .

Also by Dorothy Simpson in Sphere Books:
ELEMENT OF DOUBT
DEAD ON ARRIVAL
LAST SEEN ALIVE
CLOSE HER EYES
PUPPET FOR A CORPSE

0 7474 0128 4   CRIME   £2.99

A selection of bestsellers from SPHERE

FICTION

WILDTRACK	Bernard Cornwell	£3.50 ☐
THE FIREBRAND	Marion Zimmer Bradley	£3.99 ☐
STARK	Ben Elton	£3.50 ☐
LORDS OF THE AIR	Graham Masterton	£3.99 ☐
THE PALACE	Paul Erdman	£3.50 ☐

FILM AND TV TIE-IN

WILLOW	Wayland Drew	£2.99 ☐
BUSTER	Colin Shindler	£2.99 ☐
COMING TOGETHER	Alexandra Hine	£2.99 ☐
RUN FOR YOUR LIFE	Stuart Collins	£2.99 ☐
BLACK FOREST CLINIC	Peter Heim	£2.99 ☐

NON-FICTION

CHAOS	James Gleick	£5.99 ☐
THE SAFE TAN BOOK	Dr Anthony Harris	£2.99 ☐
IN FOR A PENNY	Jonathan Mantle	£3.50 ☐
DETOUR	Cheryl Crane	£3.99 ☐
MARLON BRANDO	David Shipman	£3.50 ☐

All Sphere books are available at your local bookshop or newsagent, or can be ordered direct from the publisher. Just tick the titles you want and fill in the form below.

Name_____

Address_____

_____

Write to Sphere Books, Cash Sales Department, P.O. Box 11, Falmouth, Cornwall TR10 9EN

Please enclose a cheque or postal order to the value of the cover price plus:

UK: 60p for the first book, 25p for the second book and 15p for each additional book ordered to a maximum charge of £1.90.

OVERSEAS & EIRE: £1.25 for the first book, 75p for the second book and 28p for each subsequent title ordered.

BFPO: 60p for the first book, 25p for the second book plus 15p per copy for the next 7 books, thereafter 9p per book.

Sphere Books reserve the right to show new retail prices on covers which may differ from those previously advertised in the text elsewhere, and to increase postal rates in accordance with the P.O.